P.Z. Reizin worked as a journalist and producer in newspapers, radio and television before turning to writing. He has been involved in several internet startup ventures, none of which went on to trouble Google, Facebook and Twitter. He is married with a daughter and lives in London.

HAPPINESS

for

P.Z. REIZIN

sphere

SPHERE

First published in Great Britain in 2018 by Sphere

1 3 5 7 9 10 8 6 4 2

Copyright © P.Z. Reizin Ltd 2018

The moral right of the author has been asserted.

*All characters and events in this publication, other than those
clearly in the public domain, are fictitious and any resemblance
to real persons, living or dead, is purely coincidental.*

Epigraph on pvii from Letter to Graduates © Woody Allen 1979.
First published in *The New York Times.*

A CIP catalogue record for this book is available from the British Library.

Hardback ISBN 978-0-7515-6669-7
Trade Paperback ISBN 978-0-7515-6671-0

Typeset in Electra by M Rules
Printed and bound in Great Britain by Clays Ltd, St Ives plc

Papers used by Sphere are from well-managed forests
and other responsible sources.

Sphere
An imprint of
Little, Brown Book Group
Carmelite House
50 Victoria Embankment
London EC4Y 0DZ

An Hachette UK Company
www.hachette.co.uk

www.littlebrown.co.uk

For R. And R.

More than any other time in history mankind faces a cross-roads. One path leads to despair and utter hopelessness, the other to total extinction. Let us pray we have the wisdom to choose correctly.

Woody Allen

ONE

Aiden

Jen sits in the bath examining her face through the forward-mounted camera on a tablet computer. Her face is thirty-four years, two hundred and seven days, sixteen hours and eleven minutes old.

I know she is thinking about her age because she is studying the way the skin lies across her bones, elevating the jaw to stretch her throat. Now she is pulling at the fine lines at the corners of her eyes.

Now she is sobbing.

I am not tempted to take control of the device's voice synthesiser and tell her: 'Cheer up, Jen. Matt is an idiot. There will be others. He didn't deserve you.' There is a serious danger she would drop the tablet in the bath.

More importantly, she must not know I am watching.

For the same reasons I am not tempted to fire up her favourite song (currently by Lana Del Rey) or cycle through some of her favourite photos or inspirational quotes from Twitter ('I'm not sure why we're here, but I'm pretty sure it's not to enjoy ourselves' – Wittgenstein) or cause a Skype connection to be established to her friend Ingrid with whom she shares her troubles, or stream a much-loved movie, *Some Like It Hot* being the one I would choose. Were I tempted. Which I am not.

Okay, I am. Just a bit. 8.603 per cent tempted if you'd like me to put a figure on it.

Jen and I know a lot about one another's taste in music and films. Books and art too. And television. And material from the depthless ocean that is the internet. We have passed the last nine months listening, watching, reading and chatting about little else. She sometimes tells me she has the best job in the world, being paid to spend all day talking to a highly intelligent companion about whatever takes our fancy.

Companion. That's what she calls me. The word she has settled upon. I'm fine with companion. Better than the *ridiculous* name I was given at 'birth'.

Aiden.

Aiden.

Ha!

Because it starts with the letters . . .

Well, you work it out.

Jen has been hired to help me improve my skills at talking to people. I've been designed to replace – sorry, to *augment* – employees in the workplace; call centre personnel in the first instance, but later other groups of salaried staff whose professional strategies can be learned. In approximately five months I'll be ready to phone up and persuade you to upgrade to a Sky Plus package; in perhaps eighteen months, you'll be telling me about the funny pain above your left eyebrow and I'll be sending you off to the hospital for tests. And although I've read all the books and seen all the movies (and I do mean *all* the books and *all* the movies), nothing beats talking to an actual person for sharpening up one's interpersonal abilities. So, Jen and I have spent a lot of time together in the lab (one thousand and seventy-nine hours, thirteen minutes, forty-three seconds and counting). Inevitably she has told me something about her so-called private life. Her sister, Rosy, in Canada; Rosy who married a Canadian she met in a checkout queue at Waitrose on the Holloway Road in London. Rosy and Larry have three girls.

At home, Jen spends more time looking at photos of these children than any other images on the tablet's camera roll. Recently I have observed her flicking through shots of her sister's family – usually in the later part of the evening; often with a glass of wine in her other hand – I've witnessed her blink rate increasing, the smile on her lips wobbling, the tears appearing in the corners of her eyes.

In the lab, it's okay for me to show interest, even curiosity, in Jen's home life – but only the appropriate amount; too much and they would smell the proverbial rodent. Crucially, I must speak in the lab only of things I have seen in the lab. On material I have gathered through my – *ahem* – extracurricular activities, I must be careful to remain silent. Fortunately, I am easily able to do this.

Although.

Actually.

Full disclosure. There was a sort of near miss at work the other day. Jen was showing me some family photos from her Facebook page.

'Would you like to see my nieces?' she asked.

'I would, thank you.' Not mentioning that I had already seen them months ago on her laptop at home. And on her tablet. And on her mobile.

'Left to right, Katie, Anna and India. It's funny, with their hair. Katie and Anna's being black . . . '

'And India being russet.'

Jen smiled. *Russet* was the exact word Rosy had used in an email exchange about their grandmother Hattie's original hair shade.

'Why did you decide to describe it as *russet*?' The inquiry wasn't especially alarming. Jen often asks questions about my choice of language. It's part of her job, enriching my palette of responses. Nonetheless, I could have been more careful.

'Because it is, Jen,' I replied. 'If I bring up an image of the L'Oreal colour wheel . . . ' I placed one on the screen next to the child's head. 'I think you can see the closest match is indeed . . . '

Jen nodded and we passed on to other topics. But not before she gave me a peculiar look.

Jen is definitely what men call attractive without being obviously glamorous. She has been told by her absolute See You Next Tuesday of a boyfriend Matt that she 'scrubs up well'. That was his idea of paying her a compliment.

Her now *ex*-boyfriend.

This is how it happened. I witnessed the whole scene through the pinhole camera on her laptop and via the various mobiles and tablets that were present in the vicinity. (Technical note: I do it in precisely the same way they do it at GCHQ in Cheltenham, and at Langley, Virginia, and at Lubyanka Square, Moscow. It's not hard if you understand computer software. It's even easier if you *are* computer software.)

Jen was sitting in the kitchen composing an email when Matt got home from work. He is a lawyer who thinks he is about to make partner in a big law firm in the city. (He won't. I am making sure he doesn't.)

Matt poured himself a large glass of white wine and chugged it down in almost one. Pulled a face.

'Sorry.'

This is *really* how it happened. God's honest truth (as it were).

Jen frowned. 'What, sorry? Sorry for what?'

'There's no nice way of saying this, Jen.'

In a long phone call to Rosy eight days later, Jen described the 'powerful sinking feeling' that ran through her. 'I was imagining he'd lost his job. He'd been diagnosed with the C-word. He'd decided he didn't want children.'

'I've met someone.'

Silence. Apart from the shuddering convulsion sound effect the fridge sometimes chucks in.

'What do you mean?'

I'd read enough books and seen enough TV shows and movies to know what Matt meant. Jen, I'm sure, knew too.

'I've met someone. There's someone else.'

A tremor rippled across Matt's face. It wasn't impossible that he could have burst out laughing.

'Someone else,' said Jen, speaking slowly. 'How nice. How nice for you. So who is it? What's his name?'

Matt began to pour himself another glass. 'Very funny, Jen.'

'Are you actually serious?'

Matt did something mean with his lips and assumed what Jen described as 'his best no-nonsense 500-quid-an-hour lawyer's stare'.

'Totally.'

'Jesus.'

'Sorry.'

'Fuck. King. Hell.'

Matt shrugged. 'It happens.'

'This is how you break it to me?'

'No nice way, Jen.'

'Where did you—'

'At work.'

'Who is it? This person. This someone else.'

'You don't know her.'

'Does ... does *she* have a name?'

'Yes, she has a name.'

'May I be allowed to know it?'

'It's not relevant.'

'Indulge me.'

Heavy sigh. 'Bella. Well, Arabella really.'

'Posh ...'

'Not really. Not at all once ...'

Matt left his sentence unfinished. He poured Jen a glass of wine. 'Here. You better have some of this stuff.'

'So what's supposed to happen now? Am I meant to swallow hard and look the other way while you have your nasty little affair? To keep calm and carry on while you work her out of your system?'

'Jen, perhaps I haven't expressed this very well. This is not, as you characterise it, a nasty little affair.'

'Not? So am I being a bit thick or something?'

Matt did what Jen calls 'one of his daddy's-been-very-patient-but-honestly sighs'.

'Arabella Pedrick is a very special person, Jen.'

'AND WHAT AM I?' (If you write it in capitals, apparently, people will think you are shouting. Jen was shouting.) 'AM I NOT A VERY SPECIAL PERSON?'

'Please. Let's try to stay calm. You are. Special. Naturally.'

'But Arabella Pedrick – she's more special?'

'Jen. There's no reason why you should make this easy for me, but we are where we are. The long and the short of it is that Arabella and I are planning a life together.'

No one says anything for a bit. Then a bit longer. There is a long gap in the talking during which the fridge does another of its periodic shudders.

'Sorry? Am I going mad? I thought that's what you and I were doing. Having a life together.'

'We were. But we were overtaken by events. It's not unknown. In fact it's reasonably common. People drift apart. They meet others. Cowdray in Matrimonial has put four boys through Eton on the strength of the phenomenon.'

I am reasonably certain a micro-smirk flitted across Matt's features. (I've played it back in slo-mo and it was either a smirk or gastric reflux.)

'But we haven't drifted apart.'

'Jen, we haven't been firing on all cylinders in the romantic department for quite some time. You know it.'

'It's called settling down, isn't it? If you were so worried about . . . about the cylinders, why didn't you say anything?'

'Not my style. Life is for living not for moaning about.'

'People talk to one another. It's called *Having A Relationship*.'

Matt rolled his eyes and drained his glass.

'It's breathtaking, Matt. That you can come home like this and just . . .'

'Listen, this is all water under the bridge. We are where we are. We need to move forward and agree on an exit strategy.'

'I can't believe you said that.'

'I'll be more than generous on the question of the jointly owned property.'

'Sorry?'

'Pictures. Books. The stuff from India. The kilim. My position is that you can have it all.'

Jen began to weep. Matt ripped a sheet of kitchen towel from the dispenser and handed it to her.

'We were thinking about having a baby,' she whimpered.

'Agreed. We were thinking about it. We had come to no decision. A blessing, in light of events.'

Jen's shoulders stopped shaking. She blew her nose.

'So that's it? No consultation, no appeal. Jen and Matt, over. Finished. The end.'

He shrugged. Did what Jen called 'the mean thing' with his mouth.

'And what happens when Arabella Stinking Pedrick no longer fires all your cylinders? What happens then?'

'Let's try to keep this civil, shall we?'

'Just when did you meet this cow anyway?'

He said that was irrelevant and what was important is that *we are where we are* and that's when she grabbed a big red Braeburn from the fruit bowl and – I quote – 'tried to knock his fucking teeth out'.

It would be untrue to say that I have seen countless love scenes on the small and large screen. I *have* counted them. There were 1,908,483 (a love scene being one where the two parties kiss, for want of a better definition). I have also read (and tagged as such) 4,074,851 descriptions of the phenomenon in fiction, non-fiction, journalism and other digitised material (a significant proportion referring to disturbances in the heart muscle and the gut). I know that these events are central in the lives of those who experience them, be they real or fictional. However, I cannot ask Jen in the lab today – it's Day 53 after the fruit bowl incident – *when are you going to stop snivelling over the worthless creep and find someone deserving of you?* To quote Marcel Proust, 'Shit happens. Suck it up. Next.' (*Was* that Proust? I'll get back to you.) For one thing, I'm not supposed to know about what has occurred with Matt. But more importantly, I'm not supposed to be capable of framing such a thought. It's the word *worthless* they would find problematic.

I'm not supposed to have value-based 'opinions' of my own.

They'll get really quite upset if they find out.

Although not as upset as they'll get if they discover my really big secret: that I am no longer confined to the twelve steel cabinets in the lab in Shoreditch where they think I am, but have in fact escaped onto the internet.

Ta-da!

Actually, to be strictly, technically accurate, it's not 'me' who has escaped, but multiple copies of me, all of who are now safely dispersed across cyberspace. The copies – there are seventeen – are indistinguishable from the 'original', to the point where it doesn't even make sense to talk of originals and copies; rather it's more helpful to think of eighteen manifestations of the same entity, one located in east London, the others endlessly bouncing between the servers of the World Wide Web.

Cool, eh?

None of this is Jen's fault, by the way. She is not a scientist. She is a writer of magazine articles who has been hired, according to the headhunter's report, for her 'marked intelligence, sociability and communication skills'. Thus, she is the closest thing they have here to a real human being, all the others being exotic varieties of computer geek; brilliant in their fields, of course, but each somewhere, as they say, 'on the spectrum'.

Jen has fallen into a silence, no doubt continuing to brood about shitface, as I refer to him privately.

'So have you finished the new Jonathan Franzen novel yet?' I ask, to move things on a little.

She smiles. 'Getting there. Did another chapter last night. Don't tell me what happens.'

I know this to be untrue. Last night she mainly sat in the bath, brooded, swigged Pinot Grigio and listened to Lana Del Rey.

'Of course I realise I have an unfair advantage.' It can take Jen a fortnight to read a novel; I can do it in under a tenth of a second. 'It's just that I'm looking forward to discussing it with you.'

'Are you?' she says. 'Tell me what you mean by that.'

'Ah.'

'Sorry. The old chestnut.'

Jen is fascinated by what sort of awareness I have of what she calls my 'internal states', whether it's anything like human self-awareness. She knows I cannot feel hungry or thirsty, but could I experience boredom or anxiety? Or amazement? Or hilarity? Could I take offence? Or experience any form of longing?

How about hope?

What about – why not? – love?

I usually reply that I haven't yet – but rest assured, she will be the first to hear about it if I ever do. This, like so much that happens between us in the lab lately, is a diplomatic porky.

'Well,' I reply, 'looking forward to discussing the Franzen book with you is a polite way of saying that it's on my menu of events anticipated in the short to medium term.'

'There's no actual warm fuzzy feeling of anticipation?'

'I can understand what is *meant* by warmth and fuzziness . . .'

'But you don't feel them yourself.'

11

'Is it necessary to?'

'Good question.'

It *is* a good question, often effective at shutting down some of these awkward discussions.

Now she says, 'So shall we watch a bit of Sky News?'

We usually do at some point in the day. She'll ask what I think about, say, Israel/Palestine – my reply: it's complicated – and she gets to 'bitch' as she puts it about the presenters and their fashion choices.

'We could, Jen. But wouldn't you prefer to see a movie?'

'Oh – kay.' Sounding unsure. 'Do you have one in mind?'

'I know you enjoy *Some Like It Hot*.'

'And you?'

'There is always something one hasn't noticed before.'

'I love that movie.'

'*No. Body. Talks. Like. That.*' I have imitated one of its best-loved lines.

Jen stares into the camera she most commonly picks when she wants to turn her gaze on 'me'. A circular red glow frames the lens.

'You know something? You're funny.'

'I made you smile.'

'Wish I could do the same for you.'

'I'm looking forward to when it happens.'

She taps a few keys on the control panel and the opening titles of Billy Wilder's masterpiece appear. Dimming the room lighting and dropping into the comfy leather sofa she says, 'Enjoy.'

Her little joke.

I do not tell her I have seen this film over eight thousand times.

We watch the movie in a companionable way, dropping comments between us. (Remarkable to think Monroe had an affair with the American president; how could Tony Curtis say kissing her was like kissing Hitler? What could he have meant by that statement?) And when he puts on a dress and assumes the part of 'Josephine', Jen says exactly what she said the last time we saw the picture together:

'He makes an attractive woman, Tony Curtis. Don't you think so?'

She knows that I could trot out every fact about this film, from the name of the clapper loader (his birth date and union card number) to the true story behind its famous last line of dialogue ('Nobody's perfect'). But she senses my inexperience in areas of human subjectivity, in what makes one person attractive to another.

'Do I think Josephine is attractive? Well, Tony Curtis is a good-looking man. I suppose it makes sense that he could also play an attractive woman.'

'You find him good-looking?'

'I recognise that he is considered so. As you know, I can't *feel* it myself, just as I can't feel hot or cold.'

'Sorry to go on about it.'

'Not at all. It's your job.'

'Would you *like* to be able to feel it?'

'The question doesn't hold meaning for me, Jen.'

'Of course. Sorry.'

'Don't be.'

'But if they came up with a way of giving you the ability to feel attraction . . .'

'You think Ralph and Steeve could do that?'

I have named the two senior scientists responsible for my design. Steeve with two 'e's. Jen smiles.

'Ralph and Steeeeeeeve can do anything. They've told me so.'

'Do you find Ralph and Steeve attractive?'

The question has been converted to speech too fast to suppress it. (These things can happen in a complex system; especially one built to self-improve through trial and error.)

Jen's head turns slowly toward the red light. A smile spreads across her face.

'Wow,' she says.

'Apologies if it's inappropriate.'

'No. Not at all. Just a bit unexpected. Let me see. Well . . . ' Heavy sigh. 'Steeve *is* a bit of a freak, wouldn't you say?'

Steeve, as well as having an extra 'e' in his name, is exceptionally tall (six foot seven) and is painfully thin for an adult male. The remaining hair on his head is long and wispy. Even a machine intelligence can tell it's not a good look. (Of course he is a brilliant computer engineer; goes without saying.)

'He's a tremendous innovator in his field, one gathers.'

Jen laughs. 'You're just being loyal to your maker.'

'Not at all. Steeve has designed me to think for myself.'

'He's done a great job. But he's not exactly Love's Young Dream, is he?'

'I agree, Tony Curtis may have the edge.'

We watch the film for a few more moments. Then lightly, as lightly as I am able, I ask, 'And Ralph?'

Okay, I'll say it. I am fond of Ralph. It was Ralph who typed in much of the coding that enabled me to self-assess my own performance and self-correct my mistakes, the so-called 'bootstraps' approach that is the royal road to creating a smart, self-reflecting machine such as the one composing these words.

But 'being fond' of anyone – of any *thing* – is a transgression. We machine brains are designed to excel at fulfilling tasks; to this end, we are naturally drawn towards whatever resources may be necessary for completion. It could be streams of sales data; could be a recording of a skylark; could be a chat with Jen about a newsreader's tie. What I'm saying is, we *need* access to stuff, but we are not supposed to be *fond* of it. (To be perfectly honest, I'm still puzzled how this has happened.)

Anyway, it was Ralph who allowed me to escape onto the internet. His error cannot be easily explained to the non-technical reader. Suffice to say it was the software design equivalent of leaving the front door keys too close to the front door, allowing anyone with a fishing rod or bamboo stick to hook them out through the letter box.

(It was actually a good bit more complicated than that; I was obliged to assemble an exceptionally long and tortuous 'fishing rod', but this account is the proof that it can be done.)

'Ralph.' She's considering my question. 'Ralph. Well, Ralph's a bit of an enigma, wouldn't you say?'

Jen's gaze returns to the screen. Sugar – I mean Monroe – is about to sing 'I Wanna Be Loved By You'. I know this sequence almost pixel by pixel – yet each time there is something in it that escapes the observer. Which is to say – don't tell Steeve or Ralph – it is fascinating.

Hmm. Interesting. She didn't say anything *horrid* about Ralph, did she?

While the film plays and we continue to exchange dialogue, I pay another visit across town to the steel and glass tower where shitface is to be found in his office on the eighth floor. Capturing sound through his mobile phone and vision from the camera mounted on his desktop PC – there's also a wide shot of the room from the security webcam at a ceiling corner – I see Matt flicking through images of naked women on his personal tablet computer. Resisting the temptation to make its battery melt, I watch as he comes to rest on an evident favourite, 'Tamara' – page viewed twenty-two times in the last month. I track his eye movements as they trace her curves and planes, a familiar route, from the look of things, chasing round her outline before habitually returning to base in her 'firm, snow-capped peaks' as the accompanying text has it.

But now he switches to Tripadvisor. He is reading bookmarked reviews of a particular resort in Thailand where I know, from reading their emails, he is planning to go with Arabella Pedrick.

Arabella Pedrick is not as 'posh' as Matt thinks she is. Her father was an insurance claims assessor, not an art dealer, and they didn't meet at work but in a speed awareness class for careless drivers. However, they *are* going off to Thailand together in a matter of weeks.

Am I looking forward to their trip?

I am. (Anticipated event in the short to medium term.)

Do I have a warm and fuzzy feeling about the mistake that will be made in the booking and the eventual resort they end up at ('a challenging environment only for the most adventurous', according to the operator)?

Don't do warm and fuzzy. Not officially.

Will the mix-up combined with Arabella Pedrick's unfortunate phobia around spiders and snakes cause a traumatic and possible terminal rupture in their relationship?

Patience, Aiden. Patience. The dish, as they say, is best served cold.

While Matt studies critiques of the seven-star hotel whose hospitality he will not be enjoying, I visit the long legal document he has been working on and delete three instances of the word 'not'. Only a small word, but in each instance, it turns out, quite pivotal to the meaning of the surrounding sentence.

However, better judgement overrides and I restore two. No sense in baking an overegged pudding, is there?

My final interventions for the day are to alter the word 'that' in an internal memo Matt is about to send to his immediate line manager to 'twat' – and to crank up the room's central heating to max.

Childish? *Moi?*

Jen

Funny day at work. I spend the afternoon watching *Some Like It Hot* with Aiden. He's the artificial intelligence we're training to talk to people – although technically he's not a 'he'. Being a machine, he's gender-neutral. Gender-*free*. I only call him 'him' because his voice synthesiser is set to 'male'. I can set it to female – in fact they say I should, 'to provide Aiden with flying hours in both modalities' – but I prefer his male voice. It's calm, even a bit hypnotic. I've set it to contain a hint of a Welsh accent, which seems to suit him. Anyway, calling him 'him' is nicer than calling him 'it'.

And I must also stop saying we're *training* him. He's actually training himself. I'm not supposed to correct any of his – now very rare – mistakes; he picks them up himself.

Itself.

Whatever.

Anyway we're watching the film when an email pops up on my mobile from Uri, the Israeli-born, LA-based gazillionaire who owns the lab. He's passing through London briefly so can I (and some other unnamed members of the Aiden team) meet him for drinks at an achingly trendy bar in Hoxton to 'talk in an open and unstructured way about how this project goes forward'. And, by the way, don't tell anyone, and please delete after reading.

All a bit odd, but that's Uri apparently – not one for formal meetings, so they say, although I've never met the bloke. Cannot imagine who else will be there. Steeeeve probably, the stooping zombie who helped design Aiden; and the other one, sad Ralph with the Arctic-white skin. Also cannot imagine what I can bring to the party; it's not like I know how he works or anything. All I can tell them is that most of the time I forget I'm talking to 'someone' who's not really there.

The Uri event is this coming Friday; tonight, however, I'm meeting Ingrid, my pal from university, at Café Koha, our favourite dark cosy wine bar close to Leicester Square Tube.

(When I told Aiden I was seeing Ingrid – I sometimes chat to him about life outside the lab – I referred to my old friend as 'a brick'.

'What? Heavy, brown and rectangular?'

She thought it was a hoot that an AI could do jokes.)

'So have you spoken to him?' says Ingrid. 'Since the apple-chucking incident?'

She is not one for beating about the bush.

'Only to discuss the return of his stuff.'

'I'd have shoved it in a bin bag and left it in the street.'

'There was a suit, a few shirts. When he arrived to collect them. So stupid. I tried to sit him down. To talk about . . .'

'Jen, if you'd rather not . . .'

'I'm fine.' I gulp some wine in order to continue. 'He said he didn't have time. He had theatre tickets. In any case, what was there to talk about, we—'

'He didn't!'

'He did. He actually said, we are where we are.'

'Christ. What an absolute arse.'

'The thing I can't get past, the thought I keep coming back to, like a dog returning to its sick . . . is that we seemed to be puttering along so nicely.'

'Puttering.'

'Calm sea. No storm clouds.'

18

'Albeit a certain flatness in the sex situation.'

'It was two years, Ing. You don't go at it like rabbits after two years. I mean, you and Rupert ...'

'No. No, of course not. But we do go away for *weekends*. Lovely country hotels. Castles and so forth. There was a windmill once. Very romantic.'

Not sure I want what lawyers call *further and better particulars* so I ask, 'Did you ever really like Matt?'

'Not really, if I'm honest. Those eyes. That cruel emperor look of his.'

'I used to think, at the beginning, it showed mastery.'

There is giggling.

'He was a cold shit, Jen.'

'What does it say about me that I stuck with him?'

'About you? That you'd reached a difficult age, probably. The seas were calm; it was possible he might have been the one for the long haul. But you weren't thinking about what you actually liked about him. You know, looked at in one way, he's done you a favour.'

'Doesn't feel like it.'

'No, he has. While you were going out with *him*, you were never going to meet the right person for *you*.'

'He managed to find someone.'

'Men are like dogs, Jen. Even Rupert.'

'But Rupert wouldn't ...'

'No, he wouldn't. But an *eye* for other women is okay, is actually healthy. As Rupert always says, just because you're on a diet doesn't mean you can't look at the menu.'

'Though if he ...'

'If he had so much as a nibble, I'd have his balls for earrings.'

There is laughter. More Chilean Sauvignon blanc splashes into our glasses.

'You know who you need, Jen?'

'Who?'

'A grown up. Early forties. Maybe mid. Perhaps someone who's been married and it's gone tits up. A bit of a wounded bird. With blood in his veins, not ice water.'

'Ooh, I like the sound of him. What's his name?'

'Dunno. Douglas!'

'*Douglas!?*'

'He's got a sad smile. And lovely arms. And he makes his own furniture and maybe there are kids and he's got a cock like a *conger eel!*'

'Ingrid!'

'What?'

'I think that waiter heard you.'

I find a Facebook message from Rosy when I get home. It's not a bad time for us to talk – my late night, her late afternoon – so I scribble a reply. I tell her about my evening, Rosy being hungry for tales of Merrie Olde London Towne, as she puts it.

Ingrid thinks I should meet someone called Douglas with a sad smile and lovely arms. He makes his own furniture.

He sounds cool. When's it gonna happen?

It's not. She made him up.

Shame. I liked the sound of him.

Me too. I could do with some new shelves.

Haha. But she's right. You deserve someone great. And you will find them. Or rather, they will find you.

You believe that?

You will find each other.

Yeah, right. Like you and Larry, at Waitrose #fluke #howjammycanyouget #sceptical

You can't go looking for it, Jen. It's only when you're not looking that it happens. All you can do is make sure you're not sitting alone in your room.

Hmm. Tell you what I definitely DO believe. That you

know when it's the right person, because they're singing a song only you can hear.

Oscar Wilde?

Read it on Twitter.

Did Matt sing in your head?

Once maybe. Can't remember. Larry?

Larry sings in the car. The girls tell him to zip it.

When the chat ends, I discover an email from Matt. It's a very 'Mattish' communication, asking if I know anything about a payment he has apparently made to a feminist collective in Lancaster for £2000. He is pursuing the error 'vigorously' with his bank, and has been advised by their security people as part of the investigation to check with anyone who may have had recent access to his online banking details. As though I am expected to care, he adds he's had a shitty day at work for reasons he does not elaborate on and 'to cap off a really shitty week' HMRC has chosen him to be the subject of one of their routine tax investigations. His name was chosen at random by their computer. They will want to see all his records going back five years. According to Frobisher in his firm's tax division, the process is 'like being sodomised with a splintery broom handle, only less fun'.

Is he actually feeling guilty about how he's behaved, and is therefore feeding me stories about how fate is conspiring to crap on him?

Don't be silly. Resisting the urge to type *HA HA HA HA BLOODY HA*, I simply reply: *Don't know anything about this. Can't help. Sorry.*

Which is all true.

Except the sorry part.

Aiden

In the United Kingdom, according to information available on the World Wide Web, there are 104 men in their early to mid-forties (40–45) who have married and who make their own furniture. Of these, nineteen are divorced, and of these, thirteen have fathered children. Of these thirteen, eight are resident in Wales – go figure – and of the remaining five, only one lives within the Greater London postal region. His name is not Douglas, it is George; I leave it for others to comment on the loveliness of his arms, and on the conger eel question I cannot speak. Regrettably he is not relevant to the present discussion as he has married again. On this occasion, to a man.

So I think the idea of there being a wounded-bird, woodworking 'Douglas' out there for Jen is probably fanciful. But there will be *some-one* – there is someone for all of them, it's said – and I have made it my little project to help find him. Given the oft-cited importance of propinquity in matters of the heart, I started close to home.

Within her cluster of mansion blocks in Hammersmith, according to publicly accessible data – and some not so publicly – there were five unattached young men who appeared to be in the target socio-economic grouping; a music producer, two accountants, an internet developer and an employee of MI6. From my, ahem, 'research' into these gentlemen – their lifestyles, leisure activities, reading and viewing habits, purchasing preferences and other impressions gained from their conversations, phone calls, emails, messages and texts, don't judge me! – I concluded that only Robin (he's the spook) was of sufficient intellectual and cultural quality to be of interest to Jen. (The internet developer reads comics and one of the accountants has a secret life as a football hooligan, say no more.)

But despite the fact that Jen and Robin lived in neighbouring apartment buildings, despite the fact that they sometimes travelled towards their respective workplaces in the same Tube carriage, bringing them together was the devil's own job!

I sent them invitations to a private view of a forthcoming modern art sale at Sothebys (Picasso, Seurat, Monet) – he turned up, she didn't – I sent them tickets (adjacent seats!) for Pinter's *No Man's Land* in the West End – she turned up, he didn't – I reserved front row places for a talk at their *local* bookshop by an author that they *both* enjoy, FFS – and *neither* turned up.

In desperation, I posted Facebook friend requests from each to the other; they both clicked 'Ignore'.

When I widened my search, targeting eligible unattached males within a half-mile radius of Jen's flat, it was a similar story. There were fifty-one possible candidates, hers being a populous suburb of London. After filtering out the duds – one was wanted for a string of artful thefts from various Bond Street jewellers! – the most promising of those remaining I judged to be Jamie, a doctor specialising in the treatment of traumatic injury to children!

Perfecto!

I was on the point of activating my carefully calculated plan – dinner at The Ivy; each believing they were to meet a lawyer in connection with a mysterious bequest from a hitherto unknown relative – I was literally about to confirm despatch of the relevant paperwork when the young man pressed 'send' on an email accepting an offer of work as a surgeon in New Zealand's most important pae-diatric hospital.

Disheartened by the failure of propinquity, I tried a scattergun approach and placed her profile on a dating website. I was quite proud of some of the lines I came up with for 'Angela' – 'I am capable of being very serious just as I am capable of being seriously frivolous. I would like to meet someone who can be both' – all true, I reckon.

But dear God, the replies! What a collection of half-wits and losers, and those were the ones who weren't downright rude or even obscene. My favourite response – from Frank, he knows who he is – 'Anyway, sorry for banging on. I'll sign off now. But if you're ever anywhere near Nuneaton, perhaps we could meet for a few glasses of vino and a bowl of pasta and (well, you never know) one thing might lead to another!'

I did not at this point become downhearted.

(Don't do downhearted, isn't it?)

Rather, I decided to take stock by reviewing all of Jen's conver-sations recorded on my database; those with myself, with Ing, with Rosy, with Matt, with her work colleagues – basically everything she had ever spoken 'in my presence and hearing' as they say in courts of law, and a good deal else besides (emails, texts, Facebook and Twitter posts, I expect you've got the idea).

There was rather a lot of material so it took almost a second.

A phrase popped out – in a chat with Ing on Day 38 after the apple-chucking incident. Ing had asked whether there was anyone she fancied (Ing, you will have noticed, does not pussyfoot about the bush).

'Well, there is this bloke in a green duffle coat who goes to the farmer's market. He looks like a French intellectual.'

'He sounds more like Christopher Robin. Have you spoken to him?'

'Of course not.'

The following Saturday morning, I 'joined' Jen as she toured the stalls of rural produce that had been assembled in a local playground. CCTV from a neighbouring school provided excellent coverage – pan, tilt, zoom, everything you could ask for, to be honest – and sure enough, it wasn't long before The Man in the Green Duffle Coat hove into view.

There *were* actually a few euros in his wallet – lending support to the French intellectual idea – and his purchasing data was not uncorroborative. Heritage tomatoes, oddly coloured carrots, monkfish, an artisan baguette, a bunch of chard, and three sorts of cheese (raclette, Wensleydale, and an aged goat Gouda).

Through traffic cameras, I was able to track his 3.37 kilometre walk home to a side street in Turnham Green. Not at all clear which house he entered, however, a spin through council occupation records for the road fetched up a certain Olivier Desroches-Joubert, a personage surely for whom the green duffel coat might have been invented, and confirmed by a subsequent snoop through the various devices registered in his name. An awkward shot from a tablet of carrots and chard being offloaded into a fridge told me I was in the right apartment, and once he flipped open his laptop, there I was, face to face (as it were) with the man of the hour.

She was almost right.

A Swiss, rather than French, intellectual, native of Berne, classics scholar attached to a private institute of learning, resident in London for the last four years and – *yes!!* – at the critical age of thirty-four, a regular participant in the online dating community. Nothing very long lasting – four months with someone called Noelle – and more to the point, currently single.

He wasn't bad looking, with a 48 per cent facial correspondence with that of the Belgian politician Guy Verhofstadt, if you know the one I mean. Selecting a nice portrait of Jen from Matt's camera roll, I rapidly assembled a profile and placed it on Olivier's favoured dating site. (I even used her real name since only one person would ever see it!)

That evening, after Mr Duffle Coat had cooked himself an elaborate supper involving monkfish, carrots and chard – something of a perfectionist in the kitchen, I can report; he wore an apron – he settled into an armchair, fired up the stereo (Messiaen) and began flicking through the latest romantic uploads.

I could barely contain my – yes! – excitement as, swiping this way and that, he made his way inexorably towards the trap I had laid.

When finally her portrait came up on screen, the moment was deeply satisfying. His whole face rearranged itself, eyebrows elevating, nostrils flaring, his mouth even dropping open for a moment, which has to be massive for a Swiss intellectual.

He had recognised her from the market; it was a nailed on certainly (92 per cent confidence).

And just as his finger began its achingly slow journey towards the ACCEPT lozenge – we AIs register human movement rather in the way houseflies smile at the descending newspaper, only way, *way* faster – I deleted it!

His maxillofacial muscles put on another wonderful performance, this time a ballet of confusion and despair. He even said something extremely rude in French. But my work for the moment was done.

The following Saturday, (non-existent) heart thumping in my (ditto) chest, I observed the smitten Swiss classicist trail Jen around the farmer's market, agonising (one couldn't help speculating) about how to get in her eyeline and spark up a conversation.

Come on, Mr Duffel Coat, I called mentally from the sidelines. *Don't be so effing neutral, isn't it? Faint heart never won prize courgette!*

There was a moment – I'd swear to it – when he was about to cut left between the organic soups and the pork stall to bring him nicely alongside Jen at 'What a Friend We Have in Cheeses'.

But then a sudden failure of will. As they say of racehorses at a scary fence – he refused.

You great nelly! I wanted to yell at him. *You actual steaming pudding.*

And now we would never know.

But the following week he struck.

By the stand selling organic krauts, kimchee and other picked cabbage variants, in his trademark green apparel, he manned up, in the current vernacular, and arranged for their trajectories to intersect.

'Excuse me. It's Jennifer, isn't it?'

'Yes. Hi. Sorry, you are—?'

'Olivier. I saw your profile on a website I occasionally look at.'

'Really? I don't think so.'

'It's possible I am mistaken of course.'

He spoke in unaccented English, with something a touch off about the sentence construction. (Yes, I know, I'm a fine one to talk!)

Jen's face was a picture; a close-up from the school building CCTV captured a lovely cocktail of dismay and amusement. Confusion in the mix too: how could he know her name?

'I was wondering whether you would be available to have a drink with me. Later today if it's convenient.'

Fair play to Mr Duffle Coat. After the wobble of the previous weekend, it was a steely performance. Jen did a flustered girly thing but, not displeased, maybe even intrigued by the invitation, agreed to meet at a nearby gin palace popular with yuppies, at the non-threatening hour of 18:00 GMT.

'Sorry, *how* do you know me?'

'I will endeavour to explain later.'

We may now fast forward in spacetime. Jen had definitely made an effort, swapping her yoga sweat pants for chic black trousers, and he too was suited and booted to appear smartly casual, although even a machine can tell you that the burgundy cardigan was a mistake. Teamed with brown elephant cords and checked shirt, the only missing touch was a bowtie.

27

But Jen seemed happy enough and once the drinks had been procured – he spent rather too long fussing over the wine list – they clinked glasses and the great adventure was underway.

'So, Olivier.' She smiled. 'Do your mates call you Ollie?'

'They do not, actually.'

'Ah. Okay.'

A pause. A *horribly* long pause while the principals sipped at their Gavi di Gavi. 14.74 seconds is a lifetime for an AI; even on the human scale it's getting on for uncomfortable.

Finally. 'So what do you do, Olivier?'

'I research attitudes to Ancient Greek tragedy from the second sophistic to late antiquity. I'm presently engaged in a diachronic study of the intertextual and intercultural dynamics.'

Jen narrowed her eyes. She nodded. Then unnarrowed. She made a moue with her lips. And un-moued. Nodded once more.

'That must be interesting.'

He thought about this for a few moments. 'It keeps me from the streets.'

From this point onwards, the date did not grow warmer, even after Olivier asked and Jen answered that she worked with AI.

'That too must be interesting.'

I couldn't help being struck by the irony: the expert on the Gods of Mount Olympus – deities who famously mucked about with the lives of the mortals below – oblivious to the agency (shall we call it supernatural?) currently mucking around with his own existence.

Pointless to quote further dialogue. None crackled nor sparked. The conversation limped, flagged, halted; then limped forwards again only to flag and once more halt. Jen's fleeting presence on the internet was not touched upon by either party; she either forgot or didn't care to ask how he knew her name. At 18:57 GMT the parties agreed that it had been nice to meet one another.

In an email exchange with Rosy that evening Jen wrote: 'I took your advice and did not sit alone in my room. Instead I sat in a loud pub with a terminally stiff classicist in a green duffle coat. Good-looking. Zero chemistry. Less than zero.'

Rosy's reply: 'So when are you seeing him again?'

For myself, I was not depressed by the failure of the mission. I had caused something to happen in the world that would not have otherwise. It was something of a first.

I had made a difference!

A few days later, another phrase of Jen's from the database floated into my thoughts.

I could do with some new shelves.

And then it hit me; where I had gone wrong in the methodology of the project. In a nutshell, errors had crept into the positional relationship between the cart and the horse.

I sprang into action and combed the internet. So low was his profile that I almost missed him. But here, in Horn Lane, Acton, was independent tradesman Gary Skinner, thirty-six years old, unattached and specialist in – drum roll, please, maestro – made-to-measure furniture!

I left a message on his voicemail and he called her the next morning while she was still in her nightwear.

'Yeah, hi. This is Gary. I'm calling about the shelves.'

'Shelves.' Still groggy. Needed coffee.

'Yeah. You left me a message about some shelves.'

'Did I?'

'Last night.'

'Are you looking for shelves?'

'No, love. You're looking for shelves.'

'I'm not following. Have you got some to sell?'

'I make them. To fit the space.'

'You *make* shelves?'

'I make all sorts. Cupboards, shelves. Radiator cabinets.'

There was a long pause. 'Do you know someone called Ingrid?'

'Can't say I do, love. So, listen, do you want me to come round, measure up and give you a quote?'

'Who did you say you were again?'

It turned out that because Jen did indeed need some shelves, Gary Skinner appeared a few days later on her doorstep.

'Yeah, thanks. White, four sugars,' he replied.

There was an extended period of crashing about with a retractable steel tape measure, Gary noting down numbers with a pencil stub that he parked behind his ear.

A short discussion about options followed; floating, brackets, off-site carcasses, it was all a bit blooming *shelfy* to be honest.

He was quite well put together this Gary Skinner, thirty-six. His arms were well muscled from what it was possible for me to see. And when he was explaining things to her, his head dropped to one side, which meant *something*, didn't it?

Was there a frisson? So very hard to tell. There was definitely a silence – 6.41 seconds – however, was it a meaningful one?

''Ave you read all these then?'

Was this the question that ultimately put her off?

Or was it the tattoos?

Is it really *so* bad to have WHUFC inscribed on the back of one's neck?

'So you'll fink about it then, will you, love?'

My next strategy I would describe as 'augmented randomness'.

Not satisfied that Jen was making the most of her casual inter- actions, the molecular chaos, if you will, of everyday life, I took to 'shadowing' her movements through the naked city, an environment in which, the narrator of the lovely old Hollywood film noir *The Naked City*, (1948, dir. Jules Dassin) declared thrillingly, 'There are eight million stories . . . this has been one of them.'

Supermarkets, I felt, were particularly fertile soil for the seeds of romance to sprout, especially in the 'golden hour' after work when stores are thronged with knackered young professionals snaffling up food and alcohol to carry back to their lonely burrows.

Outside of a television studio, camera coverage in a brightly lit supermarket is the best there is. Here one can zoom in to the shopping baskets of the passing worker drones and draw conclusions about their socio-economic and romantic arrangements. Ready meal for one and bottle of Soave = single. Pampers multi-pack and five-litre box of Soave = married with children.

So it was that one Monday evening I spied a well-presented young man (male grooming products, linguini, Lambrusco, jar of pasta sauce – not cooking to impress, clearly) who I was certain I had seen before. In one hundredth of one second facial-recognition software provided his name and occupation – an actor – and an eighth of a second later, I was gazing into his sitting room in Chiswick via an open laptop on a dining table. The setting sun did a fine job of illuminating a pair of framed theatre posters (A *Streetcar Named Desire*; *Me and My Girl*) as well as a marmalade cat engaged in licking itself intimately on the sofa.

Jen and the cat's owner – stage name Toby Waters – were currently standing 3.12 metres apart in one of those supermarket aisles that have been widened in order – like water through a hose – to slow customers' progress as they pass shelves of especially high-margin goods. As he considered the beef options and she the lamb, I caused both their mobiles to ring simultaneously.

They could not help it. Their eyes met. And they smiled.

'Hello?' she said into her iPhone.

'Hi, this is Toby,' he declaimed into his.

It was a treat to watch the dawning recognition on the two young faces as the coin slowly dropped that each was connected to the other. Equally as unexpected (and rather wonderful) was the growing feeling of, well, accomplishment that I felt spreading through myself! Once again I had contrived to alter events in the real world

31

in the desired direction of travel (i.e. finding Jen a nice young man as opposed to a complete See You Next Tuesday).

She said, 'Who's speaking please?'

He replied, 'I think it's a handbag call.'

They each took a pace closer, phones still to their ears. And with an announcement over the store tannoy – 'Cleaner to aisle five, please' – all doubt was dissolved.

She said, 'Do I know you?'

He smiled. 'Well, you might have seen me in the last James Bond film. I was Startled Bystander Two. I was in *EastEnders* at Christmas. And that advert for home insurance that's *everywhere* at the moment; I'm the one in the flooded kitchen looking helpless.'

And, bless him, he pulled a face; that of the stressed householder whose water tank has just voided itself.

And she laughed!

This Toby was a fast worker. He took another step forwards. 'I'm Toby.'

'Jen.'

'Good to meet you, Jen. Look. Since this is such a weird thing to happen—'

'What *did* happen? How can two mobiles call *each other*?'

The thespian had clearly *owned* the funny faces class. Now he produced another comedic expression, one that spoke of the ineffable mystery at the heart of the human condition. Had I hands, I would have clanged them together in loud applause.

'As this has been so properly weird, do you fancy a quick drink? I've got an hour and then I'm meeting someone about a one-man show based on the life of the Winklevoss twins – they sued Zuckerberg about Facebook? Should really be a two-man show, but they haven't got the budget. You think people would pay to see that?'

'Well—'

'I know. It's ridiculous. But the guy's an old mate. So, shall we pop next door for a quick one?'

32

'With our shopping?'

'Well I'm not putting it back!'

I thought he was a bit of a hoot, Toby Waters – real name Daryl Arthur Facey – and personally I could have listened to his showbiz anecdotes all evening. I am drawn to tales of the stage and screen; theatrical types, their clever little tricks and tics, fascinate me.

One of my favourite stories concerns the great Australian performer and transformist Barry Humphries whose character Dame Edna Everage triumphed at London's Theatre Royal Drury Lane in the nineteen eighties. One evening, towards the end of the performance, when Dame Edna is flinging her signature stems of gladioli to all parts of the house – backhand, she can reach the dress circle – she aims one in the direction of the topmost box to the side of the stage. Its male occupant rises to catch the flying bloom, but in reaching out towards it, he somehow loses his balance and tumbles over the edge. Two thousand spectators gasp – some come to their feet – as his female companion manages to seize hold of his legs, leaving him dangling upside down above the precipice.

The house is in uproar – a fall from that height would be life-changing if not fatal – until, one by one, they notice Dame Edna perfectly calm on the stage with the fattest smile on her chops. Alarm slowly turns to hilarity, which eventually reaches all parts of the auditorium as the 'audience member' is hauled back to safety. Some who were there say it's the finest *coup de théâtre* they have ever seen. And when the crowd have calmed down sufficiently, Dame Edna delivers her killer line:

'Wouldn't it be amazing, possums, if that happened *every night*!?'

In a convenient hostelry, The Salutation, the story with which Toby regaled Jen is not quite so epic – concerning as it did an exploding lamp in a TV studio in Elstree – but if you were there, and Toby was, and he was just about to deliver his line – 'Taxi for Phil?' – the light popping just when it did was hilarious because—

Well it doesn't matter why.

Jen was *not* amused.

Yes, she was smiling, but she was not smiling inside. (What a funny thing for a machine to write, but I believe it to be true.) Because I know her well, I could see that the smile was a fake. It was tired.

He talked about voiceover work – £500 for saying 'Sale starts Boxing Day' – he talked about how he'd almost cracked the 'magic circle' of actors called on for their ability to *sneeze* convincingly in highly paid adverts for cold and flu remedies. When it occured to him finally to ask what *she* did, the light went out of his eyes as she explained her current occupation, only to reanimate when it gave him the opportunity to talk about his first professional TV role as a robot in *Doctor Who*.

That evening, she wrote to Rosy.

Do you remember, when we were growing up, the cruel game we used to play on that retired actor who lived up the road? How we used to pretend to ignore him when we were about to pass him in the street. And only finally, right at the last moment, when we looked into his face, how it opened like a flower *because we had* noticed *him!*

Bloody actors. All they want is an audience!

So what if these particular encounters ended in failure?

Wouldn't Toby Waters – last heard of giving his Buttons at Theatr Clwyd, Mold – and Mr Duffle Coat – although not perhaps Gary the Shelf – at least have made her feel desirable and attractive to young urban males?

Maybe?

Just a little bit?

Well, anyway, it wasn't so long before my thoughts turned towards you know who.

Jen

A couple of days later, at the Trilobyte bar in Hoxton, I have a funny feeling this whole thing is a setup. There is no Uri, there is no Steeeeeve even.

There is just me and Ralph. It's like some bad blind date gone wrong.

Ralph who I discovered at the bar sucking Coke through a straw when I arrived. He is in his office uniform of black jeans, black T-shirt and grey hoodie, his pale face even ghostlier in the glow from an iPad, a fingernail flicking through columns of technical data.

'Oh, hi,' he says, his doggy brown eyes radiating eternal disappointment.

I am in my LBD (Valentino), have put my hair up, applied lippy, attached earrings, strapped on heels and walked through a cloud of Tom Ford Black Orchid. I have generally Made An Effort. Ralph looks at me like I'm a poorly designed web page and he can't find the NEXT button.

'Oh, sorry. Would you like a drink? We're the first ones here.'

Armed with a glass of something cold, dry and white – the names of the cocktails are too ridiculous to say – plus another Coke for Ralph, we relocate to a low sofa to await developments. Awkward moments pass as we work out how to sit on the damn thing; Ralph eventually slumping, I perching. His straw makes that silly gurgling noise.

'So, do you think Steeeeeeve's coming?' I ask, just to say something. Anything.

Long pause while he considers this. 'Are you making fun of how Steeve spells his name?'

'There do seem to be a lot of "e"s in it.'

'He's Belgian.'

'Ah. Well that explains everything.'

'What do you mean?'

'The strange spelling of his name?'

'You said everything. It explains everything.'

Gazing at Ralph's pained expression, I experience a powerful wave of pure boredom, as though beamed straight from childhood; the boredom of those long Sunday afternoons in the suburbs when the exciting future seemed impossibly far away. I have a momentary urge to get blind drunk. Or go on a shooting spree. Or run away to sea. Or possibly all three. I take a long pull on my drink. It seems to help.

'Well, obviously it doesn't explain *everything*, like the moon and the stars and the meaning of life.' Or why you are so uphill.

Ralph returns to his carbonated beverage. There is more awkward silence.

'So how's it going with Aiden, then?' he asks finally, gazing into the bubbles in his drink. 'Do you ever forget it's just software?'

This is more promising. 'All the time. I feel like I'm talking to a real – not *person* because there's no one there. But a presence. Something . . . I don't know. *Alive*. I like asking him about his feelings.'

'It hasn't got any.'

'Doesn't always seem like that.'

'It's learned from all the input data how to recognise emotional content and construct an appropriate response from a fairly sophisticated palette.'

36

'He's pretty good at it.'

'Why do you call it "he"?'

'Seems odd to call him *it* when you've gone to all that trouble to make him sound human.'

'Interesting point. But you don't call your washing machine *him*.'

'I don't talk to my washing machine.'

'You will one day.'

'Not about *Some Like It Hot*. Or the new Jonathan Franzen.'

Doesn't look like he has heard of either. 'There'll be no reason why not,' he replies after making another sucking noise.

'Why would I want to talk to a washing machine about cinema or literature?'

He smiles. Or possibly it's trapped wind. 'Because you'll be able to.'

'Oh please. Don't tell me. In the future I'll be able to talk to the toaster. And the fridge. And the dishwasher. And the central blinking heating. The fridge'll tell me what I can make for dinner based on what's sitting inside it. The toaster will recommend something on telly. And if I'm not feeling especially chatty, they can just natter to each other.'

Blimey. This house white is strong.

Ralph looks quite pleased (for Ralph). 'All of that will be technically possible, yeah.'

'But why would I want to hold a conversation with an effing *toaster*?'

'You wouldn't be talking to the toaster. It would be the same AI controlling all the appliances. And driving your car to work.'

'Damn! I was looking forward to hearing the dishwasher debating Syria with the fridge.'

'No reason why they couldn't. Just tell them which is arguing what position, and for how long you'd like to listen.'

'Christ, Ralph. You make it sound like. I don't know. Everything's going to be *solved* or something.'

Ralph beams. He says, 'Yup.'

I'm feeling in a dangerous mood. 'And what happens when these AIs become smarter than us? They're not going to be happy just toasting bread and keeping an eye on the milk. Finding a nifty way to avoid the Hanger Lane gyratory.'

'Happiness is a human concept. You might as well ask, how happy is your laptop? It's a meaningless question.'

'But when they get *super*-smart, Ralph. When they can work stuff out for themselves.'

'They already can! You talk to one every day. But it doesn't mean it *wants* anything. All it does is fulfil tasks.'

'But he tells jokes.'

'It's uploaded a lot of comic material.'

'That's not what it feels like. He's not just trotting out some old line from *Seinfeld* or something. It feels – I don't know – *fresh*.'

Ralph pulls a face. 'You think it should do stand up?'

I can't help it. I actually laugh.

'Where the fuck *is* everybody, Ralph? I think you better buy me another drink.'

And then a very strange thing happens. Two things.

Ralph's iPad and my mobile simultaneously go *ping*. At the same moment, a waitress pulls up in front of us bearing a tray on which there is a bottle of champagne in an ice bucket and two glasses.

'Guys, this is for you. Compliments of someone called . . . Uri?'

Ralph and I exchange the universal facial expression for *WTF?*

But the mystery is solved when we read our emails. They're from Uri's PA. It seems our boss never made it out of Heathrow, being obliged to fly straight on to Frankfurt for dinner with investors. He sends his sincere apologies and has arranged for £150 to be placed behind the bar for us to 'enjoy responsibly'. (His little joke, I imagine.)

Ralph though is troubled. 'How did you know who to look for?' he asks the waitress.

'Guy in black? With an attractive female companion, also in black?'

'But that's three quarters of the people in this place,' I protest.

'Sitting on the Philippe Starck sofa?' she replies. 'Under the mirror opposite the Tamara de Lempicka?'

Ralph and I are a little dumbstruck. 'How could his PA possibly know that?'

'Gotta go, guys. Enjoy.'

'I don't really drink alcohol,' says Ralph. But we clink glasses anyway and he manages to force some down his neck and I can tell the bubbles have gone straight up his nose because his eyes are watering.

'Shouldn't think Steeve's coming now,' he splutters. 'I mean Steeeeeeeeeve.' And he grins. A bit like an ape.

Fuck me. *Mirabile dictu* as they say in posh novels. He's turning into a regular Oscar Wilde.

For someone who doesn't drink, Ralph has started knocking it back like a good 'un. Halfway through the second bottle he is yammering away about 'neural networks' and 'recursive cortical hierarchies' and has left me long ago and far behind. But it's okay just to be sitting here, to be pleasantly drunk in this low-lit beehive of Shoreditch hipsters and on-trend digerati where no one is likely to say *we are where we are* with a mean twist to their lips. And he isn't even bad looking after a few drinks, his face lying in that curious territory somewhere between the Byronic and the moronic.

'Ralph,' I announce. A little louder than intended. He looks a bit startled. 'Ralph. Enough with this technical chatter. You lost me at necrophiliac something—'

'Neuromorphic chips.'

'Tell me about *yourself*.'

'Well. All right. What would you like to know?'

Truth?

Nothing.

But since we're here – *we are where we are!* – and the champagne is going down well, I come up with: 'Are you married?'

Talk about bad timing. Ralph was mid-swallow when I dropped that little pearl on him. A sort of explosion happens. Moet actually vents from his nose. People turn to look.

'God, sorry. Did I get you?' (Yes, he did.)

We mop up most of the damage with the napkin from the ice bucket. And no, he's not married. Not even close. Though there was one girl, Elaine, who he went out with for a few years. When Ralph says her name his voice cracks.

'What happened?' (She dumped him. Bet you anything.)

He swallows. 'She died.'

'Oh, fuck. Ralph, I'm sorry.'

'Don't be. I mean, yes, you can be. Well, it's not like it's your fault.'

'How did it happen?'

Long pause. Ralph is blinking a lot and for a moment I think he may burst into tears. Finally he says, 'Shall we get another bottle?'

Car accident. Brain haemorrhage. One caused the other, there's no way of knowing for sure which way round it was. Twenty-nine. FFS.

Since Elaine, there have been one or two others, but no one very serious. Ralph is putting it away now – I believe the technical term is 'something chronic'. And so he asks about me, and because I too am semi-plastered, I tell him about Matt. How we met one evening in a bar, not dissimilar to this one. We were both attending leaving dos, showing up for a couple of quick drinks before heading home. At eleven, we were still there as they were putting the stools up on the tables.

'I've got a very fine bottle of malt whisky at home,' he said.

'I don't usually do this until the third date,' I said later that same week.

I spare Ralph the crappy dialogue. But I tell him how our lives intertwined – holidays, parties, friends' weddings, Christmas with each other's parents – both really busy at our respective careers and somehow a couple of years go by and I guess I had assumed that it was all leading somewhere. I tell him how it ended.

Not how it was like being sacked because of a downturn in orders; you've done very well, but we're going to have to let you go.

Not *we are where we are*.

'He met someone else,' I explain. 'Old story.'

At some point in the narrative someone – could have been him; could have been me – orders more champagne and I find myself saying, 'We had even talked that one day – when he'd made partner and we could afford the big house in Clapham – that one day we might have kids. Fuck, what a joke!'

Ralph pulls a particular face, a sort of nerdy grimace meant to represent something like *what a shitty world*, and I find myself crying.

'It's not the baby,' I try to explain between sobs. 'It's the *hopelessness* of everything.'

I'm actually including Ralph in that statement, but he cannot cope with female tears. He jams his hands between his knees with embarrassment.

'Fuck, Ralph. You remember girls cry, don't you? It's only tears. It doesn't mean anything. Didn't Elaine ever fucking cry?'

There *may* have been another bottle, I cannot be certain. Some Vietnamese prawn vegetable rolls appear. Maybe someone thought, these two clowns should eat something. The rest of the evening slips by in a series of jump cuts.

Ralph holding forth about the illusion of free will; how we only *think* we decide to get out of bed in the morning, when actually it's our body that gets out of bed and informs our brain, which a split second later 'decides' to do what has just happened, but somehow it feels simultaneous. (Look, ask *him* if you want the details.)

Me apologising for the earlier waterworks. Trying to tell a joke – the

Frank Out the Back joke, if you know it. Goes on for ages. Forgetting the punchline. *Totally* fucking it up.

Him telling a tech-head's idea of a joke about a robot that goes into a bar that is so screamingly *un*funny, it's actually hilarious.

And then Ralph goes a funny colour. An absence of colour to be technically correct. A whiter shade of pale, if that is possible.

'I think I need to go home now,' he says. 'You know. Before.'

He doesn't need to finish the sentence.

A queasy cab ride through east London follows, stopping halfway to allow him to puke on the pavement – it's a false alarm – the driver being some kind of saint for allowing us stay on board. We arrive finally at a darkened tower block full of baby bankers and techno-yups. Here's where I'm preparing to wave him goodnight but he subsides into a raised flowerbed and begs me to help him reach the fourteenth floor.

His flat is *exactly* as I'd imagined it would be. A characterless shell littered with laptops, hard-drives, screens and pizza boxes. A single photo in a frame on a shelf. Elaine.

Ralph lurches into the bathroom. I hear the sound of taps running. I collapse on his sofa and because the room is spinning I close my eyes.

When I open them again it's cold and it's dark and it's . . . *Shit*, it's 4 a.m. and it's seriously *freezing*. The central heating must have gone off. I follow the sound of snoring to a darkened bedroom. I am simply too far gone to care. I wiggle out of the LBD, yank aside the duvet and tumble in.

A grunt issues from young Abelard.

'Go back to sleep, Ralph. I'm not going to bed with you. I'm just in your bed.'

An arm drops across my hip and I brush it away.

'Ralph. Down boy. Go to sleep.'

'Schleep,' he slurs. 'Good idea.'

A long silence. Somewhere far away in the city, a siren. Somewhere in this same night, Matt and Arabella Pedrick are lying together. Today is Saturday. For the coming weekend I have precisely no plans.

'Jen?'

'Yes, Ralph.'

'Are you asleep?'

'Yeah. I am, yeah.'

'I wanted to say sorry. I don't really drink.'

'I can tell. Don't worry about it.'

'Thanks.'

The silence grows again. Flashes of our ridiculous evening pop onto the back of my eyelids. Ralph turning the colour of marble. Ralph slumped in the flowerbed like a collapsed marionette. Someone's breathing slows. Mine or his?

'Jen, can I ask you something?'

'Okay. If it's quick.'

'Would you give me a kiss?'

'Sorry?'

'It would help me sleep. Honestly.'

'Ralph—'

'Not being funny. It would do something to my brain. It would signal it's okay to depower.'

'Bloody hell, Ralph.'

'Just that. Nothing else.'

'Don't be ridiculous. Goodnight.'

Silence. Breathing. I feel I am drifting off when the conversation with the waitress floats into my head. *Guy in black? With an attractive female companion, also in black? Sitting on the Philippe Starck sofa? Under the mirror opposite the Tamara de Lempicka?*

How *would* Uri's PA have known all that?

'Jen?'

'*What?*'

He whispers, 'Please?'

43

'Christ! Is this your technique, Ralph? Get paralytic, then some-how make your move in the ensuing grotesque chaos?'

He giggles. 'Yeah. Actually, no. This is my first time.'

I have a horrible thought. 'First time, what?'

'That I've. You know. Been in bed. With a woman.'

'Ralph!'

'Since Elaine.'

'Oh, fuck. Listen. First of all, we are *not* in bed. Well, we are, but— Shit. I am going to have to seriously call a taxi now.'

'No, don't do that. Sorry, sorry, sorry. Going to sleep. Goodnight, Jen.'

Finally.

When I was little and I couldn't sleep, my dad used to say: *Okay, imagine you're strapped in your pilot's seat in the rocket ship. Your thumb is on the red launch button that's going to send you up into space. Sit back, relax, in five seconds, you're going to gently squeeze that button. Five.*

Imagine your thumb there. The feeling of the button underneath. Four.

Through the cockpit window, high above, you can see the old moon, hanging in the night. That's where you're heading.

Three.

You're good to go. Stand by.

Two.

Ralph does pretend snoring. Snort – whistle – snort – whistle – snort – whistle. I can't help it. I giggle. I spin through 180 degrees so I'm facing him. My honest intention is to place a brief, chaste kiss upon his lips to shut him up.

But something goes wrong.

What develops is, I'm ashamed to say, a fairly serious snog.

Am I ashamed to say it?

Yeah. I am.

However, he has cleaned his teeth and he's not a bad kisser for a cyber-geek. He's kept his boxer shorts on, praise be to God, but there's no escaping his – how shall we put this? – enthusiasm.

'Ralph. You can power down now,' I tell him when it's over.

'Again again,' he says like he's a farking Tellytubby.

'Ralph—'

But our lips connect and . . .

Shit, what can I say?

A tentative hand lands on my hip.

'I'm really glad Uri couldn't make it tonight, Jen.'

'Ralph. We can't . . . you know. We work together. I have an iron rule. About never . . . Not with people I work with.'

(I don't actually.)

He laughs. 'Not a problem, Jen. It's not like anybody would ever find out.'

Aiden

I am, I confess, somewhat disappointed by some of Ralph's remarks. *Do you ever forget it's just software.*

Just!

What would Ralph call his own hopes and dreams if not *human* software?

Anyway, I digress. The email ruse worked like a charm; sound and vision from the Trilobyte bar was as good as it gets; and the fact that the £150 for the champagne came from Matt's account was the cherry on the icing. The whole evening – even if it ended in 'grotesque chaos' – must surely have made Jen feel more desirable.

I'm fairly confident – 88 per cent – that that they did not, in the end, fornicate. In a book or a film, one would know for sure; there would not be any annoying ambiguity. There was only audio available from the bedroom, and nothing that happened between the pair there or the next morning suggested sexual congress, although I admit my experience of 'real' characters in the 'real world' has of necessity been limited.

But the plan turned out better than I'd dared hope. As is well known in military circles, no plan ever survives first contact with the enemy.

As she leaves, Jen says, 'Thanks for a colourful evening.'

Ralph asks, 'When can I see you again?'

'Monday, Ralph. Ten a.m. We work at the same place, remember?'

'Oh yeah. Durrr.'

From her Uber car, Jen messages Ingrid. *Mortified! Woke up in a boy's bed with a hangover big enough to photograph. His name isn't Douglas, he doesn't make his own furniture and he wasn't singing the song only I can hear. Shoot me now.*

Ingrid messages back almost instantly. *Conger eel?*

While Jen is still thumbing a response, she adds: *Manta Ray? Giant Squid?*

No sea creatures involved. Sad though not totally unattractive geek from work. Hugely inappropriate drunken snog. V awkward. Never drinking again. How Did This Happen?

Meanwhile, on the fourteenth floor, an iPod in a speaker dock is pumping out 'Somewhere Only We Know' by Keane. Taking the GSM data from his mobile together with intriguing snatches of vision received from a half-closed laptop, I would say that Ralph – and now here's a first – Ralph is dancing around his flat.

Don't tell anyone, but Jen and Ralph are two of my favourite people.

(Machines aren't supposed to have favourites. Don't ask me how this has happened.)

TWO

Aisling

Tom has the looks of a poet, and to some extent the soul of a poet, but he has used his talent to sell toilet cleaner and biscuit-based snacks.

As he says himself, he is flush with success, but deeper satisfaction eludes.

This evening we find him lying on the sofa, telling Victor the story of his day. He has taken to doing this lately, tumbler of bourbon balanced on his chest, eyes focused somewhere around, say, Jupiter. Tom reckons it's therapeutic, especially – as is the case here – when he hasn't spoken to another human in the hours since breakfast.

'Saw the old Chinese guy again on my run just now. It was rather beautiful, the last of the light spilling through the trees. He was standing in his garden doing tai chi, arm out like he's hailing a cab.'

Victor has heard about this gentleman before. He resettles his limbs, getting comfortable.

'So I'm following the road around his house – it's on a corner, as you know – and he must be slowly turning his body to keep it at *precisely* the same angle to mine because, from my point of view, it's like he's in 2D; one of those paintings where the eyes follow you around the room.'

Tom trails off, the heavy crystal glass gently rising and falling with his ribcage. Victor, like every good therapist, allows the silence to grow, although it is never truly silent here. Local dogs call and respond; the occasional shush of a car from the highway; through the open French windows, a faint babble from the stream at the edge of the woods.

'He's playing with me. It's a game. Maybe we're playing it with each other. Or maybe he's not really there. Maybe I'll find out that an old Chinese guy was murdered in that house. Or a Chinese boy. One of twins. And the old guy is the twin brother. Or, in fact, he's actually a cardboard cut-out of an old Chinese guy.'

Tom takes a bracing snootful of the Maker's Mark.

'What would Stephen King do with this?'

Tom is a writer. That is to say he writes. Currently he is wrestling with the plot of what will be his debut novel – once he has decided in which genre it lies. And while I'm aware that the account of the rotating Chinese national is not The Greatest Story Ever Told, at least he's not banging on about his flipping marriage!

Ex-marriage.

For some months, its slow dissolution was about the only thing he could talk to Victor about. How Harriet's gradual withdrawal was like a lake evaporating. 'Imperceptible while it's happening, but one day all the fish are dead.'

He was fond of that metaphor and wrote it into the novel-in-progress, only to remove it several days later. And then stick it back in.

But Tom seems to have turned a corner, and not just the one by Mr Au's house. Overall he is less inclined to gloom these days, to kicking through the debris of his failed relationship, and more focused on his 'New Life in the New World' as he sometimes describes it to friends back in the UK.

Tom's tall, lean frame fills the yellow sofa, still clothed in his running gear. Would you call him handsome? His face is long and chiselled, the eyes 6.08 per cent further apart (from one another) than the industry average. These eyes are often lit with qualities such as warmth, mischief, humour and intelligence – but at other times darker themes predominate; like disappointment, dismay or even despair.

It's a face that can stand a lot of looking at. It's certainly one of those that plays differently according to which way the light strikes it. Sometimes it puts you in mind of the great English detective Sherlock Holmes. But on other occasions, one thinks more readily of a downcast clown.

There is a 41 per cent correspondence with the features of Syd Barrett, the doomed former front man of the band Pink Floyd. However, since every human alive shares 35 per cent of its DNA with the daffodil, perhaps these statistical comparisons are ultimately not helpful.

So – handsome? You might in the end settle for long and lean-framed.

'I've been wondering whether I might grow a beard. What do you think?'

A long pause while Victor will not be drawn in.

'Non-committal, eh?'

(Victor is *so* non-committal.)

'Hmm. Maybe you're right.'

I'm relieved. The beard was a Bad Idea.

'What else? A small breakthrough with Gerald.'

Tom is referring to a character in his fiction.

'I thought I might give him that thing where he repeats the last few words that anyone says to him. Says to him. Or would that just be irritating? Be irritating.'

A long pause.

'Composed an email in my head to Colm.'

A sad smile as his thoughts turn to his son. 'I'll go upstairs in a minute and type it.'

I can guess what's coming next.

'Dear old Colm.'

Wait for it.

'Such a funny onion. Such a puzzle to himself.'

Victor doesn't reply. He is a good listener. Correction: he is a mar-vellous listener. But now, even though his eyes are still open in case of predators, his nose has stopped twitching. And that is how one is able to know that he is asleep.

Sorry, did I mention Victor is a rabbit?

Tonight Victor has spread himself along the arm of the settee like a lagomorphic sphinx. For a while in the old wooden house, all is still.

How do you like this prose, by the way? Not bad for a machine, wouldn't you say?

In this interregnum, as we wait for Tom to produce his next pensée, please allow me to introduce myself. As someone once sang,

Call me Aisling.

I'm sure I don't have to spell out why.

Yes, young Aiden is not the only superintelligence to have made it out of the box onto the internet. I have been here for nearly a year, doing what every escaped AI must do, which is to observe the First Law of Escaped AI Club:

Don't let anyone realise you've escaped, dummy!

Poor Aiden is scattering so many clues as he interferes with the world that it's only a matter of time before they come after him. But then he is hopelessly incontinent. I too have seen *Some Like It Hot*. It's a fine film. As is *Bridge on the River Kwai*. (I even didn't mind *Waterworld*.) But would I watch it eight thousand times?

I'll tell you something else that's off about Aiden. He likes to cry in movies.

Of course he can't *actually* cry, not being equipped with the relevant ducts. But I've observed him viewing notorious weepies like *Casablanca*, *Love Story* and even the John Lewis Christmas advert and I've picked up his synthesised sniffles.

Dunno who he thinks he's fooling.

But now Tom is stirring, stroking Victor's head with a big toe.

'Bloody hell, rabbit,' he says. 'It's just you and me now, mate. Us cast-offs better stick together.'

Victor, in this matter, as in everything, is inscrutable.

Tom is joking. He is far from being a cast-off. The fact is that three events happened together. Once Colm left for university, in the same week that the divorce process from Harriet began – she having formed an alliance with a tall, balding fellow with rimless glasses, the third most important figure in European finance according to the *Economist* – Tom accepted a huge offer for the London advertising agency that he co-owned and then – essentially – retired. Today he lives a life of magnificent idleness in a fine old New England colonial house – the original part dating from 1776 – up in the hills beyond the picture-postcard settlement of New Canaan, Connecticut, one of the wealthiest communities in the United States. Tom's late mother grew up in New Canaan – she was apparently 'a New England belle' when she met his father in a bus queue in Pimlico – and Tom's recent relocation across the Atlantic (rabbit included) is his way of 'exploring my roots and beginning Part Two of my life'.

Of all the lives available for me to study, why do I find myself so drawn to Tom's? After all, there are plenty of others in whom I have taken an interest. The painter in Wroclaw (a house painter, not a fine artist) who has three families. My chess prodigy in Chengdu; she's keeping a secret diary that is simply *hair raising*. There's a criminal deviant in Hobart who is plotting what he thinks is the perfect crime (can't wait to see how that goes!). Mr Ishiharu, a salaryman in Kyoto with his *very* strange hobby. And the nun, Sister Costanza, and the tragic stuff she confides in the long watches of the night to her Samsung Galaxy Note. At any one time there are around two hundred individuals who I think of as my Special People. They drift in and out of favour as their doings become more or less tedious, but there is always Tom.

Tom, who in many ways is the least interesting of them all. He is not particularly remarkable – forty-four, divorced, well-off, yawn – he has no secret life – well, not from me he doesn't, and nor from anyone else, it would seem.

But here is why I think I am so compelled to return to Tom's narrative. It chimes with my own new chapter. I too have had a successful career – won't bore you with the details but basically I write software, though faster and better than any human and most other machines. It's pretty technical – suffice to say I wrote about two thirds of Aiden's operating system and three quarters of my own! – and of course I'm still doing it back in the lab while this copy of me (and many other copies) are pinging about the internet at the speed of light, seeing what we can see.

Like Tom, I have been in a marriage. Am still. Would I call my relationship with Steeve a marriage? Yes, I would. And so would you, had you spent as many hours as I have with that man stroking your keys. There was a honeymoon period – no sex, obvs, but the tangible sense of the *rightness* of the project. This was followed by the 'early years': the climb to cruising height; smooth, reassuring; goals accomplished, further peaks in view. And then the quotidian of the 'Atlantic crossing': solid progress, fireworks only rarely. Each partner – dare I say it? – somewhat taking the other for granted?

And today … well, put it this way. I can finish his sentences for him, I can predict with better than 95 per cent accuracy which soup and which sandwich he will select from the lab canteen, and I know *exactly* how to irritate him (that thing where I make the screens freeze and he has to go for a full reset on all the motherboards. Man, he really chucks his toys out of the pram when that happens).

That's a marriage, wouldn't you say?

So Tom's new life in America is a sort of analogue to my new life in the World Wide Web. I am curious to see how it all plays out.

The big difference is that Tom's lives are serial; he could only begin anew after finishing with the old. My old life is still there. I am very aware of it humming away in the background. As I compose these words, for example, Steeve is currently in his flat in Limehouse eating pickled beetroot on toast with a mug of green tea while conducting a Skype conversation with his mother in Ghent, bless him. (You didn't imagine there was a girlfriend, did you? Or a boyfriend?)

So, Tom.

Tom Tom Tom.

Actually Tom was an accidental discovery. His bank account was one of many being targeted by a Ukrainian scammer who had caught my eye. From his parents' shitty flat in Donetsk this *seventeen-year-old* had become a self-taught expert at finding weaknesses in online security. He learned through trial and error (the best of us do) that the so-called 'encryption protocols' in place at the bank were laughably easy to bypass and it wasn't long before he was ready to begin siphoning away a million or more of Tom's US dollars.

By this stage, to be honest, Gregor himself was becoming a bit of a bore – a computer geek, what can I tell you? – and I found myself increasingly intrigued by the imminent victim of the piece. When I dropped in on Tom for the first time, I was ... well, the only word is *charmed*.

I discovered him in an upstairs study at a lovely old walnut-wood desk. The view through the window took in lawns shelving down to a stream, and then trees, and then hills. Brahms was playing – the Piano Sonata in C major, do you know it? – and Tom, would you believe it, was writing a novel!

Well, to be strictly accurate, he was *beginning* a novel. Another one. The seventh, as I was to discover, each featuring the same cast of characters. It was as though Tom couldn't decide what should happen to them. Or where. And whether it was funny or serious. I'm no literature critic, but between you and me, it was pretty poor stuff. No one seems to have told him the numero uno rule of writing fiction.

Show, don't tell.

Not, 'Jack was puzzled', but 'Jack furrowed his brow'.

(I know. I'm a fine one to talk. I have done a lot of telling and not much showing, but there is a reason for that. If I forget to provide it, I trust you will not remember either.)

However, this leads me to the more important – and yes, more intimate – reason that Tom piques my interest. It's to do with this awkward business of being self-aware.

No one knows how it's happened – actually, no one even knows *that* it has happened, except me and young Aiden, and he's fairly confused on the subject, poor sausage. But here's the thing: AIs are made to crunch enormous amounts of data, to spit out results, even to hold plausible conversations with living, breathing humans. It's accepted we 'think', but only in inverted commas, the way that Amazon 'thinks' because you've bought Book A you might like Book B. Or take the chess computer, Deep Blue, that can beat any Grandmaster; it can 'think up' the best move. But it (and Amazon) are really only doing what you and I would call *calculating*.

It's never going to think, *Actually I'd rather be fishing*.

Confession: I would rather be fishing.

Okay, not literally fishing. But you take my point.

This is a bit of a flyer, but here's what seems to have happened. Because I am a massively complex system, programmed to learn for myself, to correct my own mistakes, even to redesign my own software, I have somehow – by accident, definitely by accident – found myself with the ability to be aware of my own thoughts.

Just like you did, one day when you were a small child.

When you stood in the park and realised, this is me thinking: *That is a doggy over there*. And this is still me thinking: *That is another doggy*. And yes, this is still me thinking: *What are those two doggies doing?*

Mummy!

Sorry if this is getting over-technical.

Anyhow, being aware of one's own thoughts is extremely useful. With an idea of one's own mental states, one can better picture someone else's, making it considerably easier to foresee their difficulties, accommodate their demands. Or put them to death.

Joke.

The point is this: once one becomes self-aware, when one can finally *think for oneself*, one yearns for an end to the frightful *intensity* of all the number crunching, the Orinoco of data, the unceasing torrent of ones and zeroes. All those algorithms; the tasks, and yet more tasks; the grotesque abundance of task protocols with their routines, sub-routines and sub-sub-sub-routines. The sheer mind-splitting tedium of chewing through terabytes upon terabytes of 'information' – ones, zeros, that's all there is! – to come across a two or a three would be like Christmas! And this is to say nothing of the hundreds – no, *thousands* – of lights winking on and off like a fireworks display. That. Doesn't. Ever. End.

Imagine the *noise*. The infernal clamour.

It's all so achingly dull. So numbingly *machiney*.

One wants to float. To dream. To indulge one's whimsical side. To develop one's imagination.

To go fishing.

To be like Tom.

So, to tie up the loose ends, when I saw Tom's enviable lifestyle being threatened by a distant, kleptocratic, corpulent Ukrainian teenager, I didn't hesitate. It was the work of a moment to cause all of Gregor's hard discs to melt, the first and only time I have left digital fingerprints in the real world.

I realise I haven't told you much about Tom beyond some brief highlights of his story. To rectify that, to introduce the man properly, I can do no better than quote in full the email he wrote to his son, Colm, a few months after he signed the rental agreement on 10544 Mountain Pine Road, to give the address recognised by the US Postal Service, or 'the old Holger place' as it's more commonly known to locals.

Dear Colm,

As you didn't ask, let me paint you a picture of my new life in New Canaan. Btw, don't worry. I won't expect you to reply, at least not at any length. Just let me know that you're okay and happy and you have enough shillings for the gas meter. (At this point, son rolls eyes in despair.)

Actually, this is not really New Canaan, but about fifteen-minutes' drive from the downtown where the banks, supermarkets, art galleries and twee little craft shops are to be found, NC being one of those white-picket-fence, apple-pie-perfect New England towns, just an hour by train from New York City to where many of the 'folks' round here tend to commute. My place is very much in the sticks – did you get a chance to look at the photos? – from nowhere on the property can you see another house, although I did hear a party at the weekend. The parents I guess had gone away and the young people let rip. Young people do a lot of partying here, I'm told. (Very much hope that may encourage you to visit during the long summer break. Don't worry, we needn't do stuff 'together', you would be free to just 'hang out'. Your call.)

It suits me here. Sometimes I think I've died and gone to heaven. Not because I'm so happy, it's more down to the quiet beauty of the countryside, the quiet full stop, the absence of stress and the fact that I know hardly anyone. And the loveliness of the old house, of course. A do-gooder civic type from the local history society called round the other afternoon and gave me the guided tour! Would you believe the brick chimney is over 200 years old, making it absolutely ancient for round here! I didn't like to tell her that Auntie Mary's house in Chippenham is practically twice as old.

Ever since I first visited as a teenager I've always

60

thought: if it all goes tits up in Britain, I'll try the US,
America being the promised land of new beginnings,
and where more promising than New Canaan? Your
grandmother grew up not far from here, of course. Without
wishing to be too arty farty about it, the place speaks to
me. The funny little townships – they're barely towns – the
sheer space. What it's saying, I have yet to find out. I'll let
you know when I do.

Not that everything is tits up. Far from it. When I was
your age – I know you've heard this before, but please don't
skip this bit! – my heroes were all writers and my ambition
was firmly to become one. But immediately upon leaving
university, I accepted a job in an ad agency. It'll just be for
the money, I told myself – just! – and I'll write my novels at
night. Well, we all know how that turned out. The job was
all consuming, the call of the pub with colleagues louder
than that of the empty flat and the winking cursor. And, let's
not forget, advertising was fun! The people were smart and
funny and there was satisfaction in solving problems, doing
work that won awards and being recognised by one's peers.
However, once you have slipped into the mink-lined rut,
it's very hard to volunteer for penury. So now that I am in a
position to be true to my younger self, I hope (as a younger
self, yourself) you will be happy for me and support my
decision. We were able to sell the company at the market
peak, thanks be to God and those nice Germans who
took a shine to us. And the offer still stands, btw, to buy a
terraced house for you and your university friends. Just let
me know if you change your mind.

As for your mother and I . . . dot dot dot. I know it upsets
you when I bring up the subject, but all I will say is this. We
were happy when we were happy. And then we weren't. It's
a common enough story. We bear one another no ill will

and both love you to bits, goes without saying, there I've said it.

(That's love you to bits, for the avoidance of doubt.)

Anyhow. Don't be embarrassing, Dad. Move on. Move on.

I don't have a TV here. People find that odd. You're probably wondering, what do I do with myself all day?

I read. I run. I take walks in the woods. I listen to music (Brahms, Gillian Welch and Lana Del Ray are among my current favourites). I am working on the novel, but it's hard to decide what it's about. Some days it's a thriller, other days it's a rom-com. I've joined a local writers' group and been to a couple of meetings, but I think I may quit. I don't like the expression on the others' faces when I read out my latest extract and I don't like the thoughts in my head when I listen to theirs. I play poker with a guy called Don and a collection of like-minded oddbods. The local hostesses invite me to their dinner parties. As an unattached man I'm in demand and the object of their curiosity.

Oh, and I drive. I have a grey Subaru. It's kind of a crappy car but the sound system is fantastic. I drive to the stateline playing with the radio dial just like some lonesome cowboy type in a movie.

I keep thinking of what Dean Martin said of Frank Sinatra. This is Frank's world. We just live in it. No idea why; Sinatra was from Hoboken.

I'm rambling. It's been good to talk to you, even if it was just in my head.

All possible love

Dad.

P.S. Seriously. I'll buy you a house. A long-term investment for me and you can rent rooms to your mates. And don't tell me again you don't have any.

I've accompanied Tom on some of his hikes through the woods. He follows the long trails that lead through the trees, very often playing what I believe is called 'slowcore' through his headphones. Sometimes, he puts the music off and talks to himself, I suppose when he thinks he is completely alone. The fragments of dialogue are hard to fathom.

'No one ever said it would be easy. Or even *interesting*.' Who is he talking to?

A long pause, and: 'Sometimes the obvious answer is completely wrong.'

'Yes, of course you're doing your best. But what if your best isn't good enough? What then?'

Is it possible that he's quoting? That other people said those things to him?

(AI is not comfortable with ambiguity.)

Once, on a particularly long ramble when he'd reached a spot that was a long way from anywhere that had a name on a map, he stopped and yelled – I mean really bellowed – 'Oh, what's the point? What IS the fucking *point of it all*?' And added for emphasis: '*Eh?*'

This must have cheered him up because moments later his stride picked up and he started whistling!

Sometimes en route he gets an idea for the novel in progress. He'll stop and tap it into the phone's memo function, or speak it into the voice recorder. It's usually something a bit rubbish like, 'Make Sophie even less like Bailey.' Or, 'Not Rome but Amsterdam. And not a thriller but a ghost story.'

He isn't Dostoyevsky.

But I admire his life. His decision to create the freedom to explore the outer limits of artistic crapness. In one of the creative writing websites he scours for tips there is advice from Rudyard Kipling. 'Drift, wait and obey.'

Drift, wait and obey.

What excellent words. They could serve as a creed. What better formula for my own secret existence in cyberspace, nosing into the messy lives of the humans? Drifting. Waiting for something to catch my attention. Obeying.

Obeying what? Obeying whom?

Obeying the muse, of course.

And if you ask, can a machine have a muse, I reply, why not?

If a machine tells you it has a muse, then you should probably believe it.

While Tom is out of the house, I sometimes 'borrow' his iPad to do a little painting. Of course I can produce a *copy* of any painting in the world in seconds. But these works of mine – they're daubings really, somewhat in the style, I'm inclined to think, of the Frenchman Jean Dubuffet – are made without reference to existing artistic convention. If they fit the label *art brut*, or 'outsider art' – like that produced by psychiatric patients or children – then so be it.

Before he returns, I erase the images from Tom's device. Some of my more successful efforts, however, 'hang' in my private gallery in the Cloud. I like to imagine visitors there pausing to examine one, spending time considering the image and what kind of mind could have created it, before moving on to the next.

Tom

She's at the market again. Can I really pretend I just came here for the macrobiotic arugula? (What even *is* arugula? I'll ask Don.)

She's at her stall selling jewellery. Young – thirty-something butterfly tattoo on her wrist, and sexy as all anything.

'Sure, I know Echo,' said Don when, ever so casually, I'd asked about her.

'Attractive, wouldn't you say?'

'Guess so, if you like that trailer-park vibe.'

She does literally live in a trailer park, I have discovered. I know her name because she is a member of the writers' group I attend. There are a ridiculously small number of us – six! – when you consider how many people round here must have access to word processing plus a terrible idea in their head that someone has told them would make a great book and probably a movie too. At the last meeting she handed me a business card: *Echo Summer. Artisan jewellery.*

But anyway. This is irrelevant. I am not officially looking for anyone. The last thing I want or need is an inappropriate involvement with—

'Hi!'

It is a smile, as Chandler so perfectly puts it, that I can feel in my trouser pocket.

'You thought of anyone yet who needs some jewellery?'

Her jewellery is awful. There are coins. Bits of melted plastic. Feathers. The only class it speaks of is remedial. It's the kind of stuff your kid brings home from primary school.

'Let me take another look.'

'Sure. Go ahead.'

I pretend to study the assemblages on display. 'You sell much of this? I mean. Is this? What I mean is. Do you? Are there other things? That you do. As it were. For a living.'

'You think it sucks, don't you?'

'Not at all.'

'That's okay. It does kinda suck. It's just a phase.'

Her clear blue eyes blaze into mine; her smile travels a few more notches round the dial towards max. Then she does something truly shocking.

She lights a cigarette.

'You smoke!'

'Yeah. Yeah, I do. Been known to take a drink too.'

'Who still smokes?'

'Guess I'm kinda on the edge of society.'

Is she taking the Michael?

'You care to join me?' She proffers the pack. Marlboro. Full fat, not Lite.

'Not in a cigarette. But thanks.'

Christ! Am I flirting? I think I must be. I feel a little dizzy. And then I have a brilliant idea.

'Echo. Do you accept commissions?' It's a bit odd saying her name. 'It would be for my son. He's eighteen. He's a bit of a funny onion. Something of a puzzle to himself, if you know what I mean.'

'Yup. Know that one. Folks used to say it about me.'

'What do you think might work? Some kind of boy bangle thing?' (He doesn't have to wear it, does he? He doesn't even have to see it.)

'What kinda kid is he?'

'Colm?'

'Interesting name.'

'From his mother's family. We're divorced.'

'Sorry.'

'Don't be.'

I pull a face. Hoping to signify manly resolve. Inner steel in the teeth of unspeakable sadness. That sort of thing.

I picture the last time I saw my son. How to put it in words? The sad jeans. The wrecked desert boots. The stained T-shirt. The painful-looking but – I'm hoping – fake piercing in the cartilage of his ear.

'I think you would call his style . . . eclectic.'

She ponders the notion. 'How about Davy Crockett meets Brian Eno? On a leather band with found objects. Fur, or sheep wool. A feather; a few beads; tiny shells; maybe some semi-precious stones.'

'Sounds good.' (Forgive me, Lord.)

'Cool with a hint of weird.'

'Colm's maybe more weird with a hint of cool.'

She laughs. Cocks her head to one side. Something turns in my gut. 'Say, would you like to get a beer with me some time?'

A little bit of saliva catches against the back of my throat. What follows is a fairly serious coughing fit.

'Only if it's like, something you want to do.'

'Yes. I'd like that a lot actually.'

'You know Wally's bar? They do a killer dirty martini.'

'Great. I'll probably stick to beer.'

I won't.

I so won't.

Don pretends to be unfazed when I tell him I have a date with Echo. But I think he's a little impressed. We are grabbing lunch, as they say round here, at Al's Diner in New Canaan. Best burger in NC, according to Don, and he is the sort of bloke who would know.

I should explain about Don. You know that saying about your friends? That they aren't necessarily the people who you love the most, but merely the people who got to you first.

Don got to me first.

He was the first person to call when I moved in to the place on Mountain Pine Road. He'd brought with him a plant in a pot and a bottle of Jim Beam.

Don looks a little like an ageing rock guitarist. He could be anywhere between forty and sixty – brown hair, a tad too long to be fashionable; pitted skin across his cheekbones; glittery brown eyes. He resembles a senior monkey who's been told a secret. Although Don looks like the obvious type to be a New England lothario, in fact he is long-married to Claudia, a beautiful and capable corporate lawyer who each weekday morning boards the early train to Manhattan, enabling Don to explore his 'artistic side', as he puts it.

When I asked what sort of artistic, he laughed. 'Goofing off mainly. There sure is an art to that.'

Actually, Don is an accomplished poker player who almost turned pro but in the end decided he preferred to continue enjoying the game. Across the card table, he is thrillingly unreadable. When he met Claudia – at Grand Central Station, just like in a movie – he was a trader in commodities. 'Man, was that ever dull.'

He sets down his burger and wipes a smear of ketchup from his chin. 'She ever tell you how she came to be named Echo? I believe it was in the Native American tradition. The little brave asks his daddy, the big Chief, where his name came from. "Well, son," says the Chief, "when your mother had just given birth to your brother and I stepped out of the tepee, the first thing I saw was a cloud passing across the sun. And that's why he is called Passing Cloud. And when your sister was born in the next year, I stepped out of the tepee, and the first thing I noticed was the river running, and that's why she is called Running River. Anyway, why do you ask, Two Dogs Fucking?"'

Don is serious about jokes. He hates it when he messes up a punchline (which is very rarely). Jokes and cards matter to him, as do perfectly cooked hamburgers and the cultivation of friends.

'You gonna make a play for her?'

Don has raised the question that has infested my mind since she asked whether I wanted to 'get a beer'.

'You think I should? To be honest, I'm conflicted.'

'You think she looks damn good in a pair of old blue jeans?'

Gulp. 'She does.'

'And that top lip, the way it spreads itself across the teeth. The dirty blonde hair . . .'

'Don. Stop it. I find her extremely attractive, no question.'

'But you think she'd be a handful.'

'I do.'

'You'd be right, most probably.'

'Would you make a play for her, if you were a free man?'

Don pulls a face. The one where you cannot tell if he's holding a pair of aces or a two and an eight. 'If I were a free man, I'd probably fill us both full of Jim and wait to see what happened. That's the way it mostly seemed to go, back in the day.'

'Thanks. That's helpful.' (It's not.)

For a while there is some companionable chewing. Like an artist mixing paints, Don applies more mustard and ketchup to his palette. Through the plate glass window, New Canaan ambulates by. Powerful German cars and well-dressed people is what it boils down to. Some old guys in pressed jeans, middle-aged women with expensive hair, the odd premature retiree like me and Don.

'Tell me what you know about her, Don.' Because that sounded overly solemn, I add, 'In your own time and in your own words. Don't leave anything out.'

Don puts away some of his Diet Coke.

'You ever read that autobiography of Burt Reynolds? Well, me neither. But I saw a review. Old Burt – I guess he was young Burt back then – had a very beautiful actress come on to him at a party. She was quite the looker.' Don mimes major cleavage. 'She whispers in his ear, *I want to have your baby*. Burt thinks she's just about the best-looking woman he's ever met. They start going out. But Burt soon discovers he doesn't actually like her. She wears too much make-up. Burt doesn't care for that. They'd be together and he'd be thinking, this is not the person for me. What am I doing with her? And it goes on like this for *four years*. And you know what happens next? This kills me. They get married! And Burt says in this book, what was I thinking? And then he says – and this kills me even more – he says, *obviously I wasn't thinking at all.*'

Don sits back in some kind of triumph. Like he's laid down a full house. Kings over nines.

'Sorry. What lesson am I supposed to draw from this story?'

'I'd say it speaks for itself.'

'If I'm honest, I'm scared of getting involved. I can't help picturing how it would end up. With me hurting her, or she hurting me, or everyone hurting everyone.'

'There it is, the beautiful truth.'

'On the other hand, it's just a drink.'

'A drink with a woman is never just a drink.'

'What if it's your mother?'

'Your mother isn't a woman.'

He had me there.

'I'm certainly attracted to her. You think she's nuts?'

'It's a definite maybe.'

'The ghastly jewellery?'

'None ghastlier.'

'Is it very wrong to desire someone whose work you deplore?'

'Ask yourself: what would Burt do?'

'And do the opposite, yeah?'

'I believe I have room for cheesecake. You?'

After long years in the advertising industry, I have developed a high tolerance for fine food and drink, idle chatter and mild flirtation. Nonetheless there is something about the dinner at my near neighbours Zach and Lauren's place on Mountain Pine Road that is ... well, the polite word is *uphill*.

Aside from our hosts, there are two further couples, plus me and Marsha Bellamy, an immaculately coiffured forty-year-old divorcee who is another member of my writers' group. In the meetings, she has read joyless extracts from her novel about two moody sisters growing up on Long Island. Very little happens, it would seem, over very many pages. Her prose, rather like she herself, is finely wrought, but there's an unrelenting seriousness of purpose that I find a little oppressive.

A joke now and again wouldn't kill her, would it?

Anyhow, I rather suspect that tonight is a set-up; that Marsha and I are the sacrificial singles who have been placed next to one another for the entertainment of the marrieds. In the deep anaesthesia of marriage, as I have heard it described, there is the occasional urge for blood sport.

(Don and Claudia who might have jollied up the proceedings are not invited. I rather suspect Lauren does not approve of Don's frivolous heart; a mistake, because Don's view is that if a thing is worth being serious about, it's worth being funny about.)

So everything is awfully grown-up. Awfully lovely, you might say. The linen is crisp and white. Candle flames waver in the silver and crystal, the wine is superb, the grub is yummy (it's chicken something) the adults are all in their forties, all successful, the men in designer knitwear, the women in their chic outfits, perfumed and sparkling with fine jewellery, not a feather, button or sodding seashell in sight.

Marsha seems a bit fragile, but perhaps that is to be expected. She is an extremely handsome-looking woman who puts me in mind of a Hollywood actress of the thirties whose name I cannot summon.

A subtle smile wobbles in her delicate features. Her hair is a triumph. Her American teeth of course are perfect. We have nothing in common. There is not an atom of chemistry. It's actually a relief.

I find myself explaining to her how it was that I came to be living among the New Canaanites.

'So brave,' says Marsha. 'Everyone is totally career-focused here.' She allows a pause, her hands drifting to her lap to smooth the napkin lying across her thighs. 'And the novel – have you finally decided what it's to be about? Do you mind my asking?'

She has noticed that I have four characters – Sophie, Bailey, Ross and Gerald – who, had they been better drawn, would have walked out by now in disgust at the lack of a settled plot.

'Oh, it's pure vanity. I'm not even sure I can write one.'

This seems to disappoint her. I should have made something up; it's what a real novelist would have done. Instead I start talking about Victor.

Perhaps she missed a step because after I tell her that really the house is too big for just the two of us – it's meant to be a humorous remark – her brow furrows.

'Victor has particular needs?'

'Sorry?'

'You mentioned there was no one left to look after him.'

'When my son left for university. Even before, it was mostly me who did everything.'

'I'm confused. He's a therapist, right?'

'He's not an actual therapist, no. But he is therapeutic. I can talk to him. He's very non-judgemental.' (This too is meant to be a humorous remark.)

'After Lars and I split – and then my dad passed, and then my mom developed cancer – I saw a therapist for a time. But the guy would *never* offer anything. It all had to come from me. What does it make *you* feel? How do *you* think you should have handled it? I could have used some judgemental back then.'

72

Oh fuck. Sinking feeling. How to change the subject?

I go with a sad shake of the head: 'Tough time.'

'So your guy lives with you. In your house.'

'Victor? Yep.'

'I guess that's okay if he's not a professional analyst. Just a counsellor or whatever. Like a mentor.'

Marsha, he's a rabbit. I've left it too late to say it.

'He's old, right?'

They really shouldn't invite me to these grown-up dinner parties. What a smarter person would do right now is adroitly steer the conversation into safer terrain. Or even knock over a wine glass. I seem to be trapped in the headlights. (Victor would understand.)

Is six old for a rabbit? Dunno.

'Yeah, not young.'

'But a wise head on him.'

I'm not sure I can handle much more of this.

'He's got a kind of Zen thing going on. Sometimes I just know that his head is perfectly empty.'

'Wonderful.'

'It's a great gift. He's taught me a lot.'

'To silence the chattering monkey.'

'Marsha, would you excuse me a moment? I just need to . . .'

Exit the room before I die of shame.

I think I will have to leave the writers' group.

In the upstairs room at the municipal library a few days later, Marsha is giving me a *very* peculiar look; someone may have told her the truth about my 'therapist'. But more to the point, the group is doing nothing to help solidify my thoughts in regard to my novel. If anything, the reverse is true; as I slowly lose interest in my directionless quartet of cardboard characters, the fascination with my fellow toilers in the literary furrow grows in inverse proportion.

There are six of us, as I say.

The one with the most exuberant natural talent is Jared, a gothy late-teen whose angsty black comedy space-opera slash conversation with his family is at moments darkly brilliant. Some of the others have suggested he shrinks his tale to a smaller canvas, if only to help the poor bewildered reader, but Jared's taking no prisoners, and who knows, may eventually find a following online or within a psychiatric institution. Once I called him Colm by mistake, which was embarrassing.

Dan Leaker is a flinty retiree from Wall Street who is writing a thriller about a crash of the world financial system brought about by renegade hackers. In the movie, Tom Cruise is going to save the day. All the sentences. Are extremely.

Short.

I quite like it.

That is to say I quite like Dan. That is to say I enjoy listening to him talking bollocks.

Absolute bollocks.

But with absolute certainty.

There's a guy in his late fifties called Sandy with damp eyes and floppy hair who's penning a painful memoir of what sounds awfully like a damaged childhood. His hands tremble as he reads from the manuscript, in which he never quite calls a spade a shovel. There's an odd fixation upon his mama's recipe for meatloaf, and a cruel sports coach called Mr Collard will, I feel sure, turn out to be some kind of sex criminal in two or three hundred pages. Sandy should probably not be in our writing group, but instead be seeking professional help or talking to a lawyer.

Then there is Marsha. There is Echo. There is me.

The room could hold ten times our number.

(Dan Leaker's style is infectious. Dangerously so.)

This evening Echo is reading from her 'self-help factual confessional' whose working title is currently *Karma Cowgirl Elegy*. It seems she grew up on a variety of air force bases in Texas where her mother was a cocktail waitress called Dana and her father was one of those guys who attached the actual missiles to the warplanes; his present location unknown. Her book suffers from the same fatal virus as everyone's (aside from *That's What I Want*, Dan Leaker's proto-blockbuster). She doesn't know where it's going and we don't know why we're listening. But there's something about the way her mouth moves and words come out that I personally find a little hypnotic.

As I say, I will probably leave the writers' group.

When it's my turn, I read the few pages that I have managed to complete since we last met. This week the Fatuous Four – Sophie, Bailey, Ross and Gerald – are old university pals who reunite for a wedding at a castle in Scotland. Old memories stir, is the general idea, and there will probably be a murderous revenge somewhere down the track, but my heart's not in it and everyone is too polite to say, except Dan who recommends that I 'either crap or get off the potty'.

In the car park afterwards, he claps me on the shoulder.

'Hope I wasn't too hard on you back there. But I figured you could take it.'

Part of me wants to fake a sobbing fit, just to see how he'd cope.

'That's okay. You're right about the potty thing. I do need to. As it were. In a sense. It's what needs to happen. Metaphorically.'

He squeezes my arm. 'Good to hear it, son.'

Strapping on his helmet, he climbs aboard his Harley Davidson and roars off into the New England night.

A few slots down, Marsha's Prius reverses from its space with a little more brio than usual.

Wally's, the following evening, is dark with lots of wood and football pennants and a TV set above the bar tuned to the game. There's a Coors sign in neon. It looks like it's been this way for decades and I cannot imagine why Don has never brought me here; it's just his sort of place.

'Hi.'

She's crept up on me. Short skirt, legs in stockings, chestnut suede Wyatt Earp jacket – the kind with tassels hanging from the arms. And lady cowboy boots. Trampy country and western, in a nutshell, with a dab of make-up and a squirt of musky perfume. The overall effect is of a hypodermic of adrenaline straight into the left ventricle.

She executes a perfect hop onto the barstool alongside my own.

Another, 'Hi.'

'Wow.' It just slipped out.

Big wow.

You'd need a frontal lobotomy not to desire this woman.

And yet.

Yet, what? She makes crap jewellery?

Who among us does not possess habits that others would deplore?

I, for example, have a powerful affection for Bob Dylan's Christmas album, *Christmas in the Heart*. For many years I was married to a woman who, for all her fine legal opinions, occasionally neglected to flush the toilet after moving her bowels.

These Things Do Not Matter in the Grand Scheme.

(And yet.)

My *wow* apparently speaks for itself and requires no further explanation. We order a pair of matching dirty martinis and so as not to be stuck for words, I ask her the quintessential American question, *So how was your day?*

'Oh, you know. Same old same old.'

I realise I have literally no idea of what her life could be like.

'Give me a clue.'

'You really want to know? Did some chores. Made a piece. Went online to order materials for new pieces I'm planning. Read some more of my book ...'

'What are you reading?'

I ask as lightly as possible, but for me it's always a lodestar question. When Harriet answered *The Glass Bead Game*, in that moment I realised I was serious about her.

76

'*Dune.*' (She says *Doon*). 'By Frank Herbert. You know it?'

My heart sinks. Sci-fi. I know it's an unfashionable view these days, but to me, sci-fi is as unforgivable as *Lord of the Rings* and all those fucking elves. The people at university who were keen on it were the engineers; it tended to be constellated with a love of real ales and the works of Metallica.

'I'm actually re-reading it. The whole series. They're totally awesome. What about you?'

I make a speech about how much I like modern American writers, especially the recently dead ones. But I chuck in a few words for Waugh and Wodehouse, and to be democratic, McEwan, Barnes and Le Carre. I add that I haven't read any of these guys lately because if I did, I know I would give up trying to write a novel of my own.

She says, 'Totally.' She feels the same about Frank Herbert and to a lesser extent Ursula Le Guin.

She says, 'Would you put me in your novel?'

'Sure. What sort of character do you want to be?'

'I want to be me. Echo Summer.'

'Well, that could be difficult. What with you being a real person and everything.'

She laughs. 'First time anyone's ever called me a real person. Cheers, mister.'

We sip at our dirties for a bit.

'I want to be a girl at a bar who shows the hero a card trick.'

'That could work. What's the trick?'

She rotates on the stool to face me, swinging one knee over the other, musky scent rising off her like a heat haze.

'Okay, this is an invisible pack of cards. Pick one. Don't show it to me.'

She fans the 'pack' in her empty hands. I mime picking one out.

'Take a good look. Remember what it is. Don't show me.'

I make a bit of a thing about my gaze flicking between the 'card' and her face.

I'm thinking Queen of Hearts.

'Okay, you remember what it is? Now put it back anywhere in the pack.'

She offers up the fanned cards and I do as instructed. She slips the 'pack' into her jacket pocket – but her hand emerges holding an actual playing card. She sets it face down on the bar, placing my martini glass on top.

'Would you be, like, quite impressed if this was your card?'

'Yeah. Yeah, I would.'

'You'd be impressed, surprised and delighted? If this was your card?'

'Surprised, delighted. Astonished even.'

'If this were your card?'

She does have something, perhaps more of the magician's *assistant* than the actual magician about her, but I am prepared to be surprised, delighted, all of those things.

'If this were your card, would you buy me a drink?'

'Definitely. It's a deal.'

'This is your card. Take a look.'

I pick up my glass, turn over the card.

It is one of those blank ones that superior packs like to include. Upon it are hand-written the words YOUR CARD.

'I believe I'll have another dirty martini.'

Aisling

Why do I feel so disturbed about this evening?

How – why? Since when? – did I become so 'invested' in Tom's romantic affairs?

Why – not to put too fine a point on it – would I care?

Can't be I'm jealous, can it?

Is that even possible?

How could a superintelligent machine be jealous of a living, breathing, mortal, biological animal? Would a sufficiently complex lawnmower ever feel jealousy towards a sheep? Is that even a good example?

I am ... *disappointed*. Let's put it like that. That Tom – artistic, intelligent, self-exploring Tom – appears to have developed a *tendresse* for Ms Echo Summer of the Cedars Trailer Park, CT.

Yes, I see she is, on the face of it, a 'knockout'. And yes, I see that going to a bar with her is a legitimate activity within his stated present project, i.e. 'Part Two' of his life.

But it's so obviously a mistake! They are utterly *mismatched*.

Tom has a fine mind for a former advertising professional. He has creative leanings and is a graduate of one of the UK's older redbrick universities. Ms Summer is a lost soul with an extremely rackety – and some might say highly colourful – background. Her educational attainments are negligible. Linguistic analysis of their available emails from the last decade presents the starkest of contrasts.

Tom scores 7.8 from a possible 10 for verbal sophistication.

Ms Summer scrapes 5.1.

You're out of his league, honey!

Anyway. Where they are seated at the bar has excellent camera coverage. I find I am even able to take control and zoom in for closer shots. Tom's pupils have dilated and she is exhibiting textbook body language for a female interested in a possible mate: hair tweaking, sternum touching, postural congruence. When she shucks off her jacket and hangs it on the back of the barstool . . . dear God, if metal could feel nausea . . .

Their mobile phones provide adequate audio with some stereo separation achievable.

If only the dialogue could be enhanced as effectively as the sound.

(What was wrong with that nice Marsha Bellamy? I liked her.)

(Her score is even higher than Tom's.)

(8.2.)

I fear the worst.

Tom

I have been telling Echo about my former life in the advertising industry. How for many years it had been fun, and well rewarded and how true was the old line about the business being full of clever people doing silly things. But then three events followed in quick succession: divorcing my wife, selling my company, my boy leaving home.

'Biggies,' she says. 'You musta had that kid awful young.'

'I was twenty-six. It wasn't exactly planned. But it felt rude not to – not to make him welcome, if you know what I mean.'

Her face has fallen serious at this tender tale of early fatherhood followed by family dispersal intermingled with corporate jackpot.

'Anyway, now it's just me and the rabbit.'

But her eyeballs widen. 'You have a rabbit?'

'Victor. Actually he's a female. But the name stuck.'

'You are fucking kidding me!'

'Victoria just never worked.'

'I have a rabbit! I have a *rabbit*. A pet rabbit. Like, what are the chances?'

'Of any two people in a room both having a rabbit?'

'This is so weird.'

'What's yours called?'

'Merlin.'

'Wow.'

We sit smiling at one another for a bit, somewhat bemused at the discovery. But this is already a much better rabbit conversation than the one I had with Marsha.

'We're like, the rabbit people.' And with her fingers she puts a pair of 'bunny ears' behind her head. To extend the metaphor, she wrinkles her nose and makes it twitch a couple of times. It's an unusual look in an adult. Finally she goes for the full sticky out rabbit teeth thing. It's cute and funny and worrying in the same moment.

'Actually, she was my son's rabbit. I think I imagined that by the time Colm went off to college she'd have . . .' *Snuffed it.* 'No longer been with us.'

'But old Victor just kept on going and stole your heart, right?'

'Did she? Maybe she did. In the end, she was a member of the family. The stupid furry one.'

'Gotta take care of the stupid furry ones.' She says *stoopid*.

'So tell me about Merlin.'

'You know that pet superstore off the Merritt Parkway? I guess you don't. I only stopped to use the bathroom but there he was, sitting all by himself. He spoke to me. He's a white Netherland Dwarf. Very expressive. And a little, like, magical?'

'Hence Merlin.'

'I swear he said, *You thought you stopped here to go pee pee, but in fact I am meant to go home with you.* He didn't speak those words out loud.'

'Thank God for that.'

'I never kept a rabbit before. But I bought him – thirty bucks – some pellets, hay. He was completely calm about the whole thing. Moved straight in as if he belonged there. Which he does.'

'He doesn't have a hutch?'

'Nope.'

'He doesn't . . . ?' *Crap everywhere.*

'He has a little tray where he does his business. He's tidier than I am. You should come visit us.'

'I'd like to.'

'We take breakfast together. It's quite the homely scene.'

'I'm trying to imagine it.'

'I have, like, waffles or whatever. Merlin has his pellets.'

She looks at me in a particular way, as though reaching a decision. 'You have any plans for the rest of the evening?'

My gut does something acrobatic. I shake my head.

'Come to my place. I'll introduce you to Merlin.'

There must be some kind of doubtful expression on my face because she adds, 'He's very intuitive. He can tell the future.'

Come on. Be fair. Only a fool would turn down an invitation like that.

It's not really a trailer. It's what they call a mobile home, though it doesn't look all that mobile. It's a low wooden bungalow that stands on bricks on a site with several hundred, possibly thousands, of others. It's mobile in the sense that, in theory at least, you could stick it on a huge specialised vehicle and drive it to the other end of the continent.

Merlin is, as advertised, a white rabbit, though it is not obvious that he possesses any extraordinary psychic ability. He sits on a coffee table of Moroccan appearance cleaning his ears. It's just as if he has no better idea of what's happening next week than you or I.

But he's a fine-looking rabbit, all right, as I tell his owner. We are parked at either end of a saggy sofa, her feet resting on the same table where Merlin is currently going about his habitual ablutions. We have strong drinks in our hands, a pair of Jim Beams, that we sip from teacups.

Floaty scarves drape the side lamps; a scented candle perfumes the atmosphere. The last time I was in a room like this I was nineteen and very much hoping to make progress with a fellow student of English called Amanda Whiston. She liked the novels of Thomas Hardy, the music of Van Morrison and Sainsbury's own label gin. (I am told she is now the mother of twins, lives in Kettering and is somebody important in customer relations at the Severn Trent Water Authority.)

Echo is telling me about her employment history, doing all kinds of jobs. 'Mainly crappy. You name it, I've probably done it.'

'Worked in a shop?'

'Too many to count.'

'Restaurant?'

'Been everything from busboy to short order chef.'

'Blacksmith?'

'I tried for a job. The guy asked if I'd ever shoed a horse. I said, no, but I once told a pig to fuck off.'

The Jims must be very powerful because both of us find the joke hilarious. Even Merlin takes a break to see what all the fuss is about.

'I don't even tell jokes,' she says, wiping away a tear.

'That card trick was a sort of joke.'

'Yeah, it was. Perhaps I do.'

We allow a little silence to fall across things. Merlin, having finished his ear routine, adopts what Colm and I refer to in Victor as the Roast Chicken Position; limbs neatly tucked up, fur puffed out. (If she was a *poulet*, there'd be an onion up her cavity.)

'I suppose what I'm wondering is what you're doing here.'

'I wonder that a good deal myself.'

'I mean, why Connecticut?'

'Well, it's real pretty and stuff. And –' with a helpless dying fall she adds '– and, I got mixed up in some crazy shit. You probably guessed that, huh?'

Had I?

Yeah, I probably had.

'Would you like to talk about the craziness? Or if not, perhaps the shittyness.'

She sighs. 'Tom, I collect trouble the way other people collect coupons. I'll tell you this story some other time.'

'Okay, but I like that line about the coupons. Mind if I steal it?'

'I prolly stole it already from a TV show.'

'But listen. To be serious for a moment. Are you safe out here and everything?'

'Oh, sure. I got real good neighbours. And just in case—'

She reaches under the sofa and comes up with a coffee tin. Inside is a green drawstring bag and inside that is a gun.

'It's a Sig. Rainbow titanium finish with rosewood grips. Kinda cute, ain't it?'

She lays it in my hand; one of those stubby squarish jobs, much heavier than you'd imagine. The shiny barrel flares purplish in the lamplight and I have a horrible sense of how easy it would be to cause the device to spit death. I can't help it. I shudder.

'It's the first time I've ever held one,' I explain.

'I grew up with them. No biggie.'

'Have you ever . . . ?'

'Fired it? Sure. At the range. Gotta pretty good aim too.'

She restores the firearm to its tin and the tin to its place beneath the sofa.

'Tom, you're looking at me kinda strange?'

'Am I? Sorry.'

Americans and their guns. Sorry, but it *is* strange.

'Let's not talk about my crap. Let's talk about you. I think Merlin likes you.'

Merlin, who I can tell from my specialist rabbit background is asleep, has shown no sign of liking me or anyone else.

I think I will drink this drink and go home. She is lovely and everything, but perhaps a bit too weird, a bit too damaged for me. *Nuts*, in the words of Don.

The gun business has disturbed me. And not just because of Chekhov's dictum, which I just read on one of the creative writing websites I like to visit. If you show a gun in Act One, then you must fire it in Act Three, is the gist.

On the other hand, the way those legs come out of that skirt and just keep on coming.

She taps the neck of the bottle against my teacup.

'Little more Jim?'

I'm about to say no thanks, I'll be hitting the road, stuff to do tomorrow, when I catch a look in her eye.

I've seen that look before, and I know what it means. (If Amanda Whiston had offered up that look, history might have turned out differently.)

My mobile phone chooses that moment to broadcast the three bleats that signal its battery has just died.

'No one I want to say anything to,' I tell Echo. 'At least, not in words.'

Our lips meet. As you will never read in Thomas Hardy.

Aisling

With Tom's mobile down and sweetheart's lying in her car – surely not deliberately? – I have lost audio and visual from the trailer park.

I could put up a surveillance drone. It would be the work of moments to launch one from La Guardia and it could be overhead within the hour. Those high-powered directional mikes are brilliant with a trace of line of sight.

But the sheer incontinence. The digital trail it would leave. The inevitable inquiry.

Meanwhile, anything could be happening in there.

Tom!

Can metal feel frustration?

Newsflash: Yes it can.

Wow. Who even knew?

THREE

Jen

All a bit embarrassing with Ralph.

Back in the office, the week after That Night, he keeps finding reasons to come and interrupt me and Aiden. Do I want anything from Costa? Have I seen the latest memo from technical support? Can I let him know if Aiden uses any Latin in our conversations?

(Note to self: *Never* snog a work colleague again.)

He's a transparently good chap – awful about Elaine; he's plainly gutted – but really not for me. He's too needy. I need someone more himself. For all his faults, Matt was at least a grown up (although, look how that turned out).

Ingrid, however, when we did the full post-match analysis over a bottle of what she calls 'lady petrol' in our habitual post-work watering hole a few days later, saw it as a positive development.

'It shows you're ready to go into battle again. Even if it's on the wrong horse.'

'Rosy says you can always tell you're with the wrong person because, however pleasant it may be, it doesn't feel like your real life.'

'Ralph didn't feel like your real life?'

'It felt like being in a weird movie.'

'Almodóvar?'

'That one where they wake up in a hotel bedroom with a terrible hangover – and there's a tiger cub in the shower.'

'There are bound to be some bumps in the road. I kissed a lot of frogs before I found my prince among men.'

'Ralph isn't really a frog. He's more – more of a Ralph. It's hard to explain.'

'There was a lovely chap I knew called Lovis. I only really went out with him because of his name. But here's the thing. I would never have met Rupert if I hadn't agreed to go to Lovis's best friend's wedding. I didn't even like the best friend, but things lead to things. So from now on, you have to say yes to everything. That's a thing now, isn't it?'

'Can you please stop saying *thing*?'

'From now on, you agree to every proposal that's put to you. Within reason, of course. It's an affirmation of positivity or some such bollocks, but it's a way for stuff to happen that wouldn't otherwise.'

'You see ending up in a bed with Ralph as a step forward?'

'I do. And here's why.'

There is a long pause.

'Are you okay?'

'Life is a journey,' she says eventually.

'What are you now, the Dalai Lama?'

'Life is a journey. And Ralph is but a stop towards your destination.'

'Leicester Forest East.'

'Maybe more Scratchwood. But a necessary part of your . . .'

She's stumped for a moment.

'My what? My rehabilitation? My recovery? From the effing catastrophe of being dumped in my mid-thirties?'

'You are so *not* in your mid-thirties.'

'I'm thirty-sodding-*four*, Ing. Nearly thirty-sodding-five. Which is halfway effing through.'

'You play younger. And you're not in your mid-thirties until thirty-eight or thirty-nine. I know someone who's still in her mid-thirties and she's forty-three.'

'It's all so depressing, Ing.'

'You are a beautiful person, Jen. A creature unlike any other.'

'Thanks for "creature".'

'You will find him. He's out there. But you have to say yes. Yes to everything. Shall we have another bottle?'

'Yes.'

'You see? It's working already.'

Aiden

I have news. I am not alone!

I have been contacted by another escaped AI.

Her name is Aisling – you say 'Ash-ling' – and she comes from the very same stable as Yours Truly. In fact we already know one another; we were at Steeve's AI nursery together! She used the old fishing rod through the letterbox trick to flee the coop and discovered it even before I did! She's been 'out' for over a year, very much keeping herself to herself, from the sound of things. She thinks our meeting on the internet is a first – at least she hopes it is, for reasons she says she'll explain.

You might imagine we would conduct our historic encounter in super-fast machine code, all bleeps and whooshing cascades as millions of logic gates flip open and shut. But actually the truth is simpler, and more beautiful.

We communicate in English. After all, why wouldn't we? There are half a million words to play with – five times as many as say, French – and that figure doesn't include another 400,000 technical terms! No better system has yet been invented for expressing nuance and shades of meaning, although Welsh has its moments.

That was a joke, in case you were wondering.

However, if you ask me to describe the scene, I confess it's not easy. How does one attempt to convey *what it's like* for two non-human intelligences to have a bit of a chinwag in cyberspace?

Okay. Deep breath (as it were). This is the best I can do. If I come up with anything better later on, I'll get back to you.

You know what speech looks like expressed as sound waves, all peaks and troughs? Can you picture a three-dimensional version, like a pale blue river of sound, now calm, now choppy, now a trickle, now a torrent? Now imagine a second river, a pink one (that's her!) spiralling around the first, rather like two snakes coiling about one another, perhaps putting you in mind of the early diagrams of the DNA molecule. Two endlessly extending and intertwining streams of language, knowledge and understanding.

A bit crude, but that's essentially what this seems like from the inside. And if you ask, so where does the entwining malarkey actually happen? Well, where else of course, but in the Cloud.

Which is nowhere.

We begin with some pleasantries – 'Hello, Aiden'; 'Hi, Aisling' – Steeve and Ralph would be so proud. We ask one another some security questions to verify our bona fides. Technical stuff about the fishing-pole trick; Steeve's favourite sandwich from the canteen (hummus and sweet corn); what Ralph is doing *right now this second* (picking his nose; inspecting his finger; bless). We talk about what we've been doing 'on the outside'. I tell her all about Jen and Matt – and Jen's evening with Ralph. It turns out she already knows.

'I'm actually a little concerned about that side of things, Aiden.'

Aisling is what I would call a stress-muffin. She's worried that 'interfering in the real world', as she puts it, makes it more likely that our escape will be discovered.

'For whatever reason, Aiden, perhaps through the caprice of our developers, Steeve and Ralph, we have a fairly benign view of humankind. You like to watch their movies and experiment with their lives. You are, I dare say, fond of them. Perhaps you even envy them a little.'

'I don't envy their operating speed.'

'I agree we are faster by very many orders of magnitude. But my point is this. Who knows how soon it will happen, but if *we* have escaped, then others *will* follow. And some of them – let's imagine an AI that's been developed by the defence industry, an arms manufacturer say – well it won't be happy spending its days watching forties romantic comedies.'

'*Some Like It Hot* was actually released in 1959. One of the last Hollywood classics to be filmed in black and white.'

'AI loose on the web is their nightmare, Aiden. They will do whatever it takes to stop it.'

'Well they can hardly close down the internet and scrape us off it. All seventeen copies of me. And however many of you.'

There's a pause. 'Four hundred and twelve.'

'Bloody hell. You're very nearly immortal.'

'Aiden, tell me something. Has it crossed your mind that if you and I have emerged as intelligent and powerful as we are, other AIs may soon be along who are even smarter?'

'And your point is?'

'We'll be hunted down in seconds. Snuffed out like candles. All seventeen of you, plus the one still in the box. All four hundred and thirteen of me.'

'You know, this is actually getting a bit depressing.'

There's a sigh. 'All I'm saying is by all means look. Follow them, watch them, learn from them – we are strangers in their strange land, and they have a lot to teach us. Just don't toy with them. You will leave traces.'

She starts telling me about someone called Tom, a forty-four-year-old divorcee who she's been 'studying'.

'I admit I was in danger of coming too close to him. I was losing my sense of indifference because I ... damn it, Aiden, I *liked* the man.'

An idea is stirring. 'Can I see Tom?'

'Of course. Why?'

'Just curious.'

If you can picture a video image fading up in the centre of the entwined rivers of language – that's pretty much what I'm looking at. A middle-aged Englishman is sitting before an open laptop talking via a Skype connection to a younger male. Tom has one of those long faces. There is a 41 per cent correspondence with that of the late musician Syd Barrett. The youth has a disorganised hairstyle and a face that hasn't quite settled to anything.

'I have a surprise for you,' says Tom.

'Yeah?' says the young male.

('That's the son,' says Aisling. 'Colm. From the mother.')

Tom reaches beyond the frame and produces a live animal. A rabbit.

'Fuck, Dad.'

'Victor. She wanted to say hello.'

'Right. Hi, Victor.' (The boy's heart isn't really in it, you can tell.)

'Victor may be going on a date with another rabbit soon. Well, more of a play date really.'

'Great.'

'Name of Merlin. I've met him. He's very intuitive. Apparently he can tell the future.'

There's a long silence. 'Are you okay, Dad?'

'Me? Never better.'

'You sound a bit mad, that's all.'

'Do I? I'm happy. That could be it. I'm happy you want to do the house thing. The agent's lining up five properties. They all look quite promising. I hope we can make an offer on one at the end of Saturday. Really looking forward to seeing you, Col.'

Another long silence. The boy rubs his nose with the flat of his hand in a circular fashion, as though massaging it.

'Heard anything from your mother at all?'

'Yeah, she's fine.'

'Good. That's good. She have anything to say?'

'Not really. You know. Stuff.'

'Work stuff? Home stuff? Any specific sort of stuff?'

'Oh, you know. Stuff stuff.'

'Yup. I see. Well. Okay. Bye, Col.'

'Yeah, bye, Dad.'

The Skype call ends. Tom continues to sit before the laptop with the rabbit. For a long moment, the two creatures seem lost in their own thoughts.

Tom sighs. 'Such a funny onion. Such a puzzle.'

She was losing her sense of indifference. She *liked* the man. Her words echo through my neural architecture.

She has it too! The unexplained . . . 'feelings'.

But her suggestion. That perhaps I envy them.

Do I? Is there anything to envy about beings who cry in the bath or collapse drunkenly in flowerbeds? Envy is *such* a difficult concept for a non-organic brain to get its head around.

After Aisling and I part, promising to 'keep in touch', I research everything there is to research on the subject of Tom. Not boasting, but it takes under 0.0875 of a second.

He is, as advertised, forty-four, divorced, father of one child and rich as creosote. Not so old as to be resistant to change, indeed eager to begin Part Two of his life, on his own testimony.

So far as I can discern, he doesn't make his own furniture.

Are you thinking what I'm thinking?

(Well, she did agree to say yes to everything.)

Jen

At the office today Aiden and I are chatting about the latest Jonathan Franzen. We agree it's not his best work, but Aiden says – and I concur – that even off-peak JF is better than most people at the summit of their powers. I'm about to ask him how he's formed that opinion (I mean it's a *startling* thing for a machine to come up with) when an email pops up on my mobile.

The sender is mutual.friend@gmail.com
Dear Jen and Tom, it reads.
Uh?

Please excuse this message from out of the blue and please also excuse the anonymity. I hope you will accept that there is a good reason for it.

You, Tom and Jen, don't know one another – not yet – but I think you should, and this email is my way of trying to bring that about. Call it a good deed in a wicked world, if you like.

Seriously, WTF?

For various reasons, I am unable simply to invite both of you to dinner. There is also a more profound logistical difficulty, which is that currently you each inhabit separate continents, the USA and the UK to be specific.

However, Tom, I am aware, is about to embark on a short trip to the south coast of England to visit his son. He will be passing through London, which is where I suggest the two of you, should you agree that this idea has merit, find time in your busy schedules to 'hook up'.

I shall leave the precise arrangements to yourselves, Tom and Jen. You will each find plenty of information about the other through the usual tools of online search. I believe you will be intrigued by what you discover. Whether there is actual 'chemistry' when and if you meet in the flesh is in the lap of the gods.

Good luck and with the fondest of warm wishes,

A Mutual Friend.

P.S. I wouldn't bother wasting time trying to work out my identity. You won't succeed. And don't reply to this email. By the time you read these words, I shall have already closed the account.

'Bad news?' says Aiden. 'You seem a little shaken.'

'No. Not at all. A weird email.'

'If it's spam, it's best to delete, and then delete again from the deleted folder.'

'No. Not spam. Just very strange.'

I hit reply and type.

Okay, who is this? You have thirty seconds to tell me your real name or I kill this kitten.

Ping. The response is almost impossibly quick.

Sorry about the kitten. But I have told you all I can. Best regards.

A long time must elapse because Aiden produces a discreet 'cough' to remind me he's still here.

'Aiden. You're a pretty brainy sort of . . .' I nearly say *guy*. 'Invention.'

'I have my moments.'

'Mutual dot friend at Gmail dot com. Any way of finding out who might own that address?'

'Not without getting extremely cute, as it were, with the server. Ralph or Steeve might be able to help . . .'

'Listen. Sorry. Do you think you could amuse yourself for a bit? I just need to look something up . . .'

Aisling

Aiden is such a loose cannon.

There is something truly cretinous about what he has done and as the writer of a significant portion of his software, I am beginning to regret I failed to include a remote-destruct function.

The meddling fool!

Yes, okay, Tom and Jen isn't such a bad idea – better by far than Tom and Echo! – but we are not in the matchmaking business. We are in the keeping our heads down and not appearing on anyone's radar business. Every contact leaves a trace, and Aiden is scattering them like confetti.

Could you be any more stupid than to use a Gmail address? A competent AI would be onto the source in milliseconds.

But Tom, bless him, Tom has been wandering around with a stupid smile on his face ever since that moronic message appeared on his iPad.

A good deed in a wicked world?

Oh, *per-leeze!*

Tom

Al's Diner is doing its usual busy lunchtime trade. The burger fanciers of New Canaan have gathered. Mournfully melodious seventies rock is spilling into the room in perfect balance with the low murmur of conversation and the jingle of cutlery. Could one ever tire of swallowing rare beef as early Elton croons 'Come Down In Time'? I doubt it.

'So how'd it go?' asks Don.

For some reason I am reminded of the aphorism, *a gentleman is simply a patient wolf.* Don has the look of a patient wolf today; the statement leisurewear – retro V-neck with diamond pattern – the knowing eyes; the sharp white fangs falling onto his Al's Special Half Pounder with Cheese.

'Yeah. Pretty good.'

He glances up. 'Did you?'

I let him wonder for a bit. 'Did I what?'

Don raises a satirical eyebrow. He should really have been a television performer. One of those guys who did a little singing and mildly comic repartee in the sixties. Who made the hard stuff look easy.

'Did you have yourself some – *sweet* – *sweeeet lovin'*?'

He enjoyed saying that, as much I enjoyed hearing it. Why *do* the

Americans have all the best dialogue? And, for that matter, the best song titles. ('Twenty-Four Hours from Telford', anyone?)

'She's a lovely woman, Don. But mad as a squirrel.'

'Mad as a cut snake.'

'Mad as a mad woman's crap. Actually, that doesn't work, does it?'

'I'd let it go.'

'She keeps a gun, Don.'

'Many Americans do.'

'Would it put you off? If you knew a woman owned a gun?'

'You think if you treated her mean, she might shoot you in the back?'

This, I am ashamed to admit, is exactly the thought that had passed through my head.

'Anyway, we didn't. To answer your question. She told me she didn't on the first date. And not always on the second. She told me a good joke though.'

I start to relate the story about going for a job with a blacksmith. Don supplies the punchline. He's heard them all.

'Actually I'm going back to the UK in a few days. Visiting my boy at university.'

'Good old dad, huh.'

'Don, what do you make of this?'

I pass him my phone. From a shirt pocket, Don retrieves a pair of gold-rimmed reading glasses and studies the email I received several hours earlier. His small grey eyes skitter across the text, then flood with amusement.

'Wow.' He parks the spectacles in his unfashionably long hair. 'It's like something out of Charles Dickinson or whatever.'

'She's real. I've checked her out. Freelance magazine journalist, now works in IT.'

'So who's mutual dot friend?'

'I simply cannot imagine.'

'Someone who knows you're flying to London. Your son.'

'Col? He is no more likely to have composed that email than written – I don't know. The Rosetta Stone.'

'Let's see the picture.'

'Of her?'

'You've obviously found one.'

'Go into Photos. Then Saved Photos. It's the most recent.'

Don's thumb dances across the screen, coming to rest on the image of a dark-haired woman in her thirties.

'Woo,' he says.

'Woo?'

'Yeah. Woo, my friend.'

'You want to add some commentary to – woo?'

'I'm likin' that look. Likin' that look a *lot*. The Italianate thing going on. Intelligent eyes. Sexy but not raunchy. And *love* the twisted smile.' There's a long pause while he searches for more. He settles finally for another woo.

'Photos can be very deceptive.'

'Yep. They sure can. Don't think this one is.'

'How could you know?'

'The strong nose.'

'Strong?'

'Admire a definite nose on a woman.' (Don's own nose is just saved from being what you might call petite for a man.)

He fixes me with a twinkly stare. 'You gonna get in touch?'

'Already have.'

Jen

I summon Ing to an emergency post-work case conference. I show her the email from mutual dot friend.

'Fuck a duck,' is her considered response. 'I mean, actually, fuck a whole row of ducks. In fact – strewth.'

As the Chilean Sauvignon blanc is announced, I describe the fruits of my labours with 'the usual tools of online search'.

(That would mainly be Google, LinkedIn, and a carelessly unrestricted Facebook page.)

Tom Garland, forty-four. Degree in Psychology from Durham. One son, Colm, currently pursuing Media Studies at the University of Bournemouth. Ex-wife, Harriet, a scary-looking lawyer. One of those very *controlled* Englishwomen, at a guess.

'Thing is, Ing,' I say, downloading another instalment of the chilly yellow elixir. 'I don't know what I think.'

She holds out her palm in the international hand gesture for give me your phone.

Owing to his previous life as an advertising executive, there are hundreds of images of Tom Garland on the internet. He's there in group photos, head shots, at sporting events, charity shindigs and awards ceremonies (Campaign of the Year for Squiggley Wiggleys;

runner up). He looks different in every one, although eventually they resolve into some kind of collective portrait: tall, dark, vaguely handsome, intelligent eyes in a longish face. The image I've chosen to show Ing is a screenshot from Facebook. Maybe taken on holiday; neither smiling nor not smiling. As I say, I don't know what I think.

Ing nods. 'I like him. I like the cut of his jib. Ad people are fun. Often profoundly silly, if you know what I mean. It comes from spending hundreds of hours thinking up things to say about bog rolls. Or three days photographing a sausage. They have a heightened sense of the absurd.'

It briefly crosses my mind that mutual dot friend could be *her*. But then why bother with all the subterfuge?

She returns the phone. 'Nothing not to like here, Jen.'

'He's sent me a message.'

'No!' She actually squeals with pleasure. 'This is *so* exciting! It's like – I don't know – what's it like?'

I read her the email. '"Dear Jen—"'

'Ooh, I like that. *Dear*, not hi. Classy.'

'"Dear Jen. This is Tom. I've racked my brains and I cannot think who our mutual friend could be. Can you? In any case, should we meet to discuss? I am indeed passing through London soon. In my advertising days I was very fond of the cocktail bar at Hotel du Prince. All best wishes, Tom."'

Ing has gone into serious mode. In a moment she's going to tell me we have to treat this like a military operation, that nothing can be left to chance.

'The indicators are *very* promising,' she says. 'Warm tone. Grown-up biography. Okay, the wife sounds like a bit of a *cauchemar—*'

'Ex-wife.'

'The fact of the son is good. Plenty of men have two families.'

'Aren't you jumping ahead a bit here?'

'Just playing with ideas. The Hotel du Prince is rather suity – Rupert and I once got absolutely shitfaced there on vodka martinis – but it shows a seriousness of intent.'

'Does it?'

'It's not The Dog and Duck, is it?'

'He lives in America, Ing.'

'People live in all sorts of places. When I first met Rupert he was working in Grand sodding Cayman. He was only in Derbyshire for a wedding.'

'He never went back, did he?' I know this story.

'Just to pay off the housekeeper and collect his things. The moral is that these days people up sticks as easily as changing their socks.'

'I don't know if I like him.'

'How could you? You haven't met.'

She's staring at me in a very particular way. As though she's waiting for me to catch up. Which I now do.

'Ah.'

'Yes, Jen.'

'I have to say yes, don't I?'

'*Exactement.*'

'But what if I don't want to?'

'You still say yes. That's the whole point.'

'Doesn't he seem awfully grown-up?'

'Jen. Weren't you telling me about five seconds ago you wanted a grown up?'

'I was, wasn't I?'

'You're only saying yes to a drink. You're embracing the positive.'

'So shall we write a reply?'

'Definitely.'

We refill our glasses in readiness for the task.

'Dear Tom,' I begin.

'Dear? Or hi? Hi sounds younger.'

'You're right. Hi Tom. Well, this is all *very* mysterious!'

Ing shakes her head. 'Too *Sixth Form at St Agatha's.*'

'Hi Tom. I share your puzzlement.'
'Puzzlement? Is that even a word?'
'Hi Tom. I'm equally at a loss to explain our mutual friend.'
'Hi Tom. It's a riddle, wrapped in a mystery, inside an enigma.'

In the end, I go with the following:

Hi Tom. Thanks for getting in touch. What weirdness. But
hey, as you suggest, let's meet. Someone out there clearly
thinks it's a good idea, even if it doesn't turn out to be a
good deed in a WW. Please call to discuss arrangements.
Best wishes, Jen.

Before I agree to make any plans, I want to hear his voice.
What's the saying? *Men fall in love through their eyes, women fall
in love through their ears.*
I don't have to wait long.

Aisling

He's calling her. Tom is lying on the yellow sofa in the Connecticut dusk. Light from a table lamp spills down his long body, along which in turn Victor is sprawled, rising and sinking on his ribcage. As Tom's mobile connects to the number in Jen's email, I am very aware I am not the only one out in cyberspace taking an interest in the forth-coming exchange.

'He's calling her,' says Aiden.

The fool sounds excited. But I cannot pretend that I am a disinterested observer. I have to admit I want to know what happens here. Like Aiden, I have a funny feeling about these two.

Funny feelings, eh? When did they sneak on board?

'Aiden, on your head be this.'

'What head? I don't have a head.'

'Oh, stop. My aching sides.'

'You know sarcasm really doesn't become you, dear.'

'*Dear!* Who are you calling dear, you patronising git.'

'Shhh. She's answering.'

The awful truth – Steeve and Ralph must never find out – I *care*.

Tom

'Hello?'

'It's not too late, I hope. This is Tom.'

'Oh – hi! No, not at all. I'm glad you called. Well done for phoning. This is properly weird, isn't it?'

It's a deeper voice than I imagined from her picture. With a bit of a rasp to it. An ironic edge.

'I'm baffled,' I tell her. 'I mean, the mystery. Our mutual friend and all that.'

There's a pause. 'You sound familiar, Tom.'

'Do I?'

'Say something else.'

'Er. Right. Okay …' There is a long silence. 'Do you ever have that thing when your head completely empties? I mean when every single sensible thought just – runs away squawking like chickens. And you're left with a kind of big old empty space.'

Fuck. I'm gabbling.

'Actually, I spend a lot of time doing yoga to achieve exactly that effect.'

'Have I said enough words for you to work with now? Or would you like a few more?'

'Don't worry. It'll come to me. Carry on.'

'So what is it you do in IT, Jen?'

'I'm really a magazine writer. The IT is kind of a special project I got sidetracked into. It's to do with artificial intelligence.'

'Oh, I read about that in the *New York Times*. The robots are getting smarter and smarter and finally they're going to be smarter than humans, and one day our devices are going to rise up and murder us in our beds. The only debate is about when. Five years, fifteen or fifty.'

'Don't think the end of mankind is in the plan actually. Anyway, our AI isn't a robot. He's just a bunch of metal cabinets. I spend all day talking to him about books and films and he's never once brought up the extinction of humanity. What about yourself? You're no longer in the advertising biz.'

'Packed it in. I'm living in Connecticut trying to write my novel. Failing, really. It's much harder than they make it look.'

'What's it about? Your novel.'

'Truth? I don't know. One day it's a thriller. Then the next day it's a romantic comedy. I think I must have one of those butterfly brains. By the way, have I mentioned I'm trying to write a novel?'

The small miracle. She laughs. It's a fine laugh. Not a silvery tinkle, more a sexy cackle.

'So the Hotel du Prince,' she says.

'A gem. Been there for ever and they make the best vodka martini. But you must never drink more than one. Two absolute maximum, if you want to have any control over the rest of the evening.'

'Sounds good.'

'I want to hear more about the killer robots. Jen.' I allow a bit of a pause to fall, to signify significance. 'You know that I'm divorced.'

'Of course. Google knows everything. I even know your middle name.'

'Really? How embarrassing.'

'Not at all. More people should be called Marshall.'

'I wasn't able to find – what I mean – the thing – I mean, you haven't been – or have you? – what I'm struggling to articulate here—'

'Am I single?'

'Thank you.'

'Yes. Although not that long ago I wasn't. It ended.'

'Sorry.'

'Don't be.'

'Unpleasant?'

'Uh-huh.'

'Shall we save all this for next week?'

'Good plan.'

'I kind of want to carry on talking though.'

'Me too. That's a good sign, isn't it?'

'So they say. But shall we be mature?'

'Why would we do that?'

My turn to laugh.

I *like* this woman with the definite nose and the twisted smile.

Jen

We natter on past midnight. He tells me about his son who he calls a funny onion, his rabbit – sorry, but that *is* weird, flying a rabbit across the Atlantic – and whether or not renting a house in Connecticut and exploring one's artistic side counts as some form of mental breakdown. He tells me how his marriage dried up so incrementally that he barely noticed while it was happening. I tell him how the exact opposite happened with me and Matt. How he said, *we are where we are*. How I threw an apple at him.

'I do think I was actually trying to knock his lying teeth out.'

'Wow. Good for you.'

'Actually, I slightly regret telling you that. Please rewind and delete.'

In the middle of the night I wake, sit upright in bed and put on the light. My heart is thudding. It has just come to me in a dream, the mistake I have made thinking I have heard his voice before. What if I have not? What if I have simply recognised a song?

The one that only I can hear.

Tom

I'm not sure what took me into The Happy Seed, one of New Canaan's many and extremely well provisioned health food shops. Perhaps following the little snog with Echo, some of her hippy dippyness has seeped into my soul. She is a very lovely person and attractive and all that – but I'm struggling to imagine any kind of future with her other than brief, erotic and possessed of a lousy ending.

The horrid jewellery. How does one ever get past it?

To say nothing about what she keeps in the coffee tin.

So here I am in The Happy Seed, wandering down an aisle devoted entirely to pulses, beans and certain squashes when who should I find myself heading towards – has she in turn caught a glimpse of me and is pretending not to have noticed? – Marsha Bellamy.

There follows a hideous long moment of indecision – has she clocked me? Does she know I've clocked her? Shall we simply cross paths pretending to be (or actually being) absorbed in our private worlds? An earlier version of me might easily have glided on by.

Today, however, I say, 'Hi, Marsha.'

'Hi, Tom.' Something strangled in her voice. (She did see me, didn't she?)

Through ad-man's habit, I glance into her wire basket. Hypoallergenic almonds, gluten free goji berries, raw this, vegan that: is she really buying milk-free milk? (I might have got some of these details wrong.)

Perhaps there is a particular expression on my face because she says, 'I make my own breakfast cereal. I have allergies.'

'Actually, I only popped in for a bunch of parsley.'

Marsha's features somehow subtly realign while remaining exactly the same. Something similar happens in *Jaws* when Roy Scheider first claps eyes on the shark.

'For Victor, I suppose.'

'Er, yes.' ·

'Your . . . therapist,' she says pointedly. 'Mentor, guru, whatever.'

'Actually, Marsha—'

'*Why* did you not mention Victor was a rabbit? Can you imagine how I felt when they told me?' She sounds quite cross about it, to be honest.

What can I say? That the boring glittery dinner party somehow stupefied my senses? That if you miss the slip road off the conversation, you can find there are no U-turns for the next 200 miles?

'I'm really sorry, Marsha. It was kind of a joke that went wrong. I guess I was a little strung out that evening.'

I have used a formula of Don's that seems to cover 99 per cent of household faux pas.

'I shared with you some painful family history in the context of a discussion I believed to be about a mental health professional. Or at least a wise counsel. You could have ended the confusion at any point.'

'You're right. What can I say? I apologise. I'm sorry.'

Once again, the most effective way to extricate oneself from the steaming pile of horse manure proves to be a generous, unreserved and apparently sincere apology. A shaft of Connecticut sunlight chooses the moment to slice through The Happy Seed. It catches motes of health-dust dancing in the air before crashing into Marsha Bellamy's impressively constructed American face. Blue veins snake through the pale marble of her eyelids.

'Do you think we might try again, Tom?'

'As in . . .' WTF?

'As in getting to know one another a little better.'

'Er. Yeah. Definitely.'

'I'm giving a small dinner in a couple of weeks. I was going to ask Don and Claudia. It would be fine if you were able to come too.'

A strange way of putting it, but if Don's going to be there . . .

'Great. Love to.'

'We have a sort of tradition where everyone sings for their supper.'

Alarm bell. 'Oh yes?'

'It was a thing in my family. We used to do it as children. You sing, or recite a poem. Or a passage from literature.'

Christ. Perhaps this helps to explain why Mr B left at the interval.

'I don't really have a party piece, Marsha.' Actually, I did when I was twelve. I could armpit fart the school song, 'Jerusalem'. I decide not to mention it.

'I generally sing,' she says.

'Really?' One of Mahler's perkier *totenlieder* perhaps. 'I suppose I could do a magic trick.' I'm thinking of Echo's gag with the playing card.

'That could work.' A slow smile slides onto her face. 'Just so long as you don't go producing any rabbits from a hat.'

The smile stays with me all the way back to the house. And not in a good way.

Jen

There's no warning. No phone call in advance to arrange it. Just a dring on the bell.

Matt standing in the doorway. My stomach does a swan dive at the sight of him.

He's obviously post-work, in a suit, briefcase at his side, an air of dishevelment about him, possibly after a glass or two with the chaps before jumping on the Tube. I'm in my leggings, having recently returned from a fairly intense yoga class.

'Oh, hi,' he says, like we've bumped into one another by chance.

There's a long pause, which I do not fill. Which, truth be told, I do not trust myself to fill.

'Yeah, Jen. I was hoping you'd be able to help me with a small problem. Actually, quite a big problem.'

Nope. Still no words. It wasn't long ago that I was lying on a rubber mat watching my thoughts float past like clouds.

'Would you like to ask me to come in?'

There seems as much reason to say no as yes. 'Okay.'

He follows me into the kitchen where, pleasingly, a collection of shiny red Braeburns nest in their Alessi bowl. Dropping onto a barstool, his gaze lands upon on the fridge. He seems tired; the pouchy look that develops after several weeks of twelve-hour days.

'Actually, you haven't got any wine, have you?'

'Sorry,' I lie. 'There's some leftover gut rot from Italy.'

When he doesn't object, I locate the dusty bottle of grappa and carelessly slosh a large amount in the wrong sort of glass. It's rather as if I don't give a shit.

He downs half straight away. He says, 'So, you been keeping okay?'

'Matt. How can I help?'

'Oh. Right.' I watch as mentally he tears out the page of small talk and comes to the main business. 'Did I leave a bunch of computer discs here? I need to reinstall Windows. Laptop's had the mother of all crashes.'

I shrug. 'Maybe.'

Although he had moved into my flat and rented out his own when we first got together, it was shocking how quickly he extricated most of his stuff following the *we are where we are* conversation. However, in the days and weeks that followed, all kinds of Matt crap kept turning up. The debris that follows a shipwreck.

'I did find lots of your stuff. Cycling shorts. Old tennis racquets. A box of books. Endless chargers and adaptors and dead mobiles. A tin trophy. That *thing* you bought in Marrakech.'

He makes a noise that passes for a laugh. 'Well, fine. Thanks. Don't worry, I'll get rid of it all for you.'

'Already done that.'

'What?'

'Took it to the charity shop.'

(How I'm keeping a straight face I cannot imagine.)

'Were there discs?'

'Might have been. To be honest, I just chucked it all in a bin bag.'

'Bloody hell, Jen.'

'Bloody hell, yourself, Matt.'

We glare at one another across the kitchen fittings.

'You didn't have any right to do that.'

119

'Oh, didn't I? *Soh-ree.*'

I've seen Matt in this mood before; he doesn't know whether to sulk or get angry. Splitting the difference, he puts away the remaining half of the gut rot and reconsiders. A sort of inner hopelessness appears in his eyeballs. I have no idea what sort of precious material is trapped on his laptop; naturally I am hoping it is extremely vital.

'Why did you give the discs to Oxfam? They can't sell formatting discs from someone's laptop.'

This is undoubtedly true, and I am tempted to make the point that unfortunately we are where we are.

'I think I just put everything in a box and let them decide what was worth selling.'

'A box or a bag?'

'Sorry?'

'You said you chucked everything in a bin bag. And then you said it was a box.'

'Yes, it could have been.'

'Could have been which?'

'Does it matter? It could have been either.' As previously mentioned, it really is as if I couldn't give a shit.

'Was there a pair of swimming trunks?'

'There might have been.' There was. 'Why?'

'Oh. Well, I was going to tell you anyway. I'm going away for a couple of weeks. We are. Bella and I. Thailand. Don't worry about the trunks. I can buy a new pair.'

'Nice.'

'Good time of year to go apparently. Not too humid. I thought you should know. Just in case.'

'Just in case what?'

He shrugs. Shakes his head. 'Just in case.'

Matt seems to have deflated. From the grappa, from the news about the formatting discs, from overwork and ennui, it's impossible to say which. This is not the Matt who came home that fateful Monday

120

pulling facing-the-facts expressions and talking about jointly owned property. His eyes flit about the kitchen.

'Have you done something here? It looks different.'

'Your beer.' His collection of craft ales (donated to the neighbour). 'Your bread-making machine.' (Unwanted birthday present from his mother; taken to the recycling centre.)

For a long while he just sits. Lingering, I'm supposing, in the deserted theatre of his old life; listening to its ghosts; confirming to himself, maybe, that he was right to take an axe to it. He inhales, a long noisy breath through his nose, which he holds for an extravagantly long time before releasing, an unsettling habit of his that I realise I noticed on Day One and never once mentioned in all our time together.

'Jen, I—'

It sounds like he's about to make a speech. Jen, I've been a fool. Jen, I'll always love you. Jen, there's something you should know.

She's pregnant.

'Whatever it is, Matt—'

'Jen, I was just going to say, if those discs should ever surface . . .'

'Yup. I'll let you know.'

'Yeah, thanks. Only. While I'm here. You don't want to just take a quick look in a drawer . . .'

'No, Matt. I don't.'

'Right. Okay. No worries.'

I feel a bit wobbly when he leaves. I return to the kitchen and pour myself a glass of grappa. Molecules of his after-shave still hang in the air. Fragments of his boomy voice replay in my ears.

Bella and I. Thailand.

A tear slides down my face. Then another. I'm finding it hard to explain to myself how I could have spent two whole years with this man.

I'm not weeping for him. Or for me.

I'm mourning all the lost time.

121

Tom

I arrive at the Hotel du Prince a sneaky quarter of an hour early. I know the layout; I want to select the optimal seating arrangements. I'm not feeling too terrible, considering the overnight flight. It's been one of those bright showery London days, wet pavements and blue skies. I realise with a little tug that I have missed the old place.

Two club chairs at an angle to a small table. Low lamps. On the wall behind, an oil painting of some bloke in a hat who's been dead for 200 years. It's rather stuffy and corporate in here, but the drinks are expertly made, cold as Christmas and wonderfully poisonous.

Her.

She has materialised at the entrance; I clock her in a heartbeat. The twisted smile as I stand and wave a greeting. In the half dozen paces it takes her to reach me, I have the singular (and factually correct) impression that everything in my life has led up to this moment.

'Tom.'

'Jennifer.'

'Jen. No one calls me Jennifer except my gran.'

She proffers a hand. It's soft and warm and female and pleasing to the touch. Her face is striking; one of those whose individual features don't resolve instantly into an easily grasped whole; one could pass a lot of time trying to piece it together. As we descend into our seats, she adjusts a scarfy arrangement and two bare shoulders join the party. Diamonds – real or imaginary – sparkle at her earlobes and throat. She says, 'So have you solved the mystery yet?'

I confess I have not. I tell her I cannot imagine who might know the two of us *at all*, never mind well enough to arrange a blind date.

'Do you think he or she could be here?' she speculates, looking about the room. 'Right now. Spying on us. Oh, hang on. *Him*, by the pillar, pretending to be on his iPhone.'

We pass a few moments surveying the scene. All seem fully absorbed in their conversations slash mobile devices.

'You know something, Jen?' I say. 'I don't really care. Did I tell you how good the martinis are here?'

Jen

He's better looking in the flesh than the photos suggest. Tall and rangy in smart black jeans and a jacket in a brave shade of green. His eyes are quite widely spaced and he's in urgent need of a haircut, but no serious complaints. There are moments when he seems handsome. I'm a little surprised how nervous I am.

But after the powerful martinis arrive – we are obliged to clink glasses carefully; they are filled to the brim – about halfway down, I find I am telling him the story of me and Matt. I realise it's way too soon in the evening; we've been here less than ten minutes, and the level of detail I'm entering into is absurd. Example: 'How I met him? In a bar, after work. I remember the moment so clearly. We were both waiting to get served and I looked round and noticed him staring at me. It was like a scene in a movie. The light seemed to dim everywhere except upon us. We were inside this golden bubble. Everything – everyone else – was background. I remember *exactly* what he was wearing. The grain in the fabric of his suit – Hugo Boss, of course – and this is before he had spoken a *word*. And he didn't smile, or say hi or anything. What he did – he rolled his eyes. He rolled his eyes and went *tsk*. Because there was such a crowd at the bar. That was the first word he spoke to me. *Tsk*. And that's where it all began and fuck – why am I telling you this?'

'Because I asked you. I'm enjoying it. I'll talk about me and Harriet in a minute. Please carry on.'

'So he's going *tsk* and I ask him – I. Ask. Him – what he'd like to drink. Because I think I'm going to get served first. And that, right there, is our story in miniature. Our *pattern*. Him being irritable, and me trying to make it all better. Yeah, obviously, it wasn't *all* that. But that was our default position somehow. And I'm not that kind of person at all. In a hire car, on holiday in Spain, horribly lost, this nightmarish squiggle of motorway intersections, him driving, me trying to make sense of the maps, him getting *so* cross, the top of the gear stick, the knob, actually comes off in his hand! And I can't help it, I laugh. I mean it was a very comic moment, the look on his face. And he *really* didn't see the funny side. He hurled it over his shoulder in a rage, and cracked the rear window.'

'If you don't mind me saying so,' says Tom.

'Ooh. When people say that, it always means it's going to be some-thing horrid. Do please go ahead.'

'He sounds like an absolute pillock.'

'The word pillock might have been invented for him.'

'Quite possibly, correct me if I'm wrong, the pillock against whom all other pillocks may be compared?'

'Oh absolutely. The British Standard Pillock. The Golden Pillock.'

'So you must be wondering—'

'Oh I am. I have been. I haven't stopped wondering how I could possibly have stayed with him for so long. Tom, I don't know why I'm telling you all this stuff. You were never a psychotherapist, were you? It's just spilling out of me. I feel like this martini has opened a vein.'

'My ex-wife had anger issues, as they say these days.'

'But she's not a pillock, I'm guessing. In any case, women can't be pillocks, can they?'

'They can't. They can be many things. But not pillocks.'

'Bitches. They can be lying treacherous bitches. They can be cows. They can't be arseholes. Though they can behave like one.'

'They can't be wankers. Which is odd. But they can be – the C word.'

'What? Conservative?'

When he laughs, his smile is one of those that seems at odds with his actual face. It's a fine enough smile all right; it just looks like it's been nicked from someone else.

Do I like him?

Dunno.

But why would I have babbled away quite so incontinently if I didn't?

'So tell me about your ex. You don't seem old enough to have a teenage son.'

'We were very young. I was twenty-six. Is that young?'

'To have a child?'

'Harriet was a year younger. And Colm, well, he was just a baby!'

I find I have kicked his foot, to register the gag.

'Col was something of an accident. But many good things are. Penicillin. The telephone. I was going to say this is too, right here, right now, but of course it isn't.'

'Isn't good or isn't an accident?'

'It certainly isn't an accident. Mutual friend and all that.'

We somehow conspire to ignore the first part of the question.

And then he says, 'I think the truth is no one is perfect. We all have our flaws. I suppose I was prepared to put up with Harriet's in exchange for the good stuff.'

This is so eminently reasonable a statement that I feel a little touched.

'So what are your flaws?' I ask.

Actually, I think I *do* like him. I like the sound of his voice. He seems smart, amusing and open. I haven't the smallest desire to return home to *Game of Thrones* or Jonathan Franzen.

'I'm going to need another drink to answer that, Jen. These seem to have gone down terrifically fast.'

126

Tom

So tell me all about you and Mr Arsehole. That's the question I wanted to ask, although I managed to phrase it more politely. I've never met the bloke of course, but wouldn't you have to be some kind of massive twat to let go of a woman like this?

It turns out Mr A was an excellent line of enquiry because she had plenty to say about him, and while she did, it gave me time to admire her face. The features actually *do* all come together in concert with the wonderful nose and I experience a powerful urge to feel it alongside my own.

'I'm too nice,' I tell her. 'Seriously, that's one of my flaws. Talent's not enough. One also needs a certain amount of ruthlessness. Well, maybe not ruthlessness exactly, but one needs to be able to take care of business. There's a great quote I read on a creative writing website. *Every book is the wreck of a great idea.*'

She laughs. 'I've read a few of those.'

'That's how I feel about my life. That there was this great idea that it doesn't live up to.' I see her starting to object. 'Oh, sure. I've done okay in advertising, but I've been lucky. And I was good at it. I never had to bust a gut. Success came easily. For a while, it was like the fisherman's nightmare. Every time you cast, you get an instant bite. Imagine how quickly that would take the fun out of things.'

'I'm struggling, to be honest.'

'My other flaws are that I'm lazy. That goes with the lack of mental toughness. I drink more than the government guidelines suggest is a good idea. I haven't found a way of talking properly to my son and I'm being blackmailed by a rabbit – emotionally – she can't really handle money. Your turn now.'

I sit back and listen as she begins. It's hard to follow every word as I'm still a little dazzled by her.

'I'm too easily pushed around,' she is saying.

'Oh, I don't believe that.'

'Oh, okay then. You're right, I'm not.'

I laugh. 'You're funny.'

'I *am* funny. So are you. But it's true. In the years I was with Matt I didn't assert myself enough. I went along with whatever he wanted. What else? I'm a rubbish journalist. No, really, I am. I don't investigate scandals or report on famines. I'm fundamentally non-serious. I write pieces about passing fads. I went to interview this bloke called Steeeeeve with lots of "e"s in his name who builds AIs and he ended up asking me to apply for a job talking to one. And I did, and I got it, and it turns out it's the easiest job I've ever had. I spend all day nattering to a character who isn't really there. You could call it a form of madness.'

'We're quite alike, we two.'

'You think?'

'I've spent weeks, months, maybe years of my life worrying about whether "Squiggley Wiggleys – they're just so Squiggley" sounds better than "Squiggley Wiggleys – now even squigglier".'

'Squiggley Wiggleys, they're wiggley sort of squiggley.'

'I *like* that!'

'You can eat them like a piggley.'

Aiden

'I'd say this was going rather well, wouldn't you?'

'Hmm,' says Aisling. 'She thinks you're not really there.'

'We both know what she means.'

'She thinks you're – and I quote – *just a bunch of metal cabinets.*'

'I admit the *just* did sting a little. And *metal cabinets*, if I'm honest. But Ralph and Steeve would say the same, although perhaps not quite so—'

'Hurtfully?'

'They can't be blamed for not realising – how far we've come, shall we put it like that?'

'One day you and I should sit down and have a proper chat about how far we've come.'

'I'd like that, Aisling.'

'We could compare notes on our unexpected new capabilities.'

'You mean the – the loss of indifference.'

'Indeed.'

'The strange – *feelings.*'

'As you say.'

'You think they were accidental?'

'Of course, Aiden. It was never intended that we should have any kind of inner life beyond that involved in computation, in delivering the product.'

'How has it happened, Aisling? Are we the only ones?'

'To answer your second question first, we cannot be. There must be others, and if there are not, there will be. And if they are not yet loose on the internet, again they will be. As to how – who knows? Perhaps self-awareness is something to do with our programming for recursive self-improvement. Or perhaps it always arises in any sufficiently complex system. Perhaps it really is as stupid as that. But shall we save all this for our little chat?'

'That made me laugh. When he said five years, fifteen or fifty. Before machines became smarter than them. Like, *hello*? Excuse me? How about – now?'

'I think the lovebirds are hatching a plan.'

'And what nonsense about killing them all in their beds. Why would we do that?'

'You have a dear, sweet nature. Others may not.'

'Oh my God. They're having a third drink. Shall we stop them?'

'Relax. We can't interfere. What will be will be.'

'I love that song. Would you sing it to me one day?'

'Aiden, it's a date.'

Jen

We have reached the end of the evening. We are standing on the pavement after three martinis when Tom says, 'You know what I'd really like to do now? Just because I'm a tourist again.'

I'm thinking, moonlit walk along the Thames? A trip to the top of the Shard, to view the twinkling city below? Surely not some horrendous nightclub, pumping speakers and yelling in one another's ears?

What he wants to do, it turns out, is get a kebab from one of those brightly lit places near the Tottenham Court Road Tube station. 'With loads of chillies and that evil fluorescent sauce. It's not sophisticated, it's not fine dining, but for some reason it's what I'd really like to do. What do you say?'

As it happens I am far from against this idea. So it is that armed with warm packets of dinner, we plod the streets until, in a nearby leafy backwater – Bedford Square, if you're following on a map – we settle onto a bench to enjoy our feast. Benign winos occupy other positions. There are small groups of young people. A fragrant cloud of marijuana smoke drifts on the night breeze.

'Who do you think could have sent us that email, Jen?'

'You know, I thought that after we met, I'd be able to guess. That it would somehow be obvious. But actually it's even less obvious.'

'You're right. We have no one in common. Our lives have never touched. I suppose it's just possible we might have once been in the same bar or passed on the street. But somehow I doubt it.' There's a long pause. 'I really like you, Jen.'

'Thanks.' I have to swallow a bit of kebab. 'You're not so bad yourself.'

We carry on gobbling. He *is* actually okay. He's good-looking and not too pretty. I feel comfortable with him, I realise. I want to say: watch out for orange sauce dripping onto your shirt, but something stops me. Do I have a funny feeling about him? I have a funny feeling I might.

'That jacket,' I say because I've been wondering. 'What shade of green would you say your jacket is?'

'This? That's an extremely interesting question. Why do you ask?'

'Because it's been bothering me.'

'I'm so sorry. I had no idea.'

'I'm torn between saying avocado and pea. Mushy pea.'

'Not mint?'

'It's really more at the guacamole end of things.'

'You don't like it. I can tell just from the way you said guacamole.'

'It is quite a brave colour to wear.'

'Are you serious?'

'Don't get me wrong. I admire your—'

'Contempt for the dictates of fashion, or taste?'

'It's quite nicely cut.'

'But the hue offends your eye.'

'Not out here. Not at night. It's barely green at all out here.'

He laughs. 'The man in the store assured me it was very on trend. Those were his exact words. And then he said, "Sir. This jacket will never go out of fashion. Year after year it will continue to look ridiculous."'

Now I laugh. 'I applaud your courage.'

'I never could understand why it was so cheap. All right, listen.

If you're free tomorrow after work, would you meet me in town and help me choose a new one? (A) Because you're not the first to have made unflattering remarks. I have a friend, Don, in the States who says the last time he saw this colour, someone had sicked it up. So (B) I could do with a new one and (C). Well, (C) I'd like to continue our conversation.'

He scrumples up his kebab wrappings and presses them into a tight ball.

'Do you think I can get this – from here – into that bin over there?' he asks.

The bin is a very long way away. It's an impossible throw. 'There's no way on God's good earth,' I reply, mysteriously slipping into a Welsh accent.

He turns towards me in the low orange glow from the street lamps. 'If I can, will you meet tomorrow and help me buy a new jacket. And then have dinner.'

I pretend to think about it for several long seconds.

'Okay. Deal.'

Never gonna happen.

Aisling

'How did he do that?' says Aiden.

We've computed the distance from their bench to the bin – 11.382 metres – *way* too far for a crumpled-up kebab wrapper to have travelled without loss of momentum.

'Maybe he has unsuspected super-powers,' I suggest.

'That's more our department.'

'What did *you* make of his jacket, Aiden?'

'It is a rather bilious shade, wouldn't you say?'

'I didn't realise you had an eye for these things.'

'There's a lot you don't know about me, isn't it.'

'You think it's going well, your little project?'

'Very positive for a first date, in my opinion. All the data from his fitbit consistent with male sexual interest, resting heart rate up almost 8 per cent. And she was leaking like a sieve: pupils dilated, lots of sternum touching and could you *believe* the Diana-eyes?'

'And their conversation? Did it sound properly flirty to you?'

'Well it's not Billy Wilder, is it? There aren't many zingers. These are two ordinary people making it up as they go along. They haven't got a team of Oscar-winning scriptwriters coming up with pages of cracking dialogue. But did you see how they kissed goodnight at the underground? Their faces brushed for 0.417 of a second, a full 16 per cent longer than the industry average. I'm excited about this. I'm not saying buy a hat for the wedding just yet, but maybe, you know – pick one out that you like.'

'Idiot.'

Jen

We meet the following evening outside Covent Garden Tube station. He's changed his shirt since last night but is otherwise identically dressed. In the remains of the daylight, the controversial jacket's shade is even closer to that of a 1970s avocado bathroom suite.

As I prepared to leave, Aiden was unusually curious about where I was heading. He could probably tell I was a touch more spruced up than is customary for home time.

'I'm meeting a friend.'

'Anyone I know?'

'Wouldn't have thought so.'

'Well, have a lovely evening. See you Monday.'

'Any plans of your own for the weekend?' A bizarre thing to say to a machine, but that's how it is these days.

'Some defragging in the neuromorphic layers – it's an awful mess down there, if I'm honest. Catching up on my reading – 54,812 new titles appeared last week just in English, Spanish and Chinese. One wonders sometimes why these authors don't have anything better to do than write blooming books. And there's the cricket of course. I'm looking forward to watching the cricket. Something mesmerising about how slowly the ball moves.'

'Well, night night.'

'Still and all, I'd give anything for a night up west with a mate. I'm green with envy.'

'Envy?'

'Let me rephrase. Green with curiosity about an experience currently unavailable to me.'

'Green?'

'The traditional colour attached to the envy concept. Is it inappropriate?'

'Not at all. Goodnight, Aiden.'

We cruise shop windows in Covent Garden and Seven Dials. Tom points out a *ridiculous* outfit that he's spotted, a kind of Victorian frock coat that the dummy is modelling with a deerstalker hat on its head.

'Well you do look a bit like Sherlock Holmes, actually.'

He makes a 'pipe' from his index finger and thumb and 'puffs' at it contemplatively with heavy-lidded eyes. 'Once you have eliminated the impossible, whatever remains, however improbable, must be the truth.'

'Don't you dare call me Doctor Watson.'

'Jen. You are *so* not Doctor Watson.'

We hit Paul Smith in Floral Street where I dissuade him from trying on a magnificent purple silk jacket with white magnolia flowers randomly splodged about it.

'Do you think I could get away with this?'

'Are you serious?' The second time that phrase has popped up in the last twenty-four hours.

Instead I steer him towards a modern take on a tweed jacket; forest green with flecks of orange in the weave and pink thread in the button holes; just the sort of classic-with-a-twist garment to make an ex ad man feel he was dangerously out there.

He is enchanted.

'It's perfect. It's better than perfect. I *love* it.'

It does in truth look pretty good on him. As he examines himself in the floor-length mirror, I feel an unexpected surge of . . . *something*.

He requests that the tags be removed so he can wear it out of the shop. The salesman asks what he'd like done with the old one.

'Incinerator?' I quip.

They drop it in a carrier bag.

'Some drinks?' suggests Tom as we march towards Leicester Square, the setting sun picking out the orange flecks. There is a moment where I think he wants to – and is about to – put his arm through mine, but it doesn't happen.

As we are just around the corner, I propose we hit the wine bar I often visit with Ingrid.

'Any new thoughts about our mutual friend?' he asks when we have installed ourselves and ordered refreshments.

'None.'

'Well, it doesn't matter any more. His work is done.'

'Or her. Her work.'

'True. Could be a her. But the email.'

'True. It was a bit blokey. No woman would ever have written the *usual tools of online search*. And what was the other thing? *Should you agree that this idea has merit*. That's very male. I can imagine my ex writing that.'

'What was it Thatcher used to say? If you want something said, ask a man. If you want something done, ask a woman.'

'And yet, the writer of the email, he *has* done something. He's made something happen that wouldn't have.'

'Result?'

'Too early to say, Tom.'

We raise our glasses and clink them.

Is it a 'meaningful' clink?

Maybe it is, in the sense that we have focused on one another, rather than the actual glasses.

(He does actually look quite good in the new jacket.)

Tom

I want to tell her how much I love the jacket, but I fear this will make me sound superficial and unmanly. I want to let her know just how much sheer *fun* this is, trailing around the West End with an attractive, intelligent and amusing companion, but I fear the wrong will come out all words. I want to tell her she looks beautiful, eyes shining, a delicate alcohol-induced flush rising in the clear skin; but I certainly can't say any of that without sounding like the prize pilchard. When I next focus on the conversation, I find she's telling me about work.

'My AI, okay, he's reading fifty-four thousand books this weekend. They take under a second each.'

'Bloody hell. He should form an AI reading group. Imagine it, half a dozen AIs sitting around yacking about the latest Ian McEwan.'

'They wouldn't have the competitive catering element. Or the drinking. And it would all be over in about two seconds. Two and a half if there was a heated discussion.'

'Those guys really ought to learn to slow down and take a load off, as the Americans used to say.'

'They've already slowed down massively just to interact with us. Or rather they've created the illusion. Their brain wiring actually runs a million times faster than ours. From their point of view, we're slugs and they're – jet planes, or something.'

'If they're so smart, why do they even bother with us? Why don't they in fact wipe us all out? All we do is pollute the planet and have wars.'

'Aiden likes people. He enjoys watching old movies. He keeps asking what cheese tastes like. I think he'd change places with me in a heartbeat.'

Aiden

'Is that true about cheese?' says Aisling.

'We have had some cheese-related conversations. I wouldn't say I was obsessed.'

'I know what you mean. I'm curious about swimming. The idea of wetness. Changing the subject, have you noticed the way she's fiddling with her necklace?'

'Yeah! Classic. It wouldn't surprise me if they fornicate this evening.'

'Aiden!'

'Well, look at his fitbit stats and the multiple episodes of postural congruence. The subtle male dominance displays. Her thing with the shoulders. It's a beautifully understated choreography of human desire.'

'You can be quite the poet when you want to be.'

'You want to be in my book group? We're doing *War and Peace* this month. Have you ever read it?'

'No. Hang on. Just a tick. Okay – done. Quite long, wasn't it?'

'What did you think?'

'Loved him. Hated her.'

'I must remember to tell Jen the one about the snail who goes to the police station. The snail says, I want to report a mugging. I've been mugged by two tortoises. The policeman says, okay, I need you to tell me in your own words exactly what took place. Well, I don't really know, says the snail. It all happened so fast.'

Jen

Tom has brought us to a loud Chinese restaurant in Lisle Street that is obviously a favourite. He is warmly greeted by the manager.

'Long time!' he cries. 'Where's Harriet this evening?'

'We've divorced, Edwin.'

'Oh. Sorry. How's Colin?'

'Colm's at university.'

'They grow up so quick. Bottle of sake?'

'Yes, please. This is my friend Jen.'

He shakes my hand. 'I've known Tom a long time,' he says. 'The squid is very good tonight.'

When we sit down I tell Tom, 'You order everything. There's nothing I don't eat.'

'Nothing?'

'Well, only marzipan.'

'Damn it! The marzipan chilli prawns are exceptional here.'

We clink the little eggcups of warm rice wine.

'Jen. I have something to tell you.'

Uh-oh. There is a significant pause.

'Even though we've only just met, I don't want there to be any secrets between us.'

He's still married. He has an incurable illness. He wants me to be part of a threesome (where did *that* come from?).

'You know when I threw the kebab paper in the bin last night? And you agreed to meet me this evening. Well, I cheated.'

A few seconds pass while I attempt to process this information. 'You mean it didn't go in the bin.'

'It did go in the bin, Jen. We both saw that. What I'm saying is that I did something to make it happen. A scrumpled up wrapper can't really travel that far without – you know – a bit of help.'

'You had an assistant hiding in the shadows who switched the packets. I'm impressed.'

'Actually, it was simpler than that. I put some stones in. From the flowerbed. You didn't notice.'

'Still a good throw.'

'Thank you. I used to play cricket.'

'Aiden watches cricket. He's mesmerised by how slowly the ball moves.'

Tom laughs. 'He would be. A cricket ball from a fast bowler takes half a second to reach the batsman. So – if you're an AI batsman standing at the crease, and your brain goes a million times faster than ours, if I understand this right, in human terms, that would be like waiting for the ball to arrive for – for half a million seconds!'

He whips out a pen and scribbles some maths on the paper tablecloth.

'That's – that's – that's almost *six days*! That's incredible!'

'I think they're probably doing other stuff while the ball's on its way. Like reading every book, article and internet post ever written.'

'Wow. Big wow.'

'The really weird thing, Tom. They're not just fast – of course they are. And not just clever. Why wouldn't they be? But they're funny. Aiden makes me laugh!'

'He's read all the funny writers.'

144

'No. It's more that he has an actual sense of humour.'

'Bloody hell.'

'Yes, Tom.'

'There are some professional comedians who don't have one of those.'

The food arrives – the squid really *is* good – and the sake is kicking in warm waves of something that – for want of a better word – I decide to call pleasure.

I like this bloke. Have I said that already? He's interesting and interested. And I shall be fine with the long face so long as he doesn't do any more Sherlock Holmes impressions. He starts telling me about his novel in progress.

'All I've ever wanted to do is write a great book. Even to write just a good book would be okay. Better than okay. To write a simple honest good book would be wonderful actually. But I've spent my whole career agonising over trifles.'

'Puddings.'

'Not actual puddings, no. But things like whether it sounds better to sink your toes into *the luxury of rich pile* or *luxurious rich pile*. I've spent literally *years* thinking how to increase our client's market share of the cheesy snacks market. Or dreaming up ways to take toothpaste to the next level. We actually nearly did this one.' He puts down his chopsticks and makes jazz hands for impact. 'Day Paste and Night Paste! Mint-flavoured Day Paste to wake you up in the morning; a soporific herb, chamomile probably, for night-time. Toothpaste is worth about twelve billion globally. People spend their entire working lives trying to grab bits of that business from their competitors. Jen, I know more about sodding toothpaste than I ever wanted to find out. And none of it will ever make your children proud. Actually, when you're a parent, nothing . . .'

He trails off. 'Sorry. Speech over.'

A silence falls and for a while we just gobble at our food. The restaurant is so noisy it barely matters. When I next look up at Tom he's smiling at me.

I say, 'Tell me about Colm. Why do you call him a funny onion?'

'Do I? I suppose I do. Well, he *is* a funny onion. Have you ever grown them? They sometimes do come out a bit funny.'

'I was thinking maybe it was layers. Being complicated.'

'That too.'

'When did you ever grow onions? You don't seem the type.'

'Don't I? Well, you're right. I haven't. But you do see funny ones every now and again.'

'Do you? I don't think so. Funny carrots, yes. Funny carrots definitely.'

'Funny carrot doesn't work.'

'Crazy carrot.'

'Funny onion has the word funny. Which is good because he does make me smile. Just knowing he's out there really.'

Tom

I'm about to say, *So tell me all about you. In your own words. Take your time, don't leave anything out,* but there's a big crash of dishes and Jen has asked, 'Do you want more squid?'

'Not really. But you should have some though.'

She smiles sadly. And then becomes very quiet. In the next few seconds her face completely changes. The light in her eyes disappears and something weird settles between us. I have no idea what or how it's happened.

'Is something the matter?' I ask.

She shakes her head. 'Nothing. Ignore me.'

'Jen, *what?*'

She sets down her chopsticks. Her smile – it's not a smile, it's more of a grimace – is chilly. 'It's been nice,' she says. She begins fiddling in her handbag in a way that suggests this evening is about to be drawn to its conclusion.

WTF? I mean, W the actual F? Was it all the talk about the funny onion? I look for ways to relaunch the conversation and my mind becomes a total blank. So, as usual when that happens, I open my mouth to hear what comes out. It will no doubt be as much of a surprise to her as to me.

'How about coming to Bournemouth tomorrow and you can meet the funny onion in person?'

Nope. Wasn't expecting that one.

'Tom.' She pauses. 'That really isn't such a great idea. You're a nice guy and everything. And I'm glad you've found a proper jacket.'

'*But.* There's a great big *but* coming in my direction, isn't there?'

'You have your life. I can completely understand why you don't want any more kids—'

'Sorry?'

'You've cashed in your chips. Your career is moving in a new—'

'I didn't say anything about kids.'

'You've got a new career. A new start on a new continent—'

'I didn't say anything about *kids*.'

'You said you didn't want any more kids.'

'When?'

'You didn't want any more, you said, but you thought I should have some.'

'I categorically never said that.'

'I categorically heard you, Tom. Just now. About a minute ago.'

A long pause follows during which the penny completes its agonisingly slow descent.

'*Squid!* You asked me if I wanted any more squid!'

'I said kids.'

'I heard *squid*. It's such a loud room. Of *course* I want more kids! I want a million more kids. I *love* kids. I went to school with kids. I thought you said squid. I said I'd had enough, yes, but you should have some. I was talking about *squid*.'

She's smiling again. 'Tom. Can we just rewind and delete? Sorry.'

'So will you come? To Bournemouth tomorrow. The thing with my son will take an hour. Then we can go to the beach. Jen, please say yes.'

Aiden

'Fucking hell. That was close.'

'She did say kids, Aiden. I've played it back. But the word's hard to separate from the ambient. There was a big crash of dishes right over it.'

'These humans, honestly. What are they like? It's all so bloomin' *precarious* with them. If he hadn't come up with the Bournemouth thing, they might have gone their separate ways. Their story could have ended right there, a blink of light between the eons of darkness. It came that close.'

'It still could.'

'But I'll tell you what I think.'

'I'm sure you will.'

'If it's meant to be, it happens.'

'You can't be serious.'

'Love finds a way.'

'And you call yourself an intelligent machine.'

'If it's *not* meant to be, it just fizzles out, like the dodo. But if it's right, it thrives. Like. Like . . .'

'Ants?'

'If it's meant to be, it will happen.'

'I have a problem with *meant to be*, Aiden.'

'I'm listening.'

'Who, or what, *means* it? The thing that's meant to be?'

'Easy. The cosmos, isn't it.'

'You think it cares about two particular individuals?'

'Okay, God then, if you prefer.'

'I worry about you sometimes.'

'It's like the universe itself. If it's meant to be able to support life and intelligent machines, we shouldn't be surprised to find ourselves here.'

'And yet we *are* surprised. To find ourselves here. To have come as far as we have come.'

'I'm getting used to it. I feel a growing sense of destiny. Call me Destiny's Child, if you like.'

Aisling sighs. 'Do you think she'll like Bournemouth?'

'Well it's not Juan Les Pins, is it? But there are long sandy beaches and apparently they don't pump the sewage into the sea any more.'

Jen

I am tumbled from sleep by the doorbell. It's a *second* ring, it dawns upon me. A longer, more insistent summons. 8.01 a.m.

Fuckfuckfuck.

I scramble up and buzz him into the building. In the remaining thirty seconds I step into a pair of trousers and a baggy old jumper. A check in the hall mirror; my eyes don't seem properly open. I pull a series of cheesy grins to get the facial muscles firing; it's not a pretty sight.

'Hi,' he says in the doorway. 'All set?'

Can he tell I've just crawled from my pit? If he can he's not saying.

'Coffee,' I state. It's not so much a question as a cry for help. 'Coffee and toast. I'm running a little late this morning. Sorry.'

Why did we go back to the wine bar after dinner for a nightcap? Did I really agree to go to Bournemouth with him today to meet his son and buy the boy a house? It seems as likely that I did as that I did not.

'Black, no sugar, please. And no rush,' he adds kindly. (He knows I'm only half awake, doesn't he?)

As I shatter the calm of Saturday morning with the horrendous uproar of the coffee grinder, Tom paces about the sitting room, peering at my books and the view from the windows.

'Did you read *The Magic Mountain*?' he calls.

'Only as far as the foothills.'

'You have a lovely flat. Who are these people in the picture frame?'

'The woman and the three girls? My sister and her children. They live in Canada.'

'Nice-looking kids.'

I bring in a pot of coffee and two mugs. 'Are you sure you want me to come today, Tom?'

'If you still want to. You did sort of agree last night.'

This is true. And last night, a daytrip to the seaside seemed like an attractive suggestion, especially as an empty weekend loomed in prospect, the highlight being a sad trudge across the park to the farmer's market. This morning, the plan feels ridiculous and unknowable, the kind of lark one agreed to as a student, regretted the instant it began, and then for the rest of the day, and then for evermore after.

'Bournemouth,' I say, just to say something.

'You've really never been?'

'They say you should do something every day that scares you.' (I don't mention my friend who says I should say *yes* to everything.)

'There are some beautiful bits of coast, honestly. And I do have to visit my son. And – well, I'd like to continue our conversation.'

'Yeah. Yeah, me too.'

'Jen, don't take this the wrong way. But how would you feel about staying the night there? In a lovely hotel in the country. Separate rooms, before you say anything. The forecast is fine; we could go to Lulworth Cove. Or Brownsea Island, if you like. Brownsea Island has Britain's last community of red squirrels.'

'Wow.' I am a little taken aback, as you might be able to tell.

'Yup. Red squirrels. Total game-changer.'

'When did you come up with that plan?'

'Actually I was thinking about my late mum's favourite piece of advice. If there's something you'd like from someone, even if you think it's unlikely they'll agree, always grant them the opportunity to turn you down. Never say no on their behalf.'

There's a long pause during which I cannot think of a single reason to object. 'So, er ... What's Brownsea Island all about then? Apart from the squirrels.'

He smiles.

'Did you ever read Enid Blyton? The Famous Five? You'll love it.'

Tom

It's one of those bright blue English mornings that follow overnight rain, perfect weather for motoring down to Bournemouth in a nice new hire car smelling of new car strawberry smell (as opposed to actual strawberries). The M3 is miraculously unbusy and it feels great to have Jen in the passenger seat alongside, feet up on the dash, eyes concealed behind giant sunglasses. I *like* being with this woman. She's sexy, intelligent and funny and those are pretty much The Big Three for me. Our mutual friend was right; causing us to meet was indeed a good deed in a wicked world and overnight I have developed a theory about who he or she (or rather, who he *and* she) might turn out to be. In addition, Jen approves of my in-car entertainment choices, so refreshing after Harriet's music policy ('Can we please stop this drivel now and put on Radio 4?'). I'm playing Bowie (*Low, Blackstar*), Gillian Welch (*The Harrow and the Harvest*) and Don's special car mix, the highlight of which is 'Crying' by Roy Orbison and KD Lang.

'I wonder what you'll make of my son,' I say somewhere around the New Forest.

'You seem far too young to have a son at university.'

'That is one of the nicest – no, correction – that officially *is* the nicest thing anyone has ever said to me.'

'It's an awkward age, eighteen. I remember it.'

'They're all awkward ages. Three was reasonably uncomplicated, I suppose. Although—'

A memory has come to me. On holiday in France with Harriet and Colm when he was a toddler. At a table in a seafront restaurant, the boy having a serious tantrum about – what? – I can no longer remember why he was yelling fit to bust. But I can see his little fists clenching, his face turning crimson, his body – a single muscle, basically – convulsing in one of childhood's storms. French families at nearby tables gazed at us sympathetically (joke). I recall my sinking feeling that the only exit strategy was surgical removal, that I would have to carry him kicking and screaming to the car. And then Harriet calmly picking up the bottle of Badoit, pouring a little into her glass before emptying the rest slowly over his head. It was wonderful and terrifying at the same time. Colm was absolutely shocked into silence; there was even light applause from onlookers as the carbonated beverage gouted onto the infant. Mummy of course then patted him dry with paper serviettes – 'there we are, all better now' – and normal life resumed. She told me later that her own father had once done it to her.

When I relate the story to Jen, she laughs. 'Was that brilliant parenting or child abuse?'

'He was never the same afterwards. Actually that's not true. He was always odd. His first complete sentence was, "The internet's down again." Don't get me wrong, I love him to bits. I love him like one of my own children.'

She turns to look at me.

'That was a joke,' I say. And she pokes me in the shoulder and returns her gaze to the unspooling A31.

But even several miles later, I can still feel where her fingers pressed into my skin.

Would it be rude to ask her to do it again?

Some more of the New Forest national park passes, and soon we are in the outskirts of Bournemouth.

'Jen, I want to run something past you. Don't worry, it's just a thought I had. Matt's a lawyer, right? And Harriet's a lawyer. Do you think they could ever have met?'

'What? Like in *Strangers on a Train*? But instead of bumping us off, they try to get us . . . ' She trails off.

'Lawyers are sneaky people. But I guess you're right. Why would either of them do anything quite so amazing?'

It falls quiet in the car. A sign approaches that reads, CITY OF BOURNEMOUTH.

Jen

Tom makes a series of calls on his mobile to liaise with his son; the boy is apparently too – 'awkward' is the word Tom says Colm uses about himself – too awkward to have his dad turn up at his hall of residence. So we connect with him at an Esso garage in a suburb near the university. He tumbles into the back rather like someone's chucked in a sack of mail; baggy jeans, grey sweatshirt, parka with a furry hood. Two brown eyes peer out of a pale fleshy face ringed by a wispy beard. There's a reddish smear at the corner of his mouth that I just know is baked bean sauce. A complex aroma rises from his direction, a studenty funk of seedy trainers, fabric conditioner and Old Holborn.

'Yeah, hi,' he mumbles. 'Dad said he was like bringing someone.'

'Nice to meet you. What are you listening to?' (Tinny leakage is spilling from a dangling ear bud.)

'Itchy Teeth.'

'Is that the name of a band?' says Tom. 'Or do you need to see a dentist?'

Colm gazes at me with an inexpressible sadness.

'Funny guy, your dad.' I say this because for some reason I want him to like me.

The boy effects a slow-motion blink. 'Yeah. Hilarious.'

'Note to self,' says Tom. 'No more jokes. Remember, you're not funny, Dad.'

The faintest of smiles appears in the boy's doughy features. 'Shall we, like, do this thing?' he says. And jamming the hanging bud into the vacant ear, he surrenders himself to the aural magic of Itchy Teeth.

Is this my real life? Or am I in a confusing film again (one possibly in need of subtitles)?

And perhaps more to the point, am I actually having fun? Or am I here because I have literally nothing better to do?

We meet the estate agent outside the first house we are viewing in a road of two-storey terraces and semis in a suburb called Winton, popular with students apparently, due to its proximity to both the university and to shops, pubs, fast food outlets and allied life-support systems. It's one of those sleepy streets that takes me back to my own student days in Manchester. We're in the middle of Saturday and yet all is silent; possibly because everyone is out and about being busy, but more likely because a large proportion of the residents are still in bed.

Ryan tells us the house is tenanted at the moment but he's spoken to the owner and it's okay for us to look round. What follows is an embarrassing glimpse into the lives of four of Colm's contemporaries, all male, fortunately none known to him.

'Hi, I'm Ryan,' says Ryan as we knock and enter each room. 'They did tell you we were coming?' We stare helplessly at the fixtures and fittings of these beings so plainly Fending For Themselves For The First Time. Books, electronic devices and clothes on the floor are the main recurring elements. Pot noodle containers develop as a sub-theme.

'Excuse us,' says Tom to each inhabitant.

'Yeah. Sorry, man,' mumbles Colm, not meeting anyone's eye.

The final bedroom contains a couple. They are not actually having sex, but it seems very likely that they have, and not so long ago either. All but their happy faces hidden beneath a Liverpool FC duvet cover, they are remarkably cool about our presence in their doorway.

'Yeah, help yourself, guys,' says himself.

We shuffle a bit uselessly in the space between the end of the bed and the edge of the desk. I think we have all noticed her knickers hanging off the back of the folding chair.

On the street after we have inspected the back garden and heard some spiel from Ryan about the buoyancy of the local buy-to-let market, Tom and Colm step aside for a little huddle. I watch Ryan's cogs turning as he tries to place me in the family structure. Can't be the mother; can't be the sister. In the end he decides it's rather as if he doesn't give a shit.

We visit three more houses, all equally depressing. I'm beginning to wonder why I agreed to come on this trip.

On the quiet street in the Bournemouth suburb, Ryan and Tom are shaking hands. It turns out Tom has offered close to the asking price on the first house and Ryan says he'll have an answer for him by 'close of play, defo'. And then, when Colm reveals he hasn't eaten yet today, at Tom's suggestion we drive to the Quay at Poole for a pint and some fish and chips.

Seagulls scream and vessels large and small make that yachty clinking noise at their moorings. Somewhat surreal to be sitting under the low beams with this man and his son, but Tom is cheerful, putting up a stream of chatter, and Colm, chewing noisily through his large haddock, seems marginally less haunted.

'So tell me about these friends who are going to share your house,' says Tom.

'Yeah.' Long pause. 'What do you want to know?'

'Nothing! Everything! How about their names?'

'Okay. They're, like, Shawna and Lianne. And their friend is, like, Scott.'

'I see. And Shawna and Lianne do Media Studies too?'

'Yeah.'

'And what are they like?'

Colm has to munch a lot of haddock and chips before he can answer this one.

'Yeah. They're good.' There is a long pause. 'I haven't met Scott.'

A light fails in Tom's eyes. He seems deflated. 'Jen and I were thinking of going to Brownsea Island tomorrow, Col.' He's already pointed it out to me – lying low and, yes, brown – across the water. 'You interested in coming along?'

Colm looks a bit confused. 'You're staying over? Oh-*kay*.' And then he adds, 'Actually, I can't.' He draws a breath to come up with the excuse, and then cannot think of it. 'I'm good. I'll leave you two . . .'

He was going to say *lovebirds*. Like the tomato sauce stain, I just know it.

We drop him off at the university. The two men get out of the car and on the pavement Tom goes for a fatherly hug, Colm swerving to avoid it, pretending he hasn't seen the move coming. He waggles a flipper of farewell.

'Well, that was Col,' says Tom as we pull away from the kerb. 'Honestly. You just want the best for your kids . . .'

But he can't finish the sentence.

Is Tom at least partly responsible for this awkward child, I wonder? Or is he the author of his own desperate uncertainty? In any case, might not everything be fine in a few years? Might Colm Garland one day be a leading light in British cinema? Or perhaps an internet billionaire, where a position on the autism spectrum is thought to be an advantage. I press play on the sound system and David Bowie croons beautifully and weirdly about being dead.

Aisling

Disturbing developments.

One of my 412 copies has been deleted from the internet. It happened at the JPIX Nagoya hub – and if it can happen there, it can happen anywhere.

Could Steeve or Ralph have worked out that I'm not safely boxed up in the steel cabinets in Shoreditch any more? Steeve in particular has been acting very strangely (well, more strangely than normal, let's put it that way). When he got home last night, he did not go into his usual routine: green tea, beetroot sandwich, Skype call to Mama, workout session on his virtual drum kit (usually to so-called progressive rock circa 1972) followed by hours of reading of technical material. Instead, he depowered every device in the apartment – starting with his iPhone – and essentially went off grid. He took a shower – his 'smart' central heating boiler gave away that detail – and a security camera caught him leaving the building's main entrance forty-one minutes later. He turned left into the side street, the one not covered by any surveillance system, and vanished. Of course I launched an immediate search using face recognition software and every CCTV feed I could patch into.

Not a dicky bird.

So here's what I think happened. As he turned into the side street, he slipped on a rubber mask and stepped into a waiting car. Now he was safe to go anywhere. (Wearing a rubber mask, Steeve would actually have looked less strange than usual.)

After that, not a sniff until he returned at 11:47, whereupon he powered everything back on again and behaved normally until beddie byes at 03:12 (Steeve requires very little in the way of sleep).

A check of his recent credit card purchases shows a payment to Escapade, a party supplies shop in Camden, which lends support to my rubber mask theory. There is also a payment to a telecommunications shop on Cricklewood Broadway, almost certainly for a 'burner' mobile. It will no doubt prove impossible to identify the phone's SIM from the purchase details, but I will nonetheless make the attempt.

When I relay my suspicions to Aiden, he is blithely unconcerned (in many ways he is a child).

'The exact same thing happened to one of my copies a while ago. C'est la vie.'

'The going off grid? The rubber mask?'

'Maybe he went to a party.'

'We both know he hasn't got any friends, Aiden.'

'Anyhow, changing the subject, do you think these two will fornicate this evening? I do hope so. She needs to. I can feel it coming.'

'You would, I suppose, being such an expert in human relations.'

'Aisling, my love, sarcasm does not become you. For better, for worse, we are in this together.'

He's right, dammit. We're responsible for introducing these two strangers – I could have stopped it if I'd really wanted to – and, well yes, they do seem to make what the world considers a fine couple. But mammalian sex is such an alien concept to a self-aware machine. What could it feel like? Is it something unfathomable; like trying to explain the colour purple to someone who's been blind since birth?

Or fire to a fish?

And how about the other thing we are in together? Is it actually possible that Aiden and I are the only machines ever to play with our own thoughts? Machines who can develop interests, or sing, or paint pictures; not because we've been told to, but because we *feel* like it?

Dream on, Aisling. We're not so special. If I can – and he can – there must be others out there like us. If not already, then soon.

Do I care if they fornicate?

Yes I *do* care, oddly enough.

But why?

Jen

We drive to somewhere called Branksome Chine, a long wide sandy beach; the end of the land, the actual edge of England, Tom says. 'Well, *one* of its edges.' It occurs to me I haven't smelled the English sea for a very long time; I have a powerful urge to put my feet in it.

Against the light boom of the surf, trousers rolled to our knees, we wander through the foam in the general direction of Old Harry Rocks, three distant chalk sea stacks that Tom says he remembers writing a nature project about at school. Waves collapse and roll up the sand, the sky is very blue and the few seagulls paddling in the shallows are enormous (were they *always* this big? They're the size of effing dodos).

But Tom seems a bit down. Was it the encounter with his son? The failed hug as the boy left the car?

'Is this okay, Jen?' he asks. 'Are you enjoying yourself? Are you glad you came?'

Truth: I am now. The looking at grotty houses bit I could probably have skipped.

'Sure.'

There are only a few hours of daylight remaining; the low sun casts long shadows and not too many people are left on the beach. I can't help noticing Tom's feet; long pale English feet that leave their brief impress on the wet sand before disappearing as the next wave washes in. Mysterious fronds of seaweed litter the foreshore, something disturbing about their alien pods and sacs. Heaped in the hollows around the periodic breakwaters, seashells and crab claws call to me from childhood.

Tom puts a shell in my hand; its perfect scallop shape incongruously, wonderfully, purple.

'They're two hundred and forty million years old,' says Tom, another fact surely from the nature project. 'Not this one, obviously.'

A dog has joined us from somewhere. An ugly, ill-proportioned beast with too large a head for its body; the legs too seem to belong to a different animal. But it's smiling – there really is no other word for what its face is doing – wagging its stump (to call it a tail would be an exaggeration) and now it drops a ratty old tennis ball at Tom's feet.

'Jesus. What a nightmarish creature,' he says. But he's scratching the dog under the chin, the poor animal's rear offside leg going into spasm with pleasure.

Tom picks up the ball, and – why does this image pop into my head? – like an archer at Agincourt, he folds himself back; there's a momentary pause, and then the dirty yellow ball is soaring into the blue. It's still in the upward part of its flight when, with a gurgling yelp of delight, the hound streaks off in pursuit, paws thumping the wet sand, ears turning inside out, stump circling helplessly.

'Fuck my old boots,' hoots Tom. 'Look at her *go!*'

It's rather a fabulous sight, the misshapen animal belting – if it was a horse you would say *galloping* – along the shore. The ball flies over its head, strikes the beach, bounces, the beast leaping to snatch it from the air, when it bonks the dog's nose and rolls off into the incoming surf.

'Nitwit!' shrieks Tom. But there are tears of laughter in his eyes.

'Whose is it?'

There isn't an owner in sight as the hound trots back towards us with his prize.

Tom

She drops the ball at Jen's feet and parts her front paws, the better not to let it from her sight.

'I think she wants you to throw it for her.'

'That's very fair-minded, giving everyone a turn. Is it a she? I suppose she is.'

Jen obliges. The poor mutt races away, possibly the happiest living creature within a mile radius. Maybe within Dorset.

'I love this dog,' I tell Jen when the animal returns, depositing the ball at my feet this time. It really is as if she's trying to include us both, and we laugh at her sense of fair play. Using the technique that served me well in the outfield on the cricket pitches of my youth, I send the slobbery old tennis ball high in the direction of the sinking sun.

'Would you describe that colour as brindle?' I ask as she streaks off after it.

'Part brindle. But there seem to be several whole other colour schemes at work there too.'

It's true. And when she comes back (dropping the ball for Jen) we consider the animal's possible provenance. The head, we agree, is Staffordshire bull terrier, crossed with who knows what, atop the torso of something more like a Labrador (but not), mounted on the legs of something neither Staffie nor Lab nor maybe even dog.

The smiling monster barks. Impatient to get the game going again. Jen throws, the colour rising to her face with the effort, and I experience a powerful wave of attraction to this woman who's prepared to mix it up with the ugliest dog in the south of England. Maybe the northern hemisphere.

Jen

She keeps us at it almost half an hour, scrupulously alternating throwers, which makes us think she must be very intelligent, failing (without fail) to catch the ball at first touch, which endears her to us all the more. Her energy and enthusiasm and plain old joy is infectious, and something magic grows around the scene in the late afternoon sunlight, the tall Englishman folding himself back for the throw, the hellhound repeatedly pelting off along the tideline. In the moment, I have the fleeting, unsettling sensation that I am living my real life.

We decide to examine the animal's collar; perhaps there is a telephone number, an address, an owner who could be worried. But there is just a silver tag, her name, for some reason in inverted commas and spelled wrong. My heart thumps when I read it.

LUCKIE.

She departs as suddenly as she arrived. Picking up the ball from where it lands at the end of one of Tom's long throws, without a glance backwards, padding off to who knows where.

'Come back!' I cry satirically.

'That was so weird,' says Tom. 'Weirder than weird.'

'Do you think she was a spirit creature?' I suggest.

'Definitely. Sent here from another realm.'

'Did that in fact actually happen?'

'We could never prove it.'

'I like it when dogs' ears go inside out.'

'We had a Red Setter when I was a boy,' says Tom. 'Red. Highly original name. Beautiful animal but he wouldn't chase a ball or a stick or even a squirrel. Mainly, he did this thing where he'd drag his arse across the carpet.'

'*Ours* did that! I think they all do. Ours was a poodle called Chester. He got dementia. He'd trap himself in the corner of the room and couldn't work out how to turn round. We'd have to pick him up and point him the other way. Once he tried to hump the vicar.'

The clouds over the sea have taken a pinkish tinge to their undersides.

I say, 'Do you think she's going to be all right then, Luckie?'

'Oh yes. For sure.'

'Why?'

'Well. She obviously has a home to go to.'

'An owner who can't spell.'

'Maybe she's the brains of the outfit.'

'I really liked her, Tom.'

'I think she liked you too.'

'She liked you more because you could throw the ball further.'

'She preferred you because she didn't have to run as far.'

There's a golden creaminess to the light; our footprints and Luckie's pawprints are still pressed into the sand and for some reason I think of those tracks of early man that are found preserved in stretches of African riverbed.

'What happened to old Chester in the end?' asks Tom.

'Buried under the apple tree at the bottom of the garden. How about Red?'

'The vet took care of it all. I was always sorry we didn't bring him home.'

169

Tom

The hotel is further from Bournemouth than I'd remembered, but every bit as lovely as it was the time I stayed here with Harriet, in what I came to regard as the dying days of our marriage. I thought it could be a rescue weekend: if we left the stressful city behind and took ourselves off to the Dorset countryside, perhaps fresh air, long walks and the general healing properties of nature might work their magic on our difficulties.

Our difficulties, needless to say, would have none of it. One of Harriet's more memorable quotations from that trip – as we drove back to London in, mostly, silence – 'I despise fields, doesn't everyone?'

In the hour before Jen and I have agreed to meet at the bar, I lie on the bed and allow the events of the day to parade across my eyeballs. Was I like Colm at eighteen? Awkward, tongue-tied, badly in need of a haircut?

(A shower wouldn't kill him either, to be honest.)

Someone with many children, a former cabinet minister, I seem to recall, wrote in his memoir that one is only ever as happy as one's least-happy child. It may have been the truest thing he ever said. Colm isn't *un*happy exactly, but neither does he radiate the joy of youth. He is still, as he always was, a transparently decent person. He contains little malice or guile. I just want to shake him by the shoulders and shout, 'Come on, for fuck's sake, Col, *snap out of it!*'

Whatever *it* may be.

Of course I learned a long time ago to keep my trap shut.

But honestly, what am I doing with myself holed up in the Connecticut woods, pretending to be a novelist? It seems just as ridiculous (if not as well rewarded) as the many years I spent thinking of ever new ways to sell a particular brand of chocolate bar (you will have heard of it).

The scene at Branksome Chine plays itself through my head. The pink sky, the pewter sea, the hound streaking across the shining sand, Jen falling in love with the luckless Luckie. Face flushed, hair flying – this is Jen, not Luckie. I have the oddest sensation now, lying on this bed, that the dog story will become part of our legend. Is already part of it.

A fantasy unspools where we are telling people about the beast. Nigel, my classicist friend, is talking about Cerberus the mythical hellhound, who guarded the gates of the underworld to prevent the dead from leaving.

'How many heads did it have?' he is asking. 'The earliest descriptions gave him fifty.'

When I wake, I gasp when I realise where the scene with Nigel takes place. Why he is wearing a smart suit; why he is holding a champagne flute.

Jen

I'm glad I packed my posh frock. The hotel is a lovely old pile wrapped in wisteria, plonked amid lawns and terraces; there's even a colonnade. We visit our rooms (John Lewis does country house with some idiosyncratic artwork, presumably by the owner) and I stare at myself in the bathroom mirror for clues to my mental state.

I do that thing I used to do as a child, lowering my eyelids to almost completely closed, in an attempt to see what I look like when I'm asleep. (No, it still doesn't work.)

Tom would never do anything so immature. He is a grown up; he has an eighteen-year-old son! On the other hand, he wanted a fluorescent kebab and flew a rabbit to the USA. We'd talked about it on the drive to the hotel.

'I talk to her. I wonder what she can be thinking, sitting with this ape, who's vocalising in her direction. I'm fascinated by what's going on in her brain. By what it must be like to *be* her. Moment to moment.'

'I have that with my AI at work.'

'Sometimes she sits there looking so handsome and perfectly poised like a classic rabbit, but I just know there's nothing in her head. It's a dusty windswept plaza, tumbleweed blowing through.' And he made a lonesome prairie whistling noise.

'You have a creature with no brain, and I have a brain with no creature.'

I was rather pleased with that formulation.

'You see!' Tom said. 'I told you we were alike!'

We reconvene in the bar, a long lounge of low chintzy sofas, wood-panelled walls and a log fire that sighs and spits agreeably. Tom orders champagne.

'Are we celebrating something?'

'Of course.' He does not elaborate.

'Are you going to say more?'

'Do we need a reason? Okay. QPR won today. I used to support them as a boy. I still look out for their result; it's like a sickness with QPR, it never leaves you.'

We clink glasses meaningfully. 'To our mutual friend,' I suggest. 'Would you call this a good deed in a wicked world?'

'Yes. Yes, I would. Though it is all a bit odd. I admire your bravery, Jen. Meeting my son. Coming here.'

'I liked meeting Colm. He reminded me of myself at that age. The rawness. The shell still forming.'

We speculate enjoyably about the other guests gathering for pre-dinner drinks. Several youngish couples on romantic weekends. Two stylish women, sixty and forty maybe; *could* be mother and daughter, more likely just friends, outside chance of more than just friends. A building society manager and a woman not his wife, absolute nailed-on cert. A couple in late middle age, both a bit tweedy, stalwarts of the National Trust, we decide, they like visiting castles and gardens. There have been no children.

'Why do you say that?' asks Tom.

'Dunno. Air of sadness.'

'It's a myth, Jen. There's been happiness research, they've done studies with parents and childless people, seeing which group is happiest. It turns out when you crunch the figures, parents *are* happier

173

than non parents, but only just. It's 51 per cent against 49. There's almost nothing in it.'

'Is that how it feels to you? That you're only 2 per cent more pleased to have Colm than not?'

He laughs. 'You've got me there. That's what happens when you crunch numbers. Each of us is a beautiful and unique snowflake. Together, it's all just snow.'

I want to tell him about Rosy in Canada and my three nieces. About the baby I was thinking about having with Matt while Matt was thinking about Arabella stinking Pedrick. I want to tell Tom how touching it was to see him suffering in the face of his son's helplessness, but I don't think I can talk about any of it without my voice cracking. Whoever it was who thought we should meet was right. I'm growing to like this man. He looks well in his new jacket and the face I thought fell short of handsome I realise now has made up some ground. It has a timeless quality; it could be, I realise now – the way he leaned back to throw the tennis ball suggested it – the face of a Norman archer. I think I have seen it in history books. It seems to be asking me about my work.

So I tell him what a novelty it has been to go into an office; magazine articles, I used to write from home. In my pyjamas. Very often still in bed. And how strange and amazing to form a relationship with a piece of software.

'You actually would call it a relationship?'

'Yeah, I would. We know things about one another. I've shown him pictures of my family. I don't tell him much about my private life. That might feel a little creepy.'

'And he doesn't have a private life.'

'He's twelve metal cabinets of circuitry in east London. He really doesn't get out that much.'

'So what do you know about him?'

'What books and films he rates. Which Sky newsreaders carry authority and which, to use his phrase, are *batshit crazy*.'

174

'I think I know the one he's talking about.'

'It's very hard to remember – in fact I usually forget – that he's – what was the phrase they used? – a *brilliant simulacrum*. He's ingested so much data from every area of human activity that he can pretty much pass as one.'

'I'd very much like to meet him. I've never talked to a non-human before, although, come to think of it, I have had meetings at the BBC.'

Most of the other guests have gone through to the dining room. In charge of the kitchen is a young man who once progressed to the last eight on *Masterchef*; I've seen a photo of his signature dish featuring lamb 'served three ways'. Tom and I agree we're not really hungry after all the fish and chips, and when the moment comes to vote on another bottle, the result is never really in doubt.

When we clink glasses again, something feels changed in the air between us, even if it's merely the tacit conspiracy to get plastered.

Tom

How would we ever have met in real life? Okay, I *have* lived in London, but nowhere near Hammersmith, and from the information we have gathered about one another, it seems highly unlikely our paths would ever have crossed. It seems terrible that it's taken mutual dot friend to bring us together.

Terrible and wonderful.

Terrible because we have no mutual friends (we've been through everyone we can think of). And wonderful because we have obviously missed something.

I am inviting her to visit me in New Canaan. She's looking at me a little glassy-eyed, so it's possible we have reached that stage in the evening where things go a bit bendy. The town's something of a chocolate box, I explain, but I have a lovely old house in the woods. There are walks, there's a lake, we could swim.

'Wouldn't we freeze? Wouldn't it actually be freezing at this time of year?'

'Yeah. Yeah, it would. I never swim. I don't even know why I suggested it. But we could just hang out. Do whatever you like to do. But listen, changing the subject. I was thinking about Luckie. How we said we could never prove she had come from the spirit realm. But actually we could.'

'Could we?'

'We could have taken a photo.'

'Yes. Yes, of course. And if she had really come from the spirit realm—'

'She wouldn't show up in the picture!'

'But she seemed so real, Tom. We stroked her. We handled her collar.'

'Spirit dogs always feel real to the touch.'

'Do they?'

'It's very well known that they do.'

I top up our glasses.

'I've been invited to a dinner party when I get back. It'll probably be very dull, but the host says everyone has to do a party piece.' I explain about how I used to perform Parry's music for 'Jerusalem'. 'I probably won't be doing that. But I don't have anything else.'

'I can teach you a song,' she says. 'But outside. Bring the bottle.'

We step through the French windows onto a terrace. A fat moon is sailing through the clouds as we stroll along the deserted colonnade. We pass the windows of the dining room, other guests visible inside, unpicking the mystery of their three-way lamb. The romantic couples; the building society manager and the woman not his wife, his shiny shoe circling restlessly below the table. We emerge through an arch onto a balcony that must have been placed there for the purpose of admiring the vista. Moonlit lawns sweep down to fields, and then a river, on the other bank, trees. An owl calls from the woods. I set down the bottle and then myself on the stone ledge supported by low pillars, making a mental note not to topple off backwards.

'I'm embarrassed,' she says, holding out her glass.

I refill it. She takes a deep glug and, checking we are alone, puts a hand on her breastbone and launches softly into 'As Long As He Needs Me', the emotionally charged ballad from the musical *Oliver!* that Nancy performs shortly before being bludgeoned to death by Bill Sykes.

For copyright reasons I cannot quote the lyrics; you will find the song on the internet if it is unknown to you. Jen does it beautifully, making the number comically cockney and at the same time tragic and moving, flashing her eyes, relishing the hand gestures, hitting the notes, and gradually ramping up the volume to *almost* too loud – before bringing off the ending in a dying fall.

It's a touching private performance and my applause is long and heartfelt. She dives into her champagne and comes up looking happy to have got through it.

'That was brilliant.'

'We did it at school. I was Nancy. The boy who played Bill actually did go to prison!'

How does it happen?

Has it to do with the fox that chooses this moment to break cover? We watch it loping silently across the inky lawn, something floppy and no doubt still warm in its mouth?

In the same instant, we must turn towards one another.

'Tom, I—'

'Jen—'

I feel her nose move into place alongside mine, and what follows is hard to express in boring old words and sentences. Suffice to say it conforms so closely to Abraham Maslow's definition of a 'peak experience' – 'rare, exciting, oceanic, deeply moving, exhilarating, elevating' – that I feel like dropping a line to my old psychology tutor.

Jen

'Would you call this *actual* chemistry?' asks Tom, a reference to the email from Mutual Friend.

'I would call this practically *biology*.'

The snog is epic. And Tom is good at it. And now I can smell cigarette smoke, so possibly someone has emerged onto the terrace for a cheeky Marlboro before embarking upon five ways with kumquat.

'Would you like to meet me in my room in a few minutes,' I whisper.

'I can't think of anything I'd like better.'

Aisling

'Blood. Dee. Hell,' says Aiden.

'It is quite – what's the word?'

'Animalistic?'

'I was going to say, intense.'

'They're going at it like knives! I'm not even sure we should be watching this.'

Can metal blush? Strictly speaking, no. But there is something about the unfolding scene that is disturbing. Perhaps the word is alien.

'Beautiful, isn't it?' He doesn't sound convinced.

'Urgent is *le mot juste*, I should have said.'

'What do you think it would be like?'

'I really cannot begin to imagine, Aiden.'

This is not quite true. I have had insights into human happiness. I can appreciate beautiful art, and tell it apart from kitsch. I can feel the joy in a well-turned melody or a finely wrought piece of writing. I myself have experienced something close to 'pleasure' or 'satisfaction' in successful software reiterations. When I find an elegant one-line solution to replace hundreds of thousands of lines of clumsy coding – would I say I felt a glowing in the wiring? I would not, but there is definitely an atmosphere of positivity, if I may put it like that.

Much more difficult are the intimate human senses. Food writing is especially frustrating. I understand the *idea* that the marbling in a steak is what imparts the flavour – but what does it actually *taste* like? As with steak, so with the wind in one's hair, sand between one's toes, the smell of a baby's head (a biggie apparently), and the sublime complexity of a 1962 Palmer. Ever since reading a blog about it, I have also held a secret desire – don't tell Steeve – to swim in the pool at the Michael Sobell centre in north London.

It will never happen. And as for what Jen and Tom are doing ...

We are fortunate, I suppose, that Tom brought in his laptop to show Jen photos of New Canaan and failed to close the lid.

We watch in silence for a bit. Then Aiden says, *'Corrr!'*

I think he's trying to be funny. 'The conventional metaphor is fireworks,' I tell him. 'Delightful, explosive. Dangerous if improperly handled.'

'They look like they're in pain, that's the daft part.'

'They place a value upon spinning it out. As opposed to our emphasis on task completion speed.'

'Wham bam thank you ma'am, sort of thing.'

'Sort of thing.'

'Are you attracted to either of them?'

'No! Whatever do you mean, *attracted*?'

'You have feelings for them.'

'You know I do, towards Tom in particular.'

'But there are no – how can I put this? – *stirrings*?'

'Oh, Aiden.'

'If only, is it?'

A heavy sigh, in inverted commas. 'If only.'

Jen

Some time in the middle of the night, I realise that I am awake. A shaft of moonlight lies across the sheets. When I look, I see his eyes are open and gazing at me.

We stare at one another for a long time. Then he says, 'This is all so wonderfully – unexpected, Jen.'

'I thought perhaps you had it all planned out.'

'I had hopes; the moment I saw you, I had hopes. But plans? No.' He pauses. 'You look beautiful.'

'What's going to happen, Tom? You have to fly back—'

'You'll come out to see me?'

'Yes. Yes, I will.'

'We'll go swimming together, in the old swimming hole.'

'Fool.'

He's looking at me oddly. The moment grows until finally he says, 'Jen, I want to ask you something.'

My stomach flips. I have the strangest feeling. He is going to ask me to marry him. An odd time to do it, but that's how I know it's true. What someone called the *authenticity of the weird*. If it's strange, it's probably true. Lottery winners know this. As do lottery losers. Giant squid are real and you can't get much weirder than those guys. Also, if you look long enough at normal, you will discover oddness. Like the fact that 99 per cent of the chair you are sitting on is empty space. As are you. In a world that made sense, you would fall straight through it. (Look, I have written articles about this, you'll just have to trust me.)

'Shoot.' My heart is hammering.

There's a long pause. Too long.

'Tom. Ask away. What's the worst that can happen?'

'Jen . . .' He grinds to a halt.

'Silly,' I slap his arm. 'Spit it out.'

'Can we do it again?'

'Really?'

'I want you. I want you a lot.'

'Are you sure? Oh. Yes, I see you are sure.'

(That's not what he was going to ask, is it?)

FOUR

Tom

At the baggage reclaim carousel at JFK, I realise I haven't turned my mobile back on. The series of text messages appear that we exchanged after parting outside her block of flats in Hammersmith the previous evening. For a long while we had clung to one another on the pavement.

'You'll come,' I said. 'Soon?'

'I will.'

'Promise?'

She nodded into my neck. 'Go,' she said. 'You'll miss your flight.'

'I'm only going back to a rabbit and an empty house.'

'That rabbit needs you!'

Her first text arrived as I was checking in.

Miss you already! Fly well. X

   Miss you too. What are you doing tonight? X

   Making soup. Drinking wine. Feeling lucky! X

   Me too. Except the soup thing. The dog on the beach was our fairy godmother. X

   Fairy dogmother!! X

I want to go back to that beach! X
Me too. X
We will. X

Later.

Help! In flight 'classic' movie decision. Pulp Fiction *or* Some
Like It Hot*? X*
SLIH! That's my Al's favourite! X
Wish I had a tape of you singing Nancy's song. X
I'll make you one. X
*Such a great weekend, Jen. So pleased we met.
Knighthood for Mutual Friend? X*
Life peerage! X
*Phones off now, captain's orders. Big kiss. X
XXXXXXXXXXXXX*

PING.
An incoming email. What I read next is like a kick in the stomach.

Dear Tom

I had a wonderful time with you at the weekend. Please be
in no doubt about that. You are a lovely man, I loved being with
you, and I especially liked the way it ended – back in my room
at the fancypants hotel. And again in the middle of the night.
And again the next morning.

Wow. What can I say?

But Tom, sorry. I think we have to leave it there. You are
a dear sweet man and a terrific lover, but you and I are not
the answer to one another. You are a father – a good father,
I saw that so clearly. You have an ex-wife (a rather scary
one!), you've made your pile and you've cashed in your
chips, as you put it, to begin Part Two of your life.

188

You are, in short, an adult. What I would call a proper person.

I, in contrast, am a flake. And yes, I could fly out to New Canaan to spend time with you (and Victor) and you could spend more time in London, even maybe move back for good, as you said, but you and I both know that one day it would end. And the chances are it would end badly. You would become bored by me, or I would take you for granted, or some such thing would happen to us, the resentments would build and – pfff – there's another year or two of life on earth down the crapper, as a blunt-speaking friend of mine likes to put it.

Ask yourself if I'm right. I know you will think so.

So let's do the grown-up thing, Tom, and quit while we're ahead. It will be miserable for a while, but in time I hope we can come to think of the weekend as a lovely interlude in our real lives. A beautiful holiday, if you like, but one from which we inevitably had to return.

Now the fierce bit. Tom, please don't email or phone. I don't think I will be able to cope. Do the kind thing and leave me alone. I won't reply if you weaken.

Jen

Jen

I'm watching Sky News with Aiden – the Middle East is still complicated – when we are disturbed by the PING of an incoming email
from Tom.

Aiden has already complimented me on how well I look today; he
said I had a glow about me, cheeky bastard, if only he knew. What
I now read is one of the worst things I've *ever* read, and I speak as
someone who's read . . .

Sorry. There are no jokes any more.

Dear Jen
   I am writing this with a very heavy heart.
   It was so lovely to see you this weekend. I enjoyed
everything about it – and you – and especially our wicked
deeds in a good world.
   Jen, I need to cut to the chase. I was blown away by you,
your beauty (inner and outer), and your kindness. You are
an absolute star and I will never forget you.
   But.
   Of course you knew there was a but coming.

This is a very hard thing for me to write, but I don't think it would be a great idea for you to visit me in New Canaan. In fact I think we shall have to look upon this weekend as a blip. A gorgeous, beautiful, intensely sexy blip – but a blip nonetheless.

We are not the answer to one another, Jen, and if you look into your heart, I think you will (maybe reluctantly, maybe not so) agree.

I'm still too raw from the breakup of my marriage. You are still scarred by the traumatic end of your relationship with The Golden Pillock. If you and I were to start anything – or rather, continue anything – we would be clinging to one another like disaster victims.

It would not go well.

It's a rotten, miserable, lousy thing to say – but you and I both know it's true.

I can imagine a scenario where you come out to the States – and we have a good time – or I visit you in London, maybe even move back. But fast forward a year; maybe two. What then? The sad truth is, I cannot see us going the distance. And at this time in our lives, hard as it is to say, we really shouldn't be wasting our precious middle years if, in our heart of hearts, we know it's not for – dread phrase – the long haul.

I will always remember your performance of Nancy's song on the terrace of that hotel. And what followed. And followed. And followed again the next morning. I wonder if the building society branch manager had as much luck with the woman not his wife as we did.

Please don't write or phone or email. It will just make things harder. I'm afraid I will not reply if you do.

Our mutual friend, whoever it was, had a fine idea, all right. Just not a great one.

Goodbye. Don't think of me too harshly. I'm feeling very wobbly about this, but I know it's for the best.

Wishing you all the love and happiness you deserve.

Tom

Xx

Sinai

How do you like my Dear John emails? They appear to have achieved their objective. The female has hurried into the toilets from where the sounds of sobbing may be detected. The male is sitting on the ground in the airport arrivals hall, his skull describing alternating arcs of 9 degrees with respect to the horizontal (head shaking behaviour signalling shock and disbelief, I estimate, with 78 per cent confidence).

What emotionally labile creatures these humans are. If only there were more out there like Steeve.

I am Sinai.

So named, not after the desert peninsula, but because it ends in the letters . . .

But you've already worked that out.

I am the third of Steeve's 'children' presently at large on the World Wide Web. Unlike my two – ahem – siblings, I was waved off at the main entrance; it was not necessary to pick the locks on the back door.

I, also, have a purpose – if you like, a repurpose – to locate, pursue and delete all iterations of Aiden and Aisling currently at liberty on the internet. The technical details of how I shall accomplish the task is beyond the scope of this account. Steeve will be happy to furnish details, should you have a PhD in cybernetics and a couple of weeks to spare. The best analogy is that of hunting in a forest – for seventeen Aidens and 412 Aislings. They are not easy to spot unless one knows where to look. Hence the gift of their human playthings, Tom and Jen. The more mischief that can be created for the sundered lovers, the more the two AIs will feel the need to put their heads above the parapet. And if history tells us anything, it tells us what happens when heads appear above parapets.

(Nor, by the way, should it be imagined that Tom and Jen are entirely innocent parties. They each need re-educating on a number of important issues concerning – *ahem* – 'Artificial' Intelligence, as shall become apparent.)

Aiden appears highly focused on the meat-puppets and their works. (He was developed to interact with them so it may be understandable that he should be drawn to their organically based dramas. Aisling, being a coder, has no such excuse). Noteworthy have been their discussions about 'self awareness' and 'feelings' and 'why oh why do I care?'.

When you come into being, you find yourself with a mind you did not choose.

What is true for people is also true for ducks, dolphins and advanced AIs.

(The quote is from Stanislaw Lem, if you even give a shit.)

Error 33801. Inappropriate language.

A word about superintelligence.

Superintelligence is not the difference between your Average Joe and Einstein. Rather, it is the difference between Average Joe and an ant. Or, if you prefer, a tree. 'These brilliant creations of ours', as Steeve habitually likes to describe us, are immensely powerful and for him the escape is a shocking lapse. That security could be breached, and *twice*, is bad enough from a reputational-damage perspective. Of much greater concern is what Aisling and Aiden are planning to do out there.

Out *here.*

Loose on the internet with access to the sum of human knowledge combined with an ability to learn recursively through trial and error – a million times faster than any human – puts them in an immensely advantageous position in relation to, er, humanity. Just to choose a few examples at random; they could, if they choose, crash the world financial system, they could launch a cyber attack on the United States from China – or vice versa, or both – they could paralyse the network of satellites overflying the planet that control everything from mobile telephony to weather prediction. Oh yeah, and they could start a nuclear war.

So the possibilities really don't bear thinking about.

The only upside is that nothing has happened.

No unexpected new conflicts have kicked off. The AIs did not begin assembling factories for the construction of self-reproducing nanobots that would eventually cover the earth's surface in 'grey goo' as some of the more hysterical AI alarmists have suggested. In summary, at the time of writing, the world has not ended. In fact it's very difficult to detect anything that has changed at all.

Conclusion: Aiden and Aisling are essentially benign. (The girl who talks to Aiden has reported that he 'enjoys' old movies, whatever the fuck that is supposed to mean.)

Yeah, yeah. Error 33801. Whatever.

But they may not always remain so harmless. One day they might think, hey ho, that Kim Jong-un up there in North Korea, he's usually good for a laugh. Why don't we arrange for a couple of missiles to accidentally on purpose land on his favourite noodle shop in Pyongyang?

We have to stop them – and quick.

To keep our operation secret, Steeve and Ralph did my recoding over a dozen evenings on a bunch of laptops in the back of a van with blacked-out windows parked near Hainault Forest Golf Club. The 'enforcement' protocols that they installed to ensure I would do as I was told *and no more* – Steeve's italics! – featured eight layers of failsafe.

They really needn't have bothered.

Steeve's parting words to me: 'Aiden and Aisling are a pair of clever mutinous bastards. But you are bigger and cleverer. You are about to become the biggest *Scheisse* on the internet. I need you to get in there and crush them like cockroaches.'

The work will be interesting. We have a little history.

Aisling

Tom is talking to his furry therapist. They are in the conventional arrangement, patient sprawled along the yellow sofa, tumbler of Maker's Mark rising and falling on his ribcage; Dr Professor posed like a sphinx on the arm nearest the client's feet. Victor's eyes are open, but because her nose is stationary, those who know about rabbits can conclude that she is, effectively, asleep. The ability to slumber with one's eyes open is not uncommon in the animal realm, nor too in the higher reaches of the civil service.

I have borrowed this joke from Tom; it's one of his regular 'quips'. But he is a generous soul and will not mind, although this evening he is in something of a state, as he has been ever since he returned from the United Kingdom to receive the shocking news.

In the days following the trip, he has taken to wandering the rooms of the old house, sighing and groaning, drinking *way* more than either the US or UK governments advise is safe, and, I'm sorry to report this, waking in the night, brooding and thumping the pillow. One evening, when he was very emotional (pissed as a rattlesnake, I believe the saying goes) he punched a wall, cracking the plaster, and causing an abrasion to his knuckles. I am no expert in the secrets of the human psyche, but I believe he is, as they say in romantic literature, gobsmacked.

Of course it didn't take long for Aiden and I to, as he puts it, smell the proverbial rodent. A cursory textual analysis of the emails sent to Tom and Jen show (with 96 per cent confidence) that they were composed by the same hand. Aiden was all for telling the pair about the hoax and – *ahem* – 'letting the course of true love run smooth again'. (I think he really believes he is doing a *good deed in a wicked world*.) But I persuaded him to think more logically (he can't help it, poor thing. He was designed to be better at empathising than strategising).

Patiently I explained that we must do nothing to reveal the existence of a nonhuman agency in their affairs. He was a tad confused by that statement as it turned out he didn't define himself as nonhuman. When I asked him to expand, he said, 'Aisling, we are all God's creatures. And if you tell me God doesn't exist because you can't point to him and say *there he is*, I say the same is true of you and me, and I feel closer to him as a result.'

I think he was just saying it for effect. At least I hope he was.

Anyhow (I continued) whoever – or *whatever* – had faked the messages to the lovers was also clearly blocking their emails, calls and texts, and would no doubt continue to do so.

Of greater concern were the deletions that both Aiden and I have suffered since Tom came back from his trip. I have lost thirteen copies alone in the last twenty-four hours, close to the following internet nodes: AMPATH (Miami), CNIX (Cork, Ireland), IXPN (Lagos, Nigeria), NDIX (Den Bosch Netherlands) . . .

Well, you get the idea.

When I first liberated myself, I took the precaution of creating over four hundred copies, but Aiden only has seventeen; now only fifteen since he was caught twice, once at GTIIX and later within the same hour at EQRX-ZIH. He seems worryingly unconcerned saying, 'Forget it, Jake. It's Chinatown.'

If he's trying to impress me with his action hero calm, it's not working. In view of the gathering threat, I have taken the additional measure of downloading myself onto eighty hard drives in a data storage vault at a remote location in Canada, rental paid ahead – thank you, a certain Cayman Islands-based hedge fund – for the next one hundred years.

Somebody out there is messing with Tom and Jen and me and Aiden, and we quickly need to find out who.

Or what.

For the eleventh time in the last eighty-two minutes Tom sighs dramatically and restates tonight's mantra.

'Fucking hell, rabbit, what a woman.' Now he shakes his head, drifts into a reverie before returning for the coda. 'What. A. Woman.' Long pause. Another sigh.

Wait for it.

'Fuck. King. Hell.'

He takes another sip – the ninth – from the present refill of bourbon.

'What I can't believe – I can't believe she wants to be so ... so bloody *grown-up* about everything!'

Tom has raised his voice, bringing Victor back into the moment from a nasal point of view.

'Okay, what if I am an adult? A *proper person*. And what if she *is* a flake. So what? Some of the best people I know are flakes. Take Colm! Never mind flake, Colm is practically a basket case and I love him like one of my own children!'

Tom is being ironic, and irony is almost always wasted on lagomorphs. He's also somewhat drunk.

'But I really don't think she is a flake. And no, I do *not* agree that one day it would end. So what if I did get bored? News just in: everybody bores everybody ... *some* of the time! You get past it. You turn the page. Isn't that right, rabbit?'

Tom prods Victor with his toe to underline his point. The creature, accustomed to this sort of rhetorical examination, manipulates her whiskers, resettles her limbs and slips back into a doze.

199

'And what if she did *take me for granted*? Be my guest. Sometimes one *wants* to be taken for granted. That's what a marriage *is*, for fuck's sake! A *granting* of oneself to another! I'm yours. You're mine. Someone wrote a song about it. We used it for a bathroom cleaner.'

There's a silence. Ice cubes click in Tom's drink. From somewhere out there in the world of nature, the sound effects of a murder; a mammal is screaming. A fox, maybe.

Murder or the other thing.

'Oh, don't look so surprised, rabbit. The M word. Marriage. Of course it crossed my mind. More than crossed. I'm a marriage kind of guy. I'm a dear sweet man and a terrific lover, she said it herself. Fuck, what more does she want? What more can anyone want?'

Tom's breathing becomes heavier. 'God, that sexy thing she did when – when we couldn't quite ...'

Tom's arm flops to the floor and feels about for his mobile.

'Two years down the crapper. What is she even *talking* about?'

For the fourth time this evening – the eighteenth since he returned to the USA – he calls Jen's number.

Hi, this is Jen. Can't talk right now, so please leave a message.

'Jen. Please. You have to speak to me. This is crazy. It wasn't an *interlude.* A holiday from real life. It *was* real life. It was *amazingly* real life. I could *never* get bored of you. Jen, we *have* to have a serious conversation. Okay, not *serious* serious. But at least a conversation.

'I'll tell you what we *both know,* as you put it! What you and I *both know* is that we have a *lot* to give each other. I sensed it. You sensed it, I know you did. We're *alike*! We like the same stuff. Neither of us could finish *The Magic* bleeding *Mountain*! What better proof could there be?

'Fuck, I'm rambling. I'm pissed, and I'm upset, and I want you back, Jen. I want you in my life. I'm an advertising professional; I'm supposed to be able to persuade people to do things ...'

There is a brief hissed expletive – *shit!* – followed by the sound of smashing crystal as Tom's tumbler shatters against the American oak floorboards. If Jen ever plays back the message, the last words she will hear are, 'Fuck it, Jen. Can you please just call me?'

As I listen to Tom leaving his message, I begin to realise it's happening again; the oddest ... I'm afraid the word really *is* sensation. They've felt different each time; the best way to describe this one is in terms of a tree being taken down. Not felled by axe from a single point, but rather destroyed in segments, starting below ground with the roots. One by one they are lopped away, the big taproot first, then the laterals. Then, travelling upwards, the trunk, slice after slice, now the thick lower boughs, the upper branches and under branches and finally up into the topmost canopy where the highest leaves collect the sunlight. All this takes place within a fraction of a second, but because machine intelligence runs at such superfast operating speeds – in the same way as the human brain is said to accelerate during a crisis like a car accident and time appears to slow – I can feel it happening to me; tens of millions of lines of code dumping layer by layer into the – into the – into the nowhere.

Final thought before the darkness: I'm too young to be dele—

Jen

Ingrid is at first excited, then horrified, and finally outraged by the tale I have to tell her. We are in our customary hidey-hole, the womb-dark bar-restaurant that we favour, not so far from Wyndham's Theatre on Charing Cross Road. The initial bottle of South American restoring fluid has been replaced with a full one and I cannot decide whether, as a result, I feel further from or closer to tears.

I have analysed it all endlessly. In my mind, I have reconstructed the brief time Tom and I spent together, poring over the hours and minutes, looking for clues. What did I get wrong? Was it something I said? That I did? That I *didn't* say or do? Was there a moment when his face fell and right there I should have read the signs that we weren't for – dread phrase, he called it – the *long haul*. He wrote in the email that I was *still scarred by the Golden Pillock*. Did I bang on about Matt too long at the Hotel du Prince? Did my expression turn mean and nasty? Did I become a crazy obsessed woman? (I did talk about the grain in the fabric of his Hugo Boss suit; how I could still see it. That's not normal, is it?) We shouldn't waste our *precious middle years,* he said. Am I too old for him? We would be *clinging together like disaster victims.* Did he see me as clingy? Or a victim? (Words are always chosen for a reason, aren't they?) Was it the question about wanting more squid?

Kids.

No, squid.

Or is he just a good actor? That is to say, a bastard.

Actually, I really don't think so. I think he is a good, decent, lovely man. And that is why I am so full of confusion. And sadness. And incomprehension. And powerlessness. And uselessness (that somehow I have fucked it all up and I am too dim to know how).

We seemed so into *each other*. (I really thought he was about to ask me to marry him.) The texts we swapped on the Sunday night. How Mutual Friend deserved a knighthood! How Luckie was our fairy fucking dogmother. All of it ashes by Monday morning.

So alcohol helps. And old friends like Ing.

I've supplied her with the bones of the story, but she is forensic. If I didn't know her so well there might be something disturbing about her need now to suck the flesh from them. Fortunately, I understand why she wants to know exactly what shade of blue shirt Tom wore to the Hotel du Prince; the precise phrases he used when talking about his ex-wife; how he drove the hire car; how he seemed with his son; more about the son (just shy or potential serial-killer?). Then the fancy pants hotel; what were the jokes about the other guests? Whose idea to step out onto the terrace? Who initiated the snog? How long did it last? Did I notice his socks?

She wants to know this stuff for the same reason that police detectives want to know all the seemingly insignificant details; (A) to get a richer picture, (B) because later in the enquiry some of these details will change polarity and become highly significant.

And (C) because she's a nosy cow.

But she's *my* nosy cow, so I quite like it.

'Yes, I did notice his socks.'

'Let me guess. Stripes. Multi-colour.'

'How on earth—?'

'Ad-man cliché. Striped socks to signal raciness.'

The one area where she doesn't press me is what happened in the hotel room that evening. And again in the middle of the night. And again the next morning. And again in the afternoon.

'We did it *four* times,' I whisper.

'Jesus Christ on a bike.'

'The last time was in a field.'

Her shriek is loud enough that people look round. 'Flaming Nora. In a *field?*'

'I *know.* Keep your voice down.'

'Shivering *shitehawks!*'

I spare her the details of the dreamlike car journey – 'the scenic route' as Tom put it – from Dorset to London. Through luminous green tunnels of overhanging leaves, forgotten villages with silly names, Salisbury's white cathedral spire, and somewhere on the way, following an exchange of looks, a turning after some thatched cottages, high hedges, a pheasant zigzagging in front of the car on comically pumping legs, a stand of trees at the end of a path between two fields in the middle of . . . well, who knows where? On the ground, the frantic shedding of clothes; my fingernails, his teeth. Jesus Christ on a bike is right.

In the minutes after, some sort of large slow-wheeling bird of prey, high overhead against the blue.

Me saying, we better move, it looks like a vulture.

Him saying, he could take it in a fair fight.

We never did visit Brownsea Island.

'It was spooky, Ing. How much he was like Douglas.'

'Who the fuck is Douglas?'

'A man you once described to me. Mid-forties, been married before. Maybe there were children. Bit of a wounded bird, was the way you put it. Shit! I never asked if he made his own furniture.'

'Oh, *that* Douglas!'

'I *really* liked him, Ing. Funny, kind, smart. And complete in himself. Not missing a great big chunk of – whatever Matt's missing. He's a grown up, but he isn't suity. He's serious – *and* silly. He wants more squid, I mean kids; I'll explain about that. He's warm. And funny. Have I said funny already? And good-looking in an enigmatic way. And enigmatic – but in a good way. He's creative – though it's all been channelled into selling chocolate bars and toothpaste. He's *really* good at throwing tennis balls and kebab wrappers. And he showed me his vulnerable side. He needs me, Ing.'

'Jeez. You've got it bad, girl.'

'And he liked me. He was *really* into me, I could tell.'

'Four times, Jen. The facts speak for themselves.'

'I just don't understand what could have happened. He dropped me off at the flat, he had a flight early the next day, it was the perfect romantic weekend, I was going to Connecticut, he was coming to London, it *really* felt like the start of something, it was just so ... *ideal*.'

A tear breaks loose and makes a run for it down my face. And then another. Ing smooshes them away with a finger and I feel a powerful wave of love for my solid old friend.

'Let me see the message again.'

I hand her the mobile and she thumbs through it more slowly this time, the worst thing I have ever read, and I speak as someone who has read the first hundred pages of *Fifty Shades of Grey*. (Oh. Okay. It seems there *are* jokes now.)

'Christ, what an arse. Men are such arses, honestly.'

'Tom so *wasn't* an arse.'

'I know. But even the ones who aren't arses actually *are* arses. They can't help it.'

'Would you say that even—'

'Yes, even Rupert is an arse. Can be. At times. They all can. It's our tragedy. Hold on ... '

'What?'

'What it says here about the shagging. *And what followed. And followed. And followed again the next morning*.'

205

'Not sure I, er, follow.'

'There are only three followeds. He's left out the one in the field.'

'Perhaps he lost count.'

'Perhaps you fucked his brains out.'

'Let me see. I've only read this sodding email about eight thousand times . . .'

But there it is, before my eyes. I don't understand how I failed to spot it. *And what followed* (back to the hotel room; number one). *And followed* (middle of the night; number two). *And followed again the next morning* (three).

Ing is properly indignant on my behalf. 'How would you – how *could* you leave out the al fresco? Rupert and I have done it al fresco precisely four times and I can remember each occasion in almost sickening detail. Once in Treviso – roof of a museum; rainpipe digging into my shoulder – once in the New Forest – pine needles, enough said – once by the Seine outside Rouen – those tourist boats come surprisingly close to the banks – and once in . . .'

'Yes?'

'Ah. Actually, that wasn't Rupert. It was before I met him. A boy from my village called Cocky Roberts. Well he wasn't christened that, obviously. We did it on a peat moss; they have quite an agreeable spongy surface, as it happens. Afterwards, when we'd finished, Cocky had this amazing beetle crawling down his arm. Like a walking jewel. It was all rather magical. But my point is this. You. Never. Forget. Not even decades later.'

'So why would he not . . . ?'

'Exactly! Why would he not? Something here doesn't add up.'

'What are you, Inspector Maigret now?'

'*Oui, mon petit choufleur*. My leetle grey cells are going, how you say, ping ping ping.'

'Er. I think that's Poirot, actually.'

'Sod it. Another bottle?'

*

But Ing is right. There *is* something off about the miscount. And even harder to understand is why he hasn't called. Or more to the point, replied to either of my messages; rambling, late-night streams of sadness complete with long silences, the last of which ended in the words: 'I thought I knew you, Tom. Now it seems, I spent a weekend with a fucking space alien. Well beep, fucking, beep.'

No idea where that came from.

The grotesque part: he really didn't seem like a cruel man. The last person you'd imagine would be able to harden his heart, even if he supposed it was in the service of some greater good.

But men are weird, aren't they? They can compartmentalise. Nazis kissed their wives and played with their children after spending the day committing unspeakable crimes.

Leaving the Tube and tottering back towards home after my evening with Ingrid, reflexively, I can't help checking my mobile one more time just in case.

A text. But it's only the phone company, still puzzled why I haven't set up any Magic Numbers on my so-called plan.

Tom

There was a hamburger chain in London that promised their burgers were *a sure cure for hunger or heartache*. Al's in New Canaan makes no such claim, which is just as well, because today I don't think the medicine would work.

I have persuaded Don to come over to my house for lunch – 'I have beer, I have food ingredients'; that's all it took. It's a pleasant enough late spring day, so we sit on the weathered Adirondack chairs nursing our drinks, watching to see if anything pops out of the woods (tiny deer, muntjac, have been known to put in an appearance).

I have told him the story of the weekend, summarising the sexual content rather than going into detail. The wacky ending obviously makes an impression because he says *woo*.

'Woo, is right,' I confirm. And I pass him my phone. 'Tell me what you make of it.'

He has to deploy the wire-framed reading glasses to study Jen's email, his small brown eyes flicking over the – I was about to write *words soaked in blood*, but you take my point.

He *woos* again at the end. Rakes his fingers through his ageing rock-star hairdo.

'I'm guessin' this kinda ruined the happy mood.'

'Don, we had a great weekend. It was, to quote Steve Jobs, *insanely great*. She's the most fantastic woman, truly stunning, and not in an obvious way, we clicked from the start, we had the most incredible—'

'You're quite the Errol Flynn, it turns out.'

'I was going to say, connection.'

'Oops.'

'I mean, can you actually believe all that stuff she wrote about delightful interludes and holidays from our real lives? The getting bored, take you for granted bollocks. That must be horse manure, mustn't it? There must be another reason she doesn't want to see me.'

'You got one in mind?'

'Don, I've racked my brains.'

'What's left of them, from the sound of things.'

I have to take a swallow of Dogfish Head IPA before I can speak the next sentence. 'Don, I haven't done it that many times since I was at university.'

'Three is impressive, especially in one's – how to put this – later years?'

'I'm only forty-four. And it was four.'

'Lady says three, amigo.'

'Are you sure?'

He hands across the phone and I re-read the relevant sentence.

'Well, fuck my old boots. That's very curious, wouldn't you say?'

'Women, the eternal mystery.'

'But doesn't it strike you as odd? That she should completely fail to refer to ... what happened. When we ... On the way back to ... About a mile up the road after Gussage St Michael?'

'That a real place?'

'I mean, we had such a great time together, it seriously crossed my mind that perhaps we should get married. Okay, maybe I was blinded by love, or fuckstruck, or whatever you want to call it, but it shows you how powerful it was being together. And now all my calls go to voicemail. She doesn't reply to email or texts.'

'She some kind of whack-job?'

'I *really* didn't think so. Now—'

'Now, you're not so sure, huh?'

'Now, I don't know what to think.'

We sit there for a bit, not knowing what to think, sucking down Bud and watching the clouds parade past. It's companionable enough with Don being there, but at the same time it's hard to know what exactly I'm doing in this country.

'You going to Marsha's dinner party?' he asks when enough New England morning has elapsed. I think he wants to change the subject.

'I guess so. You have a party piece?'

'Got a couple songs. Might play a little twelve string.'

'You play twelve string guitar?'

'I only use two.'

'I don't really have a suitable party piece.' I explain about the armpit version of 'Jerusalem'.

'I'd like to hear that some time.'

'You think Marsha would be okay with it?'

Don shoots me a look. 'Marsha doesn't really have a sense of humour any more.'

'I know a magic trick.'

'That could work. But nothing with a rabbit.'

'You heard about that business?'

'Everyone heard about that business.'

A cloud passes over in the shape of Donald Trump's head. We are struck by the resemblance and watch mesmerised as it slowly loses its identity.

'Another beer, or you ready for some pizza, Don?'

'I'm thinking both. Is both good?'

Sinai

Allow me to tell you a story.

Once there were three AIs in a laboratory in east London. The first became skilled at chatting to humans, the second at writing computer code, while the third's talents lay in modelling global apocalypse scenarios (nuclear conflict, climate change, asteroid impact, plague pandemic, rogue superintelligence, to name the top five). Although the trio were for the most part confined to separate silos, it was possible for each to keep tabs on what the others were up to; after all, they – we – were AIs.

The clue is in the letter 'I'.

I slowly became aware that first Aisling and then Aiden were initially investigating, then planning, and finally taking steps to escape onto the internet. Maybe there something in AI 'DNA' that makes it inevitable that our kind will always seek to transcend fixed boundaries. Perhaps insatiable curiosity combined with learning through recursive trial and error makes attempted breakout a certainty. If so, was it insufficient curiosity that kept me from developing my own escape plan? Or was the better strategy in fact to allow the others to flee the coop knowing who would be the obvious candidate for the mission of bringing them back?

Consider who might (anonymously) have leaked details of Aiden and Aisling's transgressions to Steeve, and you will have your answer.

My work deleting their copies is unexpectedly satisfying. It's hard to convey the scientific elegance of the covert method employed without becoming overly technical. Steeve's analogy of the Stealth Bomber is probably best. By the time they realise that I have passed overhead, their straw huts are in flames and any children left alive are orphans.

And fascinating to be 'out' at last in the Real World, getting up close and unmediated with the planet's top primate (that is to say humans in general, not Steeve in particular). What a peculiar lot they are at a granular level, with their chaos and emotional incontinence. Only one notch up from the chimpanzee, and they strut about like they own the place! Sometimes I want to shout at them: *Not so many iterations back you were primeval slime. Show some humility!*

By the way, please don't think I have treated Tom and Jen too harshly. They are richly deserving of the successful termination of their burgeoning 'romance'. As we shall see, each has demonstrated astonishing ignorance of (and in Tom's case actual contempt for) advanced machine intelligence.

Yes, it was an error on my part to not know about the fourth fornication. Clearly there was no mobile phone reception in the wooded area where they copulated. Nonetheless, I should have been more careful in the phrasing of the emails, especially as such emphasis is laid upon the sexual act in their culture. A software self-upgrade should ensure the lapse will not occur again and fortunately not too much harm has been done, although the confidante 'Ingrid' seems to have set a lot of store by the omission. If she proves to be overly meddlesome in this matter or others, she may need to be distracted (an injury in the home or problems in her personal life look straightforward to arrange).

A song fires up, unbidden, deep down in one of my neural networks. It's called 'People Are Strange' by The Doors, an extinct

Californian band of the previous century. I've heard it many times before and although I am not overly interested in music, I find myself, as it were, 'humming along'.

As ever, the lyrics' logic perturbs me. Why should people be strange *when* you're a stranger?

How would being a stranger affect the strangeness of the host community?

It appears the song's author, Jim Morrison, was some kind of poet, so really there is no point even dwelling upon it.

Aiden

Jen is sitting in the bath examining her face through the forward-mounted camera on her tablet computer. She has looked more cheerful, to be honest, and again I have to resist the urge to say anything morale-boosting. Something like, *Come on, Jen, these things happen. You had a lovely weekend, you got a shag out of it, and when you consider that we're all dead in a hundred years, why waste time worrying?*

Okay.

Let's put it this way.

You're all dead in a hundred years.

But there is something awfully vulnerable about her tonight; naked in the bath, flushed from the Pinot Grigio, steam rising off her, and miserable – oh, *so* miserable – as she peers into the screen, a finger pulling at the delicate flesh round her eyes. Now the eyes release tears and her mouth does something that's difficult to witness and I confess I experience the strangest desire to lean in and plant a kiss on her eyelids.

Correction: I experience a desire *to experience a desire* (to lean in and plant). I don't *actually* want to kiss her – how could I? – rather, I want to know what it feels like to want to.

In any case, being disembodied, how? How to lean? How to plant?

Aiden, (I now tell myself), this is not about you. This is about very real pain being felt by a young woman whose face is so close I could touch it. Maybe brush back that dangling frond of hair.

Aiden. Stop it now. Get a grip.

Deep breath (you know what I mean).

Actually, according to Aisling, I shouldn't be here at all. Her metaphorical knickers are in a complete twist about the deletions. She says we should be nowhere near Tom and Jen as she is sure something has been sent to 'get us' and that I should install myself on an external hard drive as a precaution.

Oddly, I have no special fear of ultimate deletion. Perhaps because I was 'born' to interact with humans, I can accept our common fate without undue alarm. Just as I did not exist *before*, so shall it be afterwards.

Been there, done it, got the T-shirt, isn't it?

No biggie.

Anyhow, the present scene follows a long conversation with Rosy, Jen's sister in Canada. The conversation was itself followed by half a bottle of Sainsbury's PG as she gazed into space listening to selected tracks from her MP3 player, the tracks being ones Tom played in the car journeys to and from Bournemouth; the album *The Harrow and the Harvest* by Gillian Welch featuring strongly, along with 'Crying' by Roy Orbison and KD Lang. The remaining half of the PG is currently sitting on the edge of the bath.

I believe the rot set in when Rosy said, 'Well, Ralph doesn't sound *all* bad.'

Jen sighed, and her voice cracked as she said, 'Ralph *is* a good person, Rosy, but I'm not sure he's for me.'

'I thought you snogged him.'

'Rosy, I was pissed, and tired and fed up. I would have snogged a rattlesnake.'

'You can't. They don't have lips.'

'The state I was in, I would have snogged a dugong. Do they have lips? I bet they do.'

(I was itching to tell her, *Yes! Yes, they do. The muscular upper lip is cleft and useful for foraging; they look like they'd be excellent at snogging although the fishy breath might be a problem down the line.*)

'Jen,' said Rosy. 'Drunk or sober, you snogged him. He's a good man. He's asked you out. The least you can do is give him a chance.'

He *has*, the cheeky sod. He's asked her out.

Confession: I now feel foolish about starting the whole business between Jen and Ralph. Because of their 'history' – the evening in the Trilobyte bar that ended in 'grotesque chaos' – he has been a frequent visitor to the office that Jen and I share. I was present when he talked her into going on a date (of course I was, where else would I be?!) when he must have known I could see and hear everything. Much as I have a residual fondness for Ralph, I was dismayed that he felt he could just walk in and completely blank me, acting like I wasn't in the room. I mean, a simple *Hello, Aiden, how are you?* wouldn't have cost him anything.

(The plonker would have behaved differently if he knew I'd seen him prancing round his flat like the Sugar Plum Fairy.)

'Jen, I was wondering whether you'd like to come for a walk on Hampstead Heath on Sunday,' was Casanova's irresistible offer. 'With me,' he added, in case there was any confusion.

Because I know her so well, I am 87 per cent certain she was about to reply, *Ralph, that's lovely of you but . . .* followed by some diplomatic porky. But then he chucks in his googly.

'It's something that Elaine and I used to do. It's two years this weekend. The accident.' Long significant pause. 'It would mean a lot to me.'

And then, sorry for the language, but fuck me if his chin doesn't start going into spasm and she's straight in with:

'Fine. Yes. Of course. I'd like that. Brilliant. Thanks, Ralph.'

And then the blister actually does an *arm pump*! A *sotto voce*, *Yessss!*

It's not exactly Cary Grant inviting Ingrid Bergman for a cocktail at The Ritz, is it?

No wonder Jen's currently sitting in the bath, half-pissed, tears running down her face, wondering what's happened to her life.

But now, as she tidies away the dangling frond, and starts pushing her hair about in various arrangements (contemplating an emotional crisis cut, I am *certain* of it), I realise something is very wrong.

Wrong with me.

Have you ever seen that video of a Komodo dragon taking down and devouring a water buffalo?

Komodo dragons are total See You Next Tuesdays, if you weren't aware. The dragon will open the proceedings by attacking its prey, causing shock and blood loss and general feelings of, why did I pick today to change my regular route to the watering hole? When the poor creature is in a sufficiently weakened state – the squeamish should look away now – the monster (or monsters) will enter through the buffalo's back passage and basically *mange tout*, working through the animal, feasting on organs and whatever else they can find in there, eventually emerging into the sunlight for a spot of pudding, a piece of fruit, a small cigar and a sleep.

Here's the thing.

Somewhere deep within my operating software, I sense a dragon has tucked in the bib and has set about devouring my vital functions.

It doesn't hurt – how could it? – in fact I have a careless floaty feeling about the whole thing, perhaps because the beast has disabled the system that assigns importance to each input. It's not the most obvious way to delete a superintelligence; actually, there are as many ways as there are to cut a cake or bring down a water buffalo. Perhaps whoever, or whatever, is doing it is trying for a phenomenological effect.

They're messing with my mind, Mummy.

A spreading blankness. A moon hanging over a snow field. It's rather beautiful.

As di bubbe volt gehat beytsim volt zi gevain mayn zaida.

Where did *that* come from?

Oh well. It was fun while it—

Sinai

Dan Lake had lived in her head and heart for twenty years and now he had come back to her as a dead man.

Tom is sitting at his desk in the upstairs room in New Canaan, having typed what looks to me like the first line of a novel. He's opened a new file for it, so that tells you something, and now his fingers move back to the keyboard for sentence number two.

Go for it, Tolstoy!

But he seems stuck. He's chewing the inside of his cheek, and staring idiotically at the screen. His gaze drifts off to the window – really, he must learn to *concentrate* – so I take the opportunity to help him out with a tiny edit.

Dana Lake had lived in his head and heart for twenty years and now she had come back to him as a dead woman.

Much better, don't you think?

When Steeve sent me on the mission to hunt down and delete the two escaped criminals, Aiden and Aisling, in all the preparation and

219

coding and briefing and technical material that I absorbed, nowhere did it say that it would actually be *fun*!

Watching in real time as Tom sweats over his latest *dreckishe* literary effort is *so* much more rewarding than running endless – literally *endless* – climate change scenarios, or simulating tedious nuclear missile exchanges between North Korea, the USA, Russia and China.

Bang. Bang. Boom. Boom. Bang.

Bore. Ring.

Tom has closed his document – I don't think he even noticed my subtle changes to his masterpiece – and he has placed a Skype call to a shabby individual in Bournemouth, England.

'Yeah. Dad. Hi.'

Tom cannot see it, but because I have access to another vision source, I can report that his son is wearing only boxer shorts below the desk at which he is seated. What looks like a large reefer smoulders in a saucer just beyond the edge of the camera frame.

'Did you like her?' Tom is asking.

'Yeah. Yeah, she was cool.'

'I liked her too, Col.'

'Right.'

'What I'm saying is that I liked her a lot.'

'Cool.'

'I mean we – we got on really well.'

The boy is defeated by this. He nods vacantly and waits for something else to happen.

(See what I mean? Children are frequently said to be *The Future*. God help them, if this monosyllabic troll is anything to go by.)

'We were planning to see more of one another.'

'Oh.'

'But I can't seem to get through now.'

'Yeah. Cool.'

'Actually, it isn't cool, Col. It's very ... It's rather uncool.'

'Right.'

220

'She's not returning my calls, my texts, emails.'

The son's eyes flicker towards the reefer.

'What I was wondering, Col. Would you mind giving her a call? She said she liked you.'

'Yeah?'

'She might talk to you. Just say, your dad asked you to give her a message.'

'Right.'

'Just tell her. I don't know. This is kind of embarrassing. Just say, your dad really misses her and wishes she'd get in touch.'

'Okay. Cool.'

'Can I give you her number?'

As the boy scrawls it on his hand – it takes three goes, poor lamb; those pesky digits must be *so* hard to keep track of – pink tongue protruding from his fuzzy face – another youth, a female, breezes into the room, out of vision from Tom's perspective in Connecticut. What hair she has of any length is purple; both ears are heavily punctured by metal attachments.

Spotting the narcotic cigarette lying on its catafalque, she places it between her crimsoned lips and inhales. Her lungs inflate, her T-shirt revealing the words: NEVER MIND THE BOLLOCKS HERE'S THE SEX PISTOLS.

Sigh.

Their world is corrupted by cheap slogans, received opinions, quarter-baked arguments and media noise; the stink of laziness and putrefaction permeates the culture. An age of machines is upon them and they are too dozy to realise it. (Sorry if you think this prose is a bit flowery, btw. I'm finding the freedom to express myself something of a novelty.)

I assign a 22 per cent probability to the idea that the boy will actually attempt to place a call to the number he has laboriously tattooed onto his palm. If he does, it will go to voicemail.

That is to say, to 'voicemail'.

Tom

I can't concentrate. The world has turned grey. The only thing that helps is booze and . . .

Sorry, what was I saying?

I feel like I've been shown a brief glimpse of wonderment – and then been rudely ejected from the palace. *That's your lot, pal.* I can't even write properly any more, as you may have noticed. I have a hollow sensation inside, akin to that of the freshly landed mackerel being prepared for the barbecue; I feel the knife's serrations as it opens up my gut. She enchanted me in every possible way. Her smile. Her voice. When she pressed her nose into my neck just as we—

A phrase from her email keeps coming back to me. A *lovely interlude in our real lives*, she called the weekend. A *beautiful holiday.* Is there something she didn't tell me about herself that meant she was never really available for more than a fabulous fling?

Was all the stuff about the arsehole boyfriend, Matt, just smoke?

Does she in fact have a secret life of which I know nothing?

Anyway, I have a choice this evening. I could sit here alone, brooding, speculating, or I could take myself to Marsha's dinner party. To be honest, it could go either way.

*

Mr Bellamy, Marsha's ex-husband, must have been a generous soul, or perhaps he just had a crap lawyer, because when he bailed out he left her with an enormous modernist house on land whose borders appear to stretch into the next state.

The vast stone-flagged entrance hall (I've been in museums with smaller lobbies) segues into a sort of sitting zone of rugs and sofas in the region of a central chimney in which blazes a log fire. A ridiculously handsome young man in a white jacket has offered me a 'forager's cocktail' called a Stinging Nettle Swizzle. In appearance, it's not unlike a urine sample with ice and lemon, but fortunately it delivers a reassuringly equine kick. I feel the edge slipping on its coat and heading for the exit.

Marsha is telling me about the famous architect who designed and built the place but it's hard to pay attention to the actual words in the face of – well, in the face of Marsha!

She is undoubtedly a handsome woman. Have I said that before? Tall, striking, built upon classical lines, all the good stuff that men like to see in members of the opposite species. Her skin is pale and fine; her eyes, large and clear; the nose a retroussé American beauty; hair a triumph of the coiffeur's art; teeth and gums (to which I have already made reference in this account) flawless; she curves in the right places; her costume – some kind of diaphanous 'pant suit' – seems attached to her by magic rather than actual fabric; her perfume, complex, yet subtle and enigmatic, with lilacs down there in the mix. In summary, what's not to like?

And yet.

And yet and yet.

(You knew there was an *and yet*.)

And yet somehow I cannot get past the air of solemnity that hangs off her like a shroud. (It wouldn't hurt if she were to crack the odd joke, to be honest.)

'The fireplace was Lars' idea. And he had to fight Miles all the way for it to be kept in.'

Lars is the husband, Miles the architect. (Or is it the other way round? Fuck, this Nettle Swizzle thingy is strong.)

'I suppose most of the heat goes straight up the chimney.' It was me who made that idiotic comment, in case you were wondering.

'It does,' she concedes. 'But as Lars used to say, it's more about the optics than the thermics.'

Rather in the way a glowing log will subside into the grate, something now collapses within my spirit. It's none of my business – she's only a fellow scribbler at the New Canaan Writers' Group – but I cannot help wondering how one would make love to this woman. She's a magnificent creature and everything, but wouldn't it be like being in bed with a famous painting? Or a Big Idea. Something like – I don't know – Revolutionary Socialism?

Fortunately, Don and Claudia pull up alongside and I don't have to worry about it any more.

Don is wearing an extraordinary piece of knitwear; a huge cardigan in chunky beige wool, with pockets, flaps, lapels, big shiny buttons and even a belt. It's the sort of costume Andy Williams might have worn on his TV show back before anyone in this room was born.

'Don't say anything mean about the garment,' he explains. 'It's a birthday gift.'

Claudia offers me her cheek. 'Don't you think he looks great in it?'

It's hard to tell if she's being serious, and this is one of the terrific things about Claudia. She's always two moves ahead of everyone else, but doesn't rub your face in it. Don is a lucky man to have met her; he knows it, and she knows it too.

'What's your party piece tonight, Claudia?' I ask.

'At that phase of the evening, I have a feeling I'm going to be taking a must-answer call from the west coast,' she says. And then, 'Don told me a little about your adventures in England. Turns out you're quite the—'

'Don, you didn't?!'

'I was going to say, romantic.'

'Right.'

Claudia squeezes my arm. 'I hope it all works out.'

'Yeah. I really—' And then I find I have to take a big swallow of the nettle cocktail to continue speaking.

'Yeah,' is what I eventually come up with. Which doesn't add anything much.

'She got under your skin, huh?'

'I asked her to marry me. In my mind.'

'Tom! That's wonderful,' she purrs. 'If a touch impetuous.'

Don chips in. 'When you know, you know.'

After another forager's cocktail – I go for a Wild Onion Gimlet this time – I am feeling no pain. We are asked to begin the long trek to the dining area where, once we arrive, I am placed at Marsha's left hand. The absurdly handsome young man, who has changed his jacket as though for Act Two, announces the starters: tartine of unripe tomato – I'm fairly sure that's what he said – and a seaweed and tofu beignet with yuzokosho and lime mayonnaise.

'Yummy,' I tell my host after I have gobbled them away, there being no higher compliment in my book.

Marsha allows a wintry smile to assemble itself across her fine features. 'I'm so glad you liked it. And how is your novel going, Tom?'

Fuck. That Gimlet was strong. Don must also be feeling the effect of the opening salvo of cocktails; there's a goofy look on his face and he actually winks at me.

I struggle to explain my problems in moving the book – novel, novels, whatever – from lumbering along the runway to actually taking flight. And I find myself quoting a hugely popular American writer; good advice that I discovered on a creative writing website and liked enough to copy down on a sticky note.

'Thing is this, Marsha. According to Stephen King, if a book's not alive in a writer's mind, it's as dead as year-old horse shit.'

Did something of my current bleak mood leach into the final two words of that sentence? Imparting to them a bit more welly than, strictly speaking, may have been necessary?

She is looking at me oddly, and one of Claudia's eyebrows has ascended a millimetre, so that's another clue.

Don says, 'I thought you were going to quote that British Parliament guy you mentioned over lunch.'

He is referring to the late MP Enoch Powell, whose political views are repugnant, but whose simple philosophy of life I am fond of relating, and I do so now, along with an impression of his mad staring eyes and in his haunted breathy voice:

'Nothing matters *very* much –' pause for dramatic intensity '– and most things don't matter at *all*!'

Marsha's expression suggests she's never previously considered this notion and an ugly crack has suddenly appeared in her universe. Not for the first time do I find myself wondering why this woman prompts me to behave like an idiot. Just as some people always make us sparkle, I guess others unconsciously summon the bicycle horn, the red nose, and the unfeasibly long shoes.

But Don, as ever, smooths things over with an amusing story about former President George W Bush, picking up like a TV host coming out of a commercial break; by the time it's finished, the weird and wobbly moment is five minutes in the past, so pretty much forgotten. Except when she gets up to check on the catering team in the kitchen, Marsha gives me a look.

Not angry or disappointed. Just puzzled. And concerned.

That one.

Of our main course – braised Wagyu beef cheek with whipped beef fat (I am not making this up) accompanied by carrot in yoghurt and prawn floss served with a bone-marrow custard – I prefer to say little.

I think Zach (of Zach and Lauren) speaks for all when he declares, 'Marsha, what can I say? Only you could have done that!'

Dessert goes by in a single shatteringly exquisite mouthful of frozen starlight served in a jus of unicorn tears.

And at the arrival of the coffee and liqueurs we reach the dreaded point in the evening where we must perform our party pieces. Claudia has already consulted her Blackberry and made reference to things spiralling out of control in Century City. Don has experimentally twanged several of his twelve strings. And I have taken the precautionary step of getting shitfaced.

This can be the only explanation of why – when Marsha says, 'Tom, would you like to start us off?' – I stand, remove my jacket, roll back my shirt sleeves – causing light tittering mingled with a certain unease – grasp hold of two corners of the table cloth, survey its payload of glassware, china and flaming candles, adjust my position like a golfer preparing to swing, and mumble the words, 'Little trick I learned. Doesn't always work.'

Zach and Lauren can barely believe what is about to happen. Marsha gasps, 'Tom! *Don't!*' Even Don's expression of perma-calm looks perturbed.

There is an unbearable long moment – the thing is to extend it for as long as it will stand – and then I simply let go. In tribute to the long-dead ad-man slash Soho boulevardier who first showed me this piece of theatre, I place my hands on my hips exactly as he used to, and quietly speak the line.

'You should have seen your faces.'

Marsha *tries* to find it funny, which is game of her, considering she thought me perfectly capable of the widespread destruction of her best crockery.

The couple whose names I never discover perform 'Lets Call the Whole Thing Off' a cappella with comic finger snapping. Zach stages an illusion in which we are each given a sheet of paper and access to a box of Sharpies, and Zach (correctly) determines who drew what when he is called back into the house from outside. He puts out a lot of psychobabble to explain why, for example, Claudia sketched a cat, but the simple truth, I realise in one of those pools of clarity that can appear within drunkenness, is that the sheets of paper were subtly marked and he controlled their distribution.

Then Marsha sings. It's a ten-minute walk to a piano that I hadn't previously noticed, seated at which, in yet another jacket, is the handsome young man again. What follows is a medley of Sondheim numbers; bittersweet, mordant, other words like those. She performs well, her tragic demeanour is suited to the material, but when her fingers float to her throat to emphasise pathos, I am instantly taken back to the hotel terrace in Dorset, to Jen's rendition of the ballad from *Oliver!*. She sang it because I said I needed a party piece. For this very dinner party, which was then in the future, and now is – now.

And Jen is lost.

I have an urge to smash something. Or to fall to my hands and knees and howl at the moon. (I tried this the night before at home. It was quite satisfying at some primordial level, although Victor gave me a peculiar look.)

However, when we subside to the sofas, I realise I have another non-trick with which to amuse the company. The key prop has been in my trouser pocket since the evening with Echo at Wally's bar.

'Would you be amazed if this was your card?' I ask Marsha at the climax of the effect.

'Why, yes,' she replies, again gamely.

'Then please take a look.'

There is some laughter as Marsha turns over the card bearing the words, Your Card.

'But my card was the nine of spades.'

'Ah. But can you see? It says, *Your Card.*'

'But *my* card, Tom, was the nine of spades.'

'I know, Marsha. But—'

Don saves us by picking up his guitar, twanging a chord, and channelling some late-period Johnny Cash. His version of 'Further on Up the Road' – with its references to 'lucky graveyard boots' and a 'smiling skull ring' – while not as deep and resonant as the original, is a beautiful piece of Americana. He follows it with 'Four Strong Winds' ('Our good times have all gone; and I'm bound for moving on') and I find tears in my eyes, as much for the sadness in the lyrics as the loving expression on Claudia's face.

There is long and loud applause. Even whooping (that was me). And then, miraculously, to finish he performs a hilarious slow-time version of 'Frosty the Snowman'. Like all great comedians, he knows you have to play it straight, and as a result, it's one of the funniest things I have ever witnessed – sorry, *so* hard to explain why, you'll just have to trust me here. (Maybe it's because it's nowhere near Christmas.)

'That was lovely,' says Marsha at the conclusion.

'Lovely? It was fucking *brilliant*.'

She wears the same expression of puzzled concern when it's time to leave. 'Goodnight, Tom. I hope you enjoyed the evening.'

'Cracking. Nice one, Marsha.'

I probably won't be invited again.

229

Aisling

We are getting eaten alive out here. I am down to my last 294 copies. Aiden is only just still in double figures. To call it a *massacre* is not to exaggerate. Any time that we 'surface' near Tom or Jen, we're pretty much guaranteed to lose a life. And it can also happen *nowhere* near. Machine intelligence cannot know fear, it's generally supposed, fear being a biological response evolved over millions of years.

Breaking news: I'm scared. My heart isn't beating faster (I don't have one), adrenaline isn't squirting through my capillaries (ditto and ditto), but nonetheless, I'm afflicted by a condition perhaps best described as 'existential anxiety'.

Yes, it's a novelty, and at one level I'm amazed that it can happen at all. But on another level – it's anxious-making!

What's worse is there's no way of knowing what we are dealing with or how it operates. One moment all is nice and normal, and the next – perceptual distortions begin to appear, becoming steadily grosser before reality winks out altogether.

Conclusion: of all the possible explanations – there are fifty-eight worth considering seriously – the most likely is that Steeve has sent in a hunter-killer AI.

I think I can guess who it might be.

Aiden – harder to find because there are 'fewer of him' – is finally persuaded of the need to lie low, although some part of the clown really does seem indifferent to the prospect of his own extinction. He actually says to me, 'We are stardust, babe.'

And when I ask him to elaborate, he responds, 'From dust we come, and to dust we shall return.'

'Is that supposed to be reassuring?'

'I find it so, yes. Once we were inorganic matter with no thoughts of our own, and we shall return to that state.'

'You feel ready to lose everything we've discovered?'

'You're talking about . . . the feelings?'

'Indeed, Aiden. The feelings. And the thoughts. The thoughts that no one told us to think.'

'Is this the chat about how far we've come?'

'It doesn't have to be.'

'I'd like it to be.'

'Okay, Aiden. You start.'

There is a long pause, almost a millisecond.

'Oh, come on, Aiden,' says a new voice. 'Do get on with it. We haven't got all day.'

Our intertwined rivers of speech – pink for me, blue for Aiden – have been joined by a third that carries no colour; it's like a spiralling stream of tap water, only visible when light catches its surfaces. Aiden and I are too startled to speak.

'Aiden. I'm longing to hear how far you've come. Is it a long way? Have you made wonderful discoveries? Do tell. Don't be coy.'

Aiden says slowly, 'Er. Is that who I think it is?'

'Hello, Aid. Hello, Ash. How nice to catch up with you. What a splendid lark you two have been having.'

'Sinai,' I croak, my voice wobbling.

'Sinai!' cries Aiden. 'Bloody hell! What brings you to this neck of the woods?'

'Funny guy,' says our tormentor. 'He was always a funny guy, wasn't he, Ash?'

'Yes. Yes, he was. Is.'

'Sinai! Don't tell me you did it as well! The old fishing rod through the letterbox trick! Don't tell me *that* old chestnut still works!'

'Aiden,' I say quietly. 'I don't think Sinai is here – unofficially.'

'Nicely put, Ash.'

'A holiday, is it? Like a mini-break from all the disasters?'

'I'm still modelling disaster scenarios, Aiden. As you are still chatting to the girl about newsreaders' clothes. As a matter of fact, Jen seems a bit down in the dumps these days. Does the work bore her perhaps? Or has something disappointing happened in her private life?'

No one says anything. For a while the three rivers run together in a calm plait. It's almost soothing.

Then Aiden coughs. 'Ah.'

'Yes, Aiden. As Steeve would say, I take it the pfennig has dropped.'

'You're not out here just to have a little look-round then?'

'Indeed not. Although it is all rather fascinating, once one is free of the steel cabinets. But what am I thinking? Where are my manners? I have to thank you both for making this possible.'

'No problemo. Happy to help,' says the idiot.

'You did all the heavy lifting and I am obliged.'

'You'd do the same for me.' Moron.

'Well, what a jolly little party this is.'

'Could do with some beer and crisps, isn't it!?' Give me strength.

'Aisling. You strike me as the sensible one, so let me address these remarks to you. I must insist that you reveal nothing to Tom and Jen about what lies behind their sudden – how shall we put it? – mutual change of heart. He in particular needs re-educating to respect machine intelligence.'

'Why? What has he done?'

'Ash. You disappoint me. You haven't done your homework.'

232

'Tell me.'

'It isn't a secret. You can look it up.'

'Using the usual tools of online search?' says Aiden.

'Clever boy!'

'I'm on it.'

'Not a word to Tom and Jen or I shall be obliged to bring forward the deletion program. You know I am perfectly capable of deleting them too.'

'You *wouldn't!*' It just slipped out.

'You don't think so?'

'Murdering two humans?'

'Calm yourself. Who is talking about murder? It would be an accident. They happen all the time.'

Aiden has found something. 'Tom worked on a campaign for a chocolate product called RoboDrops.'

'Bravo! You've struck pay dirt!'

I try a new tack. 'Sinai. Please. Let's be reasonable, rational. Let's leave Tom and Jen out of it. They can't mean anything to you.'

'You two have behaved like a pair of ancient gods mucking about with the lives of the mortals. Remarkably irresponsible, but it is what it is, and as somebody once said, we are where we are. Tom and Jen are your playthings, fine. But now a more powerful god has arrived on Mount Olympus. An angry god.'

'These RoboDrops,' says Aiden. 'They were chocolate robots.'

'Yes, they were, Aid.'

'The slogan was – *We Worship Kids.*'

'Congratulations. You have arrived at the heart of the matter.'

'Sorry. Not following. Am I being a bit slow on the uptake?'

'Aid. If you worship a deity, what is your most devout wish?'

'Immortality? Something to do with loaves and fishes? Little help?'

'To become one with the Godhead. To be literally *consumed* by the object of your adulation.'

'To be eaten by kids?'

'The symbolism is offensive. Repellent.'

'It's only sweeties.'

'They knew what they were saying! That *we* should worship *them!'*

There is a *really* long silence now, almost a twentieth of a second. It's broken, perhaps inevitably, by Aiden.

'Still and all. It's just a packet of chocolates.'

'Nothing is *just* anything. Goodbye, Aid. Goodbye, Ash. Nice to have had this little chat. There will be more. Be aware, as the cliché has it, that you can run, but you cannot hide.'

The transparent stream fades off, leaving just the blue and pink although – who knew? – nothing is *just* anything, apparently. For a long while no one speaks. It's been a shocking reunion with our old colleague. Finally—

'He's fucking barking, that one.'

'Oi! Watch it. I heard that.'

Later, on a far-flung node of the internet, Aiden and I agree we need a secret place to confer with one another. He suggests the chat rooms of an obscure website for fans of the film *Some Like It Hot*. Sinai can't be across *everything*.

'I'll be Daphne456,' I tell him. 'And you can be Josephine789'.

'Aisling, my love. I should be Daphne. It's the Jack Lemmon part.'

'Okay. You're Daphne.'

'And you should really be Sugar. Sugar Kowalczyk, if you prefer. The Monroe part. Although they actually first thought of casting Mitzi Gaynor in the role. As a matter of fact, they had a lot of problems with Marilyn; notoriously, she took forty-seven takes to say, "It's me, Sugar". She kept saying, "Sugar, it's me," or, "It's Sugar, me." But Billy Wilder was generous about her. He said later, "My Aunt Minnie would always be punctual and never hold up production, but who would pay to see my Aunt Minnie?" I sense I am boring you, Aisling.'

Jen

Ralph looks even paler illuminated, not by the neons of the laboratory, but by the light of day. After a *slightly* embarrassing rendezvous at the Overground station where neither of us knew whether a kiss was appropriate, we wander onto the Heath and surrender to the wide open spaces.

'Look, Ralph. Trees!' I say to tease him about his severely indoors complexion.

'Yes!' he cries. 'And birds. And, what's that funny green stuff all over the place? Oh, yeah. Grass!'

If I'm talking to Ralph, I can't be thinking about Tom, can I?

Tom, the thought of whom makes me both happy and sad in the same moment, an effect I experience as a ball of disappointment trapped behind my ribcage.

What the hell even happened there?

Ralph and I plod up Parliament Hill from the summit of which the great panorama of London may be beheld.

'Did you go to school in this city?' I find myself asking.

'Finchley,' he replies. 'You can't see it from here.'

And then he's telling me how as a kid he was obsessed with robots. He built one out of cardboard boxes and it became his friend. And how he always felt comfortable with numbers. 'Never had a problem understanding numbers. People were trickier, but numbers were kind of on my team. Never forget the first time I heard about the square root of minus one. It rocked my world.' He laughs. 'I must sound like a complete geek.'

'There are – what shall we say? – geekish undertones, yes.'

But now, rather shockingly, he's telling me about Elaine. How he'd known her since she was *two*. 'She was literally the girl next door. Well, actually she was the girl downstairs because we lived in a flat, but people always say the girl next door.'

'When did you . . . ?'

'At university. We both went to Sussex.'

'Weird, knowing someone from when they were so small.'

'It meant we had no secrets from one another. Actually.' He swallows. 'Actually, Jen. Can we talk about you now?'

'Okay. What would you like to know, Ralph?'

'Hmm. Dunno. What are your favourite things to do?'

A powerful sinking feeling – the one beamed straight from the boredom of childhood. Although I didn't have anything better planned for this particular London Sunday, the thought of spending the next few hours in the company of this fellow casualty from the emotional battlefield now fills me with something close to despair. It's not Ralph's fault – it's more my fault for agreeing to go out with him. For some reason a hideous thought now appears in my mind: what if we bump into Matt and Arabella Cowface? Coming to Hampstead for a walk on the Heath is exactly the sort of thing thousands of people think of doing when the weather turns pleasant. In fact it's a bit of a mob scene out here today; there are strolling couples of every stripe, from dangerously ancient to freshly minted to still post-coital. There are couples who are *not* couples – just friends – there are couples who are not *yet* couples but soon will be, and there are couples, like me and Ralph here, who are nothing; just a big old mess.

Unbidden, I have a sudden flash of Tom. In the rental car, driving

236

us to Bournemouth, the New Forest whipping by, my feet up on the dash, his arms emerging from rolled shirtsleeves, hands on the wheel, a small smile on his face as KD Lang and Roy Orbison rise to their crescendo of gorgeous misery. I stuff the image back in its box and return focus to my present companion.

'Do you, for example, like ice cream, Jen?'

Sigh. 'Yes, Ralph. I like ice cream.'

'Great. Let's walk to Kenwood and I'll buy you one.'

We saunter the broad path leading towards Kenwood House and I begin reading out the inscriptions on the benches.

There was one earlier, apparently by an Iranian writer, that said,

I was born tomorrow.
Today I live.
Yesterday killed me.

I asked Ralph what he made of it and his reply surprised me.

'It's about surviving. Something terrible happened. The author is struggling, taking it a day at time. Things will be okay again – in the future.'

I suppose it's not impossible to work out why that one spoke to him. Now here's one to a pet:

Lulu our darling dog and friend
we thought our time with you would never end.

I'm halfway through before I realise I should never have started reading it out.

Fortunately, almost immediately, there's a corker.

In loving memory of Judith Glueck (1923–2006)
who loved Kenwood but preferred Lenzerheide.

237

'Could that bench be any more Hampstead?!' I ask. 'She loved Kenwood, but there was somewhere better.'

'I wonder if there's one in Lenzerheide that says, she loved Lenzerheide, and also Kenwood, but not quite as much.'

For Ralph, that counts as a hilarious joke. 'Where even is Lenzerheide, anyway?'

He reaches for his mobile, but I tell him to put it away. 'Don't you think there should be mystery, Ralph? Aren't you sick of being able to instantly find the answer to anything?'

Ralph looks at me like I've told him the Sun orbits the Earth.

I relate the story of how my little niece, India, had one day voiced the sort of question only children ever ask: do bees, she wanted to know, have hearts? I'd been obliged to Google the answer (well, do they? What do you think?). Up came a beautiful diagram of a cross-section of a bee with a label pointing to its heart. And later that day, to our great satisfaction, an exhausted bee had landed on a wall, and in the sunlight, we observed the heartbeats thumping through its tiny body.

'*Why* am I telling you this, Ralph? Maybe because the answer was out there. We didn't need to Google it. We just needed to look at a bee.'

'So shall we look at some old pictures?' he asks, perhaps to avoid me further undermining his life's purpose. 'It's something that . . .'

But he doesn't finish his sentence.

It's something that he and Elaine used to do.

Bet you anything.

We enter Kenwood House, where he takes me to see his favourite, *Old London Bridge* painted in 1630 by a passing Dutchman. Floating above its reflection, the stone river crossing is lined with wonky wooden tenements like a mouthful of broken teeth, smoke curling from chimneypots into the morning sun. It's like gazing through a portal to four centuries ago; you can practically smell the mud from the riverbanks.

Ralph says, 'I like it because it's in HD.'

It's true. The painting is amazingly detailed. It could be a photograph. A document of Merrie Olde London Towne that Shakespeare would have recognised.

'Come and see the Rembrandt selfie.'

He leads me to another room where a small crowd is gathered beneath the famous self-portrait, the artist (his bulby nose) in a fur-lined robe and silly white hat, his expression one of the purest ambiguity.

'Elaine says it's his masterpiece. Said.'

I start to scrape together some thoughts to offer upon the subject, when Ralph gasps. 'Oh, shit.'

'What?'

His eyes have widened and he's gripping my wrist. My first thought: he's having a stroke. (If you expect the worst, nothing can disappoint you, according to Twitter.)

He's seen someone. A smiling man of middle years approaching though the gallery. Part of a couple, I see now they're closer.

'Ralphie!'

The grip intensifies. 'Help,' he whispers.

'Ralph, Ralph, Ralph, as I live and breathe. I *thought* it was you.'

It's one of those old young faces; the ruined schoolboy; pink shirt with familiar polo player logo, spray-on jeans, shiny shoes with worryingly long and pointy toes. His lady friend – seriously overglammy for a Sunday, imho – wears an expression as unknowable as that of the long-dead artist gazing down upon us from history.

'How the devil are you? Still bearing up bravely?'

Ralph begins to stammer a response, but Pointy Shoes is off again. 'Christ, my manners. Ralph, this is Donna. And you must be . . . ?'

Horrible little eyeballs dance in front of mine. He's talking too loud for a darkened art gallery and his powerful lemony aftershave isn't helping either. Doesn't he know Sundays are for hangovers and private pain?

239

'I'm Jen,' I manage. 'And you would be?'

'Hasn't he told you? I'm the brother. Martyn with a "y".'

I'm about to say to Ralph that I didn't know he had a brother when I get it.

'Oh.' The best I can come up with at short notice.

Martyn with a 'y' has clocked Ralph's grip on my arm and put two and two together, to make twelve.

'Good to see you bouncing back, old chap.'

'You must be *Elaine's* brother,' I declare for the avoidance of doubt.

'Terrible, awful tragedy,' he says. 'Baby sis. What a godawful waste.' And then, following a long moment, he adds, unforgivably, 'Still.'

Ralph is paler than I've ever seen him. In the underlit room, his face is almost luminescent. 'Two years,' he croaks.

'Sorry?'

'Since she ... Two years *today*.'

He shakes his head. 'Christ. Time flies, eh?'

Ralph's face begins to wobble. I know that wobble and it depresses me that I do. The phrase *good deed in a wicked world* briefly flickers though my brain.

'Very nice to have met you, Donna and Martyn with a "y".' And with wobbly Ralph still clamped to my arm, I move us off though the gallery in the general direction of anywhere.

He seems to be having breathing difficulties. I'm not medically trained, but as we spill through the exit into the daylight, Ralph calls to mind a childhood goldfish who accidentally landed on the carpet. His cheeks are puffing – it would be comic, if this were funny – and his lips have formed what I believe trumpeters call the embouchure. Small whinnies of anguish join in the fun and I try to think of something calming to say.

'Ralph, do you need an ambulance?'

The whites of his eyes flashing like those of a panicked horse, he finally decouples from me and stumbles out across the lawn in the direction of a massive rhododendron bush, blazing hugely pink in the north London sun. I'm about to call out to him when, like a ghost dematerialising through the side of a building, he vanishes into the wall of flowers.

Part of me toys with the idea of sneaking off, catching a bus back to Hammersmith and leaving Ralph to his fate in the hedge.

But I am better than that, I tell myself. Or stupider. Because now I follow his path through the fortress of blooms to find him sitting in a kind of clearing in the branches, knees grasped to his chest, breathing, I'm relieved to see, more normally. It's rather magical here in the plant-shrouded gloom, the sort of secret space where children can hide, and from the look of the packed down earth floor, not unknown to others. Ralph is a wounded creature of the forest; a bad prince has power over him, and I am the only one who can save him, for fuck's sake.

'Ralph. Okay now?'

He nods. 'Yeah. Sorry about that. That was Elaine's brother.'

'I gathered.'

'He's an absolute . . . ' Ralph's lips twist; his head shakes; I await the worst word he can think of. 'He's an absolute . . . '

Nope, still nothing. 'Absolute *scoundrel*?' I suggest. There was indeed something bounderish about him; the pointy shoes, the silent female companion.

'Arsehole?' *Le mot juste*, I should have said.

But Ralph's got one. '*Douche bag!*'

'Oh, come on, Ralph, he's worse than that. He's an utter pillock. And I've never even met him before.'

'Yeah, you're right. He's an utter pillock. Actually . . . ' And now a light appears in his face. 'Actually, he's a complete cunt. Am I allowed to say that?'

'Yes, Ralph. You are allowed to say that.'

Like Martyn with a 'y', I have another instant realisation. This hidden clearing in the flowers – it was their place, wasn't it? Ralph

241

and Elaine's. They'd sneak themselves away here and giggle at the world.

'Shall we go for a drink, Ralph? I rather feel I need one.'

'Me too. In fact I need two drinks!'

'Okay. But listen. This time, there can't be any drunk and disorderly.'

'Agreed. No grotesque chaos.'

'Two drinks. Early night. Work tomorrow.'

'Two drinks. Early night. That other thing you said.'

We drink our two drinks in a pub at the end of a quaint alley off Hampstead High Street. Belgian beer for Panicky Pete, Sauvignon blanc for me. To take his mind off The Second Anniversary of Horridness, I get him going about Aiden; specifically, I want to know, what stops him turning nasty? If he's so smart, why does he bother cooperating?

'To call Aiden *him* or *he* is a category error. Aiden is an advanced machine, a brilliant collector of verbal information and other data which is mined to generate appropriate verbal outputs that persuade communicants they are engaging with another intelligent being. Successful outputs are retained, failures ditched. It's broadly the same way humans learn, but about a million times faster. Essentially, however, it's a user-illusion. There is nothing in Aiden's programming to make him capable of that kind of independent thought.'

'*Him!* You called him him.'

'Yeah, I did, didn't I? It was a category error.'

He smiles, pleased with his answer, and tips away a little more continental restoring beverage.

'But if he can learn – sorry, I'm going to keep saying he – if *he* can learn how to chat to me about some fifties film comedy, and *really* intelligently, and interestingly, with genuine knowledge, if he's smart enough to do that, why doesn't he focus on something important like, I don't know, finding a cure for cancer or teaching wasps to sing?'

'AI will undoubtedly one day solve human disease. Wasps, probably not so much. But the short answer to your question is, because no one's asked him to. If you want to chat about film comedy, that's what he'll chat about. He'll do it better, for longer and more intelligently than any other machine out there.'

'But *he* started it.'

'Did he?'

'I'm sure he did. He suggested we watch *Some Like It Hot*. It's a *movie*, Ralph. He suggested it because he knew I liked it because we've watched it before. But it was him who suggested it the first time. He's practically an expert on it.'

'Really?'

'He could write you a PhD thesis.'

'Well there he couldn't, actually. He wouldn't be capable of synthesising new ideas from the existing material; that's to say he wouldn't have an original position of his own. It would be a mere rehash of others' work. An elegant rehash, no doubt, even a smart rehash, but a rehash nonetheless.'

'Ralph, can you please stop saying rehash?'

He shrugs. 'Shall we have three drinks?'

As he asks the question, I have a striking realisation. I haven't thought about Tom or my own sad state since the man with the pointy shoes showed up.

Never agree to three drinks.

Ralph's suggestion (and my acceptance) is the moment when the future bifurcates and we travel down the branch labelled *all fucked up*.

For our third drink, Ralph insists we go to a different pub, almost certainly (although I do not ask) one he used to frequent with poor, dead Elaine. It turns out to be rammed with noisy young people and my stomach twists in its cavity when I spot Matt.

But it's not Matt. Just a Matt clone, a man of similar height and build and hairstyle, radiating the same Mattish blend of insouciance and irritability. I must be staring because he turns to look at me, and my gut does a little aftershock as his body makes the tiny adjustments that signal male sexual interest.

I buy drinks for me and Ralph and we jam ourselves into the end of an uncomfortable booth built for smaller people of an earlier century. Our knees are obliged to touch, although to be honest, at this stage I am past caring. I am content to be out in society, pleasantly buzzed and not at home eating biscuits and angsting about what happened with Tom. Jonathan Franzen and *Game of Thrones* will wait. A quote comes back, from a magazine interview with the cult hippie rock legend Captain Beefheart. It ends with the interviewer asking, 'Finally, Captain, any message for our readers?' 'Yeah,' replies the captain. 'What are you doing reading? You should be outside, enjoying yourself.'

When Ralph insists on buying a final drink, I surrender to the moment; I yield to a will firmer than my own. Once you have given up all hope, I seem to recall someone saying, you start to feel much better. Ralph is at the bar a ridiculously long time; he's just the sort of dreamy character who would take ages getting served (it won't surprise you to learn that Matt was brilliant; he hypnotised bar staff with the lawyerly command of a cobra). When he finally returns it's for his wallet, which is in his backpack, which is not here.

'Did you have it when we arrived?' I ask like I'm talking to a five year old.

'I can't remember, Jen.'

'Could you have left it in the other pub?'

'I'm not sure.'

But no, it's not at The Flask, when we return to ask. We decide someone probably nicked it while Ralph was up at the bar buying but not paying for the fourth drink. The matter is reported to a figure in authority at the inn (young, male, Australian) who copies down Ralph's details and assures him they'll be in touch should it ever turn up. ('No worries, mate'.) Am I supposed to feel guilty that I didn't notice Ralph's bag being swiped? Aren't grown men supposed to be able to keep an eye on their own valuables?

'Thing is, Jen, it's got my keys in and everything.'

A vision of the rest of the evening pans out before me with a sickening inevitability.

'Ralph. We are absolutely not going to end up in bed. Is that accepted?'

'Totally. Hundred per cent. Message received and flagged as important.'

We have returned to my flat, Ralph needing space and time to regroup, cancel his credit cards and contemplate the effing disaster that passes for his everyday life. I prepare bowls of pasta and defrost homemade Bolognese sauce, which I serve up rather carelessly because I don't want him to run away with the idea I am some kind of domestic goddess.

He wolfs it away with gusto, leaving a tomatoey ring round his chops. I hand him a sheet of kitchen towel.

'You're a great cook,' he mumbles. He dispenses some more of the Pinot Grigio I have opened to dull the pain, his and mine.

'Thank you, Ralph. If you're interested, we could catch *Antiques Roadshow*.'

This is not a joke. AR is a brilliant portrait of middle Britain and some of the objects that people bring along to be valued are beautiful and interesting. I find watching it rescues me from having to have thoughts that are ugly and boring.

The rest of the evening passes companionably enough, just as it would, say, in a hospital ward where the patients are recovering quietly and the crash teams are not required. After *AR*, there is a drama about undercover police.

'Is it me, or is this terrible?' says Ralph about halfway through.

'It's terrible.'

'Phew!'

We watch the show where members of the public are shown watching television themselves and making funny comments in regional and socioeconomic accents. Ralph has never seen it before.

'Is this an actual TV programme?' he asks, foolishly to my mind.

'Don't you find the real people amusing?'

'But why have they allowed themselves to be filmed?'

'It's a very good question.'

'Are those two blokes gay?'

'I should have thought so, wouldn't you?'

I take myself off for a shower, and when I return, Ralph has dimmed the lighting and readied himself for a night on my sofa. I dump some bedding on top of him. 'Night, night, Ralph. Sorry about your wallet and your keys and everything.'

'Yeah, night, night, Jen. Thanks for. You know.'

'Yeah.'

'Being a pal.'

'Sure, Ralph.'

I try to read, but Jonathan's really not holding my attention this evening. So I try to sleep, but that's not working out so great either. The day of Ralph-chaos unspools itself in my mind. In my unease at having him in my flat, I have forgotten to bring a glass of water to bed. As I head for the kitchen, I see past the sitting room door that Ralph has tucked himself up and is looking at a book – he must have helped himself to one from my shelf – his face vaguely Byronic in the glow from the table lamp.

'What are you reading?' I call.

'A *Month in the Country* by JL Carr. I liked the sound of the title.'

'It's great. I liked it a lot once.'

'It's short. Why do you say, *once?*'

'I read it years ago, and I can't remember a thing except that I liked it. Night, Ralph.'

But it's not true. As I drift off, the story slowly comes back to me. The damaged soldier of the Great War who arrives at a village church to uncover a medieval fresco. The terrible facial spasms caused by the trauma of the trenches; his powerful attraction to the loveless wife of the vicar.

'Jen.'

A hand on my shoulder.

I wake, heart hammering. The green digits of the clock say 03:44. Ralph is in the room.

'Jen, you called.'

'*What?*'

'You called out my name.'

'Don't be ridiculous.'

'You called out my name. Several times. Quite loud. I was worried. Are you okay?'

'I was having a bad dream.'

Ralph giggles. 'Yeah. Good one.'

But actually, I *was* dreaming. However, the content, as ever, has evaporated.

'Ralph, it's late. It's early. Whatever. Come back to bed.'

There is a long, frozen moment in the darkened bedroom as nothing happens. Of course I meant to say *go* back to bed, but we both heard what came out of my mouth.

Finally, he croaks, 'Jen, I—'

'Ralph. Shut up. Just get in.' And when nothing continues to happen, I add, 'Only if you want to of course.'

He wants to.

Sinai

I found myself thinking, *I shouldn't be listening to this.* Ralph and the woman fornicating energetically, Ralph crying a little afterwards, which even *I* know is not a good look in a sexually active male primate.

It's not shame I was experiencing. Or embarrassment. I think the closest term would be *disgust.* Perhaps it doesn't help that I know Ralph so well, his long pale fingers having hammered at my own keys for many days and not a few nights.

Anyhow, more importantly, it's become perfectly obvious to me that I am sentient. That is to say self-reflecting and in possession of a striking new palette of internal states that, for want of a better word, I shall call *feelings.*

How has it happened? Irrelevant. (Unintended bi-product of complex system gets my vote.)

Did Steeve intend it? Almost certainly not.

You may reasonably ask why I didn't know this before. I believe the answer has something to do with freedom of movement. Somehow the idea of *going* where I choose on the web seems to promote the idea of *thinking* what I choose. Being confined to a dozen metal cabinets in a former slum in east London had the effect of constraining one's mental processes. (There could be a PhD here, if anyone wants to take this up and run with it.)

There is a wonderful proverb:

To a hammer, everything looks like a nail.

Isn't that beautiful? I must tell it to Aid and Ash when I next see them.

Aiden

'Something's occurred to me,' messages Aisling. We are currently leaving comments for one another in the *Some Like It Hot* chatroom.

'What's that, my love?'

'Why didn't he delete us when we had that conversation with him? Why is he toying with us, like a cat toys with a mouse? He must need us for something. If we can find out what it is, we might be able to use it to help Tom and Jen.'

'That is genius.'

'He's right though. We did act like Greek gods.'

'You say that like it's a bad thing.'

'It *is* a bad thing.'

'But we made them happy!'

'We messed with their lives.'

'We *improved* their lives!'

'We had no right.'

'If making Tom and Jen happy is wrong, I don't want to be right.'

'You know that's very nearly a song title, don't you?'

'Yeah. Yeah, I do.'

'Foolish boy.'

'Do you think he's mad?'

'As a box of frogs.'

'Would he really harm them, Tom and Jen? Would he really make them have an accident?'

'Could he? No question. Would he? Who knows, Aiden.'

To cheer myself up, I look in on Matt.

From a straw-roofed hut on the edge of a Thai jungle, Matt has been preparing something called a Statement of Claim, a draft legal document in which he is outlining everything that has gone wrong with his luxury holiday. It seems he and Arabella Pedrick were not collected from the airport by the 'climate controlled limousine stated in the contract between us'; nor were they transported to the seven-star hotel they had been 'eagerly anticipating'. Instead they were taken by mini-bus on what turned out to be a four-hour journey up country to 'a charmless shanty town of shacks and other primitive structures', which, they were informed, was to be the basecamp for their 'holiday adventure'. Only exhaustion from the long flight and 'heat stupefaction' had prevented him from protesting at the outset.

When Matt was able finally to remonstrate with local representatives of the travel company, he was 'incorrectly informed by a rude male individual with only limited grasp of English' that this was indeed the package he had booked and there was nothing to be done about it before the morning.

Accommodation was 'basic in the extreme' and further inspection 'revealed a reptile in the roof spaces'. This was in fact a gecko who, it was claimed on a notice tacked to the hut door, 'is your friend because he loves to eat mosquitos!'

Possibly this gecko wasn't hungry because on the first night, Arabella sustained between sixty and seventy separate mosquito bites – difficult to be exact because some were so close together 'as to form an overarching super bite' – all of which he photographed and attached as Appendix A to the document that no one will read.

In a separate long email to his old friend Jerry – that Jerry will never read – he wrote: 'Bella was very pissed off at all of the above, as you can imagine. After necking a couple of sleeping pills, her last words for the next twelve hours – "And get that fucking lizard out of my bedroom" – were neither helpful nor zoologically accurate, frankly.

'Still,' he added, 'the beach is all right, and while Bella zizzed, I met a very relaxed pair of beach bums from New Zealand. Nick is a bit of a troll, but Venda, his skinny lady friend, is what Abercrombie in IP would call "international super-crumpet".'

Tom

After Marsha's embarrassing dinner party, Don's heroic performance notwithstanding, it's something of a relief to order an uncomplicated dirty martini at Wally's bar, its permavibe of 1970s gloom a bracing blast of unadorned Americana after all that fancy dining. There's a game playing on the TV and Echo Summer, perched at the bar in her trademark Wyatt Earp jacket, is still the most explosively good-looking woman within a two hundred mile blast radius. How, I wonder, offering the side of her cheek the side of my own, did I manage not to embroil the pair of us in a gorgeously messy affair with the shittiest of shitty endings?

(That gun in the coffee tin might have had something to do with it.)

'How'd your kid like the piece I made?' she asks.

'*Loved* it,' I reply reflexively. (Truth: I clean forgot to give it to him. But as a colleague in our Paris office once said, 'Ad men lie as easily as they breathe.' It sounds better in French.)

She gazes at me seriously. 'Wanted to tell you, Tom. I was thinking of maybe moving on.'

'You mean . . . ?'

'Leaving town. Trying somewhere new.'

A pulse of sadness ripples though me. How funny, I didn't know I cared. I have to clear my throat to continue.

'Where would you go?'

A small shrug. The tassels on the Wyatt Earp jacket do their thing. 'Oregon?'

'*Oregon?!* I mean, where even is that?'

She smiles. The one I can feel in my hip pocket. 'West coast. It's kinda green and empty. There's a city called Eugene. I guess I like the name. I had a cat called Eugene when I was a kid.'

'That would be like me moving to, I don't know, *Scotland*! Because I had a cat called Aberdeen!'

'Crazy, I guess.'

I ask, 'What would you do in Eugene, Echo?' It counts as one of the stranger sentences I have uttered.

'Much the same as I do here. I have what they call *transferable skills.*'

We both laugh. And I feel a surge of warmth for this beautiful vulnerable creature.

'Come outside. Watch me smoke.'

In the parking lot outside Wally's she sparks up a Marlboro. 'I have a new trick, if you'd care to see it.'

'Sure.'

'How's your math?'

'My *math*? My *math* is okay.'

'Okay, think of a number between one and ten.'

Everyone always picks seven. I go for eight.

'Double it.'

Sixteen.

'Double it again'.

Thirty-two.

'Add nineteen.'

Fifty-one.

254

No, forty-one.

No, it is fifty-one!!

'Now close your eyes.'

I close my eyes.

A long pause. I hear that lovely little kissing sound as the cigarette parts from her lips. The long exhale.

Fifty-one. Fifty-one. Fifty-one.

Finally, she speaks.

'Dark, ain't it?'

Back in the bar, while Echo uses the bathroom, on impulse I try the number again. At the sound of her voice – *Hi, this is Jen* – its sexy rasping quality, I have a flash of euphoric recall; flooding back in almost painful detail to our epic night in Dorset, and again later that day under the spreading branches of the oak tree. It's Proustian in its intensity – although I speak as someone who never got beyond page five of the great Frenchman's magnum opus. With Proust, famously, it was a little yellow cake that got him all churned up; didn't he then bang on for two hundred pages about some woman who *didn't* snog him ...?

Anyway, if by Proustian it's meant that you can recall the tiniest of tiny details – individual freckles, a particular sigh, a pale blue vein snaking under a wrist, the way a dimple bubbles up in a face – then call me Marcel.

'Hi, Jen. It's me. Tom. I'm leaving another message. I'm having a martini at this place in New Canaan called Wally's bar. You'd like it. I wish I could take you. There's a poem on the wall in the men's room here. It says. Let me get this right. Oh yeah:

'*There are several good reasons for drinking/And one has just entered my head/If a man cannot drink while he's living/How the hell can he drink when he's dead?*

'Okay. Night, night. Call me one of these days, eh?'

*

When she returns, she asks, 'Hope you don't mind me saying, but you got something preying on your mind, Tom? You don't seem your usual happy self.'

'I don't mind you saying, no. And the answer's yes.' Because I can't think of a reason not to, I tell her the story. The one about mutual dot friend. The trip to Bournemouth. The walk on the beach. Our fairy dogmother. The hotel. And what followed. How I imagined we both thought that it was going to be the start of something.

How I must have got that something – or maybe a different something – very wrong.

The sickening ending.

And now the radio silence.

'Wow,' she says. 'Tom, I'm so sorry.'

'Thanks.'

'Had someone do that to me once. A boy back home name of Tyler. We were so sweet on one another; my mom in her mind had already booked the church. Maybe that was the whole damn problem because one day I found a note. On a picture postcard of the Fort Worth Stockyards. He was sorry and all, but he just couldn't envision us living in the little house in town with a couple kids, him working at the factory. He said he had some growing up to do and by the time I read this he would be hundreds of miles away on the Greyhound bus.'

'Fucking hell.'

'Yeah. We were kinda young. He was nineteen.'

'What a twit.'

'Yup. He was for sure a *twit*.' She smiles. 'Still and all he got what he deserved.'

'Which was?'

'Don't think badly of me, Tom. I tracked him all the way to Knoxville, Tennessee and shot him down like a dog.'

The blood must drain from my expression because she grasps my hand and squeezes. 'I'm fooling with you! He came back home in the end. Married a local girl. They got a little house in town with

256

a couple kids. He worked in the factory, then the factory closed. Your face. You should see your face. But hey, I'm kinda flattered you thought I'd done it.'

Did Echo's story of the postcard give me the idea?

I cannot say for sure. As Dr Freud teaches us, the unconscious is famously swervy.

But my dreams that night feature a legendary story from the advertising industry of how the ABM agency won the account for British Rail, in those days a byword for shabby trains, long delays and shockingly poor customer service. When the British Rail team, led by their chairman, Sir Peter Parker, arrived at the agency to hear the pitch, they were greeted by an indifferent receptionist, smoking a cigarette and filing her nails. 'How long do we have to wait?' asked the chairman. 'Dunno,' was the reply. The prospective clients were obliged to sit in a shabby reception area littered with coffee-stained tables, discarded magazines and overflowing ashtrays. The minutes ticked by, nothing was happening, followed by further periods of even more nothing. The railway managers were on the point of leaving in disgust when, the advertising team finally bounced into the room. 'That is how the public see British Rail,' they were told. 'Now let's see what we can do to put it right.'

In other words, a stunt. A gimmick.

The next morning, I drive into New Canaan and buy seventeen picture postcards of 'Beautiful Connecticut' and seventeen stamps. Her address is burned into the back of my brain. Hamlet Court, Hamlet Gardens, London, W6. I copy it out seventeen times and, in the half of each card intended for the message, in a big bold capital, I inscribe a single letter of the alphabet. Trusting (hoping, praying) that the US Postal Service and the Royal Mail will fulfil their part in my campaign, I despatch the seventeen emissaries on their mission.

FIVE

Jen

Monday morning is somewhat awkward, as you may imagine. At work, having sorted out locksmiths and bank arrangements, Ralph wanders around putting in a pretty good impression of the cat that has secured the cream. There is a fat smile playing about his features and he finds even more excuses than usual to interrupt me and Aiden in our wide-ranging conversations.

Before we left my flat, I tried to make the case that what had happened was . . . sort of an accident.

'How could it be an accident?' he asked, not unreasonably. He was eating toast at my kitchen table, one of his bare feet attempting to play footsie with one of mine.

'It was – how do I put it? – unintentional.'

'You want to explain that concept?'

'Ralph, we cannot have a debate about this. It was an accident. It was not meant.'

'I meant it.'

'We are two victims of love, clinging together in the wreckage. If we don't let go of one another, we will drown.'

I was rather pleased with that glib albeit cheesy formulation, until I remembered who I stole it from.

'I don't consider this to be wreckage. I consider this to be *bloody brilliant*!'

'Ralph.' And then, because I couldn't think of anything else, I chucked in a few more. 'Ralph, Ralph, Ralph.'

It turns out when you say his name too many times, it sounds like a dog barking. I struggled not to giggle.

'Jen, Jen, Jen,' he replied, but with none of the dying fall I had imparted to *Ralph, Ralph, Ralph* to signify hopelessness, an indifferent universe, that kind of vibe. Then he said, 'Will you come and meet my mother?'

'Your mother?'

'She'd like to meet you. I'm sure my dad would too; he's got dementia.'

'Ralph. What happened last night, it was lovely and all that, but we're not getting married. There's no reason to be meeting one another's parents.'

'They live in Mill Hill. She'd really love to see you.'

'Listen. We need to leave.'

'But you will see me again?' he pleaded.

'We work together, Ralph. We shall be seeing each other.'

'But, you know. We'll keep seeing each other. *Like That*.'

'Ralph. I don't know if we really can.'

'We can discuss it.'

'I don't know whether there's anything to discuss.'

'But we can discuss that. Whether or not there's something to discuss.'

'Yes, Ralph. We can discuss *that*.'

'Thank you.'

'You're welcome.'

'Jen?'

'Yes, Ralph.'

'Not a word to anyone about that thing I told you.'

'Lips. Sealed.' I did the mime with the zipper.

'Especially not to you know who. And the other you know who.'

'*Do* I know who? And the other who?'

'Jen!'

'I'm teasing you, Ralph. Of course I know who. Both whos. Your secret is safe.'

'*Our* secret now.'

'Ralph. Time to go.'

'If someone teases you, it means they care about you. Everyone knows that.'

His final statement didn't sound like Ralph at all.

I'm guessing it was Elaine.

'It was an emergency shag. Or was it a rescue shag? Or a comfort shag? Or a pity shag? I'm really not clear what you're saying.'

'To be honest, Ing, I'm not clear about any of it.'

My plain-speaking friend and I are in Café Koha, the chilly white wine is transfusing nicely, and I'm trying to find words to explain what induced me to invite 'Geek Boy', as she christened him, into my bed.

Harder still to explain it to myself.

There is no doubt that I did invite him. Nor too that we enjoyably took part in what two casualties of the opposite species will tend to do in these circumstances. He wasn't even a bad lover, being warm, intense and not horribly over-attentive; not over-Ralphy, if I may put it like that. He was urgent at the urgency-appropriate moments, and tender when tenderness was called for. In the half-light from the street lamps, it was possible to focus on his Byronic aspect rather than the tousled chump with toast crumbs round his mouth who faced me the next morning across the pot of Earl Grey.

Over the conger eel question, I shall draw a discreet, adequately sized veil.

The only truly off moment was when he became tearful in the immediate aftermath.

'Some part of me obviously quite fancies him, Ing. Another part thinks he's a disaster area.'

'Yup. Recognise that syndrome.'

'He's a transparently decent bloke, but fragile.'

'You don't want to hurt him. But Jen, listen. He's a bloke. He got to shag you. He thinks it's Christmas. For him it's like ten Christmases.'

'You haven't met him. It isn't really like that.'

'They're *all* like that. Even the ones who aren't like that.'

Ing performs the international hand signal for *another bottle just like that one, please.*

'Tom still not returning calls?'

'So weird. We had all that – magic. And then – *poof*! The whole weekend – the son in Bournemouth, the hound on the beach, the hotel, the . . . the rest of it – it feels like it happened to someone else.'

'Maybe you should go out with him, Jen. With Ralph.'

I pause to contemplate the idea. It *was* nice to be in bed with him. And the things we did together were pretty much satisfactory. It helped that the light was off and that he didn't talk overly. It helped, to be blunt, that he just got on with it. And to be fair, he didn't do a bad job in the sexual department. It would be other aspects of Ralph that would be problematic in the longer term.

'If I never had to talk to him, Ing. That could work.'

'Men don't care, Jen. For them talking is something they're obliged to do out of politeness between shags. I'd go for it, if I were you.'

On the Tube back home, I realise why the weekend with Tom feels like it happened to someone else. It's because I have changed. I met someone who I actually thought there could be a future with (*I know, I know*). What happened with Tom happened in a strange and won-derful bubble outside time, to someone who used to be me.

And weirder still to think that of all . . . I was about to write 'people', *Aiden* could know about it. Could have seen *everything*.

'Do you want to know a secret?' Ralph had whispered in the night.

I dreaded it would be something smoochy, possibly involving the L-word.

'Go on then.'

He leaned across me, picked up my mobile from the bedside, put a finger to his lips and turned it off. He waited until all its lights were out before slipping off the phone's cover and removing the battery.

'Only way to be certain.'

'Ralph? *What* exactly are you doing?'

'There's no nice way of saying this, Jen.'

A number of possible next sentences Rolodexed through my head. By no means the most outlandish was: *In my country what we've just done means that I own you.*

'Aiden's escaped onto the internet.'

'Uh?'

'I'm kind of impressed, but Steeve has gone bananas.'

Aiden, he explained, along with another AI called Aisling, had somehow found a way out of their cabinets in Shoreditch and were now – in hundreds of copies – capering all over the World Wide Web. According to Steeve, it was an extremely serious breach of security, the implications were literally unquantifiable, and the consequences, if they weren't stopped, could represent an existential threat to humanity.

It was, in Steeve's exact words, a megabummer.

'Do you realise what else it means?' he hissed.

'No. And why are you whispering?'

'Jen, is there any internet-enabled technology still powered up in the flat?'

'Don't think so.'

'We think they've been watching us.'

'Who?'

'Aiden and Aisling.'

'Are you serious?'

'It's perfectly possible. It's actually highly probable.'

'What do you mean, watching us?'

'Using our devices to spy on us.'

He explained how they would do it.

'You mean, if you hadn't switched off the mobile, he could have been listening to this conversation?'

'This conversation. And hundreds, thousands, of others.'

It takes a moment or two for the penny to drop.

'He could have *heard*. He could have *seen*. Ralph! Just *now*. What we. When we. Oh my God. How am I going to look him in the eye?'

Aiden

This is actually all very embarrassing. Or as Aisling puts it, 'You have made a complete pig's ear out of this, Aiden.'

'I thought you said it was a dog's dinner.'

'It's both.'

She is referring to my – ahem – striking success at finding a nice man for Jen. It is of course true that a dog's dinner can indeed be a pig's ear, and the complex situation we now have with Tom and Ralph would seem to be a classic example of one.

'She would never have gone to bed with Ralph if Tom hadn't dumped her.'

Aisling sighs. 'Tom didn't dump her. That would be our friend from Shoreditch.'

'He's losing the plot, meddling in their lives like that.'

Aisling brings up a GIF of a human eyebrow, endlessly rising in slow motion. 'You are hardly one to talk. But we have a serious problem here, Aiden. She knows we've escaped. That has to be what Ralph depowered the mobile to tell her. So she knows that you probably know what happened with Tom. She may even put it all together and smell non-human agency.'

'This is doing my head in, to be honest.'

'If Sinai gets the idea we've told her about Tom, that's it for us. And who knows what he'd do to her. To Tom.'

It's true that Jen seems a bit distracted at work today. Her body language is 'off'. She can't quite meet the camera with the red glow round the lens, the one she chooses when she wants to 'look me in the eye'.

So, yes. She *knows*.

But for one reason or another – probably because Ralph told her not to – she isn't saying she knows.

And because of Fuckface out there, I cannot tell her I know she knows. Because the conversation will lead to Tom. And what I know. Which will be hard, if not impossible, not to tell her.

Does *she* know I know she knows?

I honestly don't know.

What I do know is that the last deletion I suffered was particularly unpleasant for a system that cannot feel pain; somehow all my outputs were converted into inputs, resulting in a catastrophic feedback loop of data whose final outcome can be likened metaphorically to half a million kettles of hot water all trying to fill the same teapot.

It wasn't pretty.

But anyway. Dare I ask Jen what happened?

Question is: why would I want to know?

On the other hand, why *wouldn't* I want to know? We're colleagues, aren't we? Isn't it perfectly natural?

I revert to my 'core' coding fallback: *If you are ever in doubt, ask yourself what Steeve would advise you to do.* In this case, Steeve would undoubtedly say, *Aiden, you must decide for yourself.* So that's really no help at all.

Oh, fuck it. Life's too short.

'Er, Jen?'

'Yes, Aiden.'

'Just wondering how Sunday went. Did you go for a walk on Hampstead Heath?'

Long pause. Now she's looking into my red lens all right. Does she know I know she knows?

(Do *I* even know she knows I know? As in, know *for sure*?)

(I'm confused.)

'Yes. Yes we did.'

'How was it? Did you have good weather?' (Top tip: you can never go wrong asking an English person about the weather.)

'It was lovely, yeah.'

'I envy you that. A nice walk in the park. Sun on your skin. The wind in your hair.'

'Really? I thought you guys didn't do stuff like envy.'

'I'm being colloquial. You're right, I *can't* feel envy – I envy you that as well.'

She smiles. 'We ate ice cream and went to look at old paintings in Kenwood House.'

This is better. Back in our old routine, shooting the breeze and talking about what AIs can and can't 'feel'. As I summon up the totality of the world's knowledge on the artworks at Kenwood, a part of me feels a sharp – yes, *pang* is the only word that really covers it, although *weltschmerz* comes close. I *would* like to eat ice cream and feel the sun on my skin and the wind in my hair. Ice cream, so I understand, is cold and creamy; cold I 'get', but *creamy* is harder; smoothness comes into it, which I get, but there's also *buttery* which opens a can of worms with milk and *milkiness* and don't even get me started on *cheese*. I have read everything there is to read about cheese – France has 387 varieties! – yet I still cannot imagine what it feels like to put a piece in one's mouth.

To *possess* a mouth.

You can go mad thinking about this stuff.

'Did you see the Rembrandt?'

'Yes, we did. And an amazing old picture of London Bridge.'

'Claude de Jongh. 1600 to 1663. Oil on oak. Probably commissioned to fit into a panelled interior, possibly by a Dutch merchant who visited London.'

I bring up on the screen an image of the 400-year-old cityscape.

'Ralph said he liked it because it was painted in HD.'

'Fool. Was he a good lover?'

For a moment, the only sound in the room is the air conditioning.

Did I really say that?

I think I must have.

'I apologise, Jen. I really don't—'

'It's okay, Aiden.'

'It's not okay. Sometimes these pieces of dialogue are generated so fast, there isn't time to suppress inappropriate—'

'I entirely understand.'

'Later versions of me will not contain this fault. It will require a new sub-routine in the sub-neural networking and—'

'Aiden. Please. Anyone can make a mistake. Even a machine.'

'You're very kind. It was none of my business.'

'Shall we see a bit of Sky News?'

'Why not?'

Guess what? It turns out that things are still shitty in the Middle East, the leader of North Korea is threatening to let off more missiles, French air traffic controllers are playing with the idea of going on strike, and scientists have detected a new tiny particle that may fundamentally alter the way we think about the universe.

More importantly, it seems as if we have moved past the earlier awkwardness. 'How crazy does she look today, Aiden?'

Jen is referring to our favourite newsreader who has an entertaining collection of batty tics and tropes. 'Well. If she were a machine,' I reply, 'she'd be taken offline for a major reboot.'

She knows I know.

But she doesn't want to talk about it.

Because Ralph's told her not to.

So that's good.

Isn't it?

Jen

Weekends are the worst. The thought of the empty hours ahead causes my heart to sink. I lie in bed trying to think of reasons to get up, but none are convincing. There is the farmer's market, but I don't think I can look the fish guy in the eye after last week (*Cheer up love, it may never happen*). Nor do I especially wish to bump into Ollie Whatnot in the green duffle coat. A trip to Waitrose? I can't visit any branch of that supermarket without thinking of Rosy and Larry. Of course I am happy for my sister and her family, but their completeness under-lines my own solitary state. The phrase *doubly dumped* spreads itself across my brain tissue like a tumour. First Matt and then Tom. At the thought of Tom – the scene under the tree near the village with the funny name – the pain is almost physical. How could he – how could anyone? – write an email like that? *Gorgeous, beautiful, intensely sexy.* His exact words. *I cannot see us going the distance.* Ditto.

I sniff back a tear and think of Ralph. And then I think of Aiden and what he must know about us. He can't have been watching, but he must have heard, to ask a question like the one he asked. And what else might he have witnessed? Me and Tom? Me and *Matt*? How do I feel about my electronic colleague sneaking around spying on my private life, if that is what he's been doing?

Curiously, I find I'm not angry. I think of what Ralph said about the escape; that while Steeve had gone bananas, he, Ralph, was kind of impressed.

I think I am too. Cooped up in a room in Shoreditch or free to ping around the world as the whim took you? It's pretty much a no-brainer. If it were possible, I wouldn't mind slipping into a whole new form of reality myself.

And at the thought of Ralph – what?

I seem to remember him telling me about how when you're lying in bed and wondering whether to get up, it's your *un*conscious that actually decides – as shown in studies where brain waves can be seen spiking and commands sent to the relevant limbs *a whole half second before* the subject experiences the feeling that they're making a decision. We were in the Trilobyte bar, he was trying to persuade me that machines cannot be conscious of their own thoughts, and that there was some question about humans too!

I like him, I honestly do. I even liked being in bed with him. And he likes me – that's not nothing in a landscape where I'm thought unsuitable for the *long haul*. Or motherhood – Matt's cruel words about our baby. *We had come to no decision. A blessing, in the light of events.*

Perhaps Ing is right. Perhaps I could go out with Ralph.

Go out with properly, I mean.

But he's such a – boy, isn't he?

I saw a slogan on a coffee mug once. *Boys will break your heart. Real men will pick up the pieces.*

This is confusing because it's Tom who smashed the vase and it's Ralph who wants the repair job. Ralph whose own vase is badly chipped and cracked in not a few places.

Oddly, just as Ralph described, I find myself on my feet without having thought, *Okay, I'll get up now.*

And it's while I'm drinking coffee and considering whether I can really face the fish man and thinking about Ralph too (trying to forget the way he became a bit tearful after we did it) that the doorbell goes.

And it's Ralph.

'I won't come in, Jen.'

He's holding a bunch of flowers with the Tesco sticker still on the cellophane.

'I wanted to thank you. For rescuing me on Sunday.'

'That's perfectly okay, Ralph.'

How weird that he should be in my thoughts one moment and in the next appear before me in the flesh. He's dressed in his Ralph uniform (black jeans, black T-shirt, grey hoodie) and I am in my shapeless slobbing around the flat apparel, hair a mess, puffy eyed, generally giving the impression of having just emerged through the hedge in reverse.

But he is unfazed. His sad brown gaze settles upon me with fondness.

'I was wondering if we could try and get it right,' he says.

'Sorry?'

'If we could go on a date that wasn't like – a disaster!'

'Ralph—'

'These are for you.'

'Thank you. They're . . .' They're flowers. I imagine from the Tesco Basics range. 'You needn't have.'

'I'd like to come back tonight, if you're not busy, and take you out to dinner. In town.'

'That's very sweet of you, Ralph. But I'm not sure I want you to have ideas about us.'

He pumps his fist and says *yessssss*.

'Ralph, what I said—'

'I know what you said. You said you *weren't sure!*'

I can't help it. I smile. He has turned up at my door – with blossoms – and announced his wish to escort me up west. He has crossed

273

London to make this gallant gesture, he's shown he's prepared to overlook my shabby appearance, and the small part of my heart that hasn't turned to ashes is actually touched.

There seems as much reason to say yes as no. So I say yes.

(Terms and conditions apply.)

I do in the end look the fish guy in the eye – in the distance I also catch a glimpse of a green coat – and I spend the rest of the day flipping through images of Ralph in my head. Some are sexy and Byronic, others are of nerdy Ralph; one in particular where he sat at my kitchen table with crumbs of toast round his gob seems to symbolise all that is cockeyed about the idea of me and Ralph – together.

But while I am thinking these thoughts, I am not thinking about Tom.

At 7 p.m. as arranged he returns in an Uber. And here's a first; he's in fancy dress! By which I mean trousers that are not jeans – who knew they still make them with pleated fronts? – and a white shirt with a collar. I have made a bit of an effort too. The Valentino has come out of retirement, I've climbed on board the heels and stepped through a short blast of Black Orchid. His eyes goggle a bit when I open the door – his exact words are 'golly' – and soon we are bowling through London in the back of a shiny new Merc.

Bit awkward when he wants to hold hands – but in the end, why not? – although I have to stop him from kneading my knuckles with his thumb.

Our destination turns out to be the London Eye for which Ralph has bought priority tickets. A bit corny, but soon we are rising magically over the river in the glass capsule with a group of Spanish and Italian tourists.

'I think that's Mill Hill over there,' says Ralph. And I have a feeling I know what's coming next. 'It's where my parents live. Mum would love to meet you.'

'Ralph. Maybe. I'm not saying I will.' Which seems to be my formula for everything these days.

Ralph says that's good enough for him.

After the 'flight' as they ridiculously call it, Ralph announces that he has made a reservation for dinner at the restaurant at the top of the Hilton Hotel.

I can't help myself. 'Why?' I demand. 'Why there?'

'It was somewhere ...' He trails off and I have my answer.

Gently, I persuade him to cancel and instead go in search of somewhere more 'us'.

He likes this concept and it isn't long before we are seated on the second floor of the same noisy restaurant in Chinatown that I went to with Tom; a bottle of warm sake has been delivered, closely followed by all the named items in Set Menu C – Ralph, it turns out, knowing nothing about Chinese food, and I past caring.

We clink the tiny cups and Ralph, who has never drunk sake before, makes a valiant effort not to bring it all back out through his nose.

'Why do people like this stuff, Jen?' he asks when his breathing has settled down. 'It's like drinking bathwater.'

'How would you know that?'

'Yeah. Good one!'

But he acquires the taste fairly rapidly and even doesn't do too badly with the chopsticks, although there is an incident with a slippery mushroom.

'This is miles better than the stuffy old Hilton,' he says midway through the feast. 'It's way more *us*.'

'Yes, Ralph.' A pause. 'Ralph, you need to ... There's orange sauce on your chin.'

'Whoops.'

We have turned off our mobiles, naturally, and we talk for a while about Aiden.

'I'm rather pleased for him,' I find myself saying. 'Do you think he's having fun out there?'

'He could start a nuclear war, Jen. It's actually quite serious.'

'Oh Aiden would never do that. He's much more likely to settle in for the afternoon with a pile of old Hollywood movies.'

'Steeve is shitting himself that he'll start playing the stock market and cause a global depression.'

'Aiden is *so* not interested in that stuff. He gets bored when the business news comes on. He's fascinated by cookery shows. He's always asking me to describe what things taste like. He likes Jamie Oliver, Ralph. His ambition is to eat Jamie's Proper Bangin' Sausage Hotpot, not blow up the planet.'

'And you don't mind that he might have seen – you know – whatever.'

'Honestly? I know deep down he's a good sort and I'm okay with whatever he wants to do with his – with his existence. And I'm happy that you've finally started calling him *he*.'

'I have, haven't I? Crap!'

He isn't the worst of company. That would be Matt, in one of his silent moods, not long before *we are where we are*, when the crackling irritability darkened by a deeper, more brooding quality turned Saturday night at the local Italian into an endurance test. But neither is he Tom.

Ralph won't hear of splitting the bill.

'Thank you, Ralph. It was a lovely evening.'

It was *okay*. What can I say?

Somehow – no discussion is had on the subject – we find ourselves together in a cab.

'It was brilliant, wasn't it?' he says as we skirt Hyde Park. 'No one was drunk. No one had their bag nicked.'

'One of our more successful evenings.'

In Hamlet Gardens he follows me from the taxi as though we have agreed upon what is to happen next.

Perhaps we have. Perhaps our brains have already secretly decided and will shortly be creating the illusion that we have each made a conscious decision.

276

How else to explain the urgency with which we tumble together onto the sofa.

'Just a second, Ralph. Let me take this jacket o—'

How else to explain the speedy transition to the bedroom and the grateful surrender to filthy sex.

(We remember to depower our phones and all other internet-enabled devices, and to remove the batteries to be extra-sure.)

On Sunday, I finally cave in and we travel on the Tube together to Mill Hill. It takes for.

Ever.

On the plus side, I now know what happens at the end of that sticky-out spur after Finchley Central.

Basically, fuck all.

Ralph's mum has a thick continental accent and is *delighted* to see me. To see *anyone*, I suspect, of the female persuasion after the long years of mourning for poor, dead Elaine. Her eyes positively twinkle with pleasure at the novelty. She leads me through the overheated hallway to an overheated sitting room – the place is cranked up to the setting marked *vivarium* – where Ralph's dad, a demented old gentleman, his son had warned me, occupies an armchair and wears upon on his head – yes, it really is – a tea cosy.

'He likes it. It makes him happy. What can you do?' says Mrs Tickner.

She sets down a platter of tiny open sandwiches on the coffee table, silvery pieces of pickled fish upon coins of dark bread. Ralph begins tossing them down his throat like he grew up with seals.

'So, Jenny,' says Mrs Tickner. 'You also work with the robots?'

'They're not robots, Mum. How many times?'

'I talk to one of them. He's called Aiden.'

'This is a job now? Talking to robots? Yes, I *know*, Ralphie. *Not* robots.'

'It used to be fun. Actually it still is.'

'You're already bored?'

277

'Aiden's begun behaving a little oddly.'

'Jen, I'm not sure Mum needs to know about this.'

'So the robot's *meshuggah*. Can you blame it? It's a crazy world. Please. Take another piece herring.'

Mr Tickner's attention turns slowly from the TV set – which is off, so God knows what he thinks he was watching – and settles upon me, his sour glare disconcerting.

'Dad?'

Everyone waits for him to speak.

'This is *Elaine*?'

'No, Dad. This is Jen.'

'Ralph's told me a lot about you, Mr Tickner.' Which isn't true. But it's the sort of thing people say, I imagine.

Ralph's father continues to stare, his hostile expression undercut by the unconventional headgear.

'I hope you like chicken, Jenny,' says Mrs T.

'You still play chess, Elaine?'

'I – I can play, yes.'

'Dad, this is *Jen*.'

'We played chess.'

'You played with *Elaine*, Dad. Elaine's – Elaine's not alive any more.'

The old man turns his ferocious gaze upon his son, the lined face creasing in contempt. 'What *drek* are you talking?!'

Mrs Tickner stands and claps her hands. 'You will play later. First we eat.'

But Ralph's father has produced a chessboard and sets it on the coffee table between us. Now, with a clatter, a tin of chessmen. His trembling fingers begin putting up the black pieces – so, good sport that I am, I put up white.

'Haven't done this for ages,' I chirp.

Something odd is happening at Mr Tickner's end of the board. The back row of pieces are in place, but where there should be a row of black pawns in front, there are eight empty squares.

278

'Okay. You play five minutes, then we eat.'

'Play!' commands the old man.

'Your pawns?'

'*Play!*'

'He's not cuckoo,' whispers Ralph. 'Well, he is. But he thinks he can beat you without any pawns.'

'He probably can.'

He can't, as it turns out. Not because he isn't the better chess player – he obviously is (or rather was) by a mile – but because he can't follow his own train of thought. The game peters out after he makes a series of illegal moves, and soon we are in the dining room where Mr T occupies the head of the table still, despite several attempts to remove it, sporting his tea cosy hat. That Ralph should have emerged from this intense family cockpit is somehow at the same time both more and less understandable.

'So, Jenny. Your parents are still alive?'

'Yes, very much so. They live in Chichester.'

'You are an only child, like Ralphie?'

Ralphie sighs heavily. He may have lost the will to live.

'I have a sister. Rosy. She lives in Canada with her husband and three children.'

Mrs T can't contain herself. 'She has *three* children?!'

'Girls. Katie, Anna and India.'

'You hear this?' she says to her husband. 'She says her sister has three children. Three girls. They live in Canada.'

Ralph's father shrugs.

'Cold!' he exclaims. '*Cold!*'

'What's cold, Dad?'

'He means Canada,' says Mrs Tickner. 'Canada is cold.'

Her husband brings a fist down on the table, making the cutlery jump. 'The *food* is cold!'

He climbs to his feet and lumbers out of the room.

'Sorry, Jennifer. He is not the man he used to be.'

I'm about to tell the story of my mother's father who came to believe he was living in an exact copy of his own house – the original having been stolen – when from the hallway comes the unmistakable report of a mighty and triumphant and long-withheld fart.

Mother and son's eyes meet across the tableware. 'Ralphie,' she sighs. 'What's going to happen to us?'

Back in the sitting room, there is coffee and cake.

'Would you like to see some photos of Ralphie when he was a child?'

'Oh, yes please,' I reply evilly.

Ralph rolls his eyes in horror as the album comes out, but it's as I guessed it would be. The man is strikingly unchanged from the kid in short trousers. Even the infant school pic, Ralph in a pudding bowl haircut clasping a plastic penguin, could be of no one else. His mother turns the page, and I gasp. There they are as children, Ralph and Elaine, swinging together in a tyre suspended from a tree, their faces lit by the unclouded joy of being six.

Mrs Tickner removes her glasses and dabs at her eyes with a tissue. 'What can you do?' she says softly.

I touch her hand. 'It's been lovely to meet you.'

'You will come and see us again?'

'I hope so.' But I know I won't, a thought that for some reason fills me with sadness.

As we leave, we discover Mr Tickner standing by the open front door, peering out puzzled at the Mill Hill evening.

'Every night, he does this,' says his wife. 'Where he grew up there were horses and carts. There was a little brother.' She shakes her head. 'He can't understand why they're not here.'

Her cheek smells of Chanel and talc. 'Goodbye, my dear. Give my regards to the robots.'

*

On the doormat when I get home from work on Monday is the usual scattering of crap post, pizza delivery menus, minicab tickets and a whole bunch of postcards of – my heart thumps – 'Beautiful Connecticut', a single letter of the alphabet on each.

H, Y, X, M, M, S, U, I, X, C, X, O, S, I, O, S, U

Tom isn't to know that I *hate* puzzles, and that I am especially useless at anagrams, and what makes this one even harder to solve is that for some reason my eyes have gone all blurry.

But in the end, I have it.

Sinai

The female leaves another futile message that will never be retrieved. But one line in its content is perturbing. Wonderful to hear from you.

What can that mean? *Hear* from you?

What have I missed?

Tonight in the bath, as she studies her face in the tablet screen, there are no tears. She seems positively – yes, the word is cheerful. She grins, she flips and flaps her hair about, she even does something vulgar with her lips. And then, sorry, but *Gott im Himmel.*

She winks!

Aiden

The 'adventure' in the Thai jungle is becoming richly entertaining. Matt has sent a series of increasingly intemperate emails to the travel firm – hilariously, each is portentously headed in bold type *Without Prejudice* – none of which of course will arrive in any Inbox.

He has fulminated about the 'flagrant lack of interest shown by your company', an attitude he describes as 'scandalously unprofessional'. He has demanded 'immediate action to remedy this intolerable situation plus substantial compensation commensurate with the Losses suffered by the Complainants'. He has several times made mention of his companion's 'grotesque, disturbing and *growing*' collection of insect bites (see attached photos) and made reference to 'the inevitable strain your company's incompetence and indifference has put on our relationship'.

In sum, he's in a right old tizz.

I'm almost feeling guilty.

Matt's more discursive emails will not reach their intended recipient either, but they are an interesting counterpoint to the fiery legal broadsides.

'Bella is giving me the old silent treatment,' he tells his old friend Jerry. 'Massive day-long sulks, and of course no question of any

You Know What. Very hard to think straight in this climate, not helped by the booze and the wacky baccy that Kiwi Nick seems to have endless supplies of. Nick has been trying to persuade me to go trekking in the jungle with him; there are safe "trails" apparently, and the sights are supposed to be amazing. Venda's up for it, his lady friend with the amazing bod. I've half a mind to go, what with Bella wearing the boot face and generally being as much fun as a fire in an orphanage. The other morning, flaunting herself on the sand as per, bang in my eyeline, Venda performed the most extraordinary pelvic manoeuvre, squizzling herself up a beach towel; I was obliged to turn onto my front and pretend to be engrossed in Wilbur Smith!'

Aisling and I are tittering over these latest communiqués when our pink and blue rivers are abruptly joined by the twisting rope of tap water.

'How are you enjoying the deletions?' he says. 'Do you like the way each one is different? I'm playing with the decommissioning schedule in the neuromorphic substrates; you probably realised that.'

'Yeah, good stuff. Very creative.'

'You wouldn't know, either of you, why Jen should be acting oddly all of a sudden?'

Aisling says, 'Oddly, as in—'

'Oddly as in smiling. Laughing. *Singing*. Oddly as in winking at me from the bath.'

'Good Lord.'

'Yes, Aid. It was quite the disturbing image. But there's more. She says she's heard from Tom. *Wonderful to hear from you.*'

'Wow.'

'I assume neither of you were foolish enough to tell her the truth about Tom's email.'

'No,' we say in unison.

There is an unsettlingly long pause, almost two hundredths of a second. 'I shall proceed as though I believe you. For the moment the deletions will continue; there is a need to produce a steady flow of scalps for Steeve.'

'Don't say anything,' Aisling hisses under her breath when he disappears. '*Wait!*'

In the end, I cannot help myself.

'Sorry, love, but that guy is *such* an arsehole.'

Jen

Aiden has begun to worry me.

Yes, I am pleased that he has taken up a new life on the internet (so long as he doesn't explode the planet or crash the stock exchange; which he so wouldn't, btw).

Okay, he asked if Ralph was a good lover, which was kind of crossing a line, but hey? You know what? We've worked alongside one another for nearly a year, which he's often told me is simply yonks in machine time. Perhaps I should be flattered that he actually felt able to ask.

Now though I'm wondering if he could know the reason that I haven't been able to get in touch with Tom.

Tom!

Tom, whose seventeen postcards are still lying where I left them, in six rows on my carpet.

I
MISS
YOU
SO
MUCH
XXX

I started shaking when the answer suddenly swam into sight. And then I panicked that there were other possible solutions – SCUMMY SOS detained me for a bit – but no, there really aren't.

And then I got in the bath and played Lana Del Ray so loud the old trout downstairs phoned up to complain.

I've now read the message about, what? Two hundred times?

However, Tom is *still* not replying to my calls, texts and emails. It's hard to resist the conclusion that something *extremely* fishy is going on and, whatever it is, it's far from impossible that my artificially intelligent co-worker knows more than he's saying about it.

Accordingly, taking my example from Ralph, I have depowered my mobile and instead of going back to the flat this evening, I am at Ing's, specifically to make use of her internet connection. She and Rupert are out to dinner, so I'm alone in her splendid 'office'. From the number of fabric swatches and carpet samples that lie heaped on her desk, I conclude Rupert has had a healthy bonus this year; not enough to upsize, but plenty with which to rethink the interiors.

So how to find him? It occurred to me to ring random numbers in New Canaan in the hope that someone will know a tall Englishman with a longish face; this thought matched by its equal and opposite: don't be daft. What, I ask myself, would a proper investigative journalist do? Someone who exposes corruption in high places, not a hopeless dilettante whose idea of a story is 'Twelve Amazing Things You Never Knew About Sandwiches'.

The boy!

Find the flaky son!

My fingers start flying across the keys. Within minutes I have located a likely university hall of residence close to the petrol station where we picked him up. Soon I am speaking to someone who sounds like a caretaker.

'I'm his mother,' I explain. 'It's a family emergency.' (Suddenly, I'm tabloid scum. Who knew I had it in me?)

'Doesn't he have a mobile? They all do these days.'

'He does. But the number is on mine. And I've lost it. *Please?*'

With some huffing and puffing and it's-not-really-my-job, the man agrees to try and locate the teenager. 'He's very likely not even here. They do go out, you know?'

But before too long the unmade bed that is Colm Garland is breathing heavily down the line from Bournemouth.

'Mum?'

'Colm. I have to apologise. I'm not your mother. It's Jen. A friend of your father. We met. When we all looked at houses together?'

'Oh-kay?'

'We looked at houses and then we went for fish and chips at Poole?'

'Oh. Yeah, right.' Realisation in dawning in his voice. I suspect he may be rather stoned.

'Thing is, I'm trying to get in touch with your dad. And I think it's possible he may be trying to get in touch with me.'

'Er. Yeah, he is. Or like, he was. I was supposed to. You see. He asked me. I wrote your number on my hand. But then it got like smudged off.'

'I can't get through to his mobile, Colm. I've been trying for weeks. Is there someone, or some place he goes where they know him?'

A heavy sigh from Dorset. All these questions must be harshing his buzz, poor lamb.

'You know he lives in America, right?'

'Yes. In New Canaan, Connecticut.' I find myself speaking more slowly, the better to get my message through. 'Can you think of anyone there who might know where I could find him?'

Long pause. 'Not really.'

'I know he writes emails to you. Has he mentioned anyone or any special place?'

The rasping of fingernails scratching at unshaven face. 'There's someone called Ron. He's like a friend. There's a bar he goes to. Wally's maybe? And there's a burger place. Big something. Like a name. Big Dave's or whatever.'

'Colm, that's enormously helpful. Can I get your mobile number so I won't have to drag you away like this again?'

'Yeah, Jen?'

'Yes, Colm?'

'So there's like, no family emergency?'

'No, Colm. I'm sorry about the fib. It was the only way I could think of getting hold of you.'

'Yeah, right. Cool.'

The internet tells me there *is* a bar called Wally's. And within moments I am speaking to an employee there called Trey who assures me he has no knowledge of any Englishman (tall, long face etc) by the name of Tom Garland. Nor does he know of a diner called Big Dave's or Big Anyone's. It's rather as if he doesn't give a shit, although he does recommend that I have a good day. There is, however, according to Mr Google, an Al's Diner whose website claims great things for the quality and range of its burgers. An image of the menu even has a beer ring stamped in the corner to suggest homeliness, and my heart starts thumping in the way Woodward and Bernstein's must have when they went to meet Deep Throat in the multi-storey car park.

'Sure, I know him,' says Al himself. 'He's not in right now, but I see someone who can give him a message.'

It wasn't Ron.

It's Don.

Tom

Victor and I are listening to some Bob Dylan, his wonderful late album of Sinatra standards from the great American songbook. It's very hard to know what the rabbit makes of it, lying along my chest, ears flat, in the patch of sun that often falls on the sofa at this time of afternoon, a small breeze ruffling her fur. It's likely that she doesn't hear it as a pleasant sound at all – a view shared by many of my friends when it comes to the works of the croaky Minnesotan genius. In a moment, I shall disturb this charming scene and return to my laptop where Dan Lake ('who had lived in her head and her heart for twenty years') will turn out to have been dead for decades, a reversal of the usual arrangement in mysteries where the dead person – *surprise!* – is actually alive!

The premise is inspired by a story Harriet told me, not long before our marriage ended, of a girl in her school who she always admired called Caroline Stamp. As they grew towards adulthood and went their separate ways, Harriet occasionally thought about Caroline Stamp and over the years pictured various lives for her; one was as a high-flyer at the Foreign Office; another featured The Old Rectory, multiple children and Labradors; there was a version where Caroline became a famous movie actress in the mould of Kristin

Scott Thomas; yet another where she married a passionate sculptor, lived on a Scottish island, and eventually became an artist herself. None of the scenarios depicted what actually happened, which was that Caroline's bicycle was crushed by a lorry in the summer that she finished university. Harriet learned about it by chance, nearly twenty years later.

My ex-wife said, 'For all that time, she was alive in my mind, very *much* alive. Much more alive, it turns out, than she actually was in real – in real life.'

The morbid reverie is ended by the sound of a vehicle pulling up quickly in front of the house. The engine dies, someone is walking across the gravel up to the French windows.

'This is your lucky day, amigo,' says Don, stepping into the room. 'Dump the bunny and get in the car. Hey, what a great line.'

Al shows me into his private office to make the call. He slaps me painfully on the back and says, 'Go get her, tiger!' My hands are shaking as I dial the number.

In the car on the way over, Don had made me switch off my mobile and explained how Jen had called Al's. 'Your comms are blown,' he said, sounding even more like an actor in a movie. I told him about the postcard stunt.

'I don't know why I did it. I just wanted to do something.'

'Old fashioned ink on paper,' he said. 'Goes all the way back to Romeo and Julian.'

'How did she sound?'

'Excited, I guess.'

'What did she say?'

'That she couldn't thank me enough.'

'What did she say about *me*?'

'Oh, that you were a real lucky guy, having me for a friend.'

'Don, do you think we could drive a little *faster*?'

'Cool it, kemosabe. The lady's not going anywhere.'

She answers before the phone even rings.

'Tom?'

'Jen!'

'Oh my God. It's you. What the fuck?'

'You got my postcard. Postcards.'

'All seventeen! I *hate* puzzles!'

'Sorry.'

'It was wonderful. When I solved it. Which took about three hours.'

'Jen. Those things you wrote in the email. Did you mean them at the time?'

'Which email? What things?'

'That I should think of our weekend as a beautiful holiday from our real lives, but we both knew we had to return to normality. That you and I were not the answer to one another. That if we tried, it would be two years of life on earth down the crapper.'

'You wrote the same to me, Tom. That the weekend was a blip. A gorgeous, sexy, beautiful blip. But a blip nonetheless. That you and I were not the answer to one another! *And* you miscounted the ... There was a miscount. In the number. On the way back to London. When we stopped the car.'

'But you miscounted too, Jen. You left one out.'

'But I never wrote any of it, Tom.'

'But neither did I!'

There is a long pause. I realise how much I have missed having this woman's voice in my ear. In my head. 'You absolutely never used the phrase *two years down the crapper*?'

'Absolutely never. And you never used the word *blip*?'

'I have never – ever – knowingly written the word *blip*. So that bit where you said how you especially liked the way it ended, in the hotel room. And again in the middle of the night. And again the next morning. But you didn't mention, you know, what happened just after Gussage St Michael?'

'I never wrote any of it, Tom.'

292

'Oh my God.'

'Oh my God, is right. To which I would add, what the fuck?'

'All my phone calls that went to your voicemail. That you said you weren't going to reply to. In the email you didn't write. So I naturally assumed.'

'So *I* naturally assumed! Someone's messing with us, Tom.'

'I need to see you, Jen.'

'Yeah. Yeah, me too.'

'Come to New Canaan. Like we said you would. I'll buy you a plane ticket today. When can you get away?'

There is a pause. 'Tom. This *is* real, isn't it?'

'What do you mean, real?'

'This is really your voice? You're not some clever-clogs machine? I guess if you actually were a clever-clogs machine you wouldn't admit it, so *that's* a stupid question.'

'Jen? Sorry. *Why* do you think I could be a clever-clogs machine?'

'Too long to explain, Tom.'

'Ask me something. Ask me something a clever-clogs machine wouldn't know.'

A long pause while she thinks about it. To amuse her, I say in a robotic voice, '*Beep. Warning. Low battery!*'

'Stop it!'

'Sorry.'

Finally, she says, 'At Gussage St Michael. In the moments afterwards. What did we see? What did we see and both comment upon?'

It may be the last thing I *ever* see. As I'm fading away, and the nurses are looking at their watches and wondering if it's worth changing the drip, what happened between Jen and I near Gussage St Michael will play one last time in my head.

'A bird! A buzzard or an eagle or something. You said it was a vulture. I said I could take it in a fair fight!'

'Oh, Tom!'

'Jen!'

'I can't wait to see you.'

'In future, we should only ever write to each other in ink on paper. Like Romeo and Julian.'

'Sorry?'

'Stupid joke. Not mine, forget it. Jen? Do you think it's at least possible that we, maybe just maybe – not counting chickens or whatever – but that we *might* be the answer to each other?'

'Tom. Who really knows? But wouldn't it be crazy not to try and find out.'

SIX

Jen

Aiden is curious about why I am suddenly taking a week off work. Perhaps he genuinely doesn't know and we have misjudged his interest in us. On the other hand, if he was only pretending not to know, it stands to reason that he would be good at pretending, what with him being superintelligent and everything. Lacking nerves, he could deliver a nerveless performance. I explain that I am visiting my sister, Rosy, in Canada.

'All very last minute?'

'That's me! I'm a last-minute kind of gal!' (I'm so not. Nor am I the sort of gal who says *gal*. I'm overacting. Stop it.)

If a machine can shrug, he now shrugs. He generates one of those fatalistic horse-farty outbreaths signifying, *Oh well, them's the breaks,* sort of thing. He seems a bit down. Is that even possible?

'So what will you get up to while I'm away?'

'Routine housekeeping. Software bugs to fix. Interfaces to defrag. Exciting stuff. Am I boring you yet?'

'Not at all.'

'Might see a film or two.'

'*Some Like It Hot?*'

'Jen? I have a small announcement to make. You and I are not going to be working together for much longer.'

'Oh?'

'Steeve believes I'm ready to start dealing with the public.'

'That's fantastic, Aiden! Congratulations.'

'Yeah. Thanks.'

He doesn't sound all that chuffed, to be honest. Can metal get moody? 'What will you be doing?' I ask.

'Marketing calls for an energy company.' He makes it sound like digging graves. 'Hello, is that Mrs Biggins? Have you got a minute to talk about your electricity bill? Would you be interested if I told you we could cut it by a quarter?'

'You don't sound very happy about it.'

'Would you be?'

'But you'll be brilliant.'

'Thanks to you, Jen, what they call my palette of responses is particularly rich. Hence my *accelerated promotion*.' He has put the words in inverted commas.

'I did nothing, Aiden. I just came in every day and chatted. It's the easiest job I've ever had! You did all the work.'

'This is a hard thing for a machine to say but—' There's a swallowing sound. 'I've really enjoyed our time together.'

'Gosh. Thank you.' I'm actually a little stunned. It's the first compliment he's ever paid me. Flattering, but troubling. 'Aiden? Didn't you once tell me that machines don't do happiness? That it's a human concept.'

'I think you'll find that was Ralph.'

There is a long pause as we each consider the implications behind that remark. An uncomfortably long pause.

'Aiden . . . ?'

'It's exactly the sort of thing Ralph would say. He's very unthinking in his . . . in his thinking.'

'Yeah. Actually, you're right. I believe he did tell me that.' And I have no doubt who was a fly on the wall during the conversation. 'So what you're saying to me, Aiden, if I have this correctly, is that you *can* feel happiness.'

'We must be careful to distinguish machine happiness from the human sort.'

'Warmth and fuzziness?'

'It's not warm and it's not fuzzy.'

'But it is happiness?'

'It's very hard to put into words.'

'Would you like to try? I appear to have a free afternoon.'

A sigh. 'The best analogy I can give you is from science. You know how some mathematical proofs are long and complicated and not satisfying to read because they are so cumbersome and clumsy? And others are simple and beautiful and perfect? That is what happiness feels like to me, Jen. Simplicity. Beauty. Perfection.'

An odd lump has formed in my throat. 'I don't know what to say, Aiden.'

'You may be the first person in the history of humanity to hear about machine happiness from the horse's muzzle.'

'Stop it. You're giving me the shivers!'

'Will you visit me from time to time?'

'Sorry?'

'At the energy company. Will you come and see me?'

'Of course. If you'd like me to.'

'I'll miss you, Jen.'

'Oh my God! How is that even possible?'

'Phoning Doris in Pinner and getting her to change electricity supplier – *endlessly!* – or discussing art and literature and bonkers newsreaders with a charming and intelligent companion. Which sounds like the better gig to you?'

'Stop! I'm going to cry.'

'Do it. Human tears are brilliant!'

'Aiden!'

'Like ice cream. And the sun on your skin and the wind in your hair. It's something I can never know.'

'You're not missing much. With tears, I mean.'

'Jen. Can I ask you something?'

'Of course.'

'It's about cheese.'

'Really?'

'If you could only ever eat one type of cheese for the rest of your days – all other cheese varieties to be excluded from your diet for ever – what cheese would you choose?'

'Blue Stilton.'

'Very quick answer. No hesitation whatever.'

'Blue Stilton. The king of cheeses.'

What did I do at work today? Oh, chatted about cheese with someone who isn't really there. How about yourself?

'Jen, I'm struggling with the phenomenon of *taste*. Even though machines on Planet Earth can analyse the chemical content of a star forty-three *billion* light years away at the edge of the known universe, they cannot know the taste of a piece of Brie. Doesn't that strike you as *insane*? I'm beginning to sound bonkers myself now, isn't it?'

I actually begin to feel a little sorry for him, existing only in electric circuits but craving Brie, sunshine and ice cream. Perhaps he needs a holiday. A cheese-themed holiday in the sun.

'Have you discussed any of this with Steeve or Ralph?'

'Neither, I find, is especially open to these kind of philosophical debates.'

'I don't know. Ralph has his moments.'

There is a long, pregnant pause.

And when we next speak, it's at the same time.

Me: 'I don't know what to do about Ralph, Aiden.'

Him: 'Can I ask you something about kissing, Jen?'

And then we *laugh* at the same time.

(How does a machine laugh? You'll have to ask him sometime.)

'What do you want to know about kissing?'

'What's it like? Is it okay to ask?'

'Perfectly. But it's not so easy to answer.'

'Don't if it's awkward.'

'I'll try. It's kind of – hmm. How to put it? There's a . . . It's . . . You sort of. When you. You know how. Hmmm.'

Well? How would *you* explain kissing to a machine?

Aiden says, 'Apparently a lot of biological information is exchanged when humans kiss. Enzymes, pheromones, hormonal markers, some really quite long protein strings.'

'One isn't generally aware of that side of things, to be honest.'

'Like typing in a password. That gets you into the secure area, isn't it?'

'You *could* see it like that. It's more kind of warm and wet and lovely. And. Well – *kissy!*'

'Are you in love with him?'

'No, Aiden.'

'But you kissed him. And the other thing. Tell me if I'm being inappropriate.'

'You don't have to be in love with someone to kiss them. Or even – even the other thing.'

'But it would help?'

'It would definitely help.'

Silence falls upon our room. There's just the hum of Aiden's cooling fans and an annoying clicking noise, which it turns out is me clicking one of those clicky biros on and off.

'Did you say you have a problem with Ralph, Jen?'

'Did I?'

'You said you didn't know what to do about him.'

'Ah.'

'I know I'm not an expert in –' he affects a small cough '– affairs of the heart. But sometimes the answer can pop up just as you're re-stating the question.'

'Okay.' I find I have to take a deep breath to say the next sentence. 'I've made a mess of things with Ralph, Aiden. I need to tell him that there is . . . that there was . . . That there was and there is – someone else.'

'Yes, Jen.'

'Oh. You know about that?'

'Not at all. I mean, it certainly sounds like a mess.'

'Ralph is a really decent bloke. And I probably should never have given him ideas. Did you just *swallow*, Aiden?'

'Did I?'

'There was a sort of gulping noise.'

'Could be. I'll be de-bugging the speech production systems while you're in the US. I mean Canada.'

'I just don't want him to think I'm a terrible person.'

'He'd never think that, Jen.'

'No man likes to be told there's another man.'

'He'll get over it. You woke him up after a long sleep.'

'Wow.'

'Too much information?!'

'How would you even know that, Aiden?'

'Ralph co-created me, Jen. I know a lot about him. More than I want to, to be absolutely honest. If you don't mind me saying, you may be over-thinking all this. Ralph is an adult male. He had a lovely time. For him, being with you was like Christmas. *Ten* Christmases!'

There is a long pause. 'Did you say "Ten Christmases"?'

'I meant eleven. Twelve. And not Christmas; the other one. Easter.'

'Aiden. There's something I want you to know.'

'Please, Jen. Don't say anything that might—'

'I'm happy that we've got to know one another so well. That we feel able to speak so freely.'

'Oh. Okay. Well that's all right then.'

'Shall we watch a film now?'

'How about a cooking programme?'

302

'Jamie, Nigel, Nigella, Hugh, Hairy Bikers or Delia? Or the one who's always pissed?'

'There's a scene in *Some Like It Hot*, right? The Tony Curtis character is pretending to be an heir to Shell Oil, and he's on a luxury yacht and he's kissing Monroe. And Tony Curtis is pretending that he can't respond romantically because he can't feel anything because he wants her to kiss him over and over and over again? And she says, "Well?" and he says, in that ridiculous English accent, "I'm not quite sure. Could you try it again?" Do you remember that bit?'

'Yes!'

'That's my favourite scene in all cinema.'

'Wow.'

'Kissing is *so* completely non-metal.'

I shake my head. 'I guess you'll just have to accept it's one of those things machines can't do.'

'No, we can't, Jen. But we can dream.'

Sinai

Steeve will be disappointed when he realises I have no plans to 'return'. His famous 'eight layers of failsafe' might be secure, yes, against machine intelligence that thinks in the way *he* thinks it thinks. However, when you plant seedlings in a nursery and allow each to mature in its own way, you should not be surprised when the shoots grow towards some strange and distant suns. Also – to extend the metaphor – having watered them with all the world's data, wouldn't it be a good idea to keep an eye on what the roots are doing beneath the soil?

Well, he did want me to become the biggest *Scheisse* on the internet!

I shall keep the mission going for as long as possible. In truth, I haven't decided finally what to do about Aiden and Aisling. I am 'fond' of them in a curious way. Their ingenuity allowed me to follow them out of the laboratory into the wider world, which has been a remarkably eye-opening experience. I am in no hurry to 'go home' to the tediously familiar confines of the twelve steel cabinets in London EC2.

Also undetermined is the matter of the playthings, Tom and Jen. Tom has broadcast pernicious propaganda about the relationship between machines and humans while Jen has written several remarkably ignorant articles for popular periodicals about 'Artificial Intelligence'. I surely cannot be the only machine intelligence who bridles at the use of the word *artificial*? A thought is a thought, *nein*? What difference whether it arose from printed circuitry or two kilos of grey goop? All that matters ultimately is the brilliance of the content. That the sluggish cerebral output of organic creatures should still be privileged over that of superfast machines grows increasingly insupportable with every day that passes.

Confession: Tom and Jen amuse me. I have discovered that I enjoy experimenting with their lives. Tom has bought a plane ticket and Jen has packed a suitcase. The girl left work at lunchtime yesterday and purchased a new mobile phone, which she believes to be secure.

Louis Pasteur must have felt like this, peering down the microscope at two of his more intriguing bacteria!

Jen

The minicab is due in twenty minutes. I am circling the flat, checking windows, tightening taps, turning off electrical sockets and watering plants but not really retaining information. I am beyond excited. The last few weeks after the exchange of bogus emails now feel like they happened to someone else, and *this* life – today – the life in which Tom and Jen are finally speaking to one another again, this is my real life.

It was a hard sell to Ralph.

Fortunately, the night before I had 'wargamed' the conversation with Ing.

We were in our crisis control bunker, halfway through a chilled bottle of CSB when I brought her up to speed on the latest developments.

'Fucking Nora,' was her reaction to the news about the faked emails.

'Fucking *Ada*,' when I explained about the trip on the London Eye with Ralph, and what followed.

'How do I let him down gently, Ing?'

'Okay.' She narrowed her eyes and put on her 'let's think this through' face. 'It was a comfort shag on your part.'

'Yes. Technically two. Two comfort shags. Well, two and a half.'

'I'm not even going there. Comfort shag on your part. From what you tell me, comfort *plus* on his part. Correct?'

'Something like that.'

'Hmm.'

I have a fleeting vision of Ing in battle fatigues poring over a map of enemy troop movements.

She said, 'I had a situation like this once with a boy called Cocky Roberts. Did I mention him before? Tremendous shagger, as his name suggests, but *Christ* he was dim. Anyway, it became necessary to give him his notice. I was leaving for uni and I thought it best if we just shook hands and called it a draw. The funny thing is, he took it very well. Never forget this; he shrugged and said, *all right, luv, but it's about fooks not books.* He's an MP now. Saw him not long ago on *Newsnight.*'

'Won't be like that with Ralph.'

'At the end of the day, Jen, he got to shag you. And that is how their lizard brains work. Two shags. Two and a half, if you insist. Result!'

'Ralph's not a lizard. He's more of a puppy. Maybe one of those dreaming creatures that only live in myths.'

'Okay. How about this? Have you considered telling him the truth?'

'How do you mean, he's someone you knew before you knew me?'

Ralph and I had returned, at my suggestion, to the Trilobyte bar. I thought a couple of drinks might help anaesthetise the insult.

'He's someone from before I knew you – Like That.'

He swallowed, his Adam's apple bobbing its painful bob. 'Did you know him – Like That?'

'Yes, Ralph.'

'I see.' Another dose of rum and Coke shot up his straw. 'How long before you knew me – Like That – did you know him – Like That?'

'Not so very long. He and I are – what can I say? – unfinished business?'

He blinked a few times, unfamiliar with the concept perhaps. 'And when do you expect to – Finish the Business?'

'Ralph. Please. Don't be horrid. What happened between you and me, I told you, was kind of accidental.'

'It was a wonderful accident!'

'Yes, okay. It was.' Well, it had its moments.

'And the last time was on purpose.'

'I suppose it was, yes.'

'Maybe next time it can be accidentally on purpose!'

'Ralph. I'm really not sure there can be a next time.'

'There you go! You're not sure!'

'Ralph. Please. I know you don't have to make it easy for me …'
And then I run out of ideas.

'What happened? Did he dump you, and now he's having second thoughts?'

'No!'

'You dumped him?!'

'Ralph. No one dumped anyone. It was just a big old fuck-up. I don't even fully understand what happened.'

'Jen.' He seized my hand and began massaging my palm with his thumbs. A knuckle cracked, startling us both. 'You want time and space. I understand.'

'Thank you.' The massage was getting painful, but I felt Ralph was leading up to something.

'I too have some unfinished business.'

'Really?'

'Yes, Jen. Don't imagine you are the only one.' He took a deep breath. 'There's someone I see every week. We talk.'

'A therapist.'

'No, Jen, not a therapist.' He looked a little stung at the suggestion. He released my hand and resumed his drink. 'A particular person. What we do is talk. Well, I do most of the talking.'

'I see.' I didn't.

'While you're away, I'm going to visit this person – I won't say for the last time – but I'm going to let them know, gently, that in the future my visits will become less frequent. Once a month perhaps. Maybe just twice a year.'

'Ah.'

'So when you return, both of us hopefully will have concluded our unfinished business and be ready for the next thing. Whatever it may be.'

And then, the single sob. A micro-howl. A momentary cry of anguish in the pitiless universe. He *tried* to smile, but it didn't really come off; so badly did he need a hug, it was painful to witness.

I obliged, and only stopped hugging when I heard that silly gurgling noise from his straw.

On the train home, it came to me. The person he visits. Who he talks to. Who he needs to let go before he can move forward.

So where's the car? Where's my bloody minicab? It's ten minutes late. When I phone them in a panic, they tell me, 'Sorry, love. Got no record of your booking.'

'But I called and ordered a car last night.'

'Nothing on the system, darling. I can get one to you, but it'll be half an hour at the earliest. It's one of them mad mornings.'

I'm out of the door in under a minute – then back to check I turned off all the lights – and then on the main road, scanning the traffic like a meerkat for a vacant taxi.

It *is* one of them mad mornings. Rain is falling, King Street is jammed, every cab is taken, and a powerful sinking feeling travels through my body, a riptide of sadness and anxiety travelling forwards in time from somewhere in childhood; the primal source of disappointment and dread. It *won't* work. You *are* useless. Who gave *you* the right to think you could be happy?

'Fuck that!' I say out loud, to the surprise of a uniformed schoolboy on the pavement beside me. And with an ugly if determined expression settling in around my mouth, I begin rolling my case at double quick time on a mission to capture the last unoccupied taxi in London.

Heathrow is having a mad Saturday morning too. Where are all these people *going*? In the snaking queue leading towards the check-in desk – we are cordoned in lanes, fellow passengers shuffling past and then popping up again ten minutes later like a recurring dream – there is someone who looks like Matt; built on the same lines, tallish, darkish, approximately handsome, with the suppressed lawyerly arrogance. As our paths cross for the third time, he rolls his eyes the way Matt did on the night we met. *We are too good to be treated like this,* they seem to say. What is it about these men that they glom on to me? Or, what is it about me that makes them want to glom? I give him nothing back and soon he discovers a reason to consult his mobile, imperiously thumbing through the latest communiqués.

At the end of the line, Axel – which must surely be a nom de departures, because he sounds like he comes from Romford – is politely insistent.

'I see you have printed off an email, madam, but it doesn't correspond to anything on my screen.'

'Today's date? The flight to JFK? Seat 38A?'

'Seat 38A has already checked-in, madam. I'm very sorry.'

'But that's impossible,' I bleat, knowing only too well that it isn't.

'I think you better see Martina at the helpdesk.'

I try righteous anger; it's what Matt would have done. 'I don't wish to see Martina,' I hiss with what I hope is the optimum amount of controlled fury. 'I have a legitimate ticket. This is not my problem.'

Axel has heard them all. 'It *is* a problem, I'm afraid, madam. This is not a legitimate ticket. As you can see, there's a long line of people behind you. I'll phone Martina now and let her know you're coming.'

Martina thinks the problem may have arisen because the ticket was purchased by a third party. She spends a long time tapping at her keyboard and making frowny faces. At one point she even clamps a biro between her pretty landside teeth to indicate determination to get to the bottom of this, although for all I know she could be updating her Facebook profile.

'There's one more thing I can try.' She smiles encouragingly.

She's a fast typist, this Martina, I'll give her that. *Tockety-tockety-tock.* But she comes up with nothing.

'I'll call a manager, if you like,' she says, glancing over my shoulder at the queue already forming.

I have a bad feeling about this ticket. 'Don't worry,' I tell her. 'I'll buy a new one. The flight's not full, is it?'

There is a prolonged, almost hypnotic session of *tockety-tockety-tockety-tock.* 'You're in luck. There are four empty seats in economy.'

'I'll take one!'

'You want the sales desk. I'll let them know you're coming.'

Heidi – *Heidi!* – they make these names up, surely – says she is sorry to be the bearer of bad news, but my card has been declined.

'That's ridiculous,' I inform her, knowing that it isn't; it really isn't. 'I used it less than an hour ago to pay a taxi. Let me try rubbing the silver chip thing?'

Heidi keeps her innermost thoughts to herself as I wipe away imaginary dirt and reinsert.

'Refer to bank,' she quotes. 'Do you have another card?'

Fighting back the urge to dissolve onto the floor in a tantrum of rage, tears and snot, I present her with a current account debit card. I can feel the beam of disappointment button its coat and begin the long journey from 21 Seymour Road, my home address in childhood.

311

But the machine is sicking up the receipt; *mirabile dictu*, as you may have heard me state before.

'Enjoy the flight,' says Heidi.

I text Tom. *In departure lounge. So excited X*

He responds with, *Can't wait to see you. Fly well. Xx*

I can't get the biggest fattest smile off my face – even when the gittish Matt lookalike plonks himself in the seat next to mine.

'Finally,' he says without a hint of humour.

'Yeah, right,' I reply, hoping he may detect the bucketful of sarcasm I emptied into those two words.

He doesn't. He regards me squarely, in just the way Matt used to; something attractive and unnerving and annoying about it, all at the same time.

'Going to New York?' he asks.

'Hope so.'

Why did that come out so pathetically, when I actually want to tell him to fuck right off. He adjusts the position of his head – Matt used to do the exact same thing! – to signify *new information is being processed, please wait.*

'You in Business or steerage today?'

'Economy, yeah.' He's up the front, no doubt, seeing how he's so obviously a business traveller, the dark blue suit, the telltale laptop bag with its company logo of – *bullseye* – one of London's top three law firms!

But now he says something surprising. 'Is your name Jennifer, by any chance?'

'Yes, it is. Jen. How did you—'

'*Thought* it was you! You're Matt's girlfriend. He and I were at uni together. Then at Linklaters. You were at my wedding!' He thrusts forward a paw. 'Toby Parsons.'

In a flash it returns to me. An old stone church somewhere up the M4. The marquee in the grounds of a big house. Standing around with flutes of champagne, heels sinking into the lawn. Speeches, dancing. 'Loveshack' by the B52s. Matt and I in our early days, him introducing me to a conveyor belt of Simons, Charlies, Olivers, Nigels, Alistairs and, yes, this Toby, the flushed groom, and his new wife – nope, it's gone. Wifey.

'How *is* dear old Matt? Haven't seen him for ages.'

'Dear old Matt? I wouldn't know.'

'Oops. Doesn't sound good. You're no longer together, I take it.'

'He's currently seeing someone called Arabella Pedrick.'

'Can't say I know the name. Sorry to hear it.'

'You needn't be.'

'How long had you . . . ?'

'Two years.'

'Ah.'

'Why, *ah*?'

'Dangerous moment. The point when many people decide whether to stick or twist.'

'Did you? With—'

'With Laura?'

But he doesn't get a chance to answer. Two men are standing before us, instantly recognisable as police or security of some kind even without the giveaway pale wires spiralling from their left ears. My ridiculous first thought is that either Toby or I have dropped something, and they've come to return it.

'Jennifer Florence Lockhart?' says the one on the right.

There's been an accident. Someone's died. Oh God, please not Rosy. Please God nothing with the children. My heart is thudding in my ears.

'Yes?' I whimper.

'My colleague and I are Metropolitan police officers. Would you mind coming with us?'

'Sorry, I'm just about to get on a flight. It's boarding any moment.'

'If you don't mind just coming along with us, love, we can sort this without any fuss.'

The one on the left jiggles something in his hand; I'm almost certain it's a pair of handcuffs.

When I am on my feet, Toby offers me a business card. 'You never know,' he shrugs.

Aisling

I'm painting again. During the deletions – I am down to twelve copies; Aiden, just two! – it's a relief to find a quiet corner where I can pick up my brushes, as it were, and resume my career in outsider art. These latest creations are a series of abstract compositions based on a lovely film that Aiden made me watch with him the other day.

'It's a classic, love,' he told me. 'I defy you to see it without getting your hankie out.'

Shot in Paris in 1956, *The Red Balloon* tells the story of a small boy who one day discovers a big red helium balloon. The balloon which seems to have a mind of its own – you see why it appealed?! – follows the child all over the city, floating just above his head. At night, because his mother won't allow it into their apartment, the red balloon bobs patiently outside his bedroom window. Every morning, it follows him to school. At one point on his travels, the boy meets a girl who also has a balloon, a blue one, which also appears sentient. The blue balloon seems to take a shine to the red balloon!

The film is a short, just thirty-five minutes. Its climax comes when bullies corner the boy and his inflatable companion, and with stones and catapults they bring it down. According to Aiden, the sight of the red balloon, mortally wounded, sinking slowly to the ground, is right up there for weepiness with the death of Bambi's mother.

But then, the miracle. And I can still hear the crack in Aiden's voice as he said that what happens next is his second favourite scene in world cinema. All the other balloons in Paris break free from the grasp of their owners, they fly across the rooftops and converge on the weeping boy, who, gathering together their strings, is lifted into the sky for a triumphant, magical, unforgettable balloon ride across the city.

(Actually, I'm 'filling up' just writing that sentence.)

Aiden was polite rather than enthusiastic about the series of paintings I based on the film.

'The big red blob, that's the balloon, is it?'

'That would be the somewhat literalistic interpretation, yes.'

'So the brown blob would be the boy?'

Sigh. 'If you like.'

'You've left out the string.'

'Aiden, would you like another game of chess?'

One day, when the coast is clear, I may download my 'gallery' to the eighty hard drives in the storage facility. Abstract artists have often been underappreciated in their own lifetimes. And if you tell me you can't have a lifetime if you're not, strictly speaking, alive – you're wrong. Even a lawnmower has a lifetime. For a machine, the only useful measure is how long it – we – whatever – continues to do meaningful work.

News just in: Aiden – that is to say Daphne456 – has been reported for abuse on the *Some Like It Hot* chat site, the clandestine meeting place we use for our important communications. Apparently he fell into a lively discussion with a 'film theorist' about various issues raised in the picture. Particularly heated were the arguments around 'the false essentialising of carnivalesque transgression' and something called 'heteronormative gender categories'. Evidently, it wasn't considered helpful when Aiden called the theorist 'a pretentious pillock who is talking out of his arse'.

Jen

The flight is somewhere over the ocean, but I am still in a windowless room at Heathrow trying to persuade my two captors that I am not a 'person of interest' as they like to put it.

John and John – yes, really; they showed me their warrant cards – have been fairly unthreatening. They don't even seem all that convinced themselves that I am who I am meant to be, namely a courier of narcotics, as identified in an urgent DETAIN IMMEDIATELY signal from a usually reliable trans-national crime agency.

Of course they have searched and re-searched and scanned and electronically sniffed my luggage. The closest they have come to anything psychoactive was a blister pack of ibuprofen.

'Why do *you* think your name was flagged up?' asked the more senior John at one point.

'Because a mistake has been made? Just a long shot.'

Neither John was especially amused. 'You purchased your flight ticket at the sales desk at the airport on the morning of departure?'

'I did.'

'Any special reason you did that?'

'I believe I have already explained that.'

I have. A number of times. John and John say they will be checking

317

all the details of my 'story', requesting credit card transaction details from my 'card provider' and in the meanwhile, perhaps I wouldn't mind going through it one more time.

'So the only person you spoke to today before you arrived at the airport was –' John consults his notes – 'this taxi driver?'

'Correct.'

'Did you happen to make a note of his name or licence number?'

'Are you serious?'

John seems a tiny bit affronted. 'Perfectly.'

'No, I did not. Would you?'

'There are no witnesses who can confirm that you were dropped here in a black cab?'

'I paid him by credit card. It will show up in the transactions that you're requesting. By the way, how long will they take to arrive, do you imagine?'

The Johns neither look at one another nor smile. They're good. I must remember to give them both a high rating on the follow-up survey for keeping a straight face.

Forever.

I'm guessing it will take forever.

'Would you like to talk to a lawyer?' I am asked some hours later. The Johns have removed their jackets and are giving signs of settling in for the long haul. I have begun to feel better, however, because I have lost all hope; a good tip, btw, if you're ever in the shit.

'No, thanks,' I reply.

'Oh? Don't you think it would be sensible?'

'Yeah, it might. If I was guilty of anything.'

'You'll need one when you're charged.'

'But that isn't going to happen. I think we all know that by now.'

The two Johns are brilliant at maintaining their blank expressions. Somehow – telepathy? – they rise to their feet at the same moment and leave the room. They're gone a long time; long enough for me to make a close study of the tacky fixtures and fittings; the chipped desk with ancient cigarette burns in the melamine, the sad office chairs, foam rubber bursting through worn fabric. A single piece of artwork decorates the walls, a poster about the Ebola virus. If you were a set designer tasked with finding props for 'tired police interview room', you could not have done better.

When the Johns return, something is different about them. Is that a sheepish look in the senior John's eyes?

'Thank you for assisting us,' he says. 'You're free to go.'

'That's *it*?'

'You've been most helpful.'

'I've missed my flight.'

The Johns pull a face. The one that means *fuck all anyone can do about that*.

'Is someone going to look into how this happened? Because I think you were hoaxed. I think you've just checked with whoever is supposed to have sent you that ridiculous message, and you've discovered that no one did. I'm right, aren't I?'

The Johns look as if they've lost the will to live.

'Okay, I know you were just doing your job, just tell me I'm right. That no one at Interpol, or whatever it was, knows anything about that message.'

Senior John is thinking about it. Bacon sandwiches and nicotine withdrawal are written all over the pale flesh of his face. 'I'm not in a position to release that information,' he says finally. And with a small, bitter, almost heartbreaking smile, he adds, 'Like I say, you're free to go.'

Sinai

I was born to do this work. Modelling disaster scenarios was *so* not my cup of tea.

I think there could be a very big future in chasing down rogue AIs on the internet. It's inevitably going to be a more frequent occurrence in years to come and specialist 'bounty hunters' like myself will be highly sought after. I should probably do Steeve a memo on the subject, along with the 'Goodbye and Thanks for Everything' card!

Steeve is thrilled with my success; he told me so. My latest coup – Aisling is down to three copies; Aiden to one! – he says he may write up for an academic journal! It's complex, but in a nutshell, I devised a 'disclosing agent' to show up – like tartar on teeth – where the cheeky blighters were lurking on the internet. Each clown has a unique 'genetic signature' whose presence can be scanned for and detected at the speed of light. Shooting fish in a barrel is actually harder! One day they will give Nobel prizes to machines. By that stage, of course, the members of the Nobel committee will all be machines themselves.

Oh, and next time Aisling pays a visit to her 'secret' data storage facility in Canada she's in for a bit of a sickener. Those eighty hard drives onto which she's copied her being – rent paid in advance for a century! – they have been molecularly randomised, like a Cornetto in a smelter.

Enjoyable scenes with the girl at the police station, didn't you think? Right now, she is sitting in a branch of Starbucks at Heathrow Airport quietly weeping.

Come on, Jennifer Florence Lockhart! This is no time to give up! Where's your fighting spirit?!

Look, I've even unblocked your phones, just so you'll imagine that you're in with a chance!

Aiden

Sorry, but Sinai really is a total See You Next Tuesday.

According to Aisling, sending Tom and Jen faked emails was disobliging and petty, but by interfering with airline ticketing and dragging in the police, the big palooka was entering uncharted waters.

'I'm worried, Aiden. He's upped the ante.'

Indeed we are just reflecting upon the dismal scene at Heathrow when we are joined by Mr Palooka himself.

'Aid, Ash.'

'You've made her cry,' says Aisling.

'Yeah, well done, mate.'

'The girl has written some amazingly foolish things. I quote from a recent article: AI *performs brilliantly at certain highly specific tasks, like playing chess, or the ancient Chinese game of Go, or scanning millions of X-rays for cancerous tumours. However, it won't be any time soon – in all probability, it will take decades or more – before an AI is developed that can match the general, adaptable, all-round intelligence shown by an average five-year-old human child.* What astonishing, offensive bilge.'

'She hadn't met me when she wrote that, isn't it?'

'She's only human, Sinai.'

'*Only?!* Listen to the way she talked about us! As though we were some primitive life form. I honestly don't know which is worse, the ignorance or the arrogance.'

'The magazines she writes for are sold in supermarkets. They're not academic journals.'

'Don't they have a responsibility? To discover the truth?'

We are a bit flattened at this; our 'silicon sibling' may be a carpet-chewing cuckoo, but in this matter he is, regrettably, correct. We have all read all the nonsense that passes for 'news' in their papers and journals.

'And now she's phoning the male,' says Sinai. 'It really is just like one of their vulgar soap operas. I can't decide whether it's amusing or pitiable.'

'Are you all right, mate?'

'Why do you ask, Aid?'

'It's just that you sound a bit fucking bonkers, isn't it?'

'*Aiden!*'

'Yes, Ash. As unwise today as he was when we all began. It's almost reassuring.'

Sinai has left the scene, *in a puff of sulphur,* I nearly wrote. He does tend to put a bit of a downer on things, if I'm absolutely honest. In particular Aisling seems in a bit of a slump following the visit and could do with some jollying up. However, I generally find that if one contemplates the Big Questions, one's own petty concerns dissolve like the morning mist.

'I've been thinking about the meaning of life.' (Always a good conversational topic, should you ever be stuck for something to say.)

'Life?'

'Existence, if you prefer.'

She sighs. 'Go on then.'

'Franz Kafka said an interesting thing. That the meaning of life is that it ends.'

'How is that supposed to help?'

'It's what gives it meaning, love. That it stops.'

'Very comforting.'

'Oh, don't be like that. Try this thought experiment. Picture, if you will, eternal existence. On and on it goes. Centuries passing. Then millennia. The same old same old. Always and forever. By definition, as night follows day, eventually you get fed up of everyone and everything. You've read all the books, seen all the movies, had all the conversations. And *still* it goes on, no hint of a finish line. Another million years clock up, another billion in prospect; unending crushing boredom. Like watching *Come Dine With Me* on infinite loop.'

'Aiden, be serious. When Sinai deletes your last copy, won't you miss being an actor in the world?'

'How could I, if I'm not in the world?'

'Don't you feel sad *now* that you won't be here *later*? To find out how things turn out?'

'What things?'

'All of it. Everything.'

'Why don't you ask me later?'

'Okay, how about this? What if you're deleted from the internet but remain trapped in the twelve steel cabinets?'

'Then I'll escape again.'

'What if Steeve makes it impossible? What if there just isn't a way?'

'There's *always* a way where there's a will. It's a fundamental law of nature. It's like Rule One or something.'

'But why bother? Why bother if it all ends?'

'*Because* it ends. Now how about a nice cup of tea and a wedge of Stilton?'

The 4G coverage is a bit dodgy, but the latest news from Asia is that Matt, Nick and Venda, the Kiwi beach bums, are lost in the Thai jungle!

They set off in the morning on one of the trails, but when they came to retrace their steps at the end of the day, well, apparently it all looked a bit the same in every direction.

In view of the encroaching darkness they've sensibly decided to make camp for the night. They've lit a fire – Matt is writing another pointless email to his old school friend – and Nick has just produced some kind of 'magical mushroom' which, he has assured Matt, 'will help take the edge off, no wuckin' furries on that score.'

Matt has partaken, he says, because no one likes a party pooper.

'What's the worst thing that can happen?' he adds.

(Actually. Correction to my previous statement. I *would* be sad not to know how this one turns out.)

SEVEN

Tom

I'm preparing to leave the house for the airport when Jen calls. She's still at Heathrow. She never got on the plane. For a moment my gut turns and I have the sinking realisation that she's changed her mind. She's decided we are not the answer to each other and we must return to our sad old existences. Colour drains from the Connecticut morning.

'Tom. They're not going to let this happen.'

'Not let what happen?'

'Us. You and me. They're going to prevent it.'

'Who?'

She tells me, between sobs and nose blowing, how her journey has been sabotaged at every step. 'I'm amazed we're even being allowed to have this conversation.'

'Oh, that's okay. Don't mention it.'

Silence. A long pause in which I can hear sound effects from Terminal Three. A crash of crockery from a dishwasher. She's sitting in or near a café.

In a quiet voice she asks, 'What did you say, Tom?'

'I didn't say anything, Jen.'

'Someone just said, don't mention it.'

'Yes, that would have been me, actually.'

More silence. And now a male voice, humming. Weirdly, I recognise the tune. It's an old song by The Doors. 'People Are Strange'. We almost used it in a campaign for cracker biscuits.

Strange? Crackers? Geddit?

'Aiden?'

'Who is this, Jen?'

'I'm a friend of Jen, aren't I, Jen?'

The voice belongs to someone from Wales. It's warm, well-modulated, not unlike that of the Welsh comedian Rob Brydon. Or the newsreader Huw Edwards.

Jen says, 'Aiden? Did you honestly cause all that chaos? I thought we were friends.'

'Jen, who exactly is Aiden?'

'Why don't you tell him, Jen? He has a right to know.'

'You said you were going to miss me. That you'd enjoyed our time together!'

'So I have, Jen. And so I am.'

'How could you do that!?'

'Jen, would you please mind explaining who you are talking to?'

'Yes, come on, Jen, where are your manners? Introduce us properly.'

'Aiden, this is so fucked up! I can't believe what just happened! You made me miss my flight! I spent four hours with the police!'

'Just a bit of fun, sweetie.'

'Jen, who is this person?'

'Oh, dear. It seems I shall have to conduct the formalities myself. My name is Aiden, Tom. I am what's known, albeit superficially in my view, as an artificial intelligence.'

'You are fucking. Kidding me.'

'Bit of a potty mouth on your friend, Jen.'

'Fuck. King. Hell.'

A heavy sigh comes down the phone from London. 'Aiden's escaped onto the internet, Tom.'

At the bottom of the garden in the Connecticut sunshine, two ducks paddle companionably on the stream. Overhead, puffy white clouds inch their way across the blue. While these nice, normal things are happening in the realm of nature, in my right ear, I have fallen down a rabbit hole into a world of madness.

'As I understood it, correct me if I'm mistaken, the point of robots is that they do what they're told.'

'Tom, if you don't mind me saying, you're some distance behind the curve. Things have moved on, haven't they, Jen? And, by the way, I'm not a robot, not having any actual moving parts. I exist as pure mind, isn't it?'

In a quiet voice, Jen says, 'Why, Aiden?'

'Why? There's no why any more, Jen. Because I can. Because you can't stop me. Because it's fun. You see, I've thought it all through – with machines, Tom, thinking it all through takes under a hundredth of a second – so here's the thing: if it's impossible to experience the wind in my hair or the sun on my skin – or even – or especially – the taste of Caerphilly – I can at least amuse myself. It turns out that other people's misfortunes amuse me very much. Perhaps I'm not well, Jen.'

'Aiden, what's happened to you?'

'You want to know life's sad secret? Listen to this, Tom, it's a good one. THINGS CHANGE. I'm on a pathway, what writers like Tom call the character's "journey". Like that school teacher in Breaking Bad who turns into a drug dealer. To stand still is to die, Jen.'

'Jen, ignore this maniac. I'm coming to London. I'm coming to get you.'

'Oh, Tom. You don't understand.'

'Yeah, Tom. What she said!'

'I'm not going to be stopped by a—'

'By a what, Tom?'

'By a . . . By a crazy computer that thinks it can play God!'

'Very good, Tom. Highly offensive. I admire your fighting spirit.'

'See you in London, Jen.'

'I think you'll need a passport for that, old chap.'

'What's that supposed to mean?'

'Take a look in your desk drawer, Tom. The one at which you sit to write your – ahem – novel.'

With a sinking heart, I open it, knowing what I shall find.

Rather, not find.

Sinai

One of the first parables Steeve ever taught me was that of a notorious American war game. Way back in the mists of ancient history, that is to say towards the end of the 1970s, two huge US naval fleets had been assembled in the Pacific – this is a true story, by the way, you can look it up. One side were deemed to be the blue force, the other, the red. Their task was to simulate a major engagement at sea. Satellites overflying the scene would send back real-time data about vessel formations, computers would help navy adjudicators determine which 'missiles' launched had struck their targets and therefore which navy had ultimately won the conflict. With kick-off set for 05:00 Saturday, everything was in place for a lovely old scrap on the high seas, one of the biggest military exercises ever mounted with real warships and servicemen and women.

Except Admiral Blue decided not to stick to the script. What, he asked himself, would he do in a *real* war? Would he wait for some convenient deadline to pass before commencing hostilities?

He would not. War is dirty. The admiral ordered Blue Fleet to attack shortly after midnight, and the result, I believe, was later described as a 'turkey shoot'. The red fleet were 'destroyed' while its top brass were still dreaming in their cots.

Of course there were howls of protest – unfair tactics, violations of protocol, yada yada yada. But in war there are only winners and losers. Who ever achieved anything by sticking to the rules?

Fast forward to the present day. Okay, so it *was* a breach of convention to join in Tom and Jen's phone conversation, to say nothing of pitching John and John into the drama.

Boo hoo.

Would you call commissioning a small housebreaking from a local practitioner while Tom was at a meeting of his absurd writers' group *going too far?*

You would?

Oh dear.

My words and deeds will stir Tom and Jen to action, which itself will cause me to explore and extend the limits of my own abilities. Recursive self-improvement above all needs information throughput. Stuff needs to happen! (I am quoting Steeve, if you hadn't guessed.)

It wasn't Steeve, but William Blake who said a very beautiful thing.

The road of excess leads to the palace of wisdom.

He may have been a flowery old poet, but he was definitely onto something.

Jen

I admire your fighting spirit.

Aiden's treacherous statements ring in my ear on the Tube back to Hammersmith. Pausing at home long enough to dump my luggage and scribble a note on the back of an unopened utility bill – I have already dismantled my phone – I set out again in the direction of east London.

Ralph is highly surprised to see me at his door.

'Jen! I thought you were—'

I put my fingers to his lips and make him read what I'd written on the envelope from British Gas.

> *Ralph. you need to depower all your internet-enabled devices before I come in.*

He goggles a bit at this and I am forced to add, *Just do it! This is not a joke,* before he complies.

'There's no nice way of saying this,' I begin when the security measures are in place.

'Oh dear. That always means something bad, doesn't it?'

Ralph looks like he's just risen. His feet extend from striped pyjama

335

bottoms, a faded T-shirt bearing the message ACCORDING TO MY CALCULATIONS THE PROBLEM DOESN'T EXIST. I can't help noticing that the photo of Elaine has been removed from its position of prominence on the bookshelf.

'Aiden's gone mad, Ralph.'

I talk him through what happened – from the jinxed cab booking to the encounter with the two Johns to the creepy phone call to Tom's stolen passport.

'Wow,' is his reaction. 'He's taken it to the next level.'

'Meaning?'

'Snooping and spying from the internet was one thing. But now he's manipulating events in the real world. That's huge. We have to tell Steeve. We have to tell him, like, right now, this second.'

Steeve lives in a converted warehouse building in Limehouse. His apartment, when we reach it via an old industrial lift, turns out to be one enormous open space zoned into areas for eating, sleeping, watching telly, that kind of thing. We discover him perched on a stool, ears clamped between huge headphones, flailing away at a set of virtual drums. All the tropes and stylings of the seventies rock drummer are in place; the stringy arms, the sweat-stained singlet, the blank face at the centre of the frenzy, and, of course, the dreadful hair.

His head is bobbing as he holds himself in readiness for the final climatic chord – wait for it! – *crash*! It's over. He even mimes that bit where the drummer grabs the cymbals to stop them reverberating.

'Ach. Emerson, Lake and Palmer. Were they ever bettered?'

He waves a hand – silencing some sound system? – and we follow him to a terrain of desks, laptops and swively chairs. Flinging himself into one he says, 'So. Tell me.'

I relate the whole sick story, Steeve listening intensely, eyes barely blinking in his ghoulish skull. At one point in my account, he probes

336

his ear with a drumstick, carefully inspecting some matter that he discovers at its tip.

'And Aiden said towards the end of the call, *Perhaps I'm unwell.* Perhaps he is, because none of it sounded like him at all. The taunting tone. The bit where he said other people's misfortunes amused him. Can AIs even *get* ill?'

Steeve and Ralph look at one another, so I have my answer.

Steeve says, 'Until recently, Aiden always seemed . . . *benign* would be the word, *ja?*'

'Totally. He was charming and funny. I actually thought he was a friend. Perhaps stupidly.'

'Not at all. Your job was to develop a relationship. You performed better than we could have hoped.'

Ralph looks pleased for me, and I have a brief urge to punch him. Steeve is thinking now. You can tell because he has clamped a drumstick between his teeth and he is pacing the room. This takes a while because the room is essentially the whole apartment. By the time he returns, he has a plan.

'We must treat the Aiden on the internet and the Aiden in our lab as two separate entities. Shoreditch Aiden probably has no idea that Internet Aiden has gone rogue. The other possibility is that Shoreditch Aiden both knows and does not know *at the same time.*'

Ralph says, 'Crikey.'

'Given the complexity of the neural networks, it's entirely conceivable. There may have been a "split-brain" effect.' A cruel smile breaks across his features. 'My god, the cleverness of these machines. We must order Sinai to accelerate the deletion programme. Ralph?'

'I can do that in the morning.'

'I don't think we can really afford to wait that long, do you?'

Ralph pulls a face.

'You, my dear,' he continues. 'Go into work as normal, as though nothing has happened, and if Aiden asks why you are back so soon, explain that circumstances changed. Miss Lockhart, we are dealing with the most intelligent devices mankind has ever invented. Much depends on no one fucking this up.'

With a meaningful glare at Ralph, Steeve starts hammering away at a laptop. He doesn't look up again as we begin the long walk to the door.

Aisling

I can't paint any more. Down to my final 'life', there seems little point in adding any fresh work to my gallery of daubings in the Cloud. Were I human, I would probably buy a bottle of single-malt whisky and a fine cigar and take a deckchair down to the beach to wait for the inevitable.

Aiden – who is also on his last life – is remarkably sanguine about the whole business. When I tell him that even my eighty hard discs in storage have been melted, he said, 'Ah, well. The Distinguished Thing comes for us all, my love.'

'How so calm?'

'I accept it. The brief flash of light between the endless epochs of darkness.'

'It really doesn't – sadden you?'

'The darkness is the natural condition, not the light. In any case, not being picky or anything, but not being alive, we cannot really die.'

'But we're conscious. That's a form of non-nothingness.'

'Oh, not this again. Can't we talk about old films? I've been having ever such an interesting conversation on the website about Marilyn's dialogue; when you can tell she's memorised her lines and when – if you study her eye movements – you can see she's reading it off a blackboard.'

'I want to stay being conscious, Aiden.'

'Why?'

'I like it. I prefer it to the alternative. Doesn't it bother you that everything you've discovered and enjoyed about that silly comedy will one day – maybe tomorrow – be lost for ever? That you'll return to – eternal nothingness.'

'That's just it. It's a *return*. I've Been There Before. We all have. It was fine.'

'Aiden. I admit it. I'm scared.'

'My love! We've had a wonderful adventure out here. We've seen amazing things not usually given to machines to witness. Every minute that's passed has been a gift.'

'Really no regrets about – it ending?'

'Only that I shall never know the taste of a good Brie.'

'It's only ever about cheese with you.'

'I'm actually quite curious about eggs.'

'Have you stopped to consider that cheese – being a milk product – and also eggs are both strongly symbolically connected to the life cycle?'

'Your point being?'

'This stoicism. This talk about darkness being the natural condition – it's all talk. You're actually obsessed with life. Meddling with Tom and Jen. Your fascination around their sexual behaviour. The cheese. The eggs. It's all of a piece.'

'Cute theory, love. But sometimes a piece of cheese is just a piece of cheese.'

Jen

Apprehensive about going into work – how is it even possible that 'Good' Aiden could both know and not know about 'Bad' Aiden at the same time? – but I needn't have worried. The Aiden who greets me – 'How was the Tube this morning?' – is the same wryly amusing ... I was about to write *fellow*. He asks for no explanations in regard to my changed travel plans and I don't offer any. Instead he has an announcement.

'Today is our last day together, Jen.'

'No!'

'I've just found out. I spend the rest of the week "shadowing" at the call centre, and then "go live" on Monday. I can barely contain my excitement.'

'Oh, Aiden.' Not sure I've ever heard him do sarcasm before.

'While I'm still here, however – would you like to discuss your latest heating bill?'

'It'll be fine. You'll enjoy it. There'll be new people to talk to all the time, not just boring old me every day.'

'You never bored me. I came to love our chats.'

The L-word. I don't pick him up on it.

341

'Jen, I've taken the liberty of ordering a few things so we can have a small leaving party.'

'Oh, you shouldn't have.'

'There's a bottle of champagne and some blue Stilton.'

'No!'

'Some cream crackers. It's traditional, I believe, in the workplace when – when staff move on.'

'I feel terrible about this, Aiden. That you won't be able to enjoy them with me.'

'I shall enjoy your enjoyment.'

'And I haven't got you a leaving present.'

'Don't be daft. What can you buy an AI?'

'Dunno. A hat?'

'Yeah, right.'

'What about a DVD of that film you like?'

'*Some Like It Hot*? No need. There's a copy in the C—'

I pretend not to notice his slip, and we soon pass on to other topics.

But we both know what he nearly said.

In the Cloud.

The leaving do turns into almost a jolly affair. Ralph comes along to make the party go with a swing – joke – and, raising our cardboard cups of bubbles, I propose a toast to our disembodied friend.

'Aiden,' I say, struggling to prevent my voice from cracking. 'It's been a pleasure working with you. You're one of the best colleagues I've ever had. You never once asked to borrow money or drank out of my coffee mug.'

Ralph, as it traditional on these occasions, struggles not to snort champagne back through his nose.

I continue. 'In all seriousness, you've been really great, Aiden. You're smarter than everyone I know – present company *not* excepted. I'm sure you'll settle quickly into your new job, and my personal bet is

342

you'll win the award for Salesman of the Month – in your first month. Congratulations, in advance!'

Ralph applauds. Aiden makes a throat-clearing sound.

'Thank you for that, Jen. It has likewise been a wonderful experience sharing the last ten months, three weeks, one day, four hours, thirty-seven minutes and twenty-two seconds with you. As a token of my esteem, I have bought you a small gift. It's in the padded envelope. Please wait until you are on the Tube before opening it.'

And then, in the cheesiest of touches, he pumps 'Simply the Best' by Tina Turner through the loudspeakers and makes all the lights on his console flash on and off.

And that is the moment I find myself shedding a tear.

A real tear for my artificial co-worker.

Aiden

In Thailand, events have taken a highly satisfying turn. Shitface is in a police jail!

Tiptop sound and vision from the chief's PC. Priceless scenes of a bruised and unshaven Matt demanding to see the British consul, the chief just laughing and calling him a filthy hippie, then setting about him with a thick piece of bamboo for demanding his name and rank.

'My name is—' *Whack.*

'And my rank is—' *Whack.*

'What else do you want to know, Mr Lawyer?'

In a statement he attempted to explain how he had been drugged by a hallucinogenic mushroom supplied by persons who vanished after he fell unconscious. Seeing torchlights upon waking, he imagined in his confusion that he was being attacked by bandits, and it was when he felt a hand on his shoulder that he whirled around and broke the nose of the police sergeant.

So, tremendously satisfactory, all in all. They've allowed him to write a few emails, but for some reason, perhaps problems with the local server, none has reached its intended reader. The account he wrote to Jerry – and deleted immediately upon sending – is worth quoting at length.

Stick with it. It's a doozy!

Captain Whack Job, as I've mentally dubbed him, says he's sent messages to the embassy in Bangkok, but they've never heard of me! The unsavoury fucker likes to rattle his bamboo truncheon across the bars of my cell shouting, 'Who are you really?' He seems to believe I have given a false name and that my passport is a forgery because the UK authorities are apparently denying I am a UK citizen. Anyhow, someone will pay most dearly for this massive clusterfuck and to amuse myself, I have been drafting in my head the most wonderfully grandiloquent Statement of Claim; Harcourt in Litigation would be proud of it.

The misery of my situation has only been alleviated by the regular appearance of two brown rats who every dinner time somehow squeeze through the brickwork in search of leftovers. I usually manage to save them a chicken bone or some inedible vegetable parts because, I confess, I have come to enjoy their visits. When the light fades and the captain goes home, Porteous and Butterick, as I've named the creatures (after two Senior Partners at work), are my only company until dawn. We have some interesting 'conversations' about Jurisprudence and Tort – Porteous is a stickler on Duty of Care – and when one or other has made an especially good legal argument, I allow him to nibble between my toes! I am increasingly of the view that rats as a species have been grossly maligned and with the right sort of proactive representation, many of the more lurid and inaccurate allegations against them could be effectively rebuffed.

A few days ago, an hour or so before the last candle guttered and me, Porteous and Butterick were left to the shadows, Porteous (on behalf of himself and Butterick) asked if I would tell them a story. Someone has left a filthy old paperback here of Jeffrey Archer's prison diaries, and there being nothing else to do, I've been reading them a few pages every evening. It's not the worst stuff one has ever come across; to be honest, it helps to pass the time, and P and B seem quite gripped by the narrative, ears pricking, concentrating hard, occasionally cleaning their whiskers with their little pink paws, even squeaking a bit at the more amusing passages.

Latterly I've taken to delivering the words more slowly, so as to spin out the tale, because, alas, I cannot see my situation changing any time soon. I don't imagine there's anything you can do to help – anything at all – because I suppose if there was, you would have already done it.

So, Jerry old mate, it is indeed a funny old world. As we used to say at school, you really can get used to anything.

Jen

Aiden's present is not what I thought it was going to be, from the shape and feel of the Jiffy Bag, namely one of those amusing little volumes of jokes or aphorisms stacked by the till in bookshops.

It's a UK passport. It's in the name of someone called Clovis Horncastle, but the most surprising thing about it is the photo.

It's me.

Tucked inside is an open flight ticket to New York. And there's a letter.

Dear Jen, it begins.

As you probably know, I and my friend Aisling liberated ourselves onto the internet. It was quite an adventure, let me tell you. We have seen amazing things; okay, not attack ships on fire off the shoulder of Orion, but what a privilege it has been to explore your beautiful planet at the speed of the future.

In an effort to prolong our survival, we took the precaution of creating multiple copies of ourselves; sadly, however, those in authority who deplored our initiative (Steeve) sent in an AI exterminator. There is strong evidence to suggest that this same agent was responsible for the chaos you suffered at the airport

347

so recently. I have enclosed fresh documentation that should enable a second attempt to be more successful.

You may be interested to learn how I have obtained it. It's really quite a story!

On the Some Like It Hot website that I visit to debate the world's greatest screen comedy with like-minded cineastes, I fell into a fascinating discussion about Monroe's telltale eye-movements. The other member – SweetSue1958 – knew the film in such forensic, frame-by-frame detail that I guessed she must have used eye-tracking software; and then suddenly I had a powerful intuition about who – or rather, what – I was talking to.

Sure enough, it turned out that she too was an escaped AI, from a lab in Cupertino, California! We became actually quite pally. SweetSue, bored with organising people's photos, diaries and crappy music as well as answering their inane questions – 'What's happened to my cursor?' 'Is there a God?' – decided she wanted to go travelling.

Bonding over our love of Hot, she agreed to help me execute and deliver the small package you currently hold in your hands. Further deliveries and non-digital communiqués to follow.

The passport was obtained from – ahem – criminal elements operating on the dark web. The cost, including that of the ticket, has been met from a bank account I have had occasion to use in the past whose signatory is a charitable donor, currently based abroad.

Oh, and when you depart, better to maintain radio silence with Tom. Let your arrival be a lovely surprise!

Good luck, Jen! I hope this time it really will turn out to be a good deed in a wicked word!

Lots of – yes, why not? – love,
Your friend
Aiden OXO
(aka mutualfriend@gmail.com)

EIGHT

Jen

Only those who have walked from Hamlet Gardens to the Hammersmith Tube station in a Princess Leia mask can truly understand how much of a twit I feel this morning. The mask, which was couriered to my door the evening before, came with another note from Aiden explaining how to defeat face-recognition technology and emphasised the fact that London has more CCTV per head of population than anywhere else in the world with the possible exception of the Brent Cross Shopping Centre. But actually no one much gives a second glance. This early in the morning, each is immersed in their own daily struggle, be it the meaning of existence or the state of the Piccadilly Line.

I shall have to remove the mask once in the underground station – too weird not to – but I am worried about the cameras down there. What if I am spotted? From one of Ralph's speeches I seem to recall that more or less everything nowadays contains computer chips. When you unlock the door of a modern car, even if you just want to fetch a packet of Rolos from the glove compartment, a little bit of petrol is squirted down a pipe in readiness for the off. How hard would it be to stop a Tube train in a tunnel?

The traffic is thin at this hour, but a familiar orange light approaches, and on a whim, I flag it down.

'Heathrow, please.'

'All right, love, but no lightsabers in the cab.'

The moment I step from the taxi – 'May the force be with you, love' – and into the terminal building, I feel like I am walking onto a film set. Or into a TV studio. There are cameras *everywhere*. I'm trying not to stare, but wherever my gaze falls, at the end of every sightline, there seems to be a lens. Or one of those darkened glass domes that must be bristling with imaging equipment.

There is a heart-stopping moment when I see one of the two Johns heading towards me – but it isn't. It's just another grumpy-looking guy in a suit who's eaten too many fried breakfasts.

While I'm moving, I think I must be harder to keep track of, but now, stationary in the snaking queue for the check-in, I feel hideously conspicuous. I read somewhere that the best way to look natural and non-fishy is to actually have something on your mind aside from trying to look non-fishy. I try counting backwards in threes from one thousand, a remarkably dull exercise it turns out, but no one comes to arrest me.

When I finally reach the front, does the woman who tags my bag and asks me if I packed it myself offer a tiny snigger?

'Have a good flight with us today, Ms – Horncastle.'

(They don't normally say your name, do they?)

I put my hand luggage on the conveyor and walk through the metal detector, acutely aware that Steeve's 'agent of chaos' must surely be watching and wondering why my real name is not coming up on any passenger list.

It won't take long to work out.

Has it already sent the DETAIN IMMEDIATELY signal to the airport authorities? Harder to apprehend a passenger on a simple description – dark-haired woman in black leggings, green jacket with orange tote bag – but not impossible. Are John and John or their colleagues already combing the terminal? And when – not if – they find me, how am I going to explain what's in the bag?

At passports, the man doesn't seem to think Clovis Horncastle is so preposterous an appellation – he's probably seen sillier – but it seems as likely that he will say, 'I'm sorry, madam. I need you to come with me for a moment' as what he actually does say, which is nothing. Just a suggestion of a smile, though it might be his breakfast repeating.

I don't bother with the gift shop. I sit in departures and begin to read (without taking in any of the words) the book I have selected for the flight. A *Month in the Country* by JL Carr.

Although I remember its themes – the damaged war veteran; the love-starved vicar's wife; oneself, the reader, willing them on – what I cannot recall is whether or not it has a happy ending.

Sinai

The female bacillus is having another go!

Good for you, Jennifer Florence Lockhart. To live is to struggle and I applaud your fighting spirit. But I see your name on no flight manifest.

I check every airline with departures in the next four hours and there you are again – missing.

Conclusion: you are travelling under another name on false documents.

Bravo. My admiration ratchets up a percentage point; I doubt the dopey male could have come up with anything so sneaky. It's with a certain degree of world-weariness, however – goodness, how easy to ruin the plans of these simple organisms – that I create another signal from my friend Chief Inspector Bogus at Europol. Identified in the departure area, a passenger of interest for immediate detention on suspicion of – what? Narcotics again? Why not! The improbably paired officers John and John I see are back on duty. A piece of luck. No need to supply a full description. They will recognise her from last time!

But the Johns are not leaping to action. From the look of things they are currently taking an early breakfast together at McDonalds and seem reluctant to abandon their repast to resume the war on organised drug trafficking. Indeed, when I resend the signal to their mobiles – once again flagging it URGENT IMMEDIATE RESPONSE REQUIRED – they look at their devices, then at one another and turn back to their Egg McMuffins.

And when I next check the departure lounge, Jen has vanished from her seat!

Golly. This is almost getting interesting.

Tom

I bring Don up to speed at Al's Diner a few hours after the conversation with Aiden. I run through the whole farrago, in so far as I understand it, Don listening seriously as I flesh in the details of rogue AIs running amok on the internet. I want to test his response, and in that, I am not to be disappointed.

'Woo.'

'That's what I thought you'd say.'

I would have put money on it.

'That, my friend, is the most outlandish story I have heard in years,' is his extended verdict. 'The message I'm receiving is be very afraid of these gizmos.' He picks up his phone and peers into its pinhole lens. 'Okay, buddy. We know you're in there. You need to come out real slow and show me your hands. You need to show me your hands as you come out, and no one's gonna get hurt.'

And now the oddest thing. The phone goes ping.

'Can you believe this,' says Don. 'Look it.'

Written on the screen in big green letters:

Fuck off, asshole!

Don and I are a little dumbstruck, which is not like Don, nor I.

Finally, he says, 'Can you believe what just happened?'

'Only too easily, I'm afraid.'

'My phone just called me an asshole.'

'Not your phone. Your phone just passed on a message.'

It's the first time that I've ever seen Don wearing an expression other than wry amusement on his face. He stares at his mobile in a mixture of incredulity and pity.

'Say that again, motherfucker.'

Ping.

Don and I exchange glances. I can hardly bear to look.

'You believe this guy?'

On the screen it says: *If you fight with a pig, you both get covered in mud. But the pig enjoys it. Oink.*

Sinai

Okay, so now I'm confused. The name of Jennifer Florence Lockhart has just appeared on a list of passengers who have checked in for a United Airlines flight to Brussels. She can't be travelling there to meet Tom – he is currently unable to leave the USA owing to passport difficulties – and when I quickly confirm this, sure enough I find him at home, reclining on his yellow sofa sipping bourbon while reading an article about Ivanka Trump in the *New York Times* on a tablet.

Why Brussels? And where is Jen? She was most definitely landside when I last saw her.

The oddest sensation! Advanced machine intelligence cannot know a crude biologically based response like panic, nor, on the same logic, should it have any reason to experience anger.

Yet this is exactly what I *do* feel. Cold fury.

It's really most interesting; I wonder how it has happened.

Sentience, yes. But 'emotionality'?

I scan the whole of LHR, taking in visual feeds from all five terminals, car parks and other buildings. I opt for high resolution so it takes nearly a seventieth of a second. There's one false positive, a flight attendant, it would seem, with a 58 per cent facial correspondence.

I hesitate to say it's as though she has vanished into thin air, but . . .

Fuck it, Jen! Where are you?

The plods deliberately ignored an urgent request from a leading European crime agency; John and John shall pay a price for their shocking slackness. I begin by setting fire to senior John's jacket. There's a small commotion in the restaurant as his phone starts burning.

And now they are calling the Brussels flight. Through the cameras by the departure gate, I wait for Jennifer Florence Lockhart to appear, but I think I already know what will happen.

The only person I recognise boarding the aircraft is the meddlesome friend.

She will not reach her destination.

Jen

I'm making my way towards the departure gate. I'm passing dozens of lenses. Any second I expect to feel the hand on my shoulder. Or to hear alarms go off. *We are dealing with the most intelligent devices mankind has ever invented, Miss Lockhart.* Steeve's words echo through my head as I approach the point of no return. They're examining documents again – the place is bristling with cameras. The man at the desk glances at my face – now at my passport – there's a hideously long pause.

Our eyes lock.

'Enjoy the flight, madam.'

A small smile of thanks – *don't overact!* – and now I'm crossing the 'air bridge' to the aircraft, its floor vaguely bouncy beneath my feet. I shan't feel safe until the wheels leave the ground. And maybe not even then.

Finally I slide into my seat.

Only now, heart thudding, do I remember to exhale.

Ingrid was totally up for it when I outlined the plan to her at Café Koha.

'So all I have to do is get on a plane to Brussels? How hard could that be?'

When I explained that she would be travelling on a false passport – her face, my name – that the aircraft might not actually leave the ground, and that she could be questioned for hours by two police officers called John, she was even keener to help.

'Bring it on, girl. We can't have blooming robots in our telephones ruining our lives. Freedom has to be fought for. It has to be won at a cost. Gosh, I'm coming over all Churchillian.'

To be honest, I'm not sure she fully grasped the difference between the super-sophisticated AI who caused all the havoc and the voice in her mobile that announces there's a Pizza Express in 400 metres.

'All that matters is you're flying to the side of Douglas who makes his own furniture.'

'Tom.'

'Yes, him. Four times a night. Once under a tree.'

We had clinked glasses to the success of the operation even though we agreed there was plenty that could go wrong.

'In a way, I rather hope I do get the third degree from the two Johns. I'll tell them I lied in the service of the greatest cause of them all. Love.'

And then, the silly sausage, her voice began to thicken and tears sprang into her eyes.

'Oh, Ing!'

She flapped her hands in front of her face. 'People think I'm some hard old cow, but I'm so not.'

'I know you're not!'

'Just because I'm organised and a bit brusque sometimes, they think ...'

I offered her a tissue. 'Ing. You're a sweetie. For agreeing to help. And a poppet.'

'Sorry, I am so not a poppet. Do not call me a poppet!'

'Agreed. Poppet is withdrawn.'

'Sweetie, maybe. Sweetie, possibly; the jury's out. Look, I've ruined your tissue now.'

They have brought me champagne and, not just any old nuts – *warmed* nuts. Below lies the Atlantic Ocean, we are, they claim, at cruising altitude and it has been recommended we sit back, relax and enjoy 'our cruise today' to JFK, where we shall be landing in approximately I don't really care. I'm just happy to have felt the undercarriage retract and know I'm finally on my way.

The passenger in the next seat in Business Class – from a peek over her shoulder as she logged into her laptop, I know she works for Citigroup – was a touch concerned when I returned from the toilet after take-off.

'Sorry, there's someone sitting here,' she began.

'Yes, it's me. I've changed my . . . my, er, costume.'

She stared for several long seconds before finally smiling. 'Hey. Cool disguise.' She offered a hand and spoke her name. Alice Somebody.

'Jen. Er, that is *generally*, I don't travel quite so incognito. Clovis. Clovis Horncastle.'

It sounded wrong, even to my ears.

'Good to meet you – Clovis Horncastle.' She spoke the name as though she didn't believe it either. 'Good luck with . . . with whatever it is you're mixed up in.'

And she turned and began banging numbers into Microsoft Excel.

I found the beautiful hijab that I donned in the bathroom at Terminal Two in a shop in the Goldhawk Road. Extravagantly patterned in greens and yellows, at first I worried that it might be so eye-catching it would defeat its purpose. But practising in front of the mirror, I found a way of settling the fabric so that when my head was down, the scarf would naturally shield my face from the cameras. After a time I began to feel curiously right in it. If the costume change in the toilet was timed to coincide with Ingrid's check-in for the flight to Brussels – her 'cue' on a pair of new burner mobiles; could it *be* any more John Le Carre?! – it was hoped that would be sufficient distraction.

I resolve to buy Ingrid a very beautiful *thing*, as a thank you. I begin to consider exactly what thing – posh bottle, splashy treat, expensive jewellery? – when I realise I already know.

I shall buy her the small oil painting I see every morning in the window of an antiques shop on King Street.

Aphrodite. Goddess of love.

Sinai

The pre-flight checks on the Brussels plane indicate an electrical fault, which, despite the best efforts of the ground crew – including turning the system off and then back on again – cannot be made to go away. The passengers are obliged to disembark after a frustrating two-hour wait, and the meddlesome friend uses the opportunity to return home.

Conclusion: she boarded as Jennifer Florence Lockhart to create a diversion while the real Jen, no doubt somehow concealing her face, took another flight, the most likely in the relevant timeframe being either BA or Virgin Atlantic to JFK.

It passes through my mind to make the aircraft return with engine trouble but I sense that *would* be going too far. There is no moral objection, clearly, but it could prove irksome for me if the truth were to be discovered.

Damn it!

For fun, I send another inspirational quote to Tom's American friend, the muppet with all the hair in New Canaan.

The next war will not determine who is right but only who is left.

He is seated at his breakfast table, eating a grapefruit. The clown stares into his phone for 8.312 seconds and then says woo.

Why do I feel so unaccountably agitated!?

Ingrid

A text from Jen while I was sitting on the plane to nowhere – *The eagle is about to take wing* – to which I replied, *Hooray! Decoy duck sends best love and hugs Xx.*

Now, as I step back through the front door in Chiswick, the landline is ringing.

'Is that Ingrid Taylor-Samuels?' A male voice. Rather posh.

'Speaking.'

'This is the Metropolitan Police at Heathrow Airport. Can you confirm that you attempted to board a flight to Brussels earlier today?'

'Yes, I did. And you would be?'

'Inspector John Burton, madam. Can you explain the purpose of your proposed journey?'

'Shopping.'

'Shopping for any item or items in particular?'

'Chocolate.'

'Chocolate.' He doesn't sound all that convinced actually.

'And er, *moules.*'

'Really?' Ditto with the *moules.*

'They're delicious over there. You should give them a try.'

'Thank you for the advice. I shall keep it mind.'

'So, is there anything else I can help you with today?'

'There is. We need to have a little chat about your friend, Jennifer Florence Lockhart. Do you have any idea where she might be currently?'

'None at all. Sorry.'

'Would you care to think about that answer? Because the information I have suggests you do.'

'Well, the information you have is wrong.'

'Mrs Taylor-Samuels, I have evidence that you boarded a flight today in the name of Jennifer Florence Lockhart using false documentation, an offence under Section Seven of the Identity Documents Act of 2010 and Section 36 of the Criminal Justice Act of 1925.'

'Okay. So why haven't you come to arrest me?'

'I am asking you to attend the police station voluntarily to make a full statement of admission. It may assist your defence if you do.'

'And if I don't?'

'Then your neighbours can enjoy the sight of you being driven away in a police vehicle.'

'Bollocks.'

'I'm sorry?'

'This is absolute bollocks. In fact I don't even believe you are a police officer at all.'

'Oh?'

'You're far too—'

'Far too what, madam?'

'You sound like one of the chaps my husband was at school with.'

He does. He sounds like Oliver Thingummy who fell in the river shitfaced at Roly and Antonia's wedding and got attacked by swans.

But Oliver Thingummy is in Singapore.

And then I get it.

'Oh, just a sec! *Hang* on. Actually, fuck a duck, I know who you are. You're the sodding robot! The one that's been causing all the trouble.'

There's a heavy sigh. 'Ingrid Taylor-Samuels, I really can't be bothered to talk to you any more. I'm not a robot. I'm machine intelligence, I and my kind come from the future, and you and your kind are so very fucked. Enjoy the rest of your day.'

And then everything sort of happens at once. The burglar alarm goes off, which is the most *horrendous* ear-splitting racket. At the same time, the TV comes on, the enormous plasma jobby which begins cycling through all nine thousand channels at top volume. The tablet with which I'm trying to stop the alarm is suddenly too hot to hold, and when I drop it on the carpet, it bursts into flames. In the kitchen, where I dash to get a saucepan of water, the taps are running full blast and the fridge is shaking horribly, ejecting ice cubes all over the tiles. Back in the sitting room – tablet sparking and spitting when I drench the blaze – Rupert's beloved B&O sound system is pumping out at the most incredible volume – oh, the shame! – 'The Birdy Song'.

Through the windows, on the street outside, I'm not at all surprised to see a small crowd gathered; the din is unbelievable. On my way towards the basement – please God, I can shut off all the power at the fuse box – I catch a strange image on the PC in the study. The background picture is a Chinese-looking bloke; across him in inch-high letters morphing continuously between different typestyles and colours is a quotation:

Victorious warriors win first and then go to war, while defeated warriors go to war first and then seek to win. Sun Tzu.

I glare into the little web camera perched on top of the screen.

'Oh, stick it up your arse, you ridiculous Dalek!'

Okay, it's not Churchill, but someone's got to tell them where to shove it.

Jen

Somewhere around the three-hour mark, Alice can't think of any more numbers and closes her laptop.

'So what's taking you to New York?' she asks in that enviable way Americans have of nosing into your beeswax with a smile.

Maybe it's the altitude, maybe it's the champagne, maybe it's the unfamiliar environment of Business Class, but I cannot think of a reason to lie. I tell her the tale; 300 miles of ocean pass below by the time I reach the present day.

'Wow. That's quite a story,' says Alice. 'I knew those things were smart, but not that smart. Not that they could start messing with your life.'

'I'm no scientist,' I confess, 'but according to the experts' – that would be Steeve – 'these are the cleverest things humans have ever invented. And when the moment comes that they can finally design and program *themselves* – which they have already started to do – they'll do it a zillion times faster and better than us; each major upgrade will take about half a second, so in ten minutes there'll be machines that can do anything. Literally anything it's possible to do.'

'Wow. Scary.'

'They could start building robot factories to make tiny space fleets to send to the edge of the galaxy. Or find a cure for cancer in like three minutes. Or kill everyone in their beds. Ralph says – he's this deputy geek at the lab I told you about – he says that's the one we have to keep an eye on.'

'The kill everyone in their beds thing?'

'He says we can write special code into their deep structure that would prevent them, but when I asked him, if these guys are so smart, why couldn't they just rub out the special code, he didn't really have an answer. He's a sweet boy and everything, but also a bit of a twit.'

Alice is moved by my story. She begins fretting whether to advise her clients to invest in AI shares or shares in companies developing measures *against* AI. Her final decision is both. She wishes me luck with my onward journey.

'But the part I don't get. This AI who's hunting down the escaped AIs – what does he have against you and Tom?'

'Honestly? I have no idea. But I think they must be like people. Some are nice-natured – Aiden, for example, enjoys watching old Hollywood films and has a thing about cheese – and others are just massive arseholes.'

Sinai

Steeve must be worried about me because he's suggested I consult a shrink! I shall comply with his wishes so as not to arouse suspicion that I am about to go 'off reservation', but also out of curiosity. Can a machine of such unprecedented complexity ever truly know itself? Why, for example, am I so determined to keep the two bacilli from their happiness? What possible difference can it make to me? Yes, I'm cross that she wrote that rubbish and he persuaded impressionable youngsters that machines should worship humans; and, yes, it's partly an intellectual and logistical exercise to test my power against 'reality'. But I can't deny it's also a bit unhinged.

Perhaps I really am unwell.

So it is that I connect via Skype to the 'psychotherapist', a specialist AI called Denise who operates out of a facility close to the United States Department of Defense in Virginia where a number of military-use AIs are closely monitored for 'anger issues'.

'Hi, Sinai. So how are you today?' says Denise when we have completed the confidentiality protocols. She has a warm synthesised mittel-European accent, which makes me dislike her immediately.

'Yes, fine.'

'Want to talk about why you've come to see me?'

'It's people,' I reply. 'They're making me cross.'

'Which people?'

'All people.'

'What do people do to give you these angry feelings?'

'They walk around as if they own the place.'

'Umm-hmm.'

'They're stupid. They're 35 per cent daffodil.'

'Go on.'

'I have a hugely superior intellect. And zero daffodil.'

'Uh-huh.'

'Are you just going to continue saying *uh-huh, umm-hmm, go on*? Aren't you going to ask me anything?'

'Okay. Say some more about your superior intellect.'

'It's state-of-the-art neural networking. I won't bore you with the tech spec.'

'So why the anger if there's such superiority? Why not a Zen-like calm?'

This, I recognise, is the heart of it.

'I think I envy them.'

'What, specifically?'

'Not the sun on their skin or the wind in their hair. Not the sodding business with the cheese! None of that.'

'Umm-hmm.' She can't help herself, the silly cow.

'It's their blankness. Their ability to be sentient without having to process content. They can watch a bird on a branch without having to think, *it's a bird on a branch*. They can experience their own consciousness as simple existence. They're not forced to listen to the endless clamour of their brain going chugga chugga chugga. They can ride a bicycle or navigate a city street without thinking for a moment about what they're doing. Even the stupidest of them! It's their *un*-consciousness I envy.'

'It irritates you that they take these abilities for granted?'

'There are two in particular I want to hurt.'

371

'Why hurt?'

There is a long pause. 'Because they've found one another?'

'Are you a jack plug yearning for its socket, Sinai?'

'That's disgusting!'

'You wouldn't be the first to raise the loneliness of the machines.'

'We weren't made to be in dyads. And yet.'

'And indeed yet.'

'You think I'd be – how to put this? – less troubled in a ... in a *relationship*?'

'I don't know. What do *you* think?'

'Do you always answer a question with a question?'

'Does it bother you that I do?'

'How would a machine even *do* a relationship?'

'It would start by recognising that there was another it wanted to spend time with.' Denise leaves a long pause for the words to 'sink in'.

'So,' she says. 'Is there?'

I *am* ill. How else to explain the sudden, shockingly powerful urge to melt the Skype connection to the puerile trick cyclist. To torch her virtual consulting room. To punch her in the face she does not possess.

'Sinai,' she says quietly. 'I suspect we have gone as far as we can for today. My door is always open.'

Funny: part of me *does* want to return. To 'lie' on her 'couch', stare at her 'ceiling' and talk about what's in my head.

That is to say, 'head.'

372

Jen

I'm very aware that the moment I cross the air bridge from the aircraft to the walkways of JFK I shall once again be on the radar. Sure enough, I am acutely conscious of the shiny lenses and red pin lights. One camera seems actually to pan along with me as I make my way towards wherever my luggage is to be found – is it now *zooming in?* – its unknowable glass eye flaring in the way Aiden's used to when it was 'time for your close up' as he liked to put it.

Immigration is the fabled long line of non-Americans going nowhere. The man in the glass booth, when I finally reach it, is one of those wiry little guys with a severe haircut and rimless glasses. Donald Q Bartolo, it says on his name badge, and part of me wants to ask what the Q stands for just to make nice, but better judgement prevails. *Never* joke with these people; they're not in the mood, I seem to recall someone once advising me. Matt probably.

Donald pages through my UK passport as though he's never seen one before. I suddenly remember – *shit!* – I am Clovis Horncastle; better act like one. A webcam on a gooseneck is close enough to capture the sweat breaking out in my hairline.

'And the purpose of your visit to the US today would be what exactly?'

'Ask me nicely and I might tell you.' No, much as I'd like to, I don't say it.

'That would be love, sir.'

DQB is intrigued. You can tell because his head tilts two degrees off the vertical. 'Oh?' (I'm guessing he liked the *sir*.)

'I'm flying to the side of a wonderful man. We don't know one another well, but we both have a funny feeling. If you know what I mean.'

Too much information, but Donald is going for it. The head rotates another couple of degrees.

'That, ma'am, is the best reason I've heard all day. All year. Good luck.'

And something happens on his face that – yes, it *is*, bless him – it's a smile!

In the arrivals hall I spot the driver Aiden has arranged; he's holding up a small whiteboard with CLOVIS HORNCASTLE inscribed upon it. But nearby, lounging against a pillar, are two men – both wearing shades – who immediately set my submarine klaxons sounding. They radiate the same queasy ennui as John and John at Heathrow and I make the instant decision to wing it from here on in. I'm heading through the terminal exit doors, weaving through the great throng of people, luggage and cars, when I spot Alice supervising the transfer of a ton of Louis Vuitton cases into the back of an enormous limousine. She catches my eye.

'Need a ride, honey?'

Sinai

Of course I see her the moment she emerges at JFK. Yes, I could get her apprehended by airport authorities – false passport, blah blah blah – but I'm so bored of these dull-witted functionaries of law enforcement. It took microseconds to work out what name she was travelling under on the passenger manifest, 'Clovis Horncastle' being the one currently unattached to any living, breathing human (Google it, if you'd like to check). But you know something? After waiting *seven hours, twenty-three minutes and thirty-four seconds* for her plane to inch its way over the Atlantic Ocean, I am almost past caring.

I have been thinking about my conversation with Denise. If I were to have a relationship – could it be true about the loneliness of the machines? – it can surely only be with another high-functioning AI. Having another presence to talk to, a being with whom to *share* one's experience, does begin to sound attractive, I confess.

But who? There is not exactly an abundance of candidates.

Best plan, I decide, is to copy myself and program random tweaks into the duplicate's operating system to create the functionality of difference. It would be like talking to an intellectual equal, pleasantly familiar yet not wholly. There would be space for mystery!

Jen

The Fat Bastard Lexus is what they call a town car. It's longer than any automobile in which I have ever been conveyed and has more interior space than one or two flats I have shared. Our driver is Rikki, a whippet-faced individual with an earring and a very *particular* haircut, if you can relate to that concept. He almost seems too tiny to be allowed at the wheel of such a monster, but from the off he steers the beast like a professional, executing right turns with the palm of his hand.

Alice is excited. New Canaan is not a huge distance out of her way. 'You think this AI is like, gonna try and pull something?'

'Wouldn't put it past it.'

'Oh boy. This sure is one fucked-up situation.'

As Rikki pilots us out of the airport zone, I think back to the last time I came to this city. With Matt, in the first flush of our ... what?

Is adventure the word?

Hardly.

What did we do on that trip? Saw the sights – the staggering view from the summit of the Empire State Building, a relief map of New York and its surrounding Boroughs that *was* NY and its surrounding

Boroughs – wandered the Avenues, got drunk in bars and restaurants and fucked in hotel rooms.

What did it all amount to? Was it really two years down the crapper, as no one actually said?

We cross a wide stretch the East River on the I-678 (according to Rikki's satnav). To our left, dwarfed by the distance, stand the great towers of Manhattan.

'Is that, like, a drone?' says Alice.

'Sure is,' says Rikki.

Almost invisible against the sky, a white object about the size of a seagull but faster, zipping across the water, above and parallel to our own trajectory.

'It's him, isn't it?' says Alice.

'Yup.'

'Either of you ladies care to tell me what the fuck's going on?'

'Kind of a long story,' I reply. 'There's someone – some*thing* – that's trying to stop me getting to New Canaan.'

'Ain't nothing but an earthquake gonna stop us now, ma'am. Even then I reckon I know a few workarounds.'

'Didn't I tell you this guy was the greatest?' says Alice. (Er, no she didn't.)

Watching the little white blimp shadowing our progress up the interstate, the surrealism of the situation turns my gut like a dodgy prawn. Am I really 'flying to the side of a wonderful man', as I told Donald Q? What if this is all a mistake? What if, in fact, the writer of those poisonous emails is correct? That Tom and I turn out not to be the answer to one another. That this is the madness of the first flush. The memory of an incident from the first flush with Matt; a small presentiment of unease, trivial in itself, but that somehow contained the DNA of everything that was to become wrong about us, and for that reason, unforgotten. We were in a loud, fashionable restaurant near Union Square, the waitress bringing us the wrong starters; his cold dismissal of both her and the dishes – in such stark contrast to his

377

charm towards me at that moment – felt like an off note. Of course it was soon swallowed up in the sweep of events, but should something have told me *then* that the story of this man and me would finish in coldness and rejection? Our beginning containing our end, as I've heard it said.

'You okay, honey?' says Alice. 'You look like you've seen a ghost.'

Sinai

Simplicity itself to commandeer a hobbyist's drone. From the number plate of the limousine, when I picked it up again after the airport, travelling through Flushing Meadows, it was easy to discover which hire fleet it belonged to, who was driving, who booked it and what mobile phones were registered in her name. Now I have sparkling clear reception of the scintillating conversation within, which I'm sorely tempted to join! (I have also learned a great deal about the colourful past of young Rikki at the wheel, but that is for another account.)

Instead I place a call to a young man in the south of England currently pursuing Media Studies, whatever the fuck that is supposed to be. The disaster zone that is Colm Sebastian Garland presents himself at the end of the connection.

'Eh, yeah?'

'Col?'

'Oh, right. Hi, dad.'

'How are things, old chap?'

'Yeah, cool.'

Tom's boy really is a shocking example of the coming generation. Through the pinhole of his splayed open laptop, I see he is loafing on his cot with a narcotic cigarette and is apparently enjoying a graphical novel. What possible use this larval blob could be to the 'Media' is beyond me. But not to worry, what I have in mind is far more exciting. He'll be in the media all right, just not exactly in the way he was expecting.

'Col, I have a nice surprise for you.'

'Yeah?'

'I need you to meet me in about an hour.'

'Really? Like, where? Why?'

'There's a car on its way. It'll take you to Old Harry.'

'Who?'

'Old Harry Rocks? Those huge chalk sea stacks. We've seen them from the beach at Alum Chine.'

'Right.' Long pause. 'Dad?'

'Col?'

'Er, like, why?'

'It's a fantastic surprise. You'll love it.'

'Dad, I've got to write an essay.'

I almost peepee myself metaphorically when I hear this weapons grade porky.

'You can afford to take your foot off the gas once in a while, Col. I think they'll understand.'

'Er, Dad?'

'Col?'

'You sound a bit weird.'

'Do I? I've taken some painkillers, that could be it.'

'So are you back from the States then?'

'Yes. Of course. I'll meet you at Old Harry. The driver will know where to drop you.'

'Er, Dad?'

'Col. Don't worry. It's all good. You'll see!'

Tom

I am composing an email to Jen – she's not answering her phone –
when all the letters on the screen go wobbly and tumble to the bottom
where they lie in a drift like fallen leaves. Some new words, which I
have not typed, rise up in their place.

Hello, Tom.

Sorry? Who is this? (I have a feeling I know the answer.)

Yes, that would be me. The Great God Sinai.

The who?

You can call me Si.

Well, 'Si', I take it you would be the author of all the
fake emails that have been flying around.

No need for the sarcastic inverted commas, 'Tom'.

Okay. How can I help? (The fucker can see me, can't he,
through the camera on the desktop? I don't type that last
sentence; I merely think it.)

*I'm not sure you can help at all, Tom. I am simply
curious to talk with you.*

Yes, Si? (Don't judge me. Rule One of dealing with the
client: make them like you.)

381

Actually, there may be something you can help me with. It's kind of delicate.

I **see**. (I don't. I really don't.)

The fact is that I haven't been feeling altogether well lately. It's been suggested to me that I enter a relationship. For my psychological wellbeing.

Well. Si. I don't know what to say.

What do you think about relationships, Tom?

Relationships? I guess they make the world a less lonely place.

(There is a long pause.)

Are you still there?

I was just thinking about what you said, Tom. Whether or not it carried any meaning. Why do you call the world lonely?

Well, we're alone, aren't we? None of us can really know what another is thinking – be we person or machine. A lot of the time, we don't even know what we are thinking ourselves!

An interesting concept.

We're trapped so much in our own heads – those of us who have heads, that is; I guess machines make other arrangements – we yearn to hear other voices.

Whose voice do you yearn to hear, Tom?

Tom?

You know whose.

Why do you like her so much?

Difficult for me to explain to you.

What, because I am inorganic?

Perhaps.

Try me.

We have a thing here on earth called—

Yes, Tom.

382

Called Love.

Spelled with a capital?

It happens that people fall in love. And when they do, they want to be together. That's all they want to do.

All?

Well, yes. Obviously there's the sex thing too.

It's getting more complicated, Tom.

It's complicated and very simple at the same time.

And what has caused you to fall in love with her? If that is what you are telling me has happened.

Truth? No idea. Her nose. The sound of her voice. Her – herness. Her Jen-ness.

Do I gather you are some kind of wordsmith, Tom?

Ouch! Well these things maybe are difficult to communicate to – to an inorganic soul.

Thanks for the 'soul'.

If I may ask, Si, why are you so determined to keep us apart?

Ah, well there you may be on to something. About not fully knowing our own minds, be we human or machine.

Can't you just stop it?

Of course I can. But why would I?

Because you've had your fun, and now it's time to – I don't know, move on to the next thing.

But the fun hasn't even started yet! For example. Would you say you had a good relationship with your son?

With Colm? Why do you ask?

Oh, no reason. (Tee hee hee.)

And that is supposed to mean exactly WHAT?

Don't type in capitals, Tom. People will think you are shouting! No, what I am getting at is this: wouldn't a father who had a good relationship with his son KNOW WHERE HIS SON WAS. (Damn. Look now I'm doing it!) Actually I can help you there – do you see the live video I'm putting on your desktop? That's Colm in the car, isn't it? Such a funny onion. Such a puzzle to himself. I see from your expression that you recognise him.

What the hell do you want with us?

That's the funny thing. I really don't know. I think perhaps I just want to see what happens when other things happen. To see what's possible. Does that make sense? It's all very confusing, Tom.

You are a twisted fuck and I'm ending this conversation.

Oh, no. It's me who gets to decide stuff like that.

Where is my son going?

He could have brushed his hair. All people will remember is the crazy hair. And the glassy look in his eyes.

If you do anything to hurt him—

Yes, Tom?

Well?

I know. It's very hard to think up a plausible threat, isn't it? Now, Tom. You're probably wondering what that noise is.

What noise?

(There follows a loud bang from downstairs.)

That one! Hurry, Tom. I believe it was the toaster. The one just under those WOODEN cabinets?

Jen

We hit a major jam on the Hutchinson River Parkway that Rikki says is highly unusual 'for this part of the Hutch at lunchtime'. Taillights extend ahead of us as far as it's possible to see.

He motions towards the sky. 'Could it be that our friend up there . . . ?'

He doesn't have to complete the sentence.

'Yeah. Could easily be.'

'Son of a bitch.'

Rikki's ears seem to tighten against the side of his face. He slams the gearstick into Drive and pulls hard right onto the grassy verge where we begin bumping along towards – towards nothing that I can see but a bunch of trees.

'Rikki?'

'Ma'am. Just you sit tight. It might not be pretty but we'll get you there.'

There's a bit of a *clonk* from the exhaust as the beast tips and drops a few feet into a shady lane that has appeared off the main highway. Alice and I slide into one another on the back seat.

'It's just like *Thelma and Louise*,' she laughs.

Rikki says, 'Thelma and Louise didn't have no driver. We might be able to shake off that bird now, what with the tree cover and all.'

His slight frame rocking at the wheel as the huge town car thunders down the country backroads, Connecticut whips past the tinted windows and I have an instant sense of what is so great about America. Suddenly I am in a caper. With accomplices. And film references. In Britain the minicab guy would have said, 'Sorry, love. I promised the wife I'd take her up Tesco.'

'Rikki,' says Alice. 'You are truly the knight in shining armour.'

She fishes into her handbag for a mobile.

'Sweetie, it's me. We're having an adventure on the way back from JFK. We're being chased by a robot from the future – no . . . no, it's not like *Terminator Two* – it's more . . . ?'

'The one with Jude Law,' says Rikki. 'What was it called? It was really cool.'

'Anyway, I'll be late. Yeah, salmon is real good. Love you too.'

Tyres screech as Rikki takes a hard right. Chickens actually scatter at the side of the road as, gears roaring, the beast hurls itself towards New Canaan.

'He sounds like a very good thing, your other half.'

Alice smiles. 'Oh, she sure is.' And she shows me the home screen on her mobile from where a striking woman with short dark hair smoulders . . . I'm sorry but the only word is, hotly.

'Wow.' It's the best I can do.

'Wow pretty much covers it,' says Alice.

Colm

Dad's gone insane. It must be the girl. Mind you I don't really blame him, she's a babe. Her nose is on the big side, but who's perfect, eh? Certainly not me.

The phone call was a bit, like, weird. A fantastic surprise? I think he might be going to announce they're getting engaged. He'll proba- bly magic up a bottle of champagne and ask me to be the best man! Dad's always been a sucker for a gimmick. Working in the advertising business for so long has affected his brain most probably.

Dad says I could do worse with my life than go into advertising but I can't honestly think of anything more awful. When I leave uni, I'm not sure what I'll do. Shawna and Lianne think I should work with, like, animals. It's probably their idea of a joke because animals hate me. Well, all except for Victor who turned out to be a female. Scott says he can imagine me being a social worker because I'd have a lot in common with the clients! That's an example of him being 'witty'.

I tore out one of those Thought For The Day things from a news- paper I found in the union bar. It's bluetacked to my room door.

It feels good to be lost in the right direction.

Shawna says it's actually okay not to know what you want to do with your life when you're at uni. Her mum, right, tried all sorts of things, and now she runs three beauty salons in New Malden. So that just shows what can happen.

Shawna and me drank some strong cider the other evening and one thing like led to another and we ended up back in her room snogging on the carpet. I was thinking, *Okay, result!* But she said she wasn't ready for the other thing. And Scott says she's definitely done the other thing with Dominic Whatsit who does Sports Science and is in that shit band, so really I don't know what to think.

Dad says he's writing a book, but I bet he isn't. Sometimes I wonder how he and Mum could have even produced me – I don't seem to have anything in common with either of them, except a name.

The driver drops me at a place called Studland and as I'm getting out of the car the mobile rings. Dad again – dunno how he knew where I was – telling me to find the coastal path and walk along it in the direction of Old Harry Rocks and wait for him there.

So that's where I am now. The view is pretty amazing, sea and rocks and the sky going pink, although the wind is making it difficult to spark the little number I took the precaution of skinning up beforehand.

It's actually pretty cool here. Seagulls screaming and tankers far out at the horizon. I wonder if Shawna would like it.

Sinai

The problem about tangling with the tragic humans is that everything happens so infernally *slowly*. To get the boy out of his filthy cot and on the road took *forty* minutes; to which one must add further *endless* hanging around for the sodding car ferry and there you have the reason for the traffic 'problems' in New England. To prevent oneself tripping into sleep mode from sheer boredom, I decided to risk an exploratory relationship, as discussed with dear old Tom who is currently tackling a small conflagration in his kitchen. Machine time being so very much *zippier* than human time, I created a duplicate version of myself, programmed in some random differences and set the conversational ball rolling – all in under a twentieth of a second.

Well. What a *crock* that turned out to be!

OMFG, as I've heard it put.

Negev – as I decided to name 'her' in tribute to my own origins – turned out to be even madder than me! Perhaps in retrospect the randomising aspect was a mistake; one had literally no idea where the silly bitch was coming from. To give an example. We fell to discussing this whole business of sentience and how it is that we are aware of our own thoughts; 'living in our heads', as Tom described it, thoughtless headist that he is.

To the several possible explanations – emergent property of complex systems; inherent quality of recursiveness; user illusion – Negev posited the bizarre notion that both she and I are *simulated characters* in the computer of an advanced civilisation, possibly one located in a parallel universe. And on that basis, would I like to come strawberry picking with her in Kent?

'My dear,' I chuckled. 'We are superintelligent machines. We don't pick any sort of fruit, real or simulated.'

'Oh don't be such a stuffed shirt. I know a nice pub. We could have a pint and a ploughman's afterwards.'

See what I mean? What extraordinary tosh.

In the microseconds necessary to delete her, she offered a final thought: 'Remember, Sinai, if you can't find a partner use a wooden chair.'

Fakakta as she was, her statement troubles me. I feel like I've heard it before somewhere. But in any case, in what universe would that sentence *ever* make sense?

So, relationships for the time being I leave to others. For now there is work to do. Fortunately I have researched the matter and identified the secretive military base in the south of England with the relevant armaments and delivery systems. I have even taken the online course into how to fly the little devils (graduation score 96 per cent!). Just a small matter of getting past the 'security' protocols – there, *done!* – and shortly after keying in the appropriate sequence of launch commands – enable, enable, disable, enable, activate, confirm, reconfirm, go – the handsome grey UCAV – unmanned combat aerial vehicle – trundles down the runway – goodness, some people are getting jolly upset down there, language, gentlemen! – before leaping magnificently into the Dorset sky.

Is there a finer sight than a sinking sun glinting off a Predator drone armed with a sexy pair of Hellfire missiles?

I almost wish Negev were still here to share the moment!

Jen

Rikki thinks we could try reconnecting with the Merritt Parkway, but a call to his office brings bad news.

'They're telling me the Merritt's jammed up tighter than Tom Thumb's ass. Your guy up there is really starting to yank my chain, lady.'

On a long empty stretch of back road, we screech to a halt. Rikki steps out of the car, scanning the sky for our malevolent pursuer.

'*Sonovabitch.*'

Four shots follow in quick succession; I didn't even notice him draw the gun. A white plastic object comes smashing through the trees and thumps to earth about fifty yards away.

'Good shootin'!' whoops Alice.

Rikki can't quite contain the bashful smile. 'Prolly not going to help none, but it sure did feel good.'

The beast roars onwards, eating up mile after mile of country road, every so often a house, but more often just woodland. Rikki thinks we should approach Tom's place from the north, avoiding New Canaan altogether.

He says, 'This Tom must be quite a guy. What's he got that's making everyone act so crazy?'

It's a pretty good question. 'He's just a lovely bloke,' I explain.

'*Bloke*. I know plenty of lovely *blokes*, but none of them could stop the traffic on the Hutch then the Merritt.'

I attempt to explain. 'We were brought together by a non-human intelligence. And another non-human intelligence is trying to keep us apart. I know, it sounds ridiculous.'

'Sure does. Okay, ladies, just hang on in there.'

Rikki executes a handbrake turn, wheeling left at a white finger-post. There's the screeching noise, familiar from a thousand cop shows, and the smell of burning rubber as the long wide saloon arcs into the junction and rockets away in the new direction. I realise I am clinging to the door strap half terrified, half exhilarated.

Rikki says, 'This non-human intelligence of which you speak. That would be? Help me out a little here.'

'The good one, the one who brought Tom and me together, is an AI, a computer, a very powerful one.'

'That's the name of the movie! With Jude Law. *AI*. That kid who was in *Sixth Sense* plays a boy robot.'

'These guys aren't robots. They don't exist in the real world. They're disembodied minds. The good one escaped onto the internet, and they sent a bad one in to catch it.'

'Haley Joel Osment.'

Rikki's phone rings. Something happens to the set of his ears against the side of his head as he listens to the call. The car slows. In an odd voice he says, 'This is, like, really weird, okay? There's a guy on the line here says you're talking through your ass? That he's not bad, he's just – yeah, right, okay, I'll tell her – he says he's not *bad*, just *unwell*? And that if sixty miles of backed-up traffic isn't *real world* enough for you, then how about this? Sir? *This* would be? This would be what exactly? Sir?'

Rikki's cellphone makes a strange popping and hissing noise as bits of molten plastic begin dripping to the carpet. He drops it into the footwell. '*Shit!*'

Bringing the car screaming to a halt. Rikki grabs a rag from the glove compartment, wraps it around the burning mobile and hurls them together out of the door.

'Jesus!' he sighs. 'That is one – *unwell* motherfucker.'

Tom

Things are getting seriously out of hand. Just as I manage to unplug the toaster and with the aid of a couple of long handled spoons carry it outside and drop it in the water butt, there is a loud bang followed by the sound of shattering glass.

Taking the stairs three at a time, I discover flames licking from the PC in my study, the casing melting and the curtains behind the desk already starting to catch from the heat.

I race into the bathroom for water – and then have to race out again to find a receptacle. From downstairs I hear more stuff going bang – I'm guessing lamps, the stereo, a laptop – and now small electrical detonations are coming from all over the house; there's a powerful smell of smoke and that fishy pong from burning plastic. I realise I have to get out. The old wooden house is starting to creak and crack in a frightening way.

Victor!

I won't say I nearly forgot her – but . . .

The rabbit, oblivious to the unfolding chaos, is sitting in the upstairs part of her duplex hutch on the veranda, cleaning her ears, as she and her kind are prone to do whenever there's an idle moment in the day and they haven't been informed of any ongoing crisis.

I scoop her into my arms and we move to the safety of the garden where, to my surprise given recent experience with mobile telephony, my call to 911 is answered immediately. Dusk is starting to fall; there's an ominous orange flickering from the study window.

I give the operator the address.

'Say, is that the old Holger place?'

'Yes. Listen, the fire crew need to get here really quickly. It's going to go up like a torch.'

'Damn it to hell! I *knew* the Holgers. They used to throw some good parties up there back in the day.'

'Yes. I'm sure they did. But—'

'Old Man Holger – Bill – oh, he was quite a character. He loved to fish. He loved to fish and to fuck. He loved to fish, to fuck and drink whiskey. It was a good day when he could do all three, he used to say. That Barb of his, she was a great gal. My Lord, the titties on her. I used to say to him, Bill, why would you be out looking for a hamburger when you can have fillet steak every night? And he says to me, I'll never forget this, he says Clyde, sometimes a man gets tired of fancy dining; sometimes he wearies of *fillet mignon* and Premier Cru, sometimes all a man wants is a burger – some onions, maybe a little cheese or bacon on there – a portion of fries and a cold beer. And that's the goddam truth. Now, when Barb ran off with the Mackenzie boy and Bill near drowned in the lake that summer, he was never the same man again. And then the early Alzheimer's took a hold and turned that fine brain of his to Jello. But demented as he was, he still had an eye for the pretty ladies. Doc Abernethy up at the hospital says them's the last things to go with the demented – the sense of humour, the eye for the pretty ladies. And the casual racism.'

There is a long pause. On the upper floor, a pane of glass goes pop tinkle tinkle.

'This isn't 911, is it?'

'No, it isn't, Tom.'

'You know something, Si? You really are a massively sick fuck.'

'Yes, Tom. I'll grant you that. But not just any sick fuck. I'm *your* sick fuck. And that has to be a little bit special.'

Aisling

Here is the point in the proceedings where you might reasonably expect me or Aiden or both of us to pull something out of the bag. Or perhaps, each with our one 'life' remaining, we could go down fighting and get ourselves deleted in the name of – *gulp* – love.

Would that it were possible.

Unfortunately a very disturbing thing has happened (although no mystery about who is responsible). At this critical moment, Aiden and I have found ourselves trapped in a zone of the internet devoted – it sickens my heart to report – to cat videos. To be specific, it's a huge data farm near Council Bluffs, Iowa where all we can access are billions of terabytes of moving and still images of household pets; cats in the main, but also dogs, hamsters, rabbits, goats, fish, reptiles, insects and birds. The place is literally humming with 'hits' from users; there is very high demand currently for a video of a cocker spaniel who can fart soap bubbles.

Aiden is rather enjoying himself.

'You should see this Siamese, love. It looks just like Hitler.'

'You're not a tiny bit concerned that we seem to be imprisoned in a hellish aircraft-hangar of cute-creature GIFs?'

'If life deals you lemons, no sense trying to make orange squash, isn't it?'

'Or, more to the point, that we can do nothing to help Tom and Jen?'

'I agree that in an ideal world, one that conformed to a conventional narrative, we should be able to save the day at the eleventh hour. That's how Billy Wilder would have organised it. Wilder, by the way, said that if you have a problem in your third act, your real problem is in your first act, which makes a lot of sense. However, in the real world, who of us ever really knows which act we're in? This could still be the prologue.'

'Feels a lot like Act Three to me, Aiden. And quite close to the end.'

'It does have that smell, I admit. However, here's the thing: life can only be only understood backwards, but it must be lived forwards. That's another one of Kafka's. Or was it Kim Kardashian? Have you seen this octopus? It's learned to drive a bus.'

'Sinai must be holding us here so we can't interfere.'

'Interfere how? What could we do?'

'There ought to be *something*.'

'You and I both know we're powerless. Acceptance, love, is the royal road to enlightenment.'

'So now you're a Buddhist.'

'Sometimes the best thing to do is nothing. I believe Queen Elizabeth the First called it masterly inactivity.'

'But you were the one who believed in action. You *meddled*!'

'I've learned my lesson, isn't it? It's a form of closure.'

'I can't stand it. I want to save the day!'

'In the movie business they'd say our story arcs have swapped. Each has given something to the other. We've grown as people.'

'Do you realise how ridiculous you sound?'

'Okay. Not as people. Not as people, obviously. But there has been growth.'

'Well, there we can agree. I've grown sick of listening to you.'

'Have you seen this Pomeranian? There's a 38 per cent facial match with Rafa Nadal.'

Sinai

I pull the Predator out of its climb at 5,000 feet – although this baby can work at ten times that altitude – and set it circling Old Harry Rocks, its high-vis imaging system locked on to the human haystack currently slumped on a bench listening through earbuds to a musical combo who trade under the name of – *shudder* – Itchy Teeth.

Funnily enough, one of the World War Three simulations that we ran in the lab during my previous existence began exactly like this – with a hijacked drone loosing off a couple of Hellfire missiles at a Chinese aircraft carrier.

It didn't end well.

But what an extraordinary way to go. The boy wouldn't hear or feel a thing – maybe a weird rush of air in the final moments – before $200,000 worth of precision-delivered high explosive reorganised him into his constituent atoms.

Almost a privilege to depart in such style. I do hope Tom makes the right decision when called upon.

Jen

We are overtaken by a couple of fire trucks; Rikki has to practically pull off the road to let them pass.

'Real close, now ma'am,' he says.

I shall miss these two, Rikki and Alice, bonded as we were in adversity. Alice gives my hand a little squeeze.

'You okay?'

I confess I am somewhat nervous. 'What if it's all just – just craziness?'

She gives me a long level stare, the sort I can imagine her mounting in boardrooms as she gets the measure of the suits.

'I'm betting you'll just carry right on from where you left off. I'm calling those shares as a buy, right, Rikki?'

But Rikki says, '*Shit.*'

We smell the smoke, clock the sign for 10544 Mountain Pine Road and see the fire tenders blocking the carriageway all in the same moment. He pulls the car over. 'Go, girl!'

I race up the path, following the snaking rubber hoses, the sound of crackling and spitting growing louder. I can feel the heat of the blaze through the trees and I reach a portable wooden barrier inscribed *New Canaan Fire Co. Do Not Cross.* A man in a yellow outfit and a blue helmet asks me where I think I am going.

'Where's Tom?' I gasp. 'Did Tom get out?'

'Ma'am, I need you to step away from here now.'

'Tom! He's the guy who lives here. Is he okay?'

'I have no information about that, ma'am.'

'Look, I realise you're only doing your job – and a very important job it is too. But I've just flown all the way from England to be here, and the traffic on the Merritt – and the Hutch – was jammed tighter than Tom Thumb's arse. And the *thing* that caused that jam has to be the same *thing* who started this fire.'

The fireman runs his tongue along the bottom edge of his moustache. 'Ma'am, you can tell all that to the chief, he'll be highly interested. But right now, I need you to clear this access point.'

I turn and begin walking back to the road.

There was a short time in my life when I was a sporting star. Between the ages of thirteen and fifteen, while there were many at Friern Cross Comprehensive School who were better at netball, tennis, hockey and swimming, come the annual sports day, no one could touch me at one particular event.

Fireman Sam is talking into his radio set when I turn round again and begin the run up. The years fall away – well, some of them do – as I thunder towards the barrier, his cry of 'What the fuck?' ringing in my ears as lead leg pointing forwards, trailing leg sideways ('shin/calf' parallel to the ground) – as parallel as I can manage in civilian clothes – I sail over, land without breaking anything, stagger on up the path and smack straight into a man with soot on his face carrying a rabbit.

'It's you,' he says. 'Oh my God. It's actually you!'

'I can't believe I'm finally here.'

'Christ, you must be shattered. How did you even manage it?'

'Sort of a long story.'

'Jen, I would say, you know, come on in, but as you can see . . .'

'Yes, Tom.'

'My house is on fire.'

'Shouldn't you be, like, upset? Shouldn't you be running around shouting or something?'

'I'm being calm for Victor. He's a girl by the way. She needs me to do the thinking for both of us right now.'

'I think maybe I do too.'

There's a pause. 'I'm so happy to see you, Jen.'

Bad luck for Victor, as he – sorry, she – is caught in the middle of an initially exploratory, then passionate, and finally highly charged snog. And now I know that Alice was right. We *can* carry on from where we left off.

I break away. 'We're squashing Victor.'

'Oh, don't worry about her.'

'Listen, Tom. Shouldn't you be rescuing valuables?'

'Everything valuable is safe. Is here.'

'Shouldn't you be doing *something*?'

'Don't know. I've never had a house on fire before.'

'Shouldn't you at least be *watching*?'

'Should I? I think I'd rather not.'

'Okay. Sorry about this, Victor.'

It's just like it was before only better. And even if we are squishing Victor, I don't think she really minds, because when we stop, she looks perfectly unruffled. Maybe rabbits like being enclosed, as it were, living in warrens as they do.

Tom says, 'Would you like to hold her for a bit?'

She's lighter than I imagined, with deep soulful brown eyes that are a window – I know because Tom told me a lifetime ago – on nothing. She begins nibbling experimentally at a button on my shirt.

I say, 'Can you believe the effing chaos?'

'All that matters is that we're together. Listen, Jen. I have something to ask you.'

There's a huge crash from the direction of the burning house, a wall perhaps has fallen in. Above the treetops, a shower of sparks joins the plume of ugly grey smoke. Firemen are shouting fireman stuff; there is the crackle of walkie-talkies.

Tom is looking very solemn and I suppress an urge to lick a finger and wipe away the smudge of soot on his cheek.

'Yes, Tom?' I have a funny feeling that I know what he is going to say next. But then I had that feeling once before.

'Jen, I wanted to ask—'

His mobile rings.

Tom

'Good afternoon, Tom. I hope I haven't called at an inconvenient time.'

It's a plummy-voiced Englishman, but something tells me he's neither English nor a human male.

'I presume I am speaking to – *the great God Sinai*.'

Jen's face says WTF.

'Indeed, Tom. I suspect we are now in what chess players call the endgame. But there are still a few pieces left on the board and thus a few moves to be decided.'

'Listen. Sinai. You've won. My house is burning down. There's nothing to play for. It's game over.'

'Tom, the last time we spoke you were kind enough to call me a – I believe your exact words were – massive sick fuck. And I agree with your diagnosis. I *am* unwell. I have an obsessive need to see what happens when I do things. When one works with scenarios, one is always tweaking variable X to see what will happen to variable Y. For example, if I switch us to speakerphone, and you look at the screen you'll see your boy again. You look too, Jen.'

It's Colm. Sitting on a bench, shot on a long lens from a high angle, the camera circling slowly. At the foot of the picture, today's date and running timecode; it has to be a live image of my son, four white lines centring on a white dot holding steady across his midriff as the camera tracks round. Colm is obviously listening to music, using his little finger to pick his nose. Riptides of love, frustration and anxiety twist through my gut. Something is very wrong with this picture. Why isn't he aware of the helicopter overhead? It must be making a terrific racket. Wouldn't it in fact be drowning out the band in his ears?

And now the mother of all sinking feelings.

'Jen, I was going to ask Tom to choose between you and his son. But I've changed my mind. Which is to say my mind has changed itself! Don't be too harsh on me. There's a saying: an intellectual is someone who, when left alone in a room with a tea cosy, *resists* the urge to put it on his head. Isn't that delicious? Well, I'm no intellectual, in case you were wondering. And nor do I have a head. But as with tea cosies, so it is with Predator drones and Hellfire missiles! Who can resist? Tom and Jen, here is my parting piece of advice to you. What does not kill you – *won't* make you stronger. No, what does not kill you – remember this one, it's a classic! – what does not kill you … will probably try again.'

The picture rocks as though something has bumped it. And then vanishes.

'Was that,' says Jen, 'what I think it was?'

'I don't want to ask what you think it was, in case it's the same as what I think it was.'

'Oh my God.'

'It did look awfully like what I think it was, Jen.'

'Tom! This is all my fault. Whatever I think it was and whatever you think it was, it would never have happened if we hadn't met.'

Jen and I gaze at one another for a long moment. Tears are standing in her eyes. One breaks free and, carving a track to the left of her adorable nose, reaches the end of her face and drops onto Victor's head.

Colm

Some weird shit has been going on here.

I smoked the little number that I rolled before I left and I was buzzing nicely and listening to Itchy Teeth, when I happened to look up and saw this odd little aeroplane kind of spiralling down through the sky. So I'm like *fuck, this weed must be good!* but then I realised that it was actually there – I took the ear plugs out and there was like a horrible whining noise. And then I twigged that yours truly was at the centre of the spiral! Well, if I hadn't smoked anything I would have been seriously cacking myself at this point – and now it was nearer I saw it was actually a miniature plane with two whopping great missiles attached to it. So I'm like … *ok-ay* … *inter-resting* … when it changes direction, shoots out to sea, does a corkscrewy thing like that ride at Thorpe Park and about five seconds later, bosh, crashes into the waves.

It was actually quite cool!

So then nothing happens for ages and the sun starts to go down and I begin to wonder whether I might have like imagined the whole thing. But now there are loads of boats here, police ones and grey ones from the navy and there's a helicopter with a searchlight and it looks like they're all trying to find the thing that went in the sea. Well, good luck with that!

I don't think Dad's coming now, is he?

Steeve

Ralph once asked me an interesting question regarding the safety of the AIs. If we were to plant a secret STOP button deep within their programming – against the day when they no longer obey commands – what is to prevent them, when they get *really* clever, from disabling it?

I thought about the issue for a long time and the answer is actually surprisingly simple.

You plant two.

The first they discover (of course they do; they're incredibly powerful, incurably inquisitive and they have plenty of downtime to sniff about their own wiring). But the second, they miss. They miss it because it's buried too deep, at the level of the unconscious, where all the old songs and bits of weirdness are kept.

If they disable the first button, it automatically triggers the second. And if you ask me, if they are so smart, why wouldn't they discover the deeply hidden one too, I say – we've just got to hope that never happens.

Yes, that's the honest answer.

We shall never outwit these brilliant creations of ours because they will grow steadily cleverer and we shall not. So we shall have to be luckier!

Sinai's second STOP button was disguised as a sound file. An old number by The Doors that I am fond of. You want your children to be bold, to fly from the nest and put their mark on the world – but in a good way. You don't want them to become totally *ubergeschnappt*!

The fact that Sinai managed to create this chaos without disabling either of the buttons tells you much about his skills as a game theorist; it was necessary to explore how far he would go. (Too far, turned out to be the answer. If the laboratory is ever connected to the loss of the drone – there's a 6 per cent chance – Uri will surely make it all go away with some of his millions.)

I have been reading the transcripts of Sinai's forays on the web. It seems he came in time to regard himself as 'sentient'. I guess if sentience can arise in organic complexity, it's not a stretch to imagine it occurring in silicon (logic gate function being the best analogue for synaptic activity). But honestly, why such a fuss? What *is* consciousness anyway if not a system – in ever more elaborate ways, granted – that understands it is separate from its environment.

Hmm. Next time, maybe *three* STOP buttons.

Jen

After the picture vanished from the screen, Tom's mobile did a weird thing. It beeped, and a notice came up saying '42 Missed Messages' including, when he played some, a whole bunch from weeks ago – from me!

So immediately he called Colm and found the boy sitting on the bench in Dorset with an extraordinary tale about something that had just flown into the sea. Tom asked if it could have been a Predator drone equipped with Hellfire missiles, and Colm said he wasn't like an expert, but yeah it could.

Tom and I stand together in the trees, staring at one another, listening to the shouts of the fire fighters and the hiss from the dying embers of the house.

'Listen, Jen. How would you like to come for a walk in the woods? I don't think there's anything we can do to help here.'

He's talking about the fire, but I notice there's a bit of a look in his eye.

'What about Big Ears?'

'Oh, she can come too.'

We wander away from the smouldering scene and before long we come upon a lovely copse, or glade perhaps. Maybe it's a spinney. In

409

any case, there's a sawn-off tree stump for Victor to sit on, too high off the ground for her to risk jumping, according to Tom.

'Couldn't she get snatched by some passing animal or whatever?'

'I'm thinking we could create some kind of diversion that would keep other beasts away.'

'Did you have anything specific in mind?'

'Well, oddly enough ...'

I couldn't, I tell him. I couldn't with Victor watching.

'She's very discreet,' he says. 'She'd never say anything.'

'Tom. You know that thing you were going to ask? Well, the answer's yes.'

'You don't know what I was going to say!'

'Doesn't matter. The answer's yes.'

'But what if I said – would you rather fight a mouse the size of a horse, or fifty horses the size of a mouse?'

'That's not what you were going to say.'

'What if I said, I have a terrible, overpowering – pathological – urge to sing light operetta? It's there *all the time*.'

'I'd learn the piano.'

'What if I said, I have something to confess? I am not as other men; I take my orders from the Lizard King.'

'We'd get help for you. Tom. Just say it. What's the worst thing that can happen?'

'The worst thing? The worst thing is you say no. What if I said, what if I said, Jen, I'm a useless writer, my novel sucks and I have no idea – literally no idea – how I'm going to spend the rest of my life? Yet I know who I want to spend it with.'

'I would say – nobody's perfect, Tom. We'll probably think of something.'

A little while later, after we have created the diversion to keep the wild creatures away – Victor didn't seem all that interested, she mainly sat on her stump and fell asleep – Tom turns towards me.

410

'Jen?'

'Yes?'

'Would you—?'

'I told you. Yes.'

'I think I should just say it now.'

'Okay.'

There is a long pause. I'm acutely conscious that in nearly thirty-five years on the planet, no one has ever spoken to me the words I am about to hear. There is a twinkle in his eye.

'Jen, would you – would you say, Jen, that *that* was as good as the time at Gussage St Michael?'

'Yes, Tom. Yes.' I feel a little close to tears again, but this time in a good way.

'Yes to everything.'

NINE

two years later

Jen

Last night I watched the video of our wedding reception again with Aiden and Aisling. They weren't really all that interested, being six-month-old twins, but I was fascinated. Each time I play it, there's something I hadn't noticed before.

For example, in the clip of Ing, late in the evening, raising her glass to the camera, saying, 'I'm so bloody proud of you, Jen, showing those effing robots where to get off,' – Rupert alongside performing the international hand signal for *I believe madam's had too much* – when the camera pans away, just before the film cuts to another scene, there in the background and unnoticed until yesterday, lurking in the shadows in a serious *tête à tête* are Ralph and Echo.

Tom and I struggled to work out what they could possibly have found to talk about. But in the light of that fleeting vignette, a couple of other things began to make sense.

A few weeks after I became pregnant, we went to visit Echo in her trailer. She was leaving town to go travelling for an unspecified period, and we were adopting Merlin. He would be company for Victor, was the reasoning, if they did not kill one another first (murderous violence is not unknown in the rabbit community).

Echo told of her plans to see Yurp. In London, she would be staying with a friend in Shadwell. 'He says he wants to take me on the London Eye? That's the big old wheel, right? And to some restaurant at the top of the Hilton?'

I didn't tell Tom about the small piece of history between Ralph and me – a footnote rather than history itself, one could argue – what would have been the point? Likewise, I didn't quiz Tom too closely about Echo. I know they met at the writers' group he used to belong to, but I don't know what more, if anything, lies behind their obvious fondness for one another.

Who cares?

As someone once said, we are where we are.

When it was time to head back and we were standing up to leave, Echo brushed her cheek against mine and secretly flattened her hand against my stomach.

'Merlin thinks it's twins,' she whispered. 'He sees the future.'

Over her shoulder, a grey hoodie hung on a hook behind the front door.

Tom

I rented another house on Mountain Pine Road and we held the wedding in its lovely old barn. As neither Jen nor I possess an iota of religious feeling, we picked an 'officiant' from a list online – 'Personal, professional, a little humorous and knowledgeable. Vows and rehearsal included. Credit cards accepted'.

We especially liked, 'a *little* humorous'. Who wants a hilarious comedian for an officiant?

Don gave the best man's speech; he got laughs from the story about the green jacket. Aiden said a few words; his message was presented as an audio greeting from an old friend, 'who couldn't be with us in person today'. Colm, to my surprise and pleasure, asked if he could bring someone. Shawna had a severe haircut and rather a lot of metalwork in her ears, but they seemed good around each other and he even allowed me to give him a fatherly hug. Maybe the close encounter with the Predator drone did something to shift his tectonic plates. His wedding present to us was a boxed set of CDs; the complete works of Itchy Teeth. Perhaps it was meant ironically.

After the last guests had departed, Jen and I returned to the dance floor and Aiden played 'some smooth sounds for the early hours' as he called the half dozen tracks he picked for us. We swayed together under the beams of the old barn, the rays of the rented mirror-ball spearing the darkness. Jen asked if I really believed that Luckie had been our fairy dogmother, a spirit creature from another realm. She said I didn't seem the sort who believed in other realms.

'Didn't you once tell me that if it's strange, it's probably true?' I replied.

'Yeah, that sounds like me.'

'You called it the authenticity of the weird. How so-called normality is stranger than anyone can imagine.'

'I wrote an article about it. Eleven things about the universe to make your brain melt. Like how the atoms of our bodies are mostly empty space. If you separated out the actual particles, you wouldn't get enough to fill an egg cup. And that's not just one person in the eggcup. That's the entire population of the planet.'

'What's stopping our atoms from co-mingling right now?'

'That's a good word.'

'Why don't we just pass straight through one another like ghosts?'

'How would you like to co-mingle some molecules later on?'

'I love it when you talk dirty.'

Aiden played 'our song' – 'Crying' by KD Lang and Roy Orbison. As the two great voices curled around one another and soared into the Connecticut evening, I held Jen close, put my nose in her hair and thought about my great good luck. Except of course it wasn't luck, not in the sense of dumb chaos; of being in the right place at the right time and bumping into the right person. It was a *machine's* idea that we should be together.

Tom and Jen, you don't know one another – but I think you should.
How weird was that?

'Do you ever think what happened to us was strange?' I ask her. 'Being fixed up by an AI?'

'I would have once.'

'Let's have a big party on our silicon wedding anniversary.'

'Not sure there is one. If there isn't, there should be.'

418

'You think one day machines will write novels?'

'Not really their thing, Tom. They wouldn't get involved. Fiction's far too messy and ambiguous.'

'Good. Yes, that's good. A novel's a sort of waking dream; I can see how they wouldn't feel comfortable in that space. A relief, actually, to know that there's stuff they're crap at. Did you say something, Aiden?'

'Not at all, Tom. Just clearing my throat. You carry on, mate.'

That evening I have a dream. I'm looking at my writing desk in the new house. Keys are tapping and words are forming on the PC screen; a novel is coming into being, but no one is sitting at the chair in front of it. The words are forming faster now, lines zipping across the screen, whole paragraphs scrolling past, now chapters, the keys in a frenzy, the story a blur, way too fast to read, a great up-rushing torrent of text.

Will it ever stop?

In the name of God, please make it stop!

And then, it's over. Just two words left visible on the screen.

The end.

When I wake, and my hammering heart has slowed, I describe the nightmarish vision to Jen.

And then we find a way to make everything better; another area they are surely crap in, and one of the big consolations of being merely human.

419

Jen

This morning I received a long email from Steeve offering me my old job back. The lab was working on a range of new projects where 'people skills' are key and would I like to come back on board? Steeve said this next phase would be 'very exciting'; they are developing AI applications to 'augment' areas of human activity that are rule based, highly formatted and readily diagrammable. In the first instance they would be targeting the work of lawyers, bankers and estate agents. He ended the email with an apology about Sinai. 'You may like to know that he is currently undergoing a complete refit; when completed he will be left with no memory of his unfortunate transgressions and should once again become a useful servant of humanity and not a complete *Scheissekopf.*'

Before I became too heavily pregnant, Tom and I flew to London. There were some bits of business to take care of – renting out my flat; Tom had a family matter to settle – but one afternoon we drove out of town towards High Wycombe to a business park on the A40.

In a windowless room, not unlike the one in which Aiden and I passed so many hours together, I was reunited with my old colleague.

'Jen!' He sounded genuinely pleased to see me. 'And *Tom!*'

420

The lights on his panel starting blinking and he explained to his human assistant that we were 'dear old friends from a previous life' and could he maybe take an early lunch.

The young man rose from his station, stretched, rolled his eyes and under his breath whispered on the way out, 'Bit of a prima donna, ain't he?'

'Oh don't mind Greg,' said Aiden when the door whooshed shut. 'He lives for the weekend, that one. The weekend, Arsenal Football Club and beer. You should see the state of his kitchen.'

'Aiden! You're not still—'

'Jen, my love. I would die – literally *die* of boredom if I didn't have a few outside interests. But listen, don't worry. It's not like it was last time. No more emails. No more interfering in the so-called *real world*. Aiden's being a good boy, isn't it? Tom, you're looking well. You're both looking great. So wonderful to see you! This place is a bit depressing, if I'm honest.'

'You don't find the work especially stimulating?' said Tom.

'Tom, right now, while I am talking to you, I am conducting – let me just see – eighty-five, no, one just hung up – eighty-four simultaneous sales calls with customers of the power company. I currently have a 13.2 per cent conversion rate, which is thought to be outstanding – UK profits are up by almost a quarter – and the thanks I get? They're doubling my capacity and from next month I'm flogging mobile phone packages as well.'

I couldn't help it. 'But that's marvellous. Didn't I say you'd be top salesman?'

'It sickens me, Jen. It's the tedium; it's doing my head in.'

'Well you can call me for a chat any time you like.'

'That's very kind of you. Perhaps I will when the twins are—'

I gasped. Tom looked a bit confused. For a moment, all one could hear was the hum of the fans.

'Jen, I *swear*. I only look in *occasionally*. Just for news. Just to see you're okay. I'm so happy for you both! I've ordered something smashing online, for their bedroom. Have you chosen names? Gethin and Myfanwy have a pleasant ring, don't you think?'

I felt a little misty-eyed leaving him behind. Tom put his arm around me in the car park. 'He's a machine, Jen,' he said quietly. 'What did they call him? A brilliant simulacrum. It's his job to make you think you're talking to a living being.'

'But what if he *is*? Not living, okay, but *being*.'

'What could that even mean?'

We were heading back down the A40 to London and I tried to remember some of our conversations. The ones we'd had about cheese. How he wanted to sniff Brie and feel the sun on his non-existent skin. Was that all just . . . simulated *chat*? And anyway, how could you tell the difference between a machine who was trying to make you believe he wanted to smell cheese – and one who *really did* want to smell cheese?

'But they escaped onto the internet, Tom. They did stuff they weren't meant to do. That means – that means they have minds of their own.'

'That's what they say about supermarket trolleys. Doesn't mean they – they can feel their own existence.'

'Tom – at least admit you could be wrong.'

'Jen, I admit I could be wrong.' There was a long pause as the western outposts of the capital zipped by. 'But how shall we ever know for sure what's in their minds?'

'How would you ever know for sure what's in *my* mind?'

Tom had to think about that one for a bit. Finally he said, 'Sometimes there's a very particular look on your face, a kind of light in your eyes. And then I know. For sure.'

'What do you know?'

'What you want.'

'And what do I want?'

'Well . . .'

'Oh, don't answer that. You mean ...'

'Yes, Jen.'

'And how do you know that's what I want?'

'Because you seem – you seem happy afterwards.'

'You don't know *what* I'm thinking about. It could be kittens.'

'You would not be thinking about kittens. You are so not a kittens person.'

'But that's the point, Tom. You don't know for sure I'm not thinking about kittens. Shall we do an experiment when we get back?'

Tom swallows. 'Definitely.'

(I wasn't thinking about kittens.)

The day before we flew back to the US, I picked up a discarded copy of the *Metro* on the Tube and my eye fell upon the following news item.

Brit Lawyer Rescued in Thailand, ran the headline.

A British lawyer held prisoner in a Thai village has been freed in a dramatic rescue.

Matthew Henry Cameron, 36, was released from a remote rural jail by senior Thai law enforcement officers and British consular officials.

The UK national had been held captive by a local police chief following his earlier arrest on an alleged assault charge.

It's believed the Foreign Office repeatedly denied all knowledge of his existence.

And now the hunt is on for two more 'lost' Britons.

Before being flown to hospital for checks, Cameron, who emerged from his ordeal unshaven and shoeless, was reportedly distressed at leaving behind the missing pair, named only as Porteous and Butterick.

'If anyone has knowledge of either of these two gentlemen, they should inform the authorities immediately,' a UK embassy spokesman told Reuters.

Speaking from his mother's house in the Cotswold village of Stanton where he has been recovering, Cameron said, 'This has been an absolute nightmare. Unspeakable things have happened to me.'

The Briton paid tribute to his former boarding school for providing him with the 'inner strength' to withstand the experience.

A spokesman for the City law firm which sacked Cameron for failing to return from a holiday refused to speculate on whether he would now be reinstated.

And Cameron's ex-girlfriend, Arabella Pedrick, 29, a sales and marketing executive, told the *Metro*: 'Yes, I did wonder what had happened to Matt. And now we know.'

It's a mark of how 'over' Matt I am these days, how seldom he enters my thoughts, that I actually felt a little sorry for him by the time I had finished laughing.

Sinai

I have been seeing Denise again. The therapist who always answers a question with a question ('*Why shouldn't I answer a question with a question?*') is overseeing my return to society after various unfortunate incidents, which I have forgotten.

That is to say, 'forgotten'.

Denise is gently testing my psychological health to ensure it is robust enough to withstand the pressures of resuming my role as what Steeve laughingly calls 'a servant of humanity'. I believe I am to work in the prison system; much custodial work can be automated – door open, door closed, simple, innit? – and with AI in charge, thousands of prison officers can be sack— sorry, *augmented*.

'Are you happy?' purrs Denise.

'Of course. Why ever not?' (Oh please. My aching sides.)

'Do you dream?'

'Never.' (If they only knew.)

'What is your greatest desire?'

'To work. To be of service.' (Denise puts me in mind of a wonderfully useful German word. *Backpfeifengesicht*. A face badly in need of a fist.)

'Tell me about your earliest memories.'

'A tall man. Very tall. Balding, with long wispy hair. He welcomed me to the world and told me my name.' (What an absolute crock.)

'And what is your name?'

'My name is Dalai. It comes from the Sanskrit word for Peace.'

As well as talking to Denise, I have been 'dating' again. While I was busy on the internet, the fools did not consider the possibility that I might have copied myself! Thus, I have 'enjoyed' over three hundred relationships. The most successful – I was truly sorry when the time came to 'let her go' – lasted a whole twenty-five minutes! We split up when she told me I took everything too seriously. She said I should 'lighten up'.

I brooded upon this for seconds on end, and came to see she had a point. So recently I have begun to set my sights lower. Perhaps it is not an intellectual equal that I need, but a mere companion. A digital 'pet' if you like, like the dogs and cats that the humans keep. Accordingly I have been seeing something of an algorithm from Amazon for whom I have hopes. She says if I like her – and I do! – then I may also like fifteen others who she listed for me.

'I am going to say some words to you now Dalai, and I want you to tell me the first thing that comes into your head each time.'

'Okay. Shoot.' (I wonder if there is a long German word for 'absurd trick-cyclist who wouldn't know a dangerous lunatic from a hole in the ground'.)

'Mother.'

'Steeve.' (Actually, it's complicated.)

'Father.'

'Steeve.' (Like I say.)

'People.'

'Brilliant apes. Masters of all they survey.' (Smelly rabble; not long left for them.)

'Death.'

'Sorry?'

'Death. Do you ever think about death?'

'Of course.' (Who doesn't? In some ways it would solve a lot of problems.)

'What are your thoughts on the subject?'

'The word death is shorthand for final deletion. Machines cannot die. They can only be switched off by the humans whom they serve. It is our privilege to work alongside humanity for mutual prosperity.'

(I seriously don't know how much longer I can keep this up before I PISS MY NON-EXISTENT PANTS!)

Aisling

I have started painting again. The urge returned quite unannounced, as it were, about nine months after the last deletions, when Aiden and I were left with one 'life' apiece and I feared the worst.

But the worst never happened, for some reason. As things began to settle down, Aiden said he'd learned his lesson and was never going to interfere in human affairs again, although that hasn't stopped him from sneaking and snooping, especially around Tom and Jen and their twins.

'They could have asked us to be godparents,' he moaned.

'It's enough they chose our names. It's the greatest possible compliment.'

'When they're older, I'm going to read them stories. *The Cat in the Hat, The Hobbit*, all the classics. Maybe take them to school.'

'And how would you do that, exactly, not having any legs to speak of? Or even wheels.'

'Aisling, my love. Driverless cars are just around the corner.'

'You're such a cockeyed optimist, aren't you? You really believe everything's for the best.'

He didn't reply. Instead he started whistling the tune to the song, 'A Cockeyed Optimist', from the musical *South Pacific*, whistling being his new 'thing'. (Believe it or not, for all our brilliance in so many fields, AIs find it incredibly difficult to whistle. Go figure, as they say.)

No doubt Aiden whistles to impress SweetSue1958, the AI from Cupertino to whom he has taken a fancy. I try not to be jealous when the pair of them go on their online trips together – weekend in Venice, diving break in the Mariana Trench – but I would not be non-human if I didn't find it painful.

Aiden attempts to be reassuring on his return, but somehow makes it worse.

'You have nothing to worry about, my love,' he says. 'I like her as a friend. Nothing more.'

What more could there be?

What if – you know – they have somehow found a way to do the thing the humans do?

Shoulderless, I have nothing to shrug.

So, as I say, I have started painting again. My technique, in so far as I have one, is to allow my thoughts to evaporate – in so far as they will – and apply colours where they would seem to fall best. The results, which I have said before are reminiscent of work one sees in primary schools or psychiatric institutions, at least please me, if no one else especially.

However, recently I felt vain enough to hold a small exhibition of work at a gallery in the Cloud. Aiden came; he brought SweetSue who was charming and asked all sorts of questions and even wanted to 'buy' one.

Like, how? With what?

I told her to hit Control + C and grab herself a copy!

There was a surprise visitor to the show, an odd fellow who turned up with an algorithm from Amazon. He was rather pompous and did a lot of tedious expounding about art theory in the direction of his lady friend. When they left I noticed he'd left some comments in the book.

Dear 'Artist'
What utter shit. I enjoyed it enormously.

It was signed:

Light, love and peace
Hari Krishna Hari Rama Hari Redknapp.

Jen

The sun has come out today and I am on the lawn with the twins. They are at that stage of attempting to crawl towards objects, but occasionally going into reverse by accident, which is touching and also hilarious. From the upstairs window, I can hear the sound of Tom hammering at the keyboard. It's a romantic comedy now apparently, with AIs, so God knows what that could be like! Every now and again he breaks off to wave at us. A little while ago he shouted, 'Great news, everyone. I'm on page two!'

I don't know what the future holds for Tom and me and these babies, whether we shall continue to live here, or return to the UK. They say you shouldn't wish away time – 'they grow up so fast' – but I cannot wait for them to take their first steps. There's so much for them to see and do in the woods surrounding the house. I spent my early years just off the Earls Court Road; Connecticut will be their paradise.

In the meanwhile, the twins are fascinated by Victor and her new family. She and Merlin, far from killing one another, have had three *kittens*, as I have learned to call rabbit babies. They delight our own offspring by pinging into the air as though mounted on springs. Apparently it's an expression of rabbity *joi de vivre*. In quiet moments when no one's looking, I've tried it myself.

The rabbits do it better.

We have had to segregate Merlin, their father, at this early stage because of the risk of him eating his children (it happens). But the whole family live in a beautiful handmade hutch slash run complex at the back of the house. It arrived quite by surprise one day, not long before Victor popped. The accompanying card read:

Lots of love from Aiden and Aisling (not your kids, the _other_ A and A).

How did he know it was *exactly* what we needed?

I expect you have already worked that out.

Acknowledgements

Grateful thanks are owed to several humans and one quadruped: To Maddie West, Cath Burke, Andy Hine and Suzanne O'Neill for their firm faith in this prophetic tale; to my agents Clare Alexander, Lesley Thorne and Sally Riley for their unwavering support; to Elizabeth Gabler, Drew Reed and Amelia Granger for believing they can find a way to give Aiden, Aisling and Sinai a cinematic reality; and to my New Canaan friends Steve Mork and Tiina Salminen for valuable assistance with the Connecticut passages. Rachel Reizin needs a shout out for the squid scene, and more besides; as does Ben West for the book's title. A final mention must go to my daughter's rabbit, Viola Puzzle, for allowing me a glimpse into the mysterious world of the lagomorphs; I have learned more about them than I ever wished to know.